Oshun's Gold

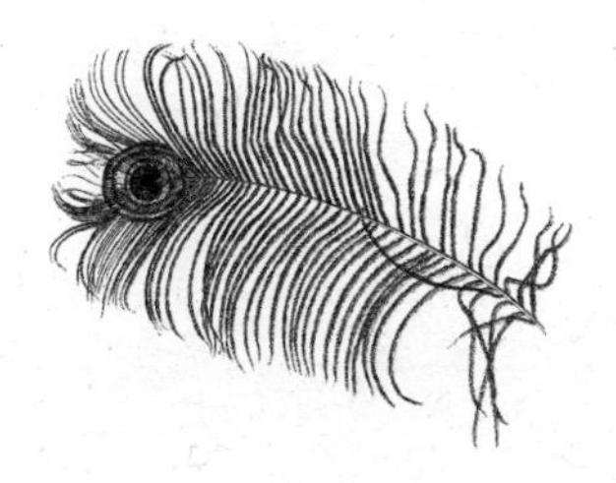

Oshun's Gold

simone brightstein

I hope this brings you
a little pleasure.
Simone Brightstein

First published in 2007 by:
Stamford House Publishing
Second Edition 2008

ISBN: 978-1-904985-68-6

Printed and bound in Great Britain by:
Stamford House Publishing
Remus House
Coltsfoot Drive
Peterborough
Cambs
PE2 9JX

For Ann

without whom this book would never have been.

ACKNOWLEDGEMENTS

A dupe lowo: Deidre Badjejo, Raul Canizares, *Awo* Fá'lókun F'átunmbi, Migene González-Wippler, Joseph M. Murphy, Philip John Neimark, Luis Manuel Núñez, Luisah Teish and Robert Farris Thompson, for their inspired and inspiring writings, which galvanized my imagination. Also to my friends, Catherine Lane and Mei Mei Sanford, who were so generous in sharing their knowledge.

To my children, Eden and Josh, my deepest love and thanks for their patience and support during seemingly endless years of work.

Cover design by Alastair Cooley
Cover photography by Mark Wright
Art by Jeanette Litterick

Prologue

OSHUN'S GOLD

by

simone brightstein

The Oshun River flows through the African countryside like melted chocolate. It meanders among the trees which grow in its depths and potters amiably around the rocks that stud its silky waters, but when it reaches the town of Oshogbo it breaks into a snappy little conga, shoogling between banks of fan-shaped hedges with yellow leaves that clink together like coins. They are called Honey Money Bush and they belong to Oshun, the goddess of love and abundance for whom the river is named.

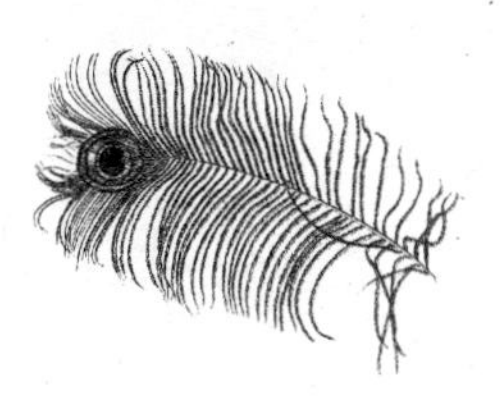

"I'm in my prying mode, Angel." Brent Lockwood waved a warning forefinger at the woman seated beside him in the cramped helicopter. "We're 5,000 feet up in a flying eggbeater, heading God knows where for God knows what and I'm dying of curiosity and claustrophobia. If there was room to move in this airborne coffin, I'd be on my knees. I'm begging you - tell me what's happening!"

Angel Zimmerman stretched her lean legs as far as they'd go in their narrow quarters: "Don't get your knickers in a knot, Tootsie. I don't know any more than you do." Angel and Brent owned The Hot Box, a boutique advertising agency which had recently bested the major players by winning an account with Glissando Beauté, a giant in the cosmetics industry. Now they were on their way to the country estate of Alix Morton, the company's president and founder, for an intensive weekend briefing.

"We're all up in the air on this one, Brent, my little cupcake." said a stunning young black woman who was cradling a *Hasselblad* camera. Keisha Adams was called the Canadian Annie Leibovitz and she had enough ego to not be complimented by the comparison.

"Very funny."

Keisha swung her camera up and fired off three shots at Brent who threw up a hand to block his face.

"Cut it out! I'm not in a photographic frame of mind."

"Anybody as disgustingly photogenic as you is fair game any time, baby."

Keisha was right, thought Angel, studying Brent dispassionately. He had curly black hair, extraordinary ice-blue eyes and was saved from being pretty by a hawk like nose. The curse of his life was that he was only five feet, eight inches tall.

"It's all my mother's fault," he'd sigh, "the blighted woman ate shortbread for the entire nine months and just before I was born she was reading a biography of Toulouse-Lautrec."

"You're wonderful as you are, darling," Angel always told him, "if you were six feet tall, the mixture would be too rich."

Angel gazed distractedly at the landscape passing below. Actually, there *was* something she'd kept from Brent and Keisha; she was Alix Morton's goddaughter. She'd stayed quiet about it when they were invited to bid on the account, never dreaming that they'd win.

To avoid accusations of favouritism, Glissando had ordered blind presentations, not an uncommon practice. The anonymous candidates had to create a fictitious product and develop an advertising campaign complete with package design. The Hot Box's entry was a sun block for children that Brent named *New Block On The Kids*. It was a clear gel that gave complete protection to face, body and hair, and was harmless if ingested.

"It'd be the first time that a major cosmetics company brought out a children's product," Angel said.

"Let's not get carried away," Brent replied, "it's only a virtual product".

"Products are often created from an advertising idea," Angel said thoughtfully as she squinted at the packaging concept she was working on. Tubes of the gel would fit neatly inside brightly coloured plastic boxes designed as alphabet building blocks. They could be used as toys when empty and would make appealing point-of-purchase displays.

The ad featured children of all nationalities and all ages, posed on and around giant cubes that spelled out the product name. A tiny Chinese girl was rubbing the gel on the shoulders of a little dreadlocked African boy; a pair of Nordic-blond twins were plastering each other's tummies with the product and one infant was taking a thoughtful taste of the gel which a freckled tyke had squeezed onto its chubby fist. The brilliance of Keisha's spontaneous style made such stunning visuals that they used many of the shots in story boards for a proposed television commercial.

"There could be all kinds of spin-offs with this," Angel said. "We could develop coloured gel crayons for older kids and call them *Colour Chips Off The New Block.* They could use them as temporary hair colours."

"Great idea," Brent agreed, "there could be a soap and shampoo with sun protection built in as well. I think we've got a real prize here."

"It's only make-believe, remember?"

"All right, don't rub it in - no pun intended. I think it's a winner."

Obviously Glissando had thought so too, and now they were churning their way to this top-secret rendezvous. "I could be right," she thought, "Glissando might have decided to manufacture *New Block On The Kids.*"

Mulling over the possibility, she saw the outline of the lake and the surrounding mountains, which hid Caprice from the outside world. The view rushed up to greet them and Angel closed her eyes in a silent prayer for a safe landing.

A canopied trolley met them at the heli-pad and chugged down a steep path to a plush lawn in the centre of which sat a sprawling yellow wooden mansion. It burgeoned exuberantly with cupolas and domes and a verandah wrapped itself around the building, billowing out into mini-porches at each corner. The roof was pavéed with rounded tiles and there was elaborate gingerbread carving everywhere in rainbow swirls of colour.

"It's a Painted Lady," gasped Keisha.

"I haven't seen one outside San Francisco," Brent said.

"That's where it's from," Angel said. "Alix Morton had it moved here when she first bought this land."

They gazed at the intricate patterns.

"How many colours do you think it has?" Keisha asked.

"Fifteen - all authentically Victorian." The voice was deep and authoritative

Angel whirled around. "Alix!" she cried delightedly.

A slim woman with a mass of white hair stood with her arms outstretched: "Hello, my Angel."

Keisha and Brent gawked in amazement as Angel was enveloped in the arms of the fabled Alix Morton.

"You look wonderful, as always," Angel said, kissing Alix's cheek lovingly.

"How is your mother? Still the queen of Bradford on Avon?

"Absolutely. She's hoping you'll be in England some time soon."

"I will, - partly for business and partly to spend time with Lucinda; we haven't seen each other since last Christmas."

Keeping her arm around Angel, Alix turned to Keisha, grey eyes good naturedly appraising her.

"You, of course, are the gifted Keisha Adams," she said. "You're as beautiful as any of your subjects, and from what I hear, twice as temperamental. But, as I always say, talent without temperament is like a flower without fragrance."

Next she gave her attention to Brent who had recovered his aplomb and stood smiling sunnily at the formidable legend.

"And this delectable elf has to be Brent Lockwood."

"That would be me, Miss Morton and I'm overwhelmed to meet you. Have you ever been told that you look like Queen Alexandra? At least, you look like pictures of her. I never met her in person - she was somewhat before my time."

Angel fixed Brent with a steely gaze that snapped his mouth shut. She turned to Alix with an apologetic smile.

"Brent tends to babble when excited, Alix. Just ignore him and he'll fizzle out."

"I find it rather endearing." Alix patted Brent on the cheek and he gave Angel a smug little smirk that made her want to kick him sharply in the shin. Brent was never more annoying than when he was being adorable.

Alix went off in search of staff to take their luggage, leaving Keisha and Brent staring accusingly at Angel. Brent broke the silence.

"You've been holding out on us, Angel girl. How do you know Alix Morton so well?"

Angel shifted her feet uncomfortably. "She's my godmother."

"Your *godmother*! Why didn't you tell us?"

"Do I know who your godmother is - or Keisha's?"

"That's different. My godmother isn't Alix *Morton* for God's sake!"

"And I don't have one," said Keisha. "How did you come to be Alix Morton's godchild?"

"She and my mother have been best friends since they were eleven years old. They met at boarding school in England and on the Queen's birthday Alix persuaded Mother that they should celebrate by lighting fireworks in bed. They almost blew up the junior dorm and became twin souls in the process."

"I don't believe she ever did anything of the sort. Look at her - beluga wouldn't melt in her mouth." Brent exclaimed.

"Don't be fooled by her appearance - the silver halo of hair, the dignified carriage - it's all a front. The woman's a loon; a world-famous, wildly successful loon, but a loon nevertheless."

"What are you saying about me, you wicked girl?" Alix had materialized with a houseman in tow.

"I was telling them about your certifiable loopiness."

"Well, children," she said, slipping her arms around Brent and Keisha, "whatever lurid stories Angel has been spinning, they're undoubtedly accurate. She was always a truthful girl."

Alix shepherded them to the porch and tucked them into overstuffed armchairs while the houseman whisked away their luggage and Cavanaugh, Alix's venerable butler, served gigantic mango Margaritas. Angel smilingly declined and took a drink from the bottle of Evian water that hung from her shoulder in a Hermés harness.

"We won't talk business tonight," said the chatelaine of Caprice. "We'll have an informal dinner and tomorrow we'll begin with a briefing during breakfast. I'm very happy to have you here and I hope you enjoy your stay."

"I'm sure we will," replied Brent.

"Who wouldn't," breathed Keisha, "it's like living inside a rainbow. Do you mind if I explore a little with my camera?"

"Go anywhere your fancy takes you, dear heart."

Keisha wandered into the huge, square front hall, her photographer's eye noting every detail. It was painted in malachite green that cleverly simulated the stone. On the far wall a pair of sconces in the shape of golden swans flanked a sixteenth century gilded sunburst mirror. A long console table held an enamelled brass statue of a beautiful African woman with her arm around the neck of a peacock.

A pair of extraordinary chairs stood on either side of the console. They were carved and painted like gigantic sunflowers with leaves and stems that twisted down to form the legs. The backs were as intriguingly worked as the fronts and the seats were upholstered in moss green tufted velvet. Keisha took several shots of them from different angles.

"They're from the era when *Belle Époque* fantasy furniture was all the rage," said Alix.

Keisha turned to see her hostess standing just behind her. "I've never seen anything like them," she replied admiringly.

"Let me show you the morning room." Alix led Keisha into a small room at the left of the hall. It was buttercup yellow trimmed in white and had floor to ceiling windows that opened onto the porch where the rest of the group was sitting.

Thick coiled tubes of fabric were shaped into couches, chairs and footstools using different chintzes in varied shades of yellow. Keisha gave a delighted laugh as she focused her camera. "They're like cartoons!"

Next was the library on the other side of the hall. Mahogany shelves were filled with leather-bound books. An old refectory table had stacks of periodicals on its gleaming surface and throughout the room were islands of deep leather armchairs and side tables with reading lamps. Alix's eccentric touch was here, too, in the form of an elaborate settee carved with two life-sized bears standing upright to support the seat. Five bears playing musical instruments were worked into the open back.

"This is Black Forest furniture," Alix told Keisha, "it was very popular in the nineteenth century."

"I wouldn't want to meet it on a dark night," Keisha replied, clicking away.

"May I save the rest for later?" she asked. "It's all so marvellous that I don't want to rush through it. Also, I'd like to take your portrait, Miss Morton, sitting in one of those amazing sunflower chairs."

"I'll consider it if you'll call me Alix instead of Miss Morton. I like to delude myself into believing I'm young again when I'm with Angel and her friends."

On the porch, Angel and Brent were in a heated, *sotto voce* discussion:

"Let's ask her *now*."

"No. Alix has her own time frame. We've gone this long without knowing, another day isn't going to make much difference."

"Not to you, Miss Calm and Collected," her partner said gloomily. He slid down in his chair, shoulders hunched, only to sit bolt upright, smiling widely as Alix and Keisha returned.

"I'm sure you could all use a rest before dinner," Alix said. "Angel, would you show Brent and Keisha to their rooms? I've put Keisha in the turret room opposite yours and Brent is in the nursery."

Alix and Angel laughed at Brent's startled expression:

"It's the old playroom," Alix explained. "It was used for the children of friends and family and it was the perfect place for kids, right on the top floor where they didn't disturb anyone. It's a guest suite now, but the name stuck. Now, let's get you settled." She led the way back into the hall where they paused and looked at the statue of the woman with the peacock.

"She is Oshun," Alix said. "The Yoruba goddess of love and abundance. She's also the patron saint of Cuba and I found this statue of her many years ago in an antique shop in Havana."

"How did an African goddess become a Cuban saint?" Brent asked.

"I'll tell you about her tonight, if you like," Alix said.

"I'd love to hear," Keisha said, caressing the statue's shoulder, "she's such a beautiful creature."

"Come on," Angel said to the other two, "I'll show you to your rooms."

"Drinks at seven," Alix called after them. She stood for a moment, still looking up the stairs, then turned briskly and went down the hall to the left of the library. At the end of this passageway was a door which had a beautifully carved sunflower above the lintel. Alix took a small golden key out of her pocket, unlocked the door and went inside, closing the door quietly behind her. She lit a beeswax pillar which stood on the window ledge and opened the double doors of a cupboard on the opposite wall. In it were several shrines. Kneeling in front of the lowest altar, she lit a red and black candle which stood in a holder on the floor. Beside it was an open bottle of rum. Alix trickled some into her mouth and then blew a fine spray of it over a cone-shaped clay object modelled like a crude head with three embedded cowry shells representing eyes and a mouth. Next she lit a cigar that had been lying beside the figure and blew smoke into its face. Rising to her feet, she saluted the object with precise gestures of her arms and legs, and spoke:

Greetings to you, EsuEleggua,
Guardian of my house.
I ask you to open my path
and to close the paths of my enemies
that they may do no harm to me or those I love.
I ask you to open my path to my mother, Oshun
and I thank you for your protection.

On a higher shelf was an altar to Oshun, filled with beautiful objects. A miniature version of the statue in the front hall stood at the altar's centre. Alix lit a beeswax taper, kindled a stick of incense from the candle flame and placed it in a cloisonné holder. She rang a little brass bell five times, intoning the name of Oshun with each chime and began her litany:

"Oshun, Goddess of Love and Beauty, Mother of the River..."

Suddenly she couldn't contain her exuberance.

"Oshun, mother of my heart, it's taken a long, long time but at last all my work is coming to fruition and I thank you, I *thank* you for all that you have done – from the very beginning..."

The beginning...almost fifty years ago when she'd first met Christopher Ross. It was in London, where Christopher was a promising young biochemist in a small pharmaceuticals firm and Alix, who was over there to research British trends in cosmetics, was working in Harrods perfumes department.

Christopher had come to buy a gift for a girlfriend's birthday but it took just one of Alix's dazzling smiles to make him fall irredeemably in love. He was a shy young man, but he hung around the perfume counter until Alix promised to go out with him that night. She was amused by his abashed persistence and enchanted by his British schoolboy beauty. He was tall and slender with a thatch of bright brown hair that kept falling into enormous blue eyes.

From his childhood in Bath, Christopher had been fascinated by the mineral waters from the famous ancient hot springs and this led him to a career in science.

When Alix began to lay the groundwork for her cosmetics company, she had no difficulty in persuading Christopher to join her and when she returned to Canada, he went, too.

She had many recipes for beauty creams, which she had discovered at the age of sixteen in the attic trunk of her Hungarian great grandmother. Nagymama was a witch and had meticulously recorded the formulas in her Book of Shadows. Her recipes were not only organic, preceding the current demand for such products, but also magical, with such fascinating instructions as: "Take two dozen rose petals, gathered in the light of the full moon."

A friend with a bad case of adolescent skin became Alix's guinea pig and she mixed up a batch of cream from one of the discovered formulae. As Christopher said when he tested it under controlled laboratory conditions several years later, it "worked a treat." Alix already knew this as her friend's skin had cleared with dramatic swiftness but it was good to have it confirmed.

From that day they never looked back, producing one carefully tested item after another until they had a superb line of skin care products. Alix was unparalleled in marketing her creations and Christopher was a genius at testing and converting the products for large-scale manufacture. Glissando was not only the first cosmetics house to use natural products, untested on animals, but also the only one to use magical practices. Herbs and flowers were planted and harvested at the correct times of sun and moon and all formulae were brewed with attention to proper magical procedures. Machinery was designed to stir ingredients clockwise, never widdershins or counterclockwise. If new employees looked askance at Alix's insistence on MCP (magically correct procedures) they quickly learned to adapt and consulted the lunar calendar as matter of factly as they checked their appointment books.

Once the company was well established, Alix took a truly daring step and created a line of products that were tailored to individual clients based on their horoscopes; not the daily readings from the newspaper but in-depth, individual astrological forecasts. This was couture skin care - wildly luxurious, incredibly expensive and so popular that there was always a waiting list of several months for Glissando's *Moon Signs Life Lines.*

Glissando Beauté had become a megaforce in the cosmetics industry - the company beside which all others were measured.

Alix loved Christopher dearly but she steadily refused his proposals of marriage. She knew herself well and marriage with children was not for her. Christopher was not happy about this but as the years went by, he considered childlessness a fair price to pay for the joy Alix brought him.

At the age of seventy, Christopher developed a mild heart condition. Alix wanted him to retire but he was stubborn in his own quiet way and refused to be put out to pasture, so they reached a compromise. Christopher went back to live in his beloved England, where he put in too few or too many hours of work at Glissando, depending on whether one was speaking to him or to Alix. In late summer he went to Canada where he stayed at Caprice, then it was back to Bath for the Christmas season. He spent much of the winter at their villa in Mustique and Alix would fly in to join him there whenever possible.

Alix had worked hard all her life, using her extraordinary talents and business sense to the utmost, but she never forgot that her success was also due to the benevolence of Oshun. She prayed to the goddess daily, and never made a decision without consulting her. The beauty of Oshun's shrine and the superb collection of objects d'art that decorated the altar were evidence of her gratitude.

Her mind returned to the present and she resumed her formal prayer: Oshun, Goddess of Love and Beauty,

Mother of the River, this is your child, Alix. Please hear me."

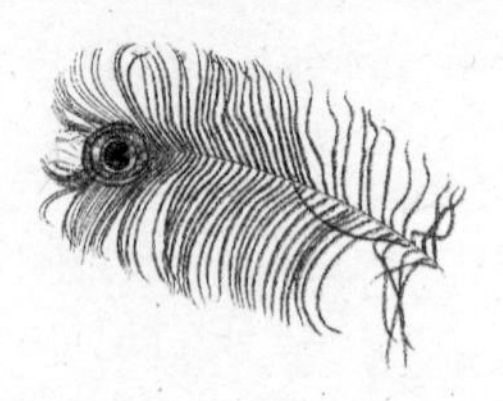

Morning teetered on the edge of sunrise and Oshun lay sleepless on the bank of her river. Sheltered by the branches of the Honey Money Bush, she tossed and turned while the prayers of her petitioners drifted up to her.

"Oshun, Goddess of Love, please send my lover back to me..."

"Mother of Abundance, help me to feed my family..."

"Oh, great and glorious Oshun, grant my request for a child..."

"Go away!" she moaned, closing her eyes and clapping her hands over her ears but the African sun chose that moment to burst onto the skyline and tattoo itself onto the insides of her eyelids. She flung both arms over her swollen eyes as a waterfall of tears poured down. Her unhappiness could be explained in one word; Chango; to give him his full credentials: Chango, the God of Fire, Thunder and Lightning: To add Oshun's editorial comments: Chango, the woman-mongering megalomaniac and, she reflected bitterly, the love of her life - may his manhood shrivel into a dried up pair of olives and a desiccated sausage.

Even in her tear-stained anguish, Oshun's beauty was matchless: copper-coloured velvet skin; huge, heavy-lidded eyes and a lush plum of a mouth curving exquisitely over white, white teeth. The upper front two had a slight gap between them, an African mark of beauty which lent a childlike charm to Oshun's smile, not that she was smiling at the moment.

Her slender body featured fine, upstanding breasts, rounded hips and superbly modelled arms and legs. But this morning, every sensuous curve was heavy with sadness and her midnight mass of hair seemed to have boulders tied to every strand. Why, oh why hadn't she left well enough alone last night? Wallowing in her misery, Oshun ran the scene through her mind yet again:

It had been the birthday celebration of Obatala, the Father of the Orisha, as the African gods are called. Obatala's name means 'Chief of the White Cloth,' and tonight, instead of his usual ajabada of plain white cotton and a fila cap, his upright figure was draped in the intricate folds of a snowy linen toga. His head was bare, displaying a close-cut crop of silver hair and, as always, he carried the symbol of his authority, an elaborately carved fly whisk of white horsehair.

Obatala was benevolence itself: even in repose his face, which looked like a brown walnut, wore a gentle smile. He never touched alcohol and had a delicate digestive system, but was the most generous of hosts and always provided the very best in food and drink for his guests.

Oshun had arrived at the party a shade after the appointed hour, early enough to show respect for Obatala and late enough to make her usual dazzling entrance. Every deity in the pantheon was there in their finest regalia, but Oshun was a vision above and beyond the call of beauty. Sweeping majestically into the palace courtyard she bowed to her host like a willow dipping its branches in the river. Her yellow gossamer robe floated around her, at once concealing and revealing her lithe figure. The assemblage murmured its admiration and Oshun caught their hearts in her smile.

Tucking his whisk under one arm, Obatala took Oshun's small hands in his, raised her up and kissed her gently on both cheeks, his laugh lines deepening as he smiled at the exquisite Orisha who was his special favourite.

A large matron in an orange and red robe and *gelé* nudged her adolescent twin daughters sharply, "You see how gracefully the Lady Oshun bowed to the great Obatala? *That's* the way to make obeisance - not tripping over each other like a pair of palsied giraffes and giggling when the Father of the Orisha condescends to acknowledge your existence."

"We were *nervous*, Mama," said Enitere, the elder by three minutes.

"Yes," chimed Ejitere, always half a beat behind her sister, "*very* nervous; weren't *you* nervous, Mama, the first time you were presented?"

"If I was, I had the good sense to hide it." Their beleaguered mother glared at her hapless daughters, but her attention was claimed again by Oshun who had taken a glass of champagne from an overwhelmed young server, turned and caught sight of something that sent her swooping across the room in full sail.

"Ummm - *um!*" said the large matron to herself. "There goes *Iyalode* over to Chango and she doesn't look happy *at* all."

Chango was flirting idly with one of Obatala's nieces. He saw the goddess bearing down on him, stopped in mid-syllable and smiled nervously.

"Give you greeting, Oshun," he babbled, "you are more radiant tonight than the sunflower, as I was just saying to Janeela." He turned to his companion for confirmation but she had beat a prudent retreat.

Oshun raised a frosty eyebrow: "Ah, yes? You were telling her, too, that she is more radiant than the sunflower?"

"No - that *you* are more radiant..."

"Look again," Oshun suggested icily, "this isn't radiance - it's fury."

Chango gazed at her with soft reproach, "There is no need for anger, my life's delight," he purred, taking Oshun's hand in his and stroking it lovingly, "out of pure politeness I was attending to the niece of our host."

Oshun snatched her hand from his grasp, "there was nothing pure about your attention or your *intention* for that matter."

"There never is, is that not so, my brother?"

The gleeful voice spoke out of nowhere, its owner materializing a split second later between Oshun and Chango. Draping his bony arms over their shoulders, the newcomer beamed happily at them.

Eleggua - I *wish* you'd stop doing that!" Oshun snapped.

"Sorry, Beautiness," he replied, putting his dreadlocked head on one side and rolling his enormous eyes in mock repentance.

Kissing him on the cheek, Oshun said, "Could you grace somewhere else with your presence? I have unfinished business with this wretched man."

"No, don't go, Eleggua." Chango dreaded being left alone with his irate beloved but Eleggua, who adored discord, cheerfully vanished, reappearing on the other side of the courtyard in the midst of a group of young women who shrieked in delighted alarm.

"That Eleggua," Chango laughed weakly, "always the clown."

"Never mind him - we were talking about you and your constant unfaithfulness."

Chango sighed. When, he asked her, would Oshun realize that these little flirtations meant nothing? He was the god of fire, filled with the passion of the moment and if the moment happened to include a likely-looking female - hell - it was part of his mandate and had nothing to do with his love for her, the most bewitching of women, immortal or human. All this and more he said to her in a voice that could best be described as sand on silk. "Always remember," he concluded, "you have my heart - you *are* my heart!"

Oshun's own heart almost melted at his words but her resolve carried her to the most important issue of all - his relationship with the goddess of the whirlwind.

"And what of Oya?"

Oya and Oshun were sometimes friends, sometimes enemies but always rivals for Chango's love.

Chango sighed. For centuries he had juggled his relationships with the two goddesses and each had tacitly ignored his philandering with the other. Now, unfortunately, the moment of truth had arrived. With a silent prayer that Oshun wouldn't make a scene in public he said:

"I cannot separate my feelings for Oya and for you, Oshun. You are my heart and Oya is my soul. Together you are my perfect love."

"I want to be your heart *and* your soul," she cried, but he made no reply. Her eyes brimmed with tears and she turned blindly away leaving him looking after her in chagrin.

For the rest of the night Oshun was feverishly gay, downing glass after glass of champagne and dancing with everyone except Chango whom she refused so curtly that for spite he spent the evening carousing with a dozen different women. His tactics annoyed not only Oshun but also Oya, who had the temper of a bull with an abscessed tooth. She twirled herself into a frenzied funnel and spun around the courtyard, extinguishing every torch with the wind of her fury. This ended the evening abruptly, pleasing nobody except Oya who took morbid satisfaction in making everyone as disgruntled as she was.

Coming back to the present, Oshun boiled her heartbreaking situation down to its essence: she was

Chango's heart but Oya was his soul! How ironic that she, the goddess of love, was second best for the only man she loved. Stinging tears swam in her eyes again but this time Oshun refused to weep. She did *have* Chango's love, she reminded herself, and if she had to share him, so be it; she'd give Oya a damned good run for her money. Dipping a slender hand into the river, Oshun washed her tears away, splashing her face until she felt able to face the day. Thus braced for the morning's onslaught, she settled back on her pillow of moss to listen to her petitioners.

Like most people, Oshun enjoyed a touch of variety in her work, so she made her daily wish granting sessions more interesting by playing little games with herself. Sometimes she answered only the first prayer to reach her, sometimes it was the most original; occasionally, just for the fun of it, she'd honour the most selfish prayer and because her personal number was five, she often granted every fifth request.

"Beauteous Goddess of Love...send me a fine young woman for my son..."

"Yo, Mama…! I've been praying to you for three weeks and you've done squat! I want an answer and I want it *now!"*

Although Oshun is kindness and generosity itself, she doesn't tolerate disrespect. Breathing a brief incantation, she dipped her fingers into the river, flicked them in the air and was immediately gratified by the voice moaning in agony as its owner doubled over, clutching his stomach.

"There's your answer, brother. A few days of dysentery will teach you not to dis *me!"*

With a satisfied nod she turned her attention back to the rest of the supplicants.

"Oshun, Goddess of Love and Beauty, Mother of the River, this is your child, Alix. Hear me, I beg you."

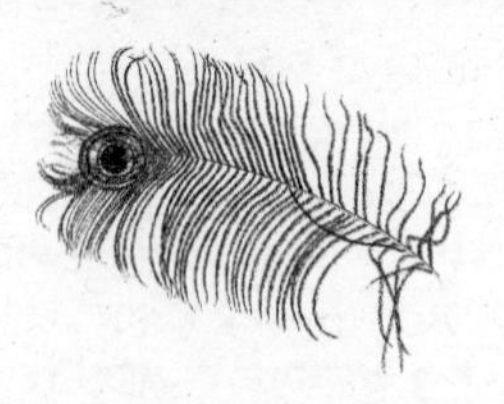

Swathed majestically in a blue crêpe hostess gown, Alix arrived downstairs just after seven to find her guests awaiting her in the hall. Angel had on a purple silk tunic and trousers, while Keisha wore a jump suit in lipstick red jersey. Brent was in a cream coloured shirt with intricate all-over pleats and black linen slacks. Alix paused at the foot of the stairs, gazing with pleasure at the group.

"What a striking picture you make. Come - drinks are set up in the library."

Accepting Brent's arm, Alix led the way to the library where she sank into an armchair, and waved to her guests to do likewise. Cavanaugh stood by awaiting orders.

"What will you have, Keisha?" Alix asked.

"White wine, please."

"Brent?"

"I know it's not the usual before-dinner drink, but I'd love one of those fabulous mango Margaritas."

"Why not? It's what I'm having," Alix smiled at him.

"Ty Nânt water, Miss Angel?" Cavanaugh inquired paternally.

"Yes, thanks, Cavanaugh. No ice, room temp."

He gave her a look which said, "as if I'd forget" and glided off, returning almost instantly with the drinks and an exquisite platter of hors d'oeuvres.

"Just leave the plate on the table, Cavanaugh, we'll help ourselves," Alix instructed.

"Very good, Miss Morton," replied the butler, disappearing silently.

"How does he do that?" Brent asked. "One minute he's doling out cocktails and canapés with the lavishness of Santa Claus on Christmas Eve and the next he's vanished like a dewdrop on a hot rock."

"It's bred in him," Alix said, "his father was the head butler at Parnham Court. I often visited there as a child and Cavanaugh and I would play together whenever I escaped to the kitchens. He was the Buttons in those days."

"What's a 'buttons'?" Keisha asked.

"It's a page, like a baby footman. Cavanaugh worked his way up the ranks under the watchful eye of his father and became a freelance butler at quite a young age. When we were children we always said he'd be my butler when we were grown ups and as soon as I began making money, I brought Cavanaugh to Canada. He's been running my household ever since."

Alix took a leisurely sip of her drink and put her feet up on a hassock: "Now - I promised to tell you more about Oshun but it needs a little background.

Oshun is a deity of Yoruba and Santeria religion and, according to their beliefs, everyone in the world, no matter what their religion of birth, is a child of one or more of the Orisha."

"Is an Orisha a god?" Brent asked.

"Yes. The word is synonymous for Yoruba and Santeria deities, male or female."

"How do you find out who your Orisha is?" Keisha asked.

"Sometimes you can tell from personality traits which match the attributes of one's Orisha, but it's properly confirmed through divination by a babalawo, or priest. There are hundreds of Yoruba deities, but the major ones were created by God, who is called

Oluddumare - and they're known as the Seven African Powers. There's Obatala, the Father of the Orisha; Eleggua, Guardian of the Cross Roads, also called the Messenger or the Trickster; Chango, the God of Fire, Thunder and Lightning; Yemaya, the Ocean Mother; Oya, Goddess of the Whirlwind; Ogun, the God of Iron and, of course, Oshun, the Goddess of Love and Abundance. In Western mythology there are gods who match the Seven African Powers: Obatala and Yemaya correspond to Jupiter and Juno, Chango to Thor, Ogun to Vulcan, and Oya to Diana."

"If Eleggua is the messenger, he corresponds to Mercury," said Brent.

"And Oshun matches Aphrodite," Angel said.

Alix continued: "When the slave trade began and captives were taken from Africa to the Americas, they were forced to convert to Catholicism. They accepted the religion but they desperately wanted to preserve their own gods, too, so they gave them the identities of Catholic saints, and created the religion known as Santeria which means 'the worship of the saints.' The merging is called syncretism and it turned Eleggua into Saint Anthony, Yemaya became Our Lady of Regla, and Oya, Our Lady of Candalera. Obatala has always been seen as both male and female and was syncretized with Our Lady of Mercy. Interestingly, although Chango is very masculine, he became Saint Barbara.

"What about Oshun?" Keisha asked.

"She is the patron saint of Cuba - *Caridad del Cobre*, Our Lady of Charity."

"I remember seeing a front-page picture of the Pope in the *New York Times* some years ago," Keisha said. "He was at a church in Cuba and there was a colour shot of him looking at a little statue of that saint."

"That was when he visited the Oshun shrine in Santiago del Cuba," Alix replied. "His trip did a great deal to bring Santeria into the open."

"The religion has different names in different countries," she continued, "and so do some of the Orisha. In Haiti, for instance, and some parts of the southern US Oshun is known as Erzulie and the religious practices vary from place to place as well, but whether it's called Santeria, Candoble, Macumba or Voodoo, it's the New World version of Yoruba, which is an ancient and powerful religion.

"I've heard of Voodoo, but not of the others," Brent said.

"Everyone's heard about Voodoo, thanks to those old Hollywood films like *Curse Of The Zombies* but it's a misunderstood religion that has been sensationalized beyond reality. It's the same thing with Santeria. It's one of the fastest-growing religions in North America, but when it makes the news, it's usually in some lurid story about the ritual slaughter of chickens and goats."

Alix reached for a smoked salmon canapé, demolished it in two neat bites, and continued: "The first time I visited Oshogbo in Nigeria, I met an amazing woman named Susanne Wenger. She's an artist who came to Oshogbo from Austria many years ago and she has devoted her life to rebuilding the shrines in the Oshun River groves. The people of Oshogbo call her *Adunni*, which means 'The Adored One'. I enjoyed being with Susanne so much and we became good friends. She has such a strong belief in what she does and she passes that enthusiasm to everyone she meets. I heard many stories of Oshun and the other Orisha from Susanne - similar to the ones Madara used to tell me."

"Who's Madara?" Brent asked. He was fascinated by Alix; she looked like the quintessential Wasp aristocrat but she was the most unorthodox woman he'd ever met.

"She was my nursemaid. I was born in Brazil when my father was the Canadian High Commissioner there. Madara was a kitchen maid at the residence and she was seconded to look after me. When we left Brazil for Father's next posting in Lagos, we took Madara with us. She loved me as if I was her own child...made beautiful dresses for me and cooked me special dishes. She loved braiding my hair in elaborate styles and to keep me quiet during those long hairdressing sessions, she told me stories about the Orisha."

"Tell us one," said Brent. "I'm getting a tad tiddly on this Margarita and I *love* to hear stories when I'm taddly…tuddly…tiddly..." He giggled into his glass and took another mouthful of the creamy orange contents.

"Yes, do," said Angel, "it's been years since I heard one of the fables and I've always loved them."

"If you insist." Alix drained the last of her Margarita and began:

"Yoruba stories are called patakis and this pataki is about the time that Oya had trapped Chango and was outwitted in turn by Oshun and Eleggua.

"Chango is the lover of both Oya and Oshun. On this particular day he was about to spend a pleasant dalliance with the beautiful goddess of love when Oya discovered he was yet again in Oshun's bed.

"She was enraged and sent a messenger to Oshun's house to tell Chango that his enemies from the North were marching on his kingdom. Chango leaped up, ignoring Oshun's wail of disappointment. He dressed in a flash and, taking his thunderstones and double-headed axe, he blew Oshun a kiss, promised to be back with her as soon as he had dealt with the marauders, and hastened to his castle to assemble his troops.

"Meanwhile Oya, who is the keeper of the gates of the cemetery, had summoned her guard of skeletons. The only thing Chango fears is the sight of a skull and, when he entered his castle, he was horrified to find himself surrounded by a bony brigade who chattered their teeth at him, snapping their ivory fingers with a sound like firecrackers. The one safe place was his private chamber and he ran to it and slammed the door shut.

" 'So, my lord,' Oya cried triumphantly: 'There you are and there you will stay!'

"Furious at being tricked, Chango paced the rooms, hurling his thunder stones against the walls and breathing flames, but to no avail. He was surrounded by Oya's terrifying troupe and there was no escape.

" 'May a herd of maddened elephants trample the devil woman into the dust! May she swallow a swarm of killer bees and may they sting her blackened heart a thousand times!'

" 'May she not hear your curses, brother or she will do even worse to you than she has done already.'

"Chango spun on his heel and saw Eleggua perched on the window ledge, grinning wickedly down at him.

" 'Oluddumare be praised that you have come!'

" 'And how could I stay away when my brother is so sorely pressed, particularly when it gives me the opportunity to outwit Lady Oya.'

" 'You have a plan? Tell it to me at once!'

" 'Softly, softly, brother. Just because those rattly beggars guarding you have no ears, doesn't mean they are deaf and Oya has the hearing of a fruit bat.'

"Chango shuddered at the very mention of his skeletal jailers. 'You're right,' he said morosely. 'The she-hound hears everything. But you, Eleggua, you will outwit her! You know me - I have no brain for this kind of thing.'

" 'You have many other qualities.' Eleggua reminded him. 'Your bravery, your genius in battle, your incomparable good looks – '

" 'And let's not forget my skills in dance and song.'

" 'Of a certainty.' Eleggua agreed cordially. 'Be of good heart, brother. I will soon have you free.'

"He flew down from the window and hurried to Oshun's brass palace where he told her how Oya had imprisoned Chango. Oshun was appalled and willingly agreed to help free her lover. Dressing herself in her finest robes, she sped to Chango's castle with Eleggua reduced to the size of a honeybee, riding on her shoulder.

"When they came to the castle, Oshun began to flirt with the skeleton guards who were beside themselves with the attentions of the ravishing goddess. It took very little persuasion to coax them into letting her visit Chango. After all, they agreed, Oya had said only that Chango must not leave. She hadn't said anything about forbidding visitors.

"Up went Oshun to Chango's chambers. The door was unlocked, for Oya knew that his dread of the skeletons would hold him prisoner more firmly than bolts and chains. Oshun slid inside and Chango, overjoyed to see her, held her closely in his arms and kissed her fervently.

" 'We have no time for that, brother,' Eleggua stretched himself to normal size. 'Oya will soon return and we must have you away from here now.'

"Oshun took off her outer robe and draped it over Chango. Then from her waist she took a pair of golden scissors and cut off her luxurious braids, which she and Eleggua attached to Chango's head.

" 'Let us go swiftly,' said Eleggua, shrinking once more and hopping onto Chango's shoulder. 'I will watch for the guard and you keep your eyes downcast so that you don't have to look at them.'

"Chango hastened down the stairs. Once at the gate he waved coyly at the guard while keeping his face modestly averted. Unseen, Oshun escaped by a side door while the guards were waving a fond goodbye to Chango.

"Chango, Eleggua and Oshun met back at her palace and long and loud was their laughter at their cleverness in outwitting Oya and her minions.

"Chango was saddened that Oshun had sacrificed her lovely hair but, as she told him, it would soon grow back and she would have done much more to assure his freedom.

"Eleggua smiled at them with a trace of sorrow for he knew that this was but one of many clashes around the triangle of Chango, Oshun and Oya and that their drama would be played out over and over through eternity."

"From hair to eternity," murmured Brent as Alix ended her story.

Keisha groaned at the pun and Angel threw the slice of lime from her drink at him, which he ducked. Cavanaugh, who had shimmered in to announce dinner, caught it deftly on his drinks tray and bowed modestly at the ensuing applause.

"I thought we'd eat in the Orangerie," Alix said, leading the way to an enchanting conservatory on the east side of the house, "it's one of my favourite rooms."

"Mine, too," said Angel, gazing with nostalgic pleasure on the white plaster walls that were painted with *trompe l'oeil* flowers and fruits. "I used to play here for hours," she told the others, "looking for the creatures that are hidden everywhere."

In between courses they searched the painted walls, finding butterflies, humming birds, lizards and ladybugs, tiny spiders and dragonflies.

"They seem invisible but when you find them you wonder why you didn't see them right away." Keisha said to Brent.

"Sometimes we can't see what's staring us in the face," he said, looking at her soulfully.

She hit him on the nose with a gardenia.

After dinner, Alix took her guests back to the library for coffee and liqueurs.

Alix, Keisha and Brent accepted coffee and cognac from Cavanaugh while Angel took more Ty Nânt.

"I've been meaning to ask you, Angel, have you begun to plan *Vegging Out* for this year?"

Alix was referring to the unique vegetarian food fair that was Angel's brainchild. She had launched *Vegging Out* five years ago and it had quickly become one of Toronto's top fund-raisers. Every restaurant in town wanted to be a part of the event, partly because it was good advertising to have a booth there and also because vegetarian cuisine, once dismissed as brown food for grey people, was now considered cutting edge: any restaurant worth its *fleur de sel* had at least one vegetarian dish on the menu. It was also a showcase for the city's leading chefs who vied for the prestigious award that was given for best dish of the show. There were lectures on different aspects of health; a huge bazaar which carried environmentally friendly products and outstanding crafts and live entertainment by the latest hot performers. Vegetarians and non-vegetarians alike flocked to *Vegging Out*, which raised enormous sums of money, all of which went to fight hunger locally, nationally and worldwide. It was a matter of some mirth to Angel's friends that she, who knew nothing about cooking, should have such success with a food fund-raiser but Angel never minded their teasing. All her friends, vegetarian or not, gave their many talents to mount the spectacular event which became more and more popular every year.

She turned to her godmother and with great enthusiasm told her of the plans for the next production.

"The Royal York has offered their main convention facilities to us which means that this year we can have all the programmes on the same floor."

“Thank God for that,” Brent cut in. He always had the job of logistics and it was a constant battle to find adequate space for everything. “I almost killed myself last year, ferrying the celebrity chefs between the demonstration cooking area and the book bazaar two floors below, in enough time for them to sign their latest best sellers and gallop back to perform - or vice versa. Nightmare City, Arizona!”

“That was nothing compared to the problems we had keeping the sound levels of the entertainers low enough so they didn’t drown out the lecturers in the next room.” Keisha said. “At one point I thought that that New Age health guru would smash a steel drum over the head of the leader of “Stone Circle Reggae” when they were playing an encore while he was beginning his talk.”

“There are always problems with any event, whether it’s a Broadway musical or a charity bash like ‘*Vegging Out’*, Angel said. “Most times the audience doesn’t know that anything is wrong and after everything’s over, the worst crises become the funniest stories.”

“Very true,” Alix agreed. “Anyway, I’m sure this year’s show will be an enormous success - it always is.”

Angel leaned over and hugged her godmother, then looked at Brent and Keisha.

“I assume,” she said with mock severity, “that you two are on board again this year?”

“Do we have any choice?” Brent asked gloomily. Keisha gave him a neat elbow to the solar plexus and said to Angel, “Don’t you worry, girlfriend. We’ll be there working our rib-pickin’ fingers to the bone for all you lentil-eaters.”

“Bless you, my children,” Angel said fondly.

Cavanaugh refilled coffee cups and offered more liqueurs. After a few minutes of small talk, Alix turned to Keisha and Brent and said:

"Would you think me terribly rude if I stole Angel away for a little while before bed? It's been so long since I've had any time with my goddaughter."

"Of course not." Brent rose to his feet.

She kissed him and Keisha on the cheek and held her hand out to Angel:

"Come on, darling. I want you to catch me up on all the family news."

Angel and Alix left the library and strolled to the morning room. They settled comfortably into the coils of the armchairs but while Alix was asking familial questions and seemingly listening to the answers, Angel had the feeling that her godmother had something else on her mind and by the time Alix had worked her way through Angel's parents, brothers and several aunts and uncles, Angel cut in:

"Alix, you don't care about Aunt Belle's rheumatism. What is it that you really want to talk about?"

Alix clasped her long arms around her knees and leaned forward, looking earnestly into Angel's eyes.

"You know how much you mean to me, darling girl..."

"Of course."

"And you know I'd *never* ask you to do anything that I felt was wrong for you..."

"Yes", Angel replied warily.

"Well, a little earlier while I was doing my evening prayer to Oshun, I had a visitation."

"Oh, Alix," Angel groaned, "not again."

"This wasn't like the last time."

"The last time? Five years ago, when you made me crazy with your announcement that Oshun wanted you to go on a mission to Nigeria and you came back three months later minus twenty pounds and suffering from nervous exhaustion? Would that be the time we're talking about?"

"It was *not* nervous exhaustion, merely a simple case of jet lag."

"I've never known jet lag to last three weeks."

"You're a darling girl, Angel, but you have a *lamentable* tendency to exaggerate. Now, as I was saying, I had the most remarkable experience today. I'd lit my shrine candle and was just beginning to pray when the candle flame shot up and started to dance like something possessed. As I watched, it took on the outline of a woman's figure and at the same time I heard the sound of tiny bells and a beautiful voice saying: 'Alix, bring me your goddaughter. It is time for her to meet me.' I was transfixed - it had been so long since Oshun had actually spoken to me - and before I could gather my wits enough to respond, the voice said again, 'Bring Angel to me, Alix - bring her tonight.' The flame grew brighter for a moment and then it shrank down to its normal size."

"Then what?"

"I thanked Oshun for her visit and told her I'd bring you to see her."

"Oh, I don't think so."

"You *must*," Alix said urgently, "You can't ignore a summons from a deity."

Angel patted Alix's hand. "My darling godmother, I know that Oshun is very real to you but I don't believe in Yoruba or any religion, if it comes to that."

"Your beliefs, or lack of them, don't matter, Angel. What is important is that you indulge me in this."

Angel had always known that her godmother marched to a different drummer in terms of her religious beliefs. Angel's mother often spoke of 'Alix's Goddess' and, as a child, Angel thought of Oshun as a kind of Fairy Godmother, often morphing Oshun and Alix into one beautiful, bountiful being. As an adult, however, she viewed Alix's beliefs with the same tolerant skepticism she had for all religions.

Although Alix Morton had been born into the Church of England, she had been a devotee of the Yoruba religion most of her life. It began when her father was appointed High Commissioner to Nigeria.

When Alix turned five, Madara took her to see a babalawo who cast the shells and declared Alix to be a child of Oshun. Madara was overjoyed. She herself was in the process of becoming a priest of Oshun and she took great pleasure in teaching Alix to pray to the goddess, showing her how to prepare the deity's favourite foods and what kinds of gifts to offer her and she dreamed that her charge would follow in her footsteps. Alix never did but she became a lifelong devotee of the goddess and kept an Oshun shrine in each of her houses and her office. She prayed to Oshun daily and delighted in finding treasures that befitted the exquisite Orisha.

Angel had never questioned Alix's connection to Oshun, but tonight she felt a new curiosity, possibly because of the interest the others had shown.

"Alix," she said tentatively, "may I ask you something?"

"Anything, dear heart."

"Why are you so devoted to Oshun?"

Alix looked at Angel quizzically. "I thought you didn't believe in any of this."

"My beliefs, or lack of them, aren't important, to quote a friend. I want to know why *you* believe so strongly."

Alix sat silently, looking into a space that was filled with very private memories.

Then: "The goddess Oshun is my life because she has *given* me my life. Everything I have accomplished, has come to me through the power of *Iyalode* and I can never begin to repay what she does for me.

"When Christopher and I were starting the firm, I prayed to Oshun for success and it was then that I had my first visitation. She came to me as she did today, in the flame of a candle - so beautiful that I had to avert my eyes. She reached out her hand and turned my face towards her, gazing at me with a love I've never felt before or since.

" 'Alix Morton,' she said in a voice like golden bells, 'you have chosen your path and it will bring you good fortune from the first step. You will have great success and enormous wealth. You love and are loved, and will never be alone, although you will not marry. You will become famous very quickly but your greatest fame will come in your later years. These are the gifts I give to you.'

"I was dumbstruck, but questions raced through my mind, tripping over each other as I tried to voice them. When I could finally speak, my throat was so dry that all I could do was croak: 'Why? Why me?'

"Oshun took both my hands in hers and I felt as if a shower of tiny jewels was cascading over me. 'You are my true child and are the instrument through which I will work. I am the goddess of love and beauty and you will help to bring beauty to the women of the world. In doing so, you will earn the success and wealth I spoke of, but there will be a price.'

"She meant that literally. 'For everything we receive, we must give back. So it will be for you. For every dollar you make, you will give five pennies to a worthy cause.'

"I was scared at the thought. Not that I was against the idea of giving, but five cents on the dollar is an enormous amount. But when I voiced my fear, Oshun just smiled. 'It is a pittance,' she said. 'In time to come, I will demand much more of you.'

"I put my fears to the back of my mind and began to think of the benefits:

" 'I'll set up a foundation,' I said, 'organizations and individuals can apply for consideration and the foundation board will give out grants. I'll make it part of our advertising campaigns - the customers will feel good about buying our products, knowing that part of their money is going to worthy causes.'

"Oshun shook her head. 'No', she said firmly.

" 'Why not?' I cried, 'surely it will be a good thing to make such a policy public knowledge?'

"She shook her head again. 'Listen to me, Alix,' she said gravely. 'Charity is a word I have always detested. To give is a privilege, whether to a cause or an individual. Sharing one's wealth is justice, and when you remember that justice is represented by a pair of scales, you realize how apt that is, for what you give helps to balance the difference between the haves and the have-nots.'

"I was profoundly impressed by her words, but I still felt that publicity was important and I said: 'If other companies see what we are doing, it could influence them to act in the same way.'

"But Oshun didn't agree.

" 'The highest form of giving is that in which neither the donor nor recipient know each other. You will give this ongoing sum anonymously and the recipients will be unknown to you. I promise you this; if you did know how your money will be used, you would be as satisfied with the results as if you'd chosen each donor personally. As for other companies, there are many ways in which you can influence them to give.'

"I stopped trying to convince her otherwise and I've followed her wishes all my life. Just as she promised, I've had success beyond my wildest dreams."

Angel was fascinated. "So," she said slowly, "Oshun isn't just a good-time goddess, granting wishes on a whim and a prayer."

"Would you think I could follow her if she was?" Alix said softly. "As I've told you, Oshun has many paths. She has all the attributes of mortals, all our weaknesses but most of all, she has our strengths multiplied a thousand fold. I am her child; she lives in me and I live in her and she gives me happiness every day of my life."

Angel hugged her godmother. "Well, if she *is* real, she couldn't have a better acolyte than you."

"Thank you, my darling. Now - will you grant my request?"

She gazed at Angel in mute appeal and Angel eyed her back cautiously.

"There isn't anything I have to *do*?"

"No, Angel. It'll be just as it was when you were a little girl, do you remember?"

"I remember you taking me into a little room, opening the door to a big cupboard and seeing a statue surrounded by candles and incense and other things."

"Yes," Alix said encouragingly.

"Then you lit the candle and prayed for a few minutes. I couldn't really hear what you were saying, except when you spoke my name. And that's all I remember."

"Well, that's all that happens."

"No weird potions? No slaughtering goats?"

"You've been reading too many lurid stories. I'm not saying animal sacrifice is never performed, but it's only on special occasions and it's not something I've personally participated in."

Angel sighed with relief. "Okay, let's go."

Alix rose briskly. "That's my girl."

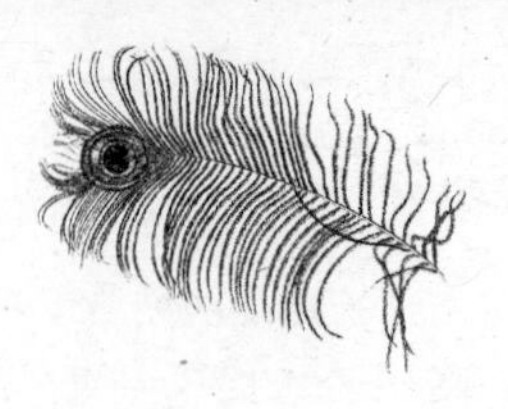

Meanwhile, back at the library, Keisha and Brent were wrapped in a passionate embrace, the intensity of which surprised them both. Pulling back slightly, Keisha took a deep breath.

"Wow! What brought that on?" she breathed.

Brent looked at her with dazed intensity, "I think it was a combination of rare wines and that combustible outfit you're almost wearing."

Keisha looked down at herself with a muffled exclamation: her jump suit, which had an oversized silver zipper snaking from her right shoulder to her left leg, was entirely undone and her beautiful brown body was very much on display. Slowly, she guided the zipper upwards, giving Brent a wicked little smile. His mouth drooped in disappointment and Keisha, now covered from toe to neck, giggled.

"You look like a little boy who dropped his lollipop in the dirt."

This was promising - women loved that little boy thing. Keeping the downturn to his mouth, Brent added a wistful under-the-eyebrows upward look. He had held it for no more than a count of three when Keisha, melting visibly, gazed at him the way she might look at an adorable puppy in a shop window.

"Come on then," she cooed. "Let's go upstairs and if you're a good boy I'll let you play with my zipper."

"Oh, yes, yes, *yes!*" said Brent, bounding to his feet.

Grabbing Keisha's hand he whisked her out of the library, through the living room, into the hall and up the stairs, ignoring her half-hearted demands to slow down. Angel, who was also on the way upstairs, pasted herself against the wall in order to avoid being flattened by the speeding blur, which waved goodnight at her. Smiling and shaking her head with a tinge of wistful envy she opened the door to her room.

Angel was filled with sleepy delight in being back at Caprice. Her bedroom, which was in one of the main towers, had been hers since she was a child and it wrapped her in remembered warmth. The walls were sponged in three shades of terracotta and the curtains, bedspread and easy chairs were in floral chintzes of soft yellow and coral. She ran her hand over the burnished mahogany of the old drum-top desk and smiled at the collection of Viennese bronzes on the round table under the window, a captivating orchestra of miniature animals. Angel loved them dearly and Alix had told her long ago that they would be part of her inheritance.

Vases of tulips and Queen Anne's lace dotted the room and there was a glowing fire in the wide fieldstone fireplace. She sat beside it, gazing into the flames and basking in the satisfaction of winning the biggest account in the short history of The Hot Box.

Then came the apprehension that always accompanied the beginning of a new project.

What if we can't do it...? What if I've dried up on ideas...? Maybe it's too much for us to handle...

The nagging thoughts went on for some time until, sighing and stretching, Angel rose from the hearth and began getting ready for bed. As she creamed her face she noted the fine lines that traced the edges of her eyes and etched lightly across her forehead:

Time for a little nip and tuck before the whole structure crumbles.

Taking a wide-toothed comb, she slid it through her thick auburn mane.

Alix says that Oshun combs her hair all the time. She makes her seem so real - while she was praying, I could almost feel Oshun's presence; funny what the power of suggestion can do....

Angel slid into bed, welcoming the softness of down pillows and the luxurious warmth of a double duvet. Turning out the bedside lamp, she lay awake for a long time, thinking about Oshun's lovely little room and the exquisite altar, hung in yellow silk and filled with treasures that Alix had presented to the deity over the years: Russian amber necklaces, perfume flasks of ancient glass, fish carved in topaz, peacock feather fans, coral beads, gold chains, all glowing in the soft light of honey-scented beeswax candles.

When she finally fell asleep, she dreamt that she stood beside a wide river that had broad stepping stones across it, each with a round, deep hollow in its centre. On the stone nearest to Angel stood an incredibly beautiful woman, dressed in a flowing yellow gown that fluttered in the breeze. There were delicate golden spirals in her ears and five gold bangles on each arm.

She smiled and beckoned to Angel and began to walk across the stones, turning at each one to repeat her gesture.

Angel followed, filled with deep curiosity but no fear and when she reached the other side, the woman stretched out her hand and pulled Angel gently to the shore.

"Who are you?" Angel asked.

The vision smiled even more widely, her face growing in radiance until it almost hurt to look at her. "I am Oshun, and you, girlfriend, are my child."

"How can I be your child," Angel asked, "I'm Jewish! I'm not terribly religious or anything, but..."

"Religion has nothing to do with it, sweet thing - you belong to me spiritually and soon we will meet in the waking world. As a reminder that you *are* my child I want you to wear these and listen when they speak. They'll liven up your life." She slid the five bracelets off her left arm and onto Angel's. Then she leaned over, pinched Angel's cheek, winked and vanished.

Angel awakened with a jolt and sat up in bed dazedly. She heard a jingle, looked down and saw five shiny gold bangles on her left arm.

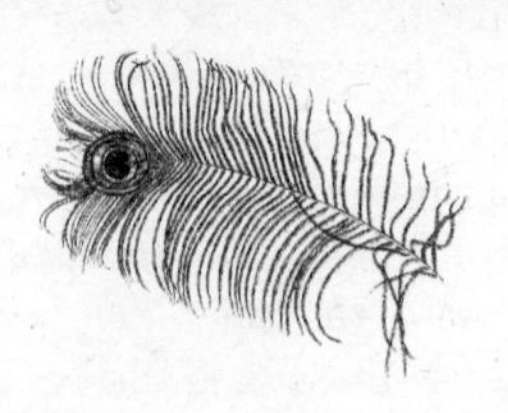

"Keisha, wait for me!"

Brent waved frantically at the slender figure which was headed down the path towards a mountain trail.

"Hurry up, then. I want to do four miles before breakfast and it's getting late."

She broke into a smooth, loping run that Brent had trouble matching. While he struggled along beside her he admired her slim, athletic build. Keisha had wonderful muscle delineation - sharply cut but not overwhelming. She had the deeply curved facial profile often seen in African carvings. Her colouring was what her grandmother would have called "high yaller" and her eyes were a warm hazel. After their night of passion, Brent more than ever fancied this intriguing young woman whose work was breaking new ground. Fashion models, rock stars, actors and politicians, were all eager to be photographed by the brilliant Keisha Adams and this added to her appeal for Brent.

They cantered along in silence for a while. Brent found his stride after the first mile and kept up with Keisha more easily. She flashed him an approving smile and said:

"Did you sleep well after you left me last night?"

"As some dazzling wit once said, I slept like a newborn baby - awake and screaming every hour."

"Cut out the smoking and cut back on the coffee."

"Thanks, Mom, but it was the crazy dream I had that was the problem."

She stopped dead in her tracks:

"What did you dream?"

"I was in a jungle and there were two black men, standing in a small clearing nearby. The younger one was tall, totally bald and extremely good-looking. He had on red and white printed trousers that ended just below the knee and he wore a heavy gold chain with a huge medallion. The other man was shorter and very thin - like a Giaccometti sculpture. He had a wild mass of hair all in braids and a strange expression on his face - not exactly evil - mischievous. He wore long trousers with one red leg and one black and a short cape in the same colours and he had strands and strands of red and black beads around his neck.

"I sensed that they knew I was there, but they ignored me and began to dance. The good-looking one was absolutely amazing. He played on a pair of small drums that were strapped to his waist and at the same time he spun on one leg until he was a blur. Every so often, he'd let out a huge shout and flames would shoot out of his mouth.

"The other one danced too, and he used a pair of rattles, one in each hand. He kept changing size - one minute he was tall, then he'd be tiny - sometimes he was so small that he'd dance on a leaf and all the time he laughed with a wild cackle. Then he stood still and pointed at me. I was scared, but he just smiled and said:

'Soon you will meet with EsuEleggua my friend, soon you will know me.'

He laughed again and said, 'Come, Chango,' to the other man. They disappeared and I woke up, still hearing that crazy laughter."

Keisha was silent for a moment, then she said shakily:

"I had a strange dream as well and it was so much like yours that it's frightening. I was in a jungle too and a hot wind began to blow, making the trees and vines sway.

A cloud of dust came, spinning like a little tornado and then it turned into a whirling woman.

"She was electrifying. Her skin was so black - it looked like the bloom on black grapes and she had angular features with cheekbones that could cut grass. Her eyes were black, long and deep set and she had a wide mouth. Her hair was cropped close to her head, like mine - in fact, she was built like me, same height and about the same weight. What was peculiar was that though she was turning so quickly, I could see her very clearly.

"She wore a purple robe with a slashed skirt lined in all the colours of the rainbow and they blended into each other as she spun. Suddenly she stopped dead, looked around and shouted 'Chango!' and flames flew out of her mouth too, just like your man.

"She saw me and said, 'Where is he? Where is Chango?'

"She spoke so angrily that I was intimidated and could only shake my head at which she stamped her foot and shouted: 'I know he is with her and when I find them they'll regret it!'

"She clapped her hands together with a noise like thunder, wound herself into a whirlwind again and tore off through the trees.

"I woke up and lay in bed without moving until it was light enough to get up. It was so real..." Her voice trailed off and they stood in silence for a moment, then Brent said hesitantly:

"Why would our dreams be so similar?"

Keisha paced slowly back and forth while she spoke.

"Well, we were talking about African deities last night. My grandmother would say that we had a visitation."

She looked at Brent half defiantly, expecting him to disparage her explanation but he just shrugged helplessly.

Keisha looked at her watch. "Hey - the meeting starts in an hour - we'd better move ourselves."

As they turned into the main gate at Caprice, they saw Angel, sitting under a tree, doing her early morning meditation while in the middle distance, Alix was performing Tai Chi with the concentration of a cobra eyeing a particularly toothsome mongoose.

"Good morning," said Angel, unfolding herself from the lotus position and wandering to the porch steps where Keisha and Brent had dropped.

"Hi," smiled Keisha

"Morning," wheezed Brent, reaching into his pocket for a cigarette.

Keisha glared at him: "Brent- you've just done a four-mile run, you're gasping for breath and now you're going to kipper your lungs. Brilliant!"

Brent sighed, looked longingly at his cigarette, put it back in the pack and shuffled off to shower and dress.

While everyone sat over post-breakfast cups of coffee, Alix called the meeting to order by tinkling her coffee spoon on her juice glass.

"I know you're wondering why there's been so much secrecy about our product but in a few minutes you'll understand why we're taking such elaborate precautions."

She asked Brent to pull down the window blinds. Opening a large cabinet to disclose a video screen, she continued. "What you're about to see will give you some history on the product and we'll go on from there."

The film opened with a long shot of African women in colourful robes and headdresses, working on the bank of a broad river. The sound of drums and a chorus of female voices were heard and the camera zoomed in for an extreme close-up of a long-fingered black hand holding a little plant with round, fleshy yellow leaves. This was followed by a quick pull back to a medium shot of a carpet of the yellow plants growing in a thick tangle on the edge of the bank. The women were picking them with great care, setting single layers of leaves into large shallow woven baskets, which were then stacked five deep. With immaculate balance, the women placed them on their heads and walked to a nearby open backed truck where the stacks were loaded and driven away.

The chant faded to the background and the camera followed the truck as it drove into a large town of tin-roofed houses. Sitting in the open back of the truck, surrounded by towers of plant-filled baskets, was Alix who looked straight into the camera and spoke:

"This is Oshogbo, a town of half a million people and one of Africa's most creative centres for art. The Yoruba, one of the three major tribes of the country, have created works that are displayed in museums around the world and Yoruba art is still being produced in the villages of the region as well as at studios here in town."

During the commentary, the screen showed superb statues, masks, batik cloths, carvings, prints and oil paintings. The scene then changed to a thickly wooded area.

"Oshogbo is also famous for its sacred forest, which houses many shrines dedicated to the Yoruba gods. The most beloved of all is Oshun, the goddess of love and abundance, an ancient deity who was born in the river that bears her name."

The scene cut back to the plant harvest at the riverbank.

"Oshun has many symbols, two of which are honey and gold, and this plant combines those attributes. Its leaves look like gold coins and they secrete a clear golden liquid that looks and smells like honey. The shrub belongs to Oshun and is treated with deep respect by the Yoruba who call it Honey Money Bush and prize it for the smoothness and firmness it reputedly gives to the skin.

"As a child growing up in Nigeria, I was fascinated by the beautiful complexions of the women of Oshogbo and when Glissando Beauté was ready to develop a new skin product, I brought a team of scientists and cosmetologists here to investigate."

In rapid sequence there followed scenes of Alix meeting with the women of Oshogbo, analytic sessions with scientists and then, in the most dramatic sequence of all, a meeting between Alix and the High Priestess of the Oshun Shrine. Months of patient work had led to this moment. Time after time Alix and her colleagues had watched the processing of Oshun's plant; always respectful, never demanding, asking questions that were at first ignored or answered incorrectly for the Yoruba don't part lightly with their religious secrets. Eventually, coming to believe in the sincerity of Alix and her team, the Oshogbons began to trust them with the facts and at last Alix was given permission to film the harvesting of the Honey Money plant.

Alix's commentary continued:

"This simple but painstaking task is performed by women of child-bearing years. After the plant has been picked it's taken to the worksheds where the gel is extracted. A special implement made of shell is used for this work; one end is scalpel shaped and very sharp, the other is carved into a shallow spoon. The leaves are opened with the blade end and the gel is gently scraped out with the spoon and put into clay jars.

"The used leaves are gathered together, wrapped in yellow muslin and, to the accompaniment of drums and chanted prayers of thanks, thrown into the Oshun river.

"When the jugs are filled, the liquid is poured into small clay pots, sealed with beeswax, stored in a mud hut and watched over by the priestesses of Oshun.

"At the annual Festival of Oshun, which is held during the last week in August, Oshun's most faithful followers are awarded a jar of the elixir.

"We knew from the preliminary studies that the fluid had powerful properties," said Alix, who was now strolling through a grove of trees which housed the spectacular Oshun shrines, "but much more work was needed and the necessary equipment was back at our laboratories in Toronto. Through the grace of the High Priestess and with a sizable donation towards rebuilding the Groves, we headed back home with fifty-five jars of the essence of Honey Money Bush."

The camera panned in on Glissando Laboratories where scientists were shown putting the extracted gel of the Oshun plant through exhaustive tests. The scene then shifted to Alix and her partner and co-founder, Christopher Matthews. Alix was seated at a large table where many flasks, bottles and pots were ranged in front of her, while Christopher sat at a nearby computer. A large distilling station was visible at the left side of the screen.

Alix opened a small container that was directly in front of her. She sniffed at the jar then took a tiny spatula, removed a small amount of the contents and ate it.

"This," she said, "is propolis - bee pollen. The propolis and this honey" - she gestured to the jar beside the pollen - "comes from African killer bees. Propolis does wonderful things for the body cosmetically and therapeutically. Both propolis and honey are important parts of our formula, which has been developed over a period of many years. Some of the other ingredients include calendula, ginkgo, mimosa, pau d'arco, hypericum, wheat germ, frankincense and myrrh. In all there are twenty-five different components and there was a lot of trial and error while we were creating the right blend in the proper proportions."

While Alix spoke she opened one container after another, putting various amounts of the ingredients into a highly polished copper bowl and thoroughly mixing each addition. While she worked, Christopher silently noted the name and amount of each element, which he recorded on the computer.

Alix paused in her work and, lifting the bowl to her nose, inhaled deeply and said:

"It smells marvellous. You know," she said to Christopher, "whenever I'm doing this work I feel almost as if I'm playing an organ...everything is laid out like a huge keyboard with all the keys and the stops and you get different fragrances which are referred to by perfumers as top notes and middle notes and so on, and that makes it seem even more like a musical composition!"

Christopher smiled in answer as, finishing the mixture, Alix poured it into a copper pot and placed it on a gas burner, adjusting the flame until it barely flickered.

"It will heat slowly until all the ingredients are blended, then it will go through the distillation process."

The camera zoomed in for an extreme close up of the pot whose contents shimmered quietly. Time lapse photography condensed a process of several hours into a few moments, melting the sludgy mass into a clear amber liquid.

Next, Alix poured the fluid into a retort, placed it over a Bunsen burner and ignited the flame. The retort had a large spiral of glass pipe attached that ended in an empty flask. The liquid began to bubble and a ribbon of steam rose from the flask, undulated through the glass spiral and flowed into the flask at the spiral's end. Unlike ordinary steam, it was as luminous as molten gold and swirled around the flask like a living thing before sinking into a shimmering pool. A slow dissolve cleared to show Alix standing at the Bunsen burner which she extinguished. She removed the filled flask from the pipes, saying:

"What we have here is called hydralate and now we're ready for the final step."

Opening a clay pot, which contained the essence of the Honey Money Bush, Alix emptied it into another copper bowl. She took an implement that looked like a chef's whisk into her right hand, the flask of oil in her left hand and, drop by drop, very much like making mayonnaise, she poured the oil into the gel, whisking steadily to blend the gel with the hydralate. While Alix brought the formula to completion, she gave a brief recap of the process.

The film closed with a shot of Alix and Christopher standing behind the copper bowl which was tilted in Alix's hands to show the glowing amber pool within. Through skillful editing, years of work had been compressed into an informative twenty minutes.

The screen went black, the blinds were raised and Alix got up from her chair. Facing the group, she said, "I'm sure you have a lot of questions, but please hold on to them until I've finished.

"Everyone knows that the greatest discovery to date in the beauty industry is the anti-aging product. We have retinol, alpha hydroxy and the fruit acid creams. Then there are the orally taken prescriptions, which also fight wrinkles and spots and which technically aren't cosmetics but medications. They're all excellent products but they have their drawbacks. A major one is the enormous investment of time before results are seen. Of course, there's also Botox, which works instantly, but it's temporary and like many of the products, it only treats fine lines with any success."

To this point, Alix had been calm and matter-of-fact, standing perfectly still in front of the screen as she spoke. Now she began to pace up and down, growing more excited with every word.

"We have something so *wonderful*, so *amazing* - something which goes much further - a formula which not only gets rid of all lines and wrinkles but restores the smooth firmness of young skin."

Angel, Brent and Keisha looked at each other in disbelief.

"Alix," Angel began, but her godmother cut her off with a peremptory wave.

"No more sagging chin lines or crepey necks! No wrinkled hands or cottage cheese thighs! We have a genuine youth restoring product and we're going to make history!"

Alix flung herself triumphantly into her chair and beamed at the three stunned faces.

Brent cleared his throat tentatively: "Alix, if this is true, it's the most incredible discovery since penicillin."

"What do you mean, '*if* it's true'?" Alix replied.

"Brent doesn't mean to doubt your word," Angel said, "but as you just said, every cosmetics company in the world has a product that claims new youth for its users."

"And most of them work to a certain extent," cut in Keisha.

Alix gestured for silence with a commanding lift of one long, bony finger.

"That's right - they work *to a certain extent.* My discovery goes far beyond that."

While speaking, she rolled up the left sleeve of her silk shirt.

"Look at my arm."

As older women's arms go, Alix's was in good shape, but it was covered with a web of fine wrinkles that spoke of age.

"Now," slowly and deliberately she folded back her right sleeve.

There was a collective intake of breath.

Alix's right arm was as smooth, firm and unlined as that of a 20-year-old woman.

"I think you'll agree that the results speak for themselves."

"Alix," Angel choked, "this is *am-m-mazing*...it's ...it's..."

"Unfuckinbelievable," Brent said.

"It's what women have been praying for since time immemorial," Alix said triumphantly.

"Not only women," Keisha said, "there are thousands of men who'd give anything to get their youth back."

Angel went over to Alix and hugged her, tears welling up and spilling over. "Alix - thank you, *thank* you for giving us this account."

Alix hugged her goddaughter back and then held her by the shoulders at arms length, looking at her with great seriousness.

"I didn't give you the account, Angel, you won it and I know you'll create a campaign that will be worthy of the product."

"We will - I *promise* you we will," Angel said fervently.

"We have a great deal of work to do in a very short time," Alix said. "How long will it take you to draft some preliminary advertising ideas?"

Angel took a deep breath and calmed herself enough to speak coherently.

"This won't be like doing a campaign for a new lipstick," she said slowly, "it's going to attract major attention all over the world."

Alix nodded in agreement.

"All the testing has been done and we're already in production. There are a very few of our people who know what the product does and they've been sworn to secrecy. That has to include the three of you and anyone else who will be working on the campaign and I must insist that you keep any others to an absolute minimum. It's utterly critical that this be kept under wraps until we're ready to go public. The cosmetics world is small, incestuous and as cut-throat as every other industry."

"Also, any other accounts you're working on will have to be re-assigned; there'll be no time in your lives for anything but Glissando."

"That won't be a problem," Brent said. "We've got two other campaigns in development but they're both at the stage where others on our staff can take over and some parts are contracted out as usual."

"Right," Angel agreed. She turned to Keisha: "What about you, K?"

"I'd set aside time to start working on a book but I can't pass up something as mind blowing as this, so my little project will go on hold for a while."

"I'm so glad." Angel said fervently. "We couldn't work with anyone else, could we, Brent?"

"Not even Annie Leibovitz," Brent said, teasingly and laughed at the indignant expression on Keisha's face.

"Well, that's sorted," Alix said briskly. "Now - what's our time frame?"

"Well, we'll have to learn all we can about the product: the components, the technical aspects of how it works..." Brent said.

"And then there's the product name, the copy slant, the packaging..." Angel ticked off the points on her fingers as she spoke.

"And don't forget the music..." Brent cut in.

"And the model," Keisha said. "We need a new face and finding the right one will take time."

"So, what are we talking about?" Alix said, "three weeks…? four?"

"More like two months," Angel answered.

"Well, that works. In two months you'll be heading off to Oshogbo."

At this bombshell they all began to speak at once but Alix waved them into silence.

"It's important that you experience the source of this miraculous fluid. Whatever work you'll have done to that point will be a plus, but who knows what inspiration you'll find over there."

"Africa!" Angel was starry-eyed with excitement.

"Back to my roots!" exclaimed Keisha. "Wait 'til I tell my family!"

"Where are they from?" Alix asked.

"I'm not sure. *They're* not sure. We've been on this side of the world for many generations. All I know is that my great-great God knows how many times great grandparents came from somewhere in A-a-africaaaaa. Well - this settles the model problem - we'll find the perfect face over there."

"You're right," Alix said. "It's an African product and it calls for an African model."

She returned to the agenda:

"The arrangements have been made: your flights and hotels are all booked, I'm sure your passports are in order, it won't take long for you to get the necessary innoculations and we'll be able to get visas with no problem as my friend, Susanne Wenger, will send you letters of invitation. The only other thing is for you to have the necessary innoculations."

"Oh, God –I'm terrified of needles!" moaned Keisha.

"You?" Angel was incredulous: "you've sky-dived, bungee-jumped and white-water rafted your way through every possible death trap. I always think of you as totally fearless."

Keisha gave a shamefaced grin: "Yeah, I don't scare easily. But I was traumatized by my first vaccination and I never got over it. Oh, I get all the shots I need and blood tests and all of that, but they have to chase me around the room with the needle until they corner me."

Angel felt guilty about making light of Keisha's phobia.

"I guess everyone has something they're afraid of," she said, "I can't stand loud noises: balloons bursting, fireworks, thunder – even dogs barking.

She turned to her godmother: "Could we use the library for a while, Alix? We have to draw up a work schedule and after that we'll have a ton of questions for you."

"Go ahead. I'll have lunch sent in."

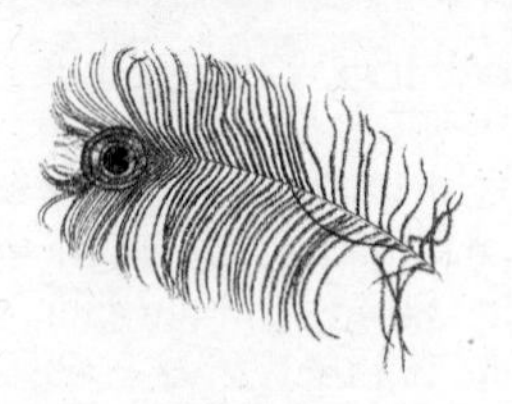

"The fewer people involved at this stage, the better," Angel said. She and Keisha were curled up in deep leather armchairs while Brent lounged in the embrace of the Black Forest bears.

"Right," he agreed. "We can produce the preliminary work between the three of us."

"Except for music," Angel pointed out, "and we need someone really good for that."

"I know just the man," said Keisha. "His name is Marc Dupré and he's hot. I shot the cover of his new CD last Fall."

"What's his background?" Angel asked.

"He's been in Toronto for the last few years, but he's from Montreal by way of New Orleans. His mother is Creole and a number of his compositions have an African influence. He's quite the musical wunderkind - started playing professionally while he was still in high school and cut his first disc when he was nineteen."

"I've heard some of Dupré's stuff. He *is* good...but I read something about him recently..." Brent clicked a pen against his teeth as he often did when deep in thought: "Oh, I remember - *FRANK Magazine* hit on him in their last issue: 'Marc Dupré - heavy on talent, high on hash.' "

"No one believes anything they read in that rag," Keisha snorted.

"Most people don't take *FRANK* seriously," Angel said thoughtfully, "still, like they say, where there's smoke there's dope."

"Yeah," Brent was still tapping his teeth, "maybe we should give him a miss. Why look for trouble?"

"Oh, please!" Brent's sanctimonious attitude irked Keisha, "like you've never taken a toke or two?"

"Not while I'm working." Brent replied primly.

"Well, that's the way most rock musicians work, Miss Priss."

"Stop it, both of you," Angel cut in, "I'm sure you're right, Keisha, both about the article and Dupré's talent. Get me his number and I'll set up a meeting with him."

"In the meantime," said Brent, "let's spend the day doing something really worthwhile like overindulgence in food, drink and sex. It's our last chance before we're locked in the grip of Glissando Beauté.

"I am going to sit under that tree," said Angel, pointing at a nearby weeping willow "and I don't want to see either of you until dinnertime. We're going to be together *ad nauseam* - excuse the pun - and I want a few hours to myself - nothing personal."

"No worries," said Keisha. "I think I'll go for a run."

"You ran this morning," Brent exclaimed.

"Only four miles and after sitting for so long I'm stiff and starved for motion. Gotta look after my body."

"I could look after your body right now," he grinned.

"Down, Igor," Keisha replied. She went off to change, leaving Brent staring after her with unabashed lust.

"This is not a pretty sight, Brent," said Angel.

"Looks damned good to me."

"I meant you, idiot. Roll up your tongue and stick it back into your mouth."

"Sorry - just remembering the joys of last night and hoping for a repeat performance."

"You may have to wait a while," Angel said. "Keisha is kind of hit and run when it comes to sex. She enjoys it and forgets about it until the urge strikes again. You ought to know - you're the original love-them-and-leave-them in both camps, if you'll pardon the expression."

"That's what makes her so intriguing. She could make me think about narrowing my options but right now I still have twice the possibilities than most people do; twice as many fields to play in and twice the number of partners to play with."

"Double the chance for jealousy if a female partner finds you talking casually to another man, double the suspicions if a male lover sees you dancing with a woman - double trouble all around, Tootsie."

Angel ruffled his hair and headed off to her tree. Brent wandered away in search of a Margarita and a hammock. Once settled comfortably, he lit a cigarette and made serious inroads into his drink as he swung gently and mulled over Angel's words.

He'd lived a life of open duality ever since university where, instead of being rejected for his switch hitting, he'd been the centre of attention. Quite apart from his exceptional good looks, Brent's charm was legendary and he used it on students and professors alike to great effect.

Brent and Angel had met during a freshman mixer and became instant friends. Her goal was to have her own advertising agency, and after graduation she worked as a layout artist for a major firm. She rose quickly through the ranks and was offered a vice presidency after five years. She was tempted to accept but decided to strike out on her own. She began The Hot Box as a one-woman operation, using freelance artists, writers and photographers as she needed them, which was how she and Keisha had met. Angel had asked Brent to join her, but he wanted to make brave new films and struggled for several years during which he made two short feature films that were artistic successes and commercial failures.

During this time, Angel's company grew quickly. She approached Brent again and again met with refusal as he had decided on a year's travel throughout continental Europe. He meandered from country to country, making friends easily and leaving them just as casually to move on to the next adventure. It was a pleasant life but one day in an Athens café, he met a man whose background was similar to his own, and who had been floating around Europe for over thirty years. As he said to Angel later, "I realized then that if I didn't come back home soon I'd be just the same way and I knew that I wanted more out of life than a hand to mouth existence."

When Brent returned, Angel tried again.

"I really need you, Tootsie. Nobody else has your combination of creativity and salesmanship. Give me a year and if it isn't for you, you can walk away with no recriminations. I think you *will* like it though and if you do I'll make you a full partner and I'll promise not to say 'I told you so.' "

Somewhat to his surprise, Brent loved it from the beginning. He enjoyed the crazy pace, the high pressure life, and the powerful rush of creating an exciting campaign. He relished the competition between agencies and excelled at luring new clients into The Hot Box fold. Best of all, he and Angel worked really well together, their blend of talents acting almost synchronistically to create campaigns that became the talk of the industry. Within three years The Hot Box was a force to be reckoned with. This win was their biggest victory to date and Brent took tremendous pride in knowing he was largely responsible for that success.

Brent smiled as he thought of how far he and Angel had come in such a short time. They were young, attractive and successful and if he had a somewhat freewheeling lifestyle - well, what the hell. It wasn't as if he didn't take precautions. *Sometimes,* he mused, *Angel is a tad over-cautious.* He finished his drink and cigarette and settled deeper into the hammock to laze contentedly in the glow of the golden afternoon.

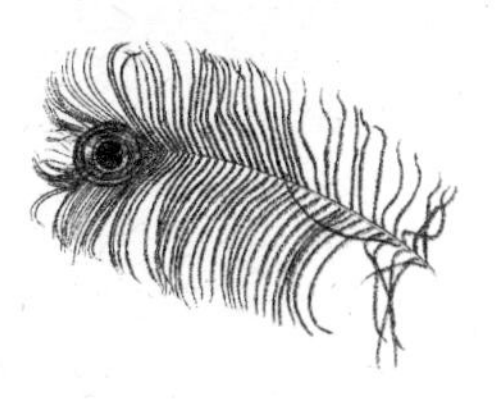

"Marc Dupré," said the faintly accented voice at the other end of the phone.

"Mr. Dupré, my name is Angel Zimmermann. I work with Keisha Adam who suggested I call you."

"Ah, yes - Hurricane Keisha. I so enjoyed the photography session I had with her and the results were spectacular, considering the material she had to work with." He gave a self-deprecating laugh.

He's probably a roly-poly little man with a guitar larger than he is, she thought while she said: "I am the Creative Director of The Hot Box Advertising Agency and we're looking for a musician and composer for a new campaign. Of course, I don't know if you're interested in commercial work..."

"What's good enough for The Stones is good enough for me, Mz'Zimmermann.

How enchanting he made her name sound, thought Angel.

Why don't you come to lunch at my studio tomorrow, and we can discuss your proposal."

"I wouldn't want to put you to such trouble," Angel said.

"Not at all -I love to cook."

Mentally adding another twenty-five pounds to the chubby frame she'd already given him, Angel took down his address and agreed to be there at twelve-thirty the next day.

Angel rang the bell of the converted warehouse in the lakefront area. The speaker box squawked and crackled before she heard a Franco-Louisiana drawl saying "C'mon in," followed by a prolonged buzz. The ancient iron cage elevator groaned and clanged its way to the top floor

"Mz'Zimmermann?" Again the liquid voice melted the two words into one. The light was dim and until her eyes adjusted, he was just a blur in the centre of a cavernous room. Gradually her pupils dilated, and when the blur sharpened into the lines that were Marc Dupré, they expanded still more.

"Oh, God," she moaned silently, *"my ideal man and twenty years too young!"* Her experience in working with announcers had taught her that the best voices were usually attached to the worst bodies, reflecting that here was the exception that proved the rule, she smiled coolly and extended her hand.

"How do you do, Mr. Dupré."

Nom d'un nom d'un nom! Marc said to himself. *Look at that flaming hair...those eyes like smoky stars...those endless legs...What should I say to make that all-important first impression? Something witty... charming...*

"How y'awl," he said, giving her hand a brief shake and dropping it as if it had scorched him.

Tingling from his touch, Angel covered her agitation by looking around the room with a feigned interest that quickly became genuine. She'd never seen such a collection of musical instruments, many of which she didn't recognize, all mixed in a jumble of wiring, control panels and speakers. Massive couches, giant easy chairs and huge cushions were grouped invitingly in different areas and a grand piano, dwarfed by the immensity of the room, squatted blackly in one corner, covered with score sheets and surrounded by drums of all shapes and sizes.

On the right hand wall of the room was a fireplace with a hearth big enough to roast a sheep and on either side of it sat a pair of sofas with a large, square coffee table in front of them.

What a sexy room. I could lose myself on one of those couches with him for at least three days.

She must think this place is a junk heap, thought Marc.

Speaking slowly in order to calm herself, Angel asked a few questions about the instruments and sank back into her x-rated reverie during his reply.

"Well," Marc said briskly, snapping Angel back into focus, "I've been going on far too long and I'm starved. Let's do something about lunch."

Centred against the far wall of the room was the kitchen area which looked like a 1950's lunch counter. The equipment, however, was ultra modern. A magnificent commercial gas range held pride of place and hanging behind it was a battery of gleaming copper pots.

Angel perched on one of the stools which were pulled up to the long counter while Marc went into the kitchen. And opened the refrigerator which was filled with orderly containers and jars. Having removed eggs, milk and other items he turned to Angel, raising an enquiring eyebrow:

"I thought perhaps a smoked salmon soufflé?"

"I'm vegetarian," Angel said.

"Vegan or ovo lacto?"

Angel was impressed by his knowledge. "I eat dairy products."

"A cheese soufflé, then." He took a wedge of cheddar cheese from the refrigerator and from the shelf behind him, brought down three bowls, plus a round-bottomed copper bowl which was hanging on the wall.

He broke an egg with one hand, opened his fingers a little to let the white slide through into a large glass bowl and deposited the yolk into a smaller one. Angel watched, fascinated.

"Do you like to cook?" he asked.

"I don't know much about cooking, but I've never seen eggs separated like that."

He smiled slightly, "I was taught by my grandmother to use the hands wherever possible."

Angel gazed at his hands, picturing the sensitive fingers sliding over her body. *Stop that!* she hissed to herself.

Marc took a small copper pan into which he put a large lump of butter, placed it on the gas range and lit a burner. When the butter was melted, he added several spoonfuls of flour, stirring the mixture carefully. After a few minutes, he poured milk slowly into the pot, blending the butter and flour smoothly into the liquid.

"Perhaps you'd grate the cheese for me?" he said to Angel, "there's a mouli in the left-hand drawer."

Grateful for something to do, Angel rummaged in the drawer, fished out the efficient little mill and shredded the cheddar. When she had finished, Marc said, "Now stir it into the saucepan and then remove the pan from the heat when the cheese is melted."

While Angel was doing this, Marc took the bowl of egg yolks. With a small whisk he beat them until they were a pale yellow and then stirred them into the cheese sauce. Admiring his precise movements, Angel idly twirled the copper bowl.

"What is this for?"

"Watch and see," said Marc. He poured a little vinegar and a pinch of salt into the copper bowl and wiped it out with a paper towel.

"Neutralizes the copper and helps the whites to rise." he said in answer to Angel's questioning look. Pouring the egg whites into the copper basin, he took a wire balloon whisk and began to beat the egg whites with a steady rhythm and in a surprisingly short time there was a cloud of white in the bowl. Marc turned the bowl upside down but the whites stayed inside. "That's how you tell they're done," he told her. He slid them into a large bowl, and, after stirring a spoonful into the cheese sauce to lighten it, mixed the sauce into the whites with quick, deft folds. A buttered soufflé dish stood nearby and Marc coated the inside with a fine sprinkle of grated cheese, poured in the cloud-light batter, then took a spatula and ran a deep groove around the top, about an inch from the edge of the dish.

"Why did you do that?" asked Angel.

"It will give the soufflé a crown," Marc replied, as he put the soufflé onto the centre rack of the oven and carefully closed the oven door. "Now we will make a salad and set the table *v-e-r-y* quietly so that the soufflé will not fall."

In addition to a large, round table in the dining area, there was a small table in a window alcove which Marc had chosen to use for lunch.

"This is my favourite place to sit," he told Angel as they put out woven place mats, Alessi stainless steel cutlery and blue pottery plates.

"It would be mine, too," she said, gazing delightedly at the central window which was an exquisite stained glass panel of a young woman picking peaches.

"I'm sure I've heard your music," Angel said, "but I have a dreadful time keeping the names of performers and songs together. I'd have researched your work before today, but this meeting was booked so quickly I didn't have time. I do apologize." She smiled charmingly and Marc felt as molten as the soufflé perking away in the oven.

"What would you like me to play for you?"

"What's the latest piece you've recorded?"

"That would be...this." He slid a disc into the console and the room filled with a familiar melody.

"I know that tune!" Angel exclaimed. "I've head it often but I don't know its name."

"It's called *'Cinnamon Honey'*."

"It's wonderful." They listened to the rest of the song in silence.

"What else have you done?"

He gathered together a small stack of CDs and handed them to her, saying "Instead of me reciting titles, listen to these at your leisure, *"hopefully in your bed, while you think of me."*

While they waited for the soufflé, Angel described the campaign to Marc as best she could without breaching confidentiality.

"Our client insists on secrecy, so I can't say any more for now", she finished. "Should we decide to work together, you'll be given all the details."

The young composer was intrigued: "I'm inclined to say 'yes' just to know everything."

"Better wait until we're sure that we're right for each other." Angel replied and then blushed at the implication of her words. Luckily, the oven timer had rung and Marc turned to open the oven door which kept him from seeing her embarrassment.

The soufflé was perfection - a delicate golden brown towering above its dish, with a crown worthy of an emperor. Accompanying it was a platter of peeled, seeded tomatoes and cucumbers which Marc drizzled with a fine olive oil from Provence and 12-year-old Balsamic vinegar.

Marc served neatly and waited for Angel to taste the soufflé. He had baked it in the French manner so that it was liquid at the centre, creating its own sauce. Angel took a small forkful, slid it into her mouth and closed her eyes with a blissful smile.

"Ummmm - *marvellous*!" she sighed.

Gratified, he reached over to pour her a glass of white Bordeaux.

"I don't drink," she said warily, half expecting him to be annoyed but he just nodded and filled his own glass.

"What can I offer you instead?"

"Water will be fine."

"Still or sparkling?"

"Still, thanks."

He poured her a glass from a deep blue bottle and they ate for a while in silence, glancing at each other every so often.

Ignoring her small protest, Marc gave them both another helping of soufflé, leaned back in his chair and said:

"So, Ahnghel - you really are like your name. You don't drink... don't smoke...you're vegetarian. You are filled with virtue."

She laughed uncomfortably. "How dull you make me sound."

"Oh - I don't think you're dull." His head tilted to one side, he gazed steadily at her with olive-black eyes. She felt as flustered as a teenage wallflower being asked to dance by the king of the prom.

Suddenly, the soufflé which had been melting in her mouth, turned into a brick in her throat. She put down her fork and pushed her plate to one side.

"Is something wrong?" Marc's measuring stare turned into a look of concern.

"No. I - I - heavens, look at the time!" She glanced at her wrist and realized she wasn't wearing a watch but decided to bluff it out. "I'm going to be late for my next meeting."

If I don't get out of here I'm going to drown in those eyes and I must *keep my head above water.*

"That's too bad." *Just as well. Another minute and I'd have lunged across the table and plunged my tongue down her throat.*

They shook hands gingerly, both feeling the jolt of electricity that leaped between their palms.

"I'll be in touch with you soon." *Steady on, girl, you're almost out of here.*

"Good. Oh - don't forget these." Marc started to hand her the CDs and dropped them.

Could you be any more of a klutz? he screamed at himself as he knelt down to pick them up.

He handed the discs to Angel and gestured mutely with one hand as he opened the door with the other. Angel clutched the CDs and, with a weak smile and an answering flutter of her fingers, slid swiftly through the door.

Once in the elevator she sagged against the wall, simultaneously congratulating herself on her escape and cursing herself for taking flight. Meanwhile, Marc was clearing away the luncheon debris and replaying their meeting in his mind, changing the ending so that Angel melted into his arms like the soufflé.

He put the last of the plates into the dishwasher and sank onto a sofa in front of the fireplace. Opened the cedar wood box on the coffee table he took out a neatly rolled joint, fired it up and drifted into a fantasy of his next encounter with Angel Zimmermann. It was a quiet evening with rain softly misting the window panes. They had just finished dinner and Angel was gazing into a leaping fire while Marc played a tune he had composed just for her.

Looking over to the fireplace, Marc was startled to see the magnificent figure of a black male appear in the flames. As he watched, the man strode out of the fireplace and stood on the hearth. Smiling at Marc, the vision picked up a flaming log and wrote letters in the air;

C-H-A-N-G-O. He pointed to himself, gave Marc a friendly nod and stepped back into the fire, carrying the log over his shoulder. Unaware, Angel continued to stare into the flames.

Marc sat bolt upright, abruptly interrupting his daydream. He looked suspiciously at the joint in his hand and then crushed it out in the ashtray.

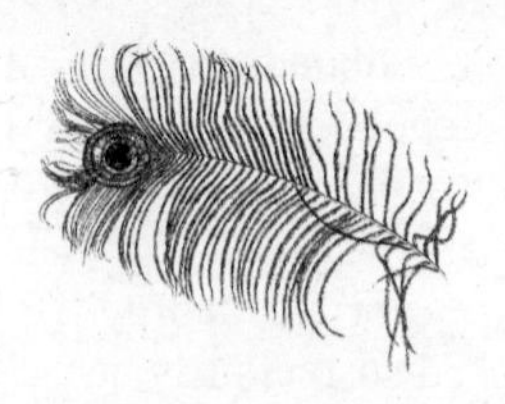

By Monday Angel had signed Marc to compose the music for the campaign. At a meeting during which he met Brent and was reacquainted with Keisha, Marc was pledged to secrecy and, after being briefed on the revolutionary new product, he put everything else aside to concentrate on creating a theme song for Glissando's discovery.

"Ahnghel, it's Marc."

Angel pressed the phone tightly to her ear as if she could get closer to the voice that made her name the most desirable sound in the world.

Be brisk - be businesslike, she instructed herself.

"Yes, M-M-M-Marc," *Godammit - I sound like a cow in heat.*

"I have finished the demo tape of the theme," he said. "When would you like to hear it?"

Angel didn't speak for a minute as she tried to get her thoughts in order. She and Marc had consulted together several times at his studio and it had been difficult for her to keep her mind on work. She wanted to touch him all the time - to put a hand on his shoulder as he sat at the keyboard or to brush his hair back where it fell over his forehead.

She had decided that once the song was written, she'd invite Marc to her apartment. By then, she'd reasoned, one of two things would have happened. Either she'd have gotten over a ridiculous crush on a man who was far too young for her or she'd have to admit that her feelings for him went deeper than a superficial flirtation. If so, she'd need to bring about a confrontation and she'd feel far more confident about doing that on her own territory.

"-Are you there, Ahnghel?"

"Oh, sorry. I was just looking through my book... How about tomorrow evening at my place? I'll order in sushi if you like Japanese food."

"That sounds wonderful. What time?"

"Eight o'clock?"

"Eight it is. I look forward to it. Goodbye."

"Bye," she said weakly.

The next night Marc arrived fifteen minutes late and very apologetic. She waved his excuses aside with a smile as she said, "I can't wait to hear the tape, but let me get you a drink first. What would you like?"

"Have you any single malt?"

"How's Cardhu?"

"Perfect - neat, thanks."

Angel poured him two fingers of whisky, gave herself a large glass of Ty Nânt and curled up on the couch.

Marc raised his glass to her, drank and turned to the tape deck. Taking a deep breath, he pushed the button.

Two hours later, they had finished dinner, and were listening to the theme for the tenth time. The music was everything Angel had hoped for and Marc was thrilled with her reaction.

"Of course," he said, "it may have to be reworked a little when we have a product name, but I think I've captured the essence of it."

Unable to trust her voice in response, Angel just nodded while she caught the corner of her lower lip between her teeth.

Ohhhh, don't do that, Marc moaned silently.

Desperate to keep his cool, he moved away from the chair in which he'd been facing Angel and sat on the floor, facing the fireplace.

She gazed at his profile as he looked into the fire and twiddled her gold bracelets. They chimed softly, saying, "Do it. Do it. Do it."

I can't. Angel hissed mentally.

"You can," tinkled the bangles.

I won't!

"You *will,*" they clanked sternly.

As if being pushed, Angel slid off her chair and curled up on the floor just behind Marc. He neither spoke nor moved but she could sense his tension. She reached out a tentative hand and touched his shoulder; it felt like wood. He sat rigidly for a moment, then turned and wrapped his arms tightly around her. They lay on the floor locked together, breathing in unison.

Suddenly Marc sat up, pulled away from Angel and leaned against the side of the fireplace. His mind lurched between fear and reason. He wanted her desperately but was terrified to begin what he knew would be more than a casual relationship.

Don't start down that road, he said to himself, *you won't be able to come back.*

Prodded by an unseen force, Angel moved to him and laid her hand on his neck. He took hold of her shoulders, turned her so that her back was to him and held her firmly against his chest.

"Ahn-ghel..." he said in a choked voice.

She leaned against him, sick with a mixture of shame and desire. "I don't know what's wrong with me...I've never done anything like this before."

Inwardly she writhed over the triteness of her words but it was the truth, even though he probably wouldn't believe her. Her stomach spasmed in anticipation of rejection.

"Ahn-ghel - I want to leave here as friends, not lovers."

That line was no better than hers and it gave her courage. She twisted back to face him, looking deep into his eyes, unsmiling and unmoving. Suddenly he gave a loud cry, threw himself on her and kissed her until her mouth was bruised. They rolled around the floor, crashing into assorted pieces of furniture. *This is more like it, Angel, my girl,* she said to herself exultantly. A few minutes later, having accumulated several light contusions, she disentangled herself, stood up, reached out her hand and with calm authority, said, "Come."

Like a sleepwalker, Marc allowed himself to be led to the bedroom. He lay down on his back, looking up at Angel who stood at the foot of the bed, inwardly quaking.

The bracelets chittered, *You have him where you want him - now, easy does it.*

Her jitters disappeared. She knelt beside him and unbuttoned his shirt.

Oh, mon Dieu, mon Dieu - I am undone. Even in the midst of his panic, Marc's writer's brain approved his choice of words.

With a note of hysteria in his failing voice he asked, "What if I told you that I am very small?"

"I don't care what size you are," she replied tranquilly.

"And if I should have only one testicle?" his fright was increasing.

"I'm told that's quite a common condition." There was a note of amusement in her voice. The more frenzied he was, the calmer she became

"I can make you come without touching you."

"I think," she said gently, "that we'll try the regular method."

She slid off his shirt. He had wide shoulders and a beautifully smooth chest.

She removed his shoes and socks, flicked open his belt buckle, peeled away his jeans and underwear and leaned back to survey the fruits of her labours. He was exquisite, like a Tanagra figurine.

"I thought you'd be thin - but you're not...and you are *very* large!" she breathed in delighted surprise.

Her admiration restored his confidence and he folded his arms behind his head and waved at her appreciatively as he said, "Take off your clothes."

She undressed with a speed that she blushed to remember and a few minutes later, they were lying side by side after a fast and furious consummation.

"Damn! I didn't mean to finish so quickly." Marc was chagrined by his lack of control.

"That's quite all right." Actually, Angel was flattered that he'd been so overcome by passion.

"Don't worry - I'll be ready again in a few minutes."

"I have every confidence in you, Marc," Angel said, keeping laughter out of her voice with difficulty.

Her confidence wasn't misplaced for even as she spoke, Marc was growing to a new and impressive height. Leaning over her, he cupped her face in his hands and kissed her with soft insistence. She buried her hands in his hair and the strands sifted through her fingers like silk fringe. He trailed his mouth down her neck to her shoulders until it reached her breasts where he began doing talented things with his tongue.

Angel lay in a blissful haze, scarcely able to believe that she was in bed with this incredibly sexy creature who seemed to be enjoying himself, and her, tremendously. A tinkle cut through the mist:

Don't just lie there, clanged the bracelets, *do something!*

Angel began running her hands down Marc's back, rubbing gently in small circles as she travelled the length of his spine. The simple motion created unusual sensations as if every nerve ending in her fingers and his back were stitched together by tiny jolts of lightning. Marc moaned. Angel stroked longer and lighter. Marc moaned louder and rolled onto his back. His penis popped into Angel's hand as smoothly as if they'd been rehearsing for weeks and she juggled it thoughtfully from hand to hand while deciding on her next move. Angel had never been an oral sex enthusiast but it occurred to her that she might have been missing out on a good thing and, after a tentative start, discovered that this was the case. Anyone who has ever tried a sport for the first time and discovered a natural aptitude for it will understand Angel's exhilaration. It's difficult to know who was happier over her new-found talent, she or Marc.

For three blissful weeks they lived in a state of total euphoria and semi-hibernation, spending every free moment in Angel's apartment or Marc's studio. When with the rest of the team, they adopted a friendly professional attitude which, they assured each other, fooled everyone. They were wrong.

"I am here as a one-man committee to find out what's going on." Brent lay, legs outstretched on the sofa in Angel's office, a glass of Sancerre in one hand and a cigarette in the other.

"What should be going on?" Angel replied innocently.

"Well, let's see," Brent blew an accusatory smoke ring at her, "usually we have lunch at least three times a week and you've been unavailable the last seven times I've asked you...you couldn't have dinner last Wednesday, Thursday or yesterday and you missed Monday Night Madness at *Imogene's* twice in a row. Questions are being asked..."

"By who?"

"By whom," he reproved.

"All right, by whom?"

"By me, your boon companion. Angel, my child, why hast thou forsaken me?"

"Don't get biblical on me, Tootsie. I've been working on the campaign, and - "

"Without me? Your partner *and*, I might add, chief copywriter of the firm. What on earth could you be working on that doesn't need my input?"

"The music."

"Oh, the *music.* Silly me, I should have known: of course, the fact that you can't carry a tune in a Hermés tote bag doesn't enter into it."

"I may not be able to sing or play an instrument," Angel said defensively, "but there's more to the musical component of a campaign than that...there's knowing the type of music and the mood of the commercial and...and..."

"And the body of work of the composer...or, perhaps, just the body of the composer?" he said slyly.

Angel flushed bright red, "I don't know what you mean."

Brent shook his head in mock sorrow, "Angel, my Angel - *when* will you learn to confide in those who love you best. I came back to the office last Tuesday evening to pick up some material because I'd decided to work at home the next day. While I was checking in, I noticed that you weren't signed out, so I thought I'd see if you wanted to go for a late dinner. I poked my curly little head into your office and what to my wondering eyes should appear but you and Marc, entwined on this very couch like a pair of amorous octopuses - or is it octopi? Being the heart and soul of discretion that I am, I tippytoed away, leaving you to the body in question. Of course, it wasn't much of a surprise - when we're all working together Keisha and I can hardly breathe from the electricity that's kicked up between you two. And now, darling, I'm all of a doodah to hear whatever you want to tell me and I *know* you want to tell me everything!"

Brent took a sip of his wine, lit another cigarette and settled even more comfortably on the couch, gazing at Angel in bright-eyed expectation.

Angel fiddled with a heap of brightly coloured paper clips.

"It's not quite how it seems," she began slowly.

"Seemed pretty hot and heavy to me," observed Brent.

"If you're going to interrupt and be *flippant* I'm not telling you anything!" Angel jumped up from her chair and paced around the room.

"Sorry darling, I promise I'll be as mum as a sealed bottle of champagne. Now, sit down and unburden yourself."

Mollified, Angel sat at the other end of the couch and swung her legs up so that she and Brent were reclining facing each other, as did they so often when deep in discussion.

"The thing is, I think I'm in love with him."

"But that's *wonderful*, Angel girl!"

"No, it isn't. I'm fifteen years older than he is."

"So?"

"So - it's dreadful!"

"Does anyone think it's dreadful to see a man with a woman fifteen years his junior?"

"No, but the double standard still prevails," Angel said morosely.

"The times, they are a-changing, as Bob Dylan so cleverly pointed out," Brent replied, "besides - there are other factors. First of all, you don't look anywhere near your age. Secondly, many men like a more mature woman - I do myself, come to think of it, and thirdly, Marc may be only twenty-five, but he's had a wealth of experience that many men of fifty would envy. I think you make a delightful couple and nobody would raise an eyebrow in your direction."

"But there's more to it than just other people's opinions," Angel sighed. "For instance - "she paused uncomfortably.

"Go on - it's just us girls."

"Well - the sex is *marvellous*, truly magical, but I often find myself worrying about how I look. It's fine when I'm underneath, but sometimes Marc wants me on top and then all I can think about is that my face has grown three more chins and my belly is hanging down to my knees."

"First of all, you may be pushing forty, but you look like someone in her late twenties. The only wrinkles you've got are those cute little crinkles at the corners of your eyes and your body doesn't have a droop to its name - yes, yes, I know", as Angel opened her mouth to protest, "you think you need to lose weight, but men don't *like* women to be so thin that they could use their shoulder blades as razors and I'll tell you a little secret; when the woman is on top, the man isn't aware that she *has* a belly- not when her boobs are dangling above his face. All he's thinking is, 'don't those look delicious and wouldn't it be great if I could get both of them into my mouth at the same time.'"

Angel laughed. “You’re incorrigible! Thanks, Tootsie, but I’m still not ready to throw caution to the wind where Marc is concerned.”

She leaned over to Brent, gave him a kiss on the cheek and stood up. “And now we’d both better get back to work. Glissando calls.”

“Right,” said Brent, sliding off the couch and doing a couple of deep knee bends to loosen his joints. “Why don’t you and Marc come out of your cosy little closet and join Keisha and me Saturday night? That new fusion restaurant is opening on King Street.”

“No, I’ll give it a miss...like I said, I can’t bring myself to go public just yet.”

“Okay,” Brent said as he strolled to the door. He left, but then popped his head back into the doorway: “By the way the answer to any of your future problems is the new Glissando potion: rub it on any trouble spot and voila - not a sag in sight. *Ouch*!” Angel had hit him with a paper clip shot from a rubber band. “All right, all right, I’m going!”

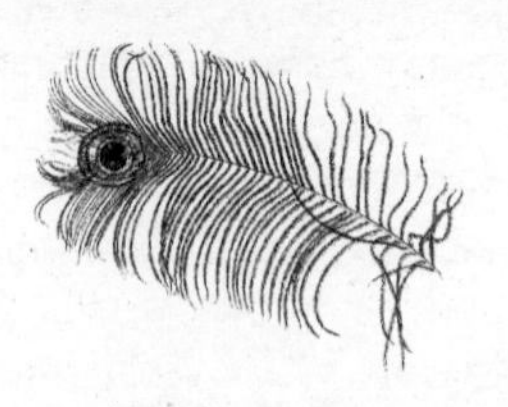

Obatala sat in his cloud palace, gazing down on the land, down to the forests, the plains, the rivers and out to the ocean. He was a placid, clear-thinking god, always in control of his emotions, never shouting or spitting fire like Chango or playing practical jokes like Eleggua. Obatala had a delicate constitution; he lived on bland, soothing foods such as milk, yams and beans and he was very fond of igbin, the large African land snails. He never drank but enjoyed the occasional mild cigar and was truly moderation personified or possibly deified.

After scanning the ocean depths for some moments he found who he was searching for.

"Yemaya," he called, "Ocean Mother, I would talk with you."

Deep within the coral walls of her underwater palace, Yemaya was lounging on a couch made of sea anemones that massaged her lavish contours with every motion. She was eating sea grapes and enjoying the first rest she'd had that day when she heard Obatala's call bubbling down through the water's depths. With a resigned sigh, she rolled off the couch, collected a few confections of which she was particularly fond and climbed into her silver seashell carriage. Settling herself among dense sponge cushions, she chirped to the eight harnessed manta rays and rose swiftly to the surface where she saw Obatala looking down at her.

"Greetings, King of the Clouds." Her beautiful green eyes crinkled as she smiled.

"Greetings, Ocean Mother. Will you come up or should I come down?"

"No, no - I'll rise to the occasion."

Obatala nodded tolerantly. Yemaya had a passion for puns and was so childishly pleased with herself whenever she delivered one that nobody had the heart to discourage her.

She soared up to Obatala and sank contentedly onto a pink-edged cloud beside him, giving a dismissive wave to her vehicle. The manta rays saluted with a curl of their front fins and drifted back down to the ocean, diving below the waves with the seashell coach which glinted briefly underwater and disappeared.

Yemaya watched it out of sight and then turned to her host.

"And how is it with you, my lord?"

"One day is pretty much like another, in fact, to tell you truthfully, Yemaya, I'm feeling a little bored these days."

"Ah - that is not good. We must see what diversions we can find to interest you. I've brought you some sea horse milk and mother of pearl biscuits. Let's relax and talk of pleasant things."

Obatala took several sips of milk and ate a crunchy little biscuit, sighing with pleasure.

"Yemaya, you always know what pleases me. My digestive system is so weak and these soothe my stomach and my soul. What would I do without you?"

"Fortunately you will never have to find out."

"Yes, constant friendship is one of the major benefits of eternity," beamed Obatala, patting Yemaya's smooth, firm arm and allowing his hand to wander towards her extraordinarily fine bosom.

Yemaya eyed Obatala indulgently while she weighed up the possible courses of action. She really wasn't in the mood for sex right now but it would probably take more energy than she wanted to expend in dissuading him. Yemaya was indolent by nature and Obatala, although gentle, could be very determined. Her good heart won out and she wound her arms around him and gave him a generous, open-mouthed kiss. Warming to her work, she pulled the fleecy cloud over herself and Obatala. Anyone who chanced to look up would have seen the cloud changing from white to pearl pink and finally to a soft red as it heated up from the activities happening within its billowing depths.

What a beautiful cloud, thought Brent, gazing at its rosy fluffiness from the airplane window. *I can't remember seeing one change shape quite like that before. It looks like a feather bed with people under the covers doing wonderfully unspeakable things to each other.*

"Would you like coffee or tea, sir?" asked the stunning blonde flight attendant, brandishing a pot of each and smiling warmly at Brent.

Everyone smiled at Brent. Angel thought, with a twinge of envy, *he was one of those charmed and charming people who breeze through life adored by all, He only has to flash that baby boy grin and everybody melts like butter on a griddle.*

Marc had fallen asleep in the seat next to Angel and she studied him minutely, her eyes measuring the length of his lean body as she remembered the feel of it against hers. His brown hair was pulled back into a pony tail and she tried to decide whether she preferred it that way so she could hold on to it while she guided his head to selected parts of her body, or whether it was better when she loosened it and let the silky mass cascade over her. She was, she realized glumly, mad about the boy.

"He's not a boy - he's a man," she scolded herself.

He's just a boy, her self sniped back.

"He's a *man*!"

He's twenty-five years old and you are forty.

"Thirty-nine!"

Only 'til next month, Mrs. Robinson!

"Shut up, bitch!!!"

Angel indulged in many such edifying chats with herself since meeting Marc Dupré. They all ended in a slanging match which she never won.

She and Marc had had a perfect eight weeks - perfect except for her daily agonies over the age difference and Marc's fondness for soft drugs and hard liquor.

The loudspeakers crackled, bringing her back to her surroundings with the announcement that they were about to land. Marc had awakened and was looking out the window. She followed his gaze to see glimpses of land through the drifting clouds.

"I wonder what's waiting for us down there?" she said.

"Strange and wonderful things," he smiled.

"Malaria, AIDS and other things too ghastly to mention," said Brent, popping his head over the back of his chair and gazing dolefully at them.

Keisha pulled his chair to the upright position, making him ricochet back to where he belonged. "Fasten your seat belt and your mouth, Cassandra," she said briskly.

"Cassandra?"

"The goddess of prophecy - very big in the gloom and doom department."

"You may scoff, my dear Keisha, but when they find our heads shrunken to the size of crab-apples, don't say I didn't warn you," he replied with offended dignity.

"Head-hunters live in Borneo, not West Africa."

"Borneo, Africa, what does it matter? I have trouble with anything north of Yonge and St Clair."

Keisha laughed indulgently and patted his cheek. "Poor baby. Never mind, I'll look after you."

"With you by my side, I can face anything - even the lack of my morning *latte*."

The plane landed with a soft thud, followed by several small bounces and taxied slowly to the glass-fronted building. Gathering their carry-on luggage, they disembarked into the maelstrom of insanity known as the Murtala Mohammed Airport.

"How long have you been a flight attendant?"

Brent poured *Moet et Chandon* into two glasses and handed one to the ravishing creature lying beside him at the edge of the hotel pool.

"I've been a trolley dolly for the past five years."

"You Brits have the niftiest expressions."

Brent looked at the alluring figure. It was a vision to behold with a mane of long, blonde hair, lazy green eyes and curved lips with those deeply indented corners that one usually sees only on children.

He looked at his surroundings: the brightly-coloured chaise longues around the pool, a thick hedge of flowering shrubs on which jewel-toned butterflies flickered in an endless ballet and a flock of hoopoes soaring in a sky which the African sun had bleached to blue-white.

Very pretty, mused Brent, *but no competition for the beautiful bundle beside me;* "So, Steve -"

"Stephen, if you don't mind, darling. 'Steve' is so effing butch, I feel I should be wearing a hard hat and a tool belt."

"Is that Stephen with a V or a PH?"

"PH. V is American, like you."

"I'm Canadian."

"Sorry. I know how you Canadians hate being taken for people from the US, but we tend to think of you all as Americans."

"Correct that tendency, young Stephen," Brent said with mock severity, "wars have been fought over semantics."

"As Richard Sheridan once said, I'm anti-semantic," chortled Stephen, now half-way through his second glass of champagne.

"Mmmmmm - a *literate* trolley dolly!"

"I think one should be well-rounded."

"And you are, in whichever direction one looks." He gave Stephen a speculative look: "I'm surprised you're in Oshogbo. I would have thought you'd spend your free time in Lagos."

"Perish the thought - everyone hates Lagos, even those who live there. No, for the usual two-day layover here, I go to Lome, but I'm on holiday this trip. I'm into ceramics and Oshogbo has a lot of talented potters and sculptors, so here I am. Besides," he gave a wicked little grin, "this time there's an added attraction."

"Which is?"

"You."

"Music to my ears. Now all you have to do is whisper demurely that you're free for dinner and whatever madness an Oshogbo night might bring."

"I thought you'd never ask. Let's go for a swim."

Stephen uncurled his slim, well-muscled body and dived into the pool in one smooth motion, followed quickly by Brent. It took them a long time to come to the surface.

Later that evening, Brent and Stephen strolled through downtown Oshogbo. The streets were red earth, packed solid from generations of feet and the smell of wood fires mingled with exhaust fumes from swarms of old cars rattling by. The two men looked with interest at the houses crowded together in irregular lines. They had thick earthen walls and corrugated tin roofs and were known as shotgun houses because the rooms were laid out in a straight line so that a bullet fired from the front door would pass through the house and exit via the back door.

"There are similar houses throughout the southern United States," Brent said to Stephen, "you could almost think you were in Louisiana or southern Georgia except for how the people are dressed."

There was colour everywhere in the gowns and headdresses of the Yoruba women and the long shirts known as *ajabadas* worn by the men, sometimes alone but often partnered with trousers, which were called *sokotos.* Many also wore the *fila*, a shaped cap that perched on one side of the head. The vibrant shades were counterpointed by the garments of women from east Nigeria who wore pure white lacy blouses and wraps

Arriving in Kings Market, they found clusters of small restaurants offering a variety of foods. Brent left the choice to Stephen and they now sat facing each other in a small *bouka* that served local specialties, including game.

"I'm probably passing up the only chance I'll ever have to try roast impala," Brent said ruefully, "but I don't want to risk it. Game has to be well hung and it's probably dangerous."

"Like some men I know," Stephen murmured.

They both ordered *ikokore,* a yam stew with seafood and ate in a leisurely fashion.

"So, you're in advertising," Stephen said. Brent had told him that much during their time at the pool.

"Yes. I'm co-owner of The Hot Box Agency in Toronto. My partner is Angel Zimmermann."

"The big, beautiful redhead?"

"That's my Angel."

"The bloke who was sitting beside her on the plane - he's Marc Dupré, right?"

"Yes."

"I have his new CD - it's brilliant. What's he doing with you, then?"

"He's going to compose the music for the commercial we're making."

Stephen nodded thoughtfully. "And the gorgeous black woman?"

"That's Keisha Adams."

"The photographer?"

Brent was impressed, "you certainly know your players."

Stephen gave a little laugh. "It's a must in my job; you never know who you'll be saying 'coffee, tea or me' to. What are you doing with all this high-priced help?"

Brent took a sip of wine while mentally rehearsing the story they'd agreed upon.

"We're in Oṣhogbo to work on a campaign for a new product by Glissando Beauté."

Stephen was intrigued. "It must be something special to bring you to Africa."

"It's a new body lotion with a time-released sun block and more Vitamin C than a bushel of oranges."

"Why would you shoot here? There are a lot more beautiful places in Africa."

This was not a question Brent had anticipated. He thought fast and spoke slowly:

"W-e-l-l, it seems that the President of Glissando, Alix Morton, has a special place in her heart for Oshogbo. She has an old friend here - Susanne Wenger."

"Ah - *Adunni.*"

"You know her, too?"

"I've never met her, but everyone knows about *Adunni*. She's pretty much a national treasure."

Making a mental note to tell the others of the addition to their cover story, Brent smiled at Stephen and, signalling to the server, said "Shall we see what they have in the way of dessert?"

"Here we are, suite 16," Brent put his key into the lock and had unaccustomed difficulty in opening the door. After a few rattles and twists accompanied by muttered imprecations, the door opened and Brent ushered his guest in. Stephen tripped on the threshold and galloped into the room with his body ahead of his feet by several inches. Making an ungraceful recovery, he landed in an armchair by the window, laughing weakly and trying to look as if he'd done it on purpose.

Brent was relieved to discover that the beautiful young Brit wasn't quite as confident as he appeared. He, himself, who was known among his peers as Control Central, felt nervous and wasn't sure why. It wasn't just that Stephen was uncommonly handsome. He'd had ravishing partners before and he was no slouch in the looks department himself, if he did say so. Was it Stephen's mind that was so alluring? Certainly he had an abundance of wit and charm but Brent never bothered with people who didn't. Life, he always said, was too short to consort with bores. God knows it wasn't because Stephen had money and position. The average flight attendant, although a mover in the basic sense of the word, isn't much of a shaker in terms of power.

No, Brent decided while he poured two large cognacs into the glasses he'd snagged from the bar on the way upstairs, none of those qualities was the reason for Brent's emotional upheaval, and with his new conquest at arm's reach, he wasn't in the mood for further analysis. Action was called for.

Knocking back the last of his cognac, he placed the glass with exaggerated care on the dresser. Stephen had ended the suspense and that, plus the liquor, swept away Brent's hesitancy. It was but the work of a moment for him to plunge over to the chair, wrap Stephen in his arms and lock him into an embrace that almost tumbled them to the floor. Coming up briefly for air, they segued into a dazzling variety of kisses and nibbles while fondling each other's backs and buttocks. Stephen employed a feathery fingertip touch, while Brent used a firm gliding stroke. There was much to recommend both techniques.

Slowly but purposefully moving a few inches at a time, Brent steered Stephen towards the bed while they kissed, caressed and undressed each other, leaving a trail of assorted garments along the way.

Once at the bed's edge, Brent eased Stephen backwards until he was lying flat on the bed, his caramel coloured skin contrasting deliciously with the white bedspread.

"Perfect landing," Stephen said, locking his hands behind Brent's neck.

"Couldn't do any less for a member of British Air - now, where was I…? Ah, yes - we began here..." He kissed Stephen in the hollow of his collar bone, "and then moseyed along to here..."he trailed his lips down to Stephen's left nipple, "and then, if memory serves me, we ended up right about...here."

“Ummmm,” Stephen sighed, “I may work in the air but I *do* enjoy a good navel manoeuvre.”

Brent chortled appreciatively and renewed his efforts while Stephen was perfectly happy to lie back and think - not of England - but of the extraordinary things that were being done to him and the marvelous things he was going to do in return. In the meantime, recalling the sage words of his dear old Auntie Ethel: “Busy Hands Are Happy Hands,” he reached underneath Brent, who was suctioning him lightly all over, and took the measure of the man, cupping his tackle and jiggling it lightly up and down while comparing Brent’s length, breadth and weight with his own. Brent won on width while he was ahead on length. All in all, Stephen felt, they were well matched. Brent, who knew exactly what Stephen was doing with these meditative caresses, had already come to the same conclusion.

Leaning over the side of the bed, Brent opened the drawer of his night table from which he took a red leather case.

“Willy wrappers?” Stephen lay on the bed, one hand propping up his blond head, an eyebrow raised inquiringly.

“Never make a move without one,” said Brent, “take your pick.” He snapped open the case to display a dizzying variety of condoms. He left the bed and poured himself a little more cognac. Offering a drink to Stephen, who shook his head in refusal, Brent retreated to an armchair where he sat sipping his drink and watching Stephen browsing through the brightly coloured rubbers.

“Mmmm, they all look delicious...let’s see...” Stephen’s hand hovered over the multitude of multicoloured tubes, pausing at *“The Scarlet Pimp”* and then hovering over *“Yellow Submarine”* before pouncing on a purple latex sheath labelled *“Grape Expectations”*.

“This one tickles my funny bone,” he said.

"If that's what you want to call it," Brent replied.

He took *Grape Expectations,* rolled it onto his tongue and blew it smoothly over the appropriate area of Stephen's anatomy. Snugly sheathed in deep purple, Stephen performed the identical task on Brent, using the flesh toned condom handed to him. Leaning back to admire his work, he collapsed in hysterical giggles. The business end of Brent's condom had two enormous blue eyes with long, curly lashes.

"I thought a little humour would relax us," Brent said. "It's called *'Here's Looking at You, Kid.'*"

"*Looking* at me? It's glaring at me as if I was picking my teeth with an oyster fork." Stephen rolled onto his back, laughing until tears ran into his ears.

"If you can't recognize a passionate gaze when you see one, my good man, I feel for you."

"Well," Stephen said, dabbing his eyes and ears on a corner of the sheet and sliding over to Brent's side of the bed, "if you're going to feel for me, I'd better make myself accessible."

The bed became a wild tangle of arms, legs and other essential parts as the two men got down to the business of pleasuring each other. They did it extremely well. Deep into the night they went while the stars peeked in the window and giggled to each other and the full moon raised a craggy eyebrow. It had seen just about everything in its time but Brent and Stephen brought the hope that there were still a few surprises left.

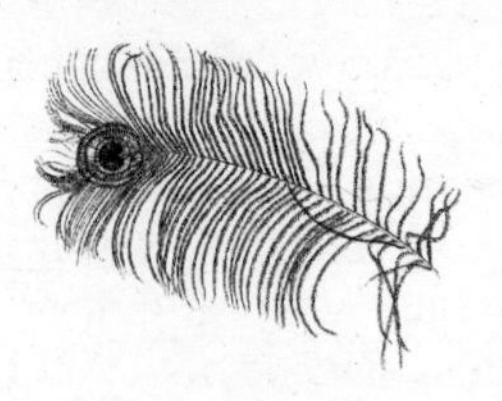

"It's *so* good to be back in Bath!" Alix kicked off her shoes and stretched out on the Regency sofa in the front room.

"It's great to have you back." Christopher planted a fond kiss on Alix's forehead before seating himself in an armchair opposite her. A low fire danced in the grey marble fireplace and the lemon yellow walls glowed in welcome.

Nine Duke Street was Christopher's ancestral home. It was a charming five-storey Georgian town house, built by famed Bath architect John Wood the Elder and had been passed down through generations of Matthews. In the mid nineteen thirties, Christopher's father died suddenly at the age of forty-five. A charming, haphazard man, he had earned a good living as a journalist, but spent everything he made and left his wife and ten-year-old son with little save the house itself.

His practical young widow had Number Nine converted into a maisonette and three flats. She rented out the flats as holiday lets and she and Christopher lived in the maisonette, which consisted of a street-level sitting room, dining room and library, and on the basement level, an enormous Georgian kitchen, a bathroom and Christopher's bedroom. Yet another flight down was a lovely little walled garden and a study, bedroom and bathroom, which were Mrs. Matthews quarters.

Duke Street is a pedestrian walkway, which links North Parade and South Parade. It has none of the cachet of the Circus or the Royal Crescent, but it is pure

Georgian, virtually untouched by time and beautifully situated near the Roman Baths and the Abbey. There was a constant demand for the flats of number nine, furnished economically but imaginatively by Mrs. Matthews, who was thus able to support herself and Christopher quite comfortably.

Although Christopher was content to live in reduced circumstances with his beloved mother, he promised himself that someday he would restore Nine Duke Street to its original splendour. When Glissando Beauté began to enjoy success, Christopher's mother happily turned the Duke Street freehold over to him and went to live with a cousin in Cornwall.

Alix and Christopher lavished time and money on the reclamation of Christopher's childhood home, furnishing and decorating in the Georgian period to which the house had been born. They both loved southwest England and had always intended it as the European headquarters of Glissando. The nearby town of Bradford on Avon had several defunct old woollen mills and they purchased the largest one for very little and gave it a costly and comprehensive conversion.

"Far less expensive than locating in London," Alix had said, "and much more pleasant."

It perfectly served their purpose and, as the mill had been an eyesore in the heart of the town for many years, the citizens of Bradford on Avon were delighted to welcome the new business to the town. Alix and Christopher further endeared themselves by hiring most of their workers locally, apart from the specialists who were recruited from all over. In addition to the mill, they bought a nearby mansion, which they turned into luxurious flats for key personnel.

Upon Alix's arrival, she and Christopher had gone straight to Glissando headquarters. A lunch party was scheduled for the next day, a combination of work and socializing, which Rob Sheffield, the managing director, always arranged when Alix was at the European base.

After hugging Alix warmly, Rob asked her for a brief rundown on the discovery.

"I don't want to tire you after your journey," he said with his charming smile, "but I'm wild with excitement and I'd love a smidgen of news before tomorrow's meeting."

Alix gave him a quick overview of the progress to date and after expressing his delight and asking a few incisive questions, he suggested that further discussion wait until the lunch meeting on the following day.

"I'll brief the staff this afternoon so that they'll be ready for the meeting," he assured Alix, "now, let's make a quick visit to the kitchen to see what Nicolai and his crew are creating for tomorrow; then I think you should head for Number Nine and put your feet up"

Before leaving for Bath, Alix and Christopher made a quick visit to Lucinda Zimmerman, Angel's mother. In one smooth motion, Lucinda flung open the front door of Westbury House and enfolded Alix and Christopher in a double hug that almost overbalanced all three of them.

Lucinda was a large, imposing woman, equally at home in the company of dukes and earls or leading a knees-up for the residents of the local old age home. Her pedigree was impeccable, coming, as she did, from landed gentry on both sides of her family. At an early age, she married a brash young Canadian tycoon, whom she had met at a weekend party in the Cotswold's. They settled in Toronto, where they had a happy but brief life together. Lucinda's husband died of an aneurysm at the age of forty-one, leaving her with a sole child, their daughter, Angel, and a considerable fortune.

Although Lucinda had enjoyed her life in Canada, she had always missed England and, when Angel was of legal age, her mother returned to her homeland where she became enchanted with Bradford on Avon. She bought Westbury House, a historic building, which like Lucinda, was large and imposing. It stood in the centre of town and with Lucinda as chatelaine, was the hub of all social and artistic activity.

Now, releasing Alix and Christopher from her grip, she looked keenly at them both.

"I'm not going to invite you in," she boomed, "the pair of you look absolutely knackered, but you must have dinner with me tomorrow night."

Now, back in Bath and comfortably ensconced in the Duke Street drawing room, Alix nibbled on a cream and jam-laden scone as she talked over the next day's plans with her partner.

"Tomorrow's meeting should be very interesting. I know Robin will go all out as usual and I'm very keen to hear what ideas they'll come up with."

Christopher nodded agreement.

"And, of course, it will be marvelous to have the evening with Lucinda. I hope she's not inviting anyone else. We have so much to catch up on."

Christopher waved the teapot at her: "Another cup, darling?"

"Yes, please. Would you like to split a scone with me? I'd love a little more but I couldn't possibly manage a whole one."

They sat contentedly in front of the fire, delighted to be together in the place they loved so dearly.

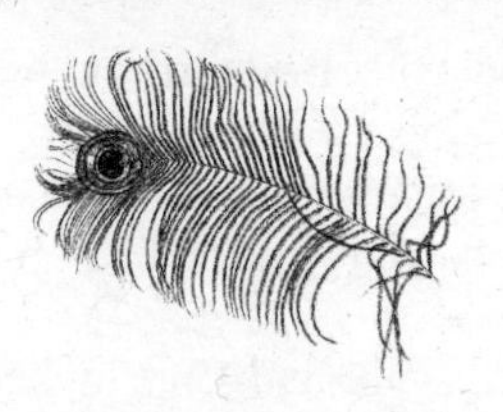

Jonathan Bernstein clenched the phone in his fist, glaring down at the city skyline while he listened to Theodore Slotkin's litany of woe. Jonathan's staff had learned to measure the intensity of his daily troubles by the appearance of his clothes. A smoothly running day meant jacket on, tie snugly fastened and shirt cuffs showing an elegant half-inch of linen. A normally frantic day had jacket on door hook, top button of shirt undone, tie loose and sleeves rolled up, while a really bad day saw the jacket thrown onto the nearest chair, tie hanging from a desk drawer knob, shoes kicked under the desk, shirt half pulled out and suspenders trailing. Today, in addition to the usual semi-striptease, Jonathan's shirt was completely out of his trousers, which was a blessing as his fly was also partly undone. His secretary, Cleo Baines, rolled her eyes over this latest breach of sartorial etiquette and let the flies fall where they may. Scooping up the papers she needed, she returned to the comparative peace of her own office, leaving her boss to squint malevolently at the panorama below.

The view from his office on the top floor of First Canadian Place could have given Jonathan great pleasure, if he allowed himself pleasure in anything. The spectacular scene usually gave him the same complacent satisfaction that he had from all his possessions, which included his glossy, interior-decorated office, his glossy, interior-decorated house and his glossy, interior decorator wife. But this was not a normal day and Jonathan wasn't getting satisfaction from anything. If he'd been a Rolling Stone, it would have made a nice little hit song.

Jonathan was Toronto's leading entertainment lawyer. His clients read like a list of MuchMusic's Top Forty intertwined with a stable of supermodels, which they usually were. This was both good and bad for business and Jonathan spent ulcer-filled days and nights disentangling his clients from situations which to the average person would be bizarre beyond belief, but which were everyday incidents in the lives of the rich, famous and crazed.

Today, however, as already noted, was not a normal day because Theodore Slotkin, Marc Dupré's agent, had discovered that Marc, incommunicado for weeks past, had now flown off to Nigeria without bothering to check his schedule. Had he done so, he would have found the Toronto Philharmonic Orchestra cooling its heels in Massey Hall, where it was waiting to record Dupré's latest oeuvre.

As orchestras go, the TPO was fairly laid back, but as the conductor Sir Trevor Hardwicke had pointed out to Theodore, there was a limit and it had been reached.

"This date was carved in stone six months ago," he said frostily.

"Yes, Sir Trevor."

"One week from today we leave on a three-month tour which, while it might afford us the opportunity of waving to Dupré as we pass over Nigeria on our way to Johannesburg, isn't going to get one blasted note recorded."

"Now, Sir Trevor, negativity isn't going to get us anywhere."

"Neither is working with Dupré. We are *done* - we are *finished* and, as we are very much out of pocket having given up a booking in order to accommodate your client, who changed dates on us *three* times, we are going to sue."

"Sir Trevor - "

"Good day to you, Mr. Slotkin. We'll see you in court!"

Jonathan's eyes glazed over as Theo related the latest chapter in his life and hard times.

"Theo, normally this wouldn't bother me at all, but you are call number 47 at the end of a day, which included (A) a crisis with Waterfall whose contract was breached because they were served Evian water instead of Ty Nânt at last night's concert. (B) a tragedy involving Lydia Mephistala who, after dying her hair its tenth colour in one year for yet another *Harper's Bazaar* cover and having the entire left side fall out, is suing her hairdresser for everything he owns, including his family jewels and (C), an imbroglio starring that lovable moppet, Dimples O'Hara and her harpy of a mother who claims that Dimples was poisoned by a bad Cube'O'Chick during the shooting of a TV spot for that epicurean delight. I wish to God she had been. These are just the highlights. Would you like to hear the low points?"

"Thank you, I'll pass. We have a *real* problem here, Jonathan. I've tracked Marc down as far as Lagos but he seems to have vanished from that point. I know he was travelling with a group from The Hot Box Ad Agency but we don't know where they're headed."

"Call the agency and ask them."

"I did. Their corporate lips are sealed and they've got Dupré hidden in the depths of West Africa. What the hell are they *doing* with him?"

"Maybe they've commissioned him to write a new national anthem," Jonathan said. "At the rate those countries change I wouldn't be surprised."

"We've got to *do* something! If we don't get him back here soon God knows how many more lawsuits I'll be slapped with!"

"Do what? Shall I leap on to the next plane and safari around West Africa looking for him?"

"What a splendid idea! You were saying just the other day that you haven't had a holiday in a dog's age. Take Stephanie to Africa for a couple of weeks. You're bound to find Marc in that time."

"Are you *mad*?"

"No more than any of our clients - you notice I say 'our clients', because you represent my entire stable..." Theo's voice trailed off in delicate innuendo.

"And what you are trying to tell me in your subtle way is that I owe you."

"Big time."

"So, if I were to agree to your crazed suggestion?"

"I would kiss your hands, feet and any other appropriate part of your anatomy and help you pack."

Jonathan sighed, pushed his intercom button and said, "Cleo, get me Mrs. Bernstein, two first class tickets to Lagos on the next available flight and three extra strength Tylenol."

"Will do, Mr. B." No request was too extreme for Cleo, who had been Jonathan's first and only employee when he opened his office, twenty-five years ago.

Theo bubbled over with gratitude. "I love you, Jonathan."

"Fuck you, Theo," Jonathan replied cordially and hung up.

Cleo came in with the pills and the information that Jonathan and Stephanie would need visas, anti malaria drugs and several assorted shots.

Jonathan nodded wearily, "Deal with it, Cleo." He grabbed the pills and gulped them down without benefit of water. Cleo shook her head and left, wondering, as she often did, what she and Jonathan Bernstein were doing in the entertainment industry.

Jonathan often wondered that himself. He'd begun a solo practice in a tiny office on Queen Street West in the days before it became Toronto's megatrendy zone. His first clients were his neighbours, mostly hard-working Italian immigrants; bricklayers and carpenters who brought their labour grievances to the young lawyer who fought and, for the most part, won for them. Jonathan's clients became successful developers and as they prospered, so did he, building a reputation as one of the best commercial lawyers in the city.

Early in his career he'd met Stephanie Cohen, the indulged only child of a wealthy Forest Hill family. She had been a bridesmaid at the wedding of Jonathan's university roommate. Jonathan had been an usher and was smitten with her blonde prettiness, but for her part, Stephanie hadn't been impressed by the dark, skinny young man who had no small talk when they danced, and who stood against the wall glowering whenever she danced with anyone else.

He badgered her all evening until she agreed to go out with him the following Saturday night, beginning a courtship in which Stephanie didn't have a chance. Jonathan showered her with attention, bringing her flowers and candy, getting first night tickets for every Broadway show that came to Toronto and taking her to the best restaurants in town. He proposed on the average of twice a month, and Stephanie refused on as regular a basis, but after a year, she succumbed to his relentless pressure and they married the following Spring.

After a three-week honeymoon in Europe, they settled down to married life. Stephanie had studied interior decorating and found a job as resident consultant to a large, glitzy furniture shop, which was owned by a friend of the family. This pleased Jonathan because it left him free to work night and day and to treat his wife with benign neglect.

Stephanie's talent was negligible but she had good taste and many connections which she parlayed into a successful career, eventually leaving the shop and opening her own consulting firm. Neither she nor Jonathan had wanted children and work, with its frequent business entertaining, filled their lives.

A gradual change in Jonathan's legal career took place when Theo began sending him work. At first it was just the occasional contract but as Theo became more and more successful, he brought in clients with more complicated needs.

Those were early days in the Canadian entertainment industry and lawyers who specialized in this esoteric area were few and far between. Using the hardheaded skills that had built his corporate practice, Jonathan became a legal legend in the world of show business. The bulk of his work came from Theo's stable, giving the two of them a virtual monopoly on the entertainment and fashion fields of the nation. Some would say it was an enviable position and on a good day, Jonathan would say it himself but, as already noted, this wasn't a good day. His intercom buzzed.

"Mrs. Bernstein on line three," said Cleo.

He and Stephanie had had very little time together lately, Jonathan thought. Perhaps this trip would help to mend the tattered fence of their marriage. Pasting a ghastly grin onto his face (you can hear the smile in someone's voice), he boomed with assumed enthusiasm: "Stephanie, sweetie - how'd you like to go to Africa?"

As he often did, Theo decided to walk home from his office. Usually, he was on his cell phone all the way but this evening he started to think about himself and Jonathan. He sometimes envied Jonathan's married state and occasionally wondered if he'd made a mistake in remaining single. Mostly, though, he was sure he was better off as a bachelor. He had a marvellous career, lots of money, more invitations than he could handle and plenty of female companionship, There were several women of whom he was fond, but the only one for whom he felt real love was Danielle Fressange, his first client and friend of many years, As he walked, his mind went back to when he and Danielle met.

Theo's first job had been PA to the president of a large talent agency. He was in love with show business and happily spent day and night at the beck and call of his employer, Patrick Monahan. Theo was always ready to do a favour for a friend and his easygoing charm gave him a large network of those who were up a rung or two on the ladder of success.

Theo had been with Monahan and Associates for a little over a year when he was summoned to his boss' office one Friday morning and told he'd be chauffeuring Mrs. Monahan on one of her frequent shopping trips. He was used to this chore and braced himself for a day of fighting traffic, wrestling with boxes and bags and listening to Mrs. Monahan's dimwitted monologues. It wasn't exactly a day on the golf course, but it got him out of the office and it was a beautiful spring morning.

Theo swept the pink Eldorado through the gates of Chez Monahan, the most ostentatious mansion on The Bridle Path, the most glaringly nouveau riche enclave in the city. He rang the bell, wincing, as always, at the chimes which played the opening bars of *There's No Business Like Show Business.* The door was opened by a maid who could have stepped out of the first act of a French farce.

"Good morning, Fifi," Theo said cheerfully. The Monahans' maids were always called Fifi, regardless of their real names, which in the case of the incumbent was Ethel Murphy.

"Bonjewer M'Sewer T'eo," said Fifi/Ethel. "Madame Mona'an is in 'er boodwah. I weell tell 'er you are 'ere."

"Merci millefois," Theo replied courteously.

"Huh?" said Fifi/Ethel blankly.

"Never mind."

While he waited for his employer's wife, Theo wandered around the broadloomed half acre that was the Monahan's living room. He had whiled away many an hour here but never ceased to be fascinated by the eclectic mayhem that was a surreal journey through the history of furnishings. Were you a fancier of seventeenth century boule cabinets? There was a superb example nestled next to the Eames leather chair and stool. Have you always wanted a close look at some really fine *pietro dura*? Feast your eyes on the pedestal table in the bay window, which was a dead ringer for the one in the Queen's Picture Gallery at Buckingham Palace. Her Majesty didn't have a fluorescent orange lava lamp in the middle of *her* table but then, she was never on the cutting edge. From Louis Quinze through Charles Rennie Macintosh to John Makepeace, they were all there, fighting each other to the death.

"Hi, Theo - sorry I'm late. Rocky added another fifty sit-ups to my daily routine - he's an absolute *torturer* - and I was so achy afterwards that I had to spend half an hour in the Jacuzzi before I had the strength to decide what to wear."

"Not to worry, Mrs. M. It was more than worth the wait."

It certainly was. He'd dine out on the description of her outfit for the next month.

Dolores Monahan stood in the centre of the room, clashing resoundingly with every period. She was wearing a sleeveless, scoop necked, micro-mini dress in metallic gold leather, studded all over with red and green crystals. Her shoes were clear plastic strips on see-through heels which made her look as if she was tottering six inches above ground level and she carried a gold Judith Lieber *minaudiere* shaped like a butterfly and pavéed with multi coloured gems. Because it was early in the day, Dolores had restrained herself in her choice of jewellery, wearing a simple diamond and emerald choker around her neck and two diamond and ruby bangles on her right arm. These were complemented by shoulder length earrings, one diamond and emerald and the other diamond and ruby.

It was a trademark of Dolores Monahan's to crossmatch her accessories. If, for example, she was wearing a black and white striped dress, she teamed it with one black stocking and a white shoe and one white stocking and a black shoe. It was a pretty delusion of hers that she set trends to be emulated by all dedicated followers of fashion. It never happened but she never stopped believing.

She had a truly amazing figure, taut and tanned with a cantilevered bosom, neatly curved hips and a splendid length of leg. Her lacquered pouff of platinum blonde hair topped a coarsely pretty face that was covered in dark pancake makeup. Her eyebrows were heavily pencilled, she sported two sets of false eyelashes and frosted turquoise eyeshadow. Nobody knew the real colour of her eyes because she had tinted contact lenses in every shade and changed them with every outfit; today she had chosen a fluorescent green. When she smiled at Theo, she revealed a blinding set of capped teeth nestled behind a thick coat of black lipstick. She was scary looking but she had a kind heart and Theo quite liked her.

"Where do I have the pleasure of taking you today, Mrs. M?"

"This is a special day, Theo. Mr. Monahan has found a new singer. Her name is Danielle Fressange (she pronounced it Dan-yell Fray-singe) and I have to take her shopping and stuff. Mr. Monahan said to me, 'Sweetieface, she's a nice little girl, but she has no style. Take her under your wing and smarten her up."

Theo knew that Danielle Fressange was to be the newest name on the Monahan roster - she hadn't actually been signed yet - and he had heard a couple of songs from her début album on the radio. She had a haunting voice and he was curious to see the new discovery from northern Quebec. He quailed at the thought of Mrs. Monahan as fashion mentor, still, his was not to reason why, but to drive the pink hippopotamus as he'd privately dubbed the Eldorado.

After a detailed discussion with the housekeeper regarding arrangements for that night's party, Mrs. Monahan hustled Theo to the car, babbling about the enormous amounts of shopping to be done. On arrival at The Park Plaza, she sent Theo in to collect Danielle while she waited in the car, spritzing a cloud of lacquer onto her already rocklike hair.

Theo hurried in, picked up the house phone and asked the operator for Miss Fressange's suite. The phone on the other end was picked up immediately with a hesitant "*Allo?*"

"Mrs. Monahan is here, Miss Fressange."

"*Merci*, I will be right down." The voice was soft and pleasantly accented.

Theo stationed himself at the bank of elevators and when the next one disgorged a slight, pretty young woman he stepped forward: "Miss Fressange?"

"Yes."

"I'm Theo Slotkin, Mr. Monahan's PA. Mrs. Monahan is waiting in the car."

He steered her through the busy lobby and out to the car where Dolores was applying another layer of lipstick.

Theo opened the back door and ushered Danielle into the seat beside his boss' wife. At the sound of the door opening, Dolores looked up from her absorbing task.

"Hiya, doll!" she squealed, "ready to shop 'til we drop?"

Danielle was hesitant. "Well, I'm not sure, Mrs. Monahan. I don't have much money to spend on clothes"

"Your wardrobe is a business expense, honey bunny - the agency picks up the bills - and call me Dolores - all Patrick's stars call me by my first name, don't they, Theo?"

"Yes, Mrs. M," Theo said pleasantly, starting the motor and deftly steering the car out into Avenue Road.

"Where do you want to go first?" he asked.

"Alan Cherry" said Dolores, "and then Holt Renfrew. From there we'll go to The Courtyard Café for lunch and after that I'm taking Danielle to my hairdresser's on Scollard Street." She turned to Danielle and patted her hand. "We'll have you fixed up in no time. Patrick said to me when he told me you were signing with us, he said 'Sweetieface' - that's what he always calls me - 'Sweetieface,' he said, 'this girl is a big talent but she's a touch short in the style department so I want you to give her a shot of glamour".

" 'Sugardingle', that's my pet name for him. 'Sugardingle,' I told him, 'you just leave that little lady with me - you won't recognize her on the night of the party.' "

While driving through the heavily trafficked streets, Theo stole frequent peeks at the new Monahan acquisition. She wasn't beautiful but she had a vivacious charm that overrode the lack of classical features. A stubborn jawline softened when she smiled, which was often; a deep dimple in her left cheek gave her an endearing lopsidedness and her tip-tilted nose just escaped being pug. She had a mop of chestnut coloured curls and dark brown eyes that scrunched closed when she laughed. Her mouth was wide and full-lipped and she had a sexy little overbite. She was petite with a trim, short waisted body, slim legs and expressive hands that were in motion with every word.

All morning the two women went from dress shop to shoe store, from milliner to jeweller and back again while Theo watched Danielle's sparkle fade. When he picked them up after lunch she was barely speaking and when they came out of the hairdresser's, his heart sank.

The shiny brown hair was now a harsh orange red and fused into an overblown upsweep with tarty little kiss curls on the forehead and in front of the ears. Her face had been transformed into a Dolores clone with a mask of tan makeup base, magenta eyeshadow and fuschia lipstick. She looked tawdry and very unhappy.

"How do you like her, Theo?" Dolores asked proudly.

"I'd never have known her," Theo replied politely.

His eyes met Danielle's in the rearview mirror. She bit her lip and turned away.

His employer's wife lavished another proud look upon her work and found it good. Looking at her left arm which sported three Swatches, she exclaimed in dismay, "it's getting late, and I have to get myself tarted up for tonight."

No change needed there, then, he thought.

"Drive me home first and then take Danielle back to the hotel. You can wait while she gets changed and then bring her to the house." She turned to Danielle. "Wear that gorgeous purple lamé mini dress with the silver fringe - and don't forget the matching boots. They're thigh high with five-inch heels," she told Theo happily, "the men will flip out when they see this little sex kitten in them!"

Danielle sat silently while Mrs. Monahan rattled on, discussing the many purchases they'd made and advising the young singer on the appropriate accessories and jewellery to wear with each outfit. By the time they reached Chez Monahan, Theo was as familiar with the merchandise as if he'd personally chosen every item. Dolores had done a mountain of shopping for herself, too, and Theo took her boxes and bags into the house.

When he returned to the car, he found his passenger huddled into a corner of the back seat, crying unrestrainedly. He opened the opposite door and slid in beside her, saying nothing. She sobbed on for a few minutes more, rummaging blindly in her handbag for a tissue.

"Here," said Theo, handing her a handkerchief from his pocket.

"*Merci*," she sniffed, mopping ineffectually at her face.

"I gather," Theo said, "that you aren't thrilled with your new look."

"I *hate* it!", she said vehemently, bursting into another flood of tears, "if my *grandmere* were to see me she would say I look like a *salope* and she would be right. I hate my hair, I hate my *maquillage* and I loathe the clothes Mrs. Monahan bought for me. And I can say nothing because she has been so kind to show me how the stars dress and if I want to be a success I must dress also this way, no?"

"No," Theo replied firmly. "You have a unique quality and it shouldn't be smothered in purple lamé. I can help you, if you'll trust me."

"I don't know anyone else here," she said with Gallic practicality, "so I'll have to."

"Good girl. Tomorrow I'll have everything you don't like returned, but right now we're going back to your hotel where you'll wash out that dreadful hairstyle and get rid of the makeup. I'm going to make a couple of calls and by the time you're out of the shower, I'll have a few surprises for you."

Theo quickly phoned a young designer whose work was already causing a buzz in the halls of fashion, a hairdresser from the salon he himself patronized, and a makeup artist who dated a friend of his.

After Theo had described Danielle to the designer, she chose four gowns from her latest collection and rushed to the hotel, picking up the other two members of the team along the way. They were all happy to help Theo, whom they adored and they were intrigued with the idea of creating a new image for the young singer.

After trying the gowns, Danielle liked a tangerine coloured chiffon dress best, but Theo and the others preferred a fluid column of cream silk jersey and she bowed to their opinion.

There hadn't been time to dye Danielle's hair back to its original shade but the same effect had been achieved by using a temporary colour spray. Then her hair was smoothly brushed back and braided into a butterfly loop which nestled at the nape of her neck, held in place by a single pearl clip.

Next it was the turn of the makeup artist, an exquisite young Oriental woman whose own makeup was beautifully executed but startling in its extreme style. She saw Danielle's apprehensive look and said sweetly, "Don't worry. I use dramatic makeup on myself because it is good for business - people tend to remember me - but I don't do this to my clients." She spent half an hour working on the young singer with a dizzying variety of creams, powders and liquids, applied with many different brushes and sponges. Danielle couldn't see what was being done to her, but Theo watched every stroke in fascination.

Finally, with great care, the gown was slipped over her head. Fortunately a pair of plain gold kid sandals and a matching evening bag were among the day's purchases, so accessories were not a problem and when Danielle asked about jewellery, Theo said firmly that she was to wear none. He relented only in the matter of the amethyst ring which she always wore; it had belonged to her beloved *'Grandmere'*.

Finally Danielle was allowed to see herself and she gazed transfixed at her image in the full-length mirror. The sleek hairstyle gave her a new sophistication, which enhanced her gamine appeal. Slate grey shadow outlined her eyes, making them enormous. Several coats of mascara turned her curly lashes into long flirtatious fringes and her strongly marked eyebrows had been left full but tweezed into a neater line. The only colour on her face was in her lipstick, a luscious raspberry red that drew attention to her voluptuous mouth.

The gown skimmed her body, touching lightly at breast and hip, and falling to her feet in Grecian folds that parted to show a slender leg whenever she moved. She looked like an ivory figurine.

Crying again, but this time with pleasure, she lunged at Theo, throwing her arms around his neck.

"Stop that," Theo said, "you'll ruin your makeup - and don't hug me," he pushed her gently away, "your dress will get crushed."

"Oh, but Theo, how will I ever thank you? I look just the way I always dreamed of - like myself but so *chic*...so...so *soignée* and you did it all, you and your marvellous friends." She smiled gratefully at the others who told her how wonderful she looked and that they would be thrilled to work for her at any time.

"Okay, Galatea, it's time to go to the ball."

Danielle looked puzzled. "Who is Galatea?"

"Did you see *My Fair Lady?"*

"I saw the film. *J'adore* Audrey Hepburn. She is my absolute favourite actress."

"You, me and everyone else in the world," Theo said. "Well, *My Fair Lady* was adapted from *Pygmalion* by George Bernard Shaw and he took the name from the story of Pygmalion, the Greek sculptor who made a statue which he brought to life. He called her Galatea."

"So - if I am Galatea, you are Pygmalion. But I shall call you Pyg for Pygmalion is too much for my mouth."

"That's no name for a nice Jewish boy," Theo said, but Pyg he now was to Danielle and Pyg he remained to her throughout their lives.

When they arrived at the Monahans', Danielle clutched at Theo. "Are you sure I look all right? Won't Mrs. Monahan be furious that I'm not as she left me?"

"You look exquisite and Mrs. M will get over her disappointment."

"You are coming to the party, too, aren't you, Pyg? You're not just delivering me like a parcel?"

"I am standard issue at all Monahan events," he assured her, "always on hand to remind Patrick of an elusive name and make sure that rival factions don't clash. I will never be far from your side, so take a deep breath and say to yourself, 'I am the most beautiful girl at the ball.' In we go!"

Just as Audrey Hepburn captivated the assemblage at the palace in *My Fair Lady*, Danielle Fressange enchanted everyone at the Monahan party. Dolores was a little upset that her protégé had retransformed herself, but her husband was pleased with the results of Theo's work.

"Class! She's got class." he said to his wife.

"But she's so *plain* looking. I thought you wanted her to look like me!"

"Sweetieface, nobody could look like you," Patrick said fondly, squeezing Dolores around the waist.

"Do you really mean that, Sugardingle?" she said.

"Of course. You're an original and you come up with something new every time. I don't know how you do it!"

Dolores had certainly outdone herself that evening. She wore a leopard patterned bustier with tiger striped Lycra leggings and both were completely covered in clear sequins. Her hair was teased into a lion's mane and thickly dusted with gold glitter. Huge amber nuggets swung from her ears and hung, multi stranded, around her neck. Slave bracelets of hammered gold clasped her upper arms and, as a final touch, she wore cat's eye contact lenses.

"Yeah," she said happily, "I bet everyone'll be copying this little get-up next season."

Later that evening, Danielle had a talk with Patrick Monahan and asked that Theodore Slotkin be her representative at the agency. Patrick balked at first, saying that he needed Theo himself but Danielle pointed out that she wouldn't be able to work nearly as well with anyone other than Theo who was so *sympathetique* to her needs and, "after all, Patreek," she smiled charmingly with a steel-edged dimple, " anyone can chaperone your stars and drive Dolores on her shopping excursions."

Patrick Monahan wasn't a stupid man. Danielle's signature wasn't on the contract yet and he sensed that if he refused, she'd back out and take Theo with her as her manager. They wouldn't have the weight of his agency behind them, but the momentum of her hit would carry them quite a distance. He didn't want to lose the young singer or Theodore Slotkin and if having him as her agent would keep both Danielle and Theo in the Monahan stable, so be it.

"You've got a deal, sweetheart," he chuckled. "Let's find young Slotkin and tell him the news."

Theo was over the moon. "I'm going to make you the biggest star this country has ever seen," he told Danielle.

"Of course you will, Pyg," she laughed. "I'm your Galatea, no?"

Theo didn't make Danielle a star - he made her a comet that blazed around the world. After the first hit came a second and a third until her début album had five songs in the top ten.

The record company wanted her as the opening act for Bryan Adams' upcoming world tour. Theo wouldn't hear of it.

"You're not opening for anyone," he said firmly. "Soon we'll begin recording your second album. It will sell even better than this one and *then* you'll go on tour - but as the headliner, *not* an opening act."

It happened just as Theo had said and by the end of their second year together, Danielle Fressange was on a par with Madonna.

Six months after that, Theo was made a full partner in the agency and a few years later when Patrick Monahan retired to travel the world and indulge his passion for yachting, Theo took over as head of Monahan and Associates. In tribute to his former partner, he kept the original name but everyone knew that Theodore Slotkin was the most powerful man in the field and they knew, too, that Danielle Fressange couldn't be pried away with a crowbar from her beloved Pyg.

A blast from a car horn brought Theo sharply back to the present. For a moment he thought he saw the pink hippopotamus across the road, where it had stood when he'd picked Danielle up that first day but realized that he'd unthinkingly stepped in front of a Jaguar coming out of the driveway at the Four Seasons. He gave an apologetic wave to the Jag's driver, smiled nostalgically and carried on up Avenue Road.

Stephanie Bernstein adjusted her designer sunglasses, clutched her carry-on bag which a small but determined boy was trying to extract from her, and snapped at her husband: "Get us out of this hellhole and into an air-conditioned hotel."

"I need as many arms as a quintet of octopuses to juggle these suitcases," gritted Jonathan from between clenched teeth, while he fought off the advances of a dozen would-be guides, "where did you think we were going - Paris for the Spring shows?"

Stephanie took a deep breath, about to respond with all the vitriol she could muster, which was considerable, but before the first lethal syllable could leave her lips, the PA system crackled and wheezed, "Would Mr. Jonathan Burston please come to the information centre? Mr. Burston, to the information centre, please."

"I think they're playing our song," Jonathan said to his seething wife. "You stay here with the bags and I'll be back in a minute with what should be our driver."

Jonathan returned triumphantly with a wiry little man who loaded the suitcases onto a cart while scolding the swarming urchins simultaneously in Edo, Fulani, Hausa, Erbo and Yoruba. Motioning to the Bernsteins to follow him, he steered them briskly through the seething throng and into an ancient black Mercedes.

Smoothly decanting Stephanie and Jonathan into the back seat, their driver loaded the luggage into the trunk, popped behind the wheel, turned around, smiled widely and, in perfect English, said "I am Salif. Welcome to Nigeria." Starting the car with a mad clash of gears and a jolt that caused the Bernsteins to clutch the upholstery, he roared out into the traffic.

No sooner were they on the highway into Lagos when Jonathan's cell phone rang. It was Theo:

"How was your flight?"

"Long, which is what I don't want this conversation to be. What's up?"

"A happy change of plans. We've traced Marc to Oshogbo and I've booked you into the Oshun Presidential Palace - best hotel there."

"Probably the only hotel there," Jonathan said grimly.

"I hear Oshogbo is a fascinating place...lots of art, fabulous fabrics. You'll find many wonderful things there."

"All I want to find is Dupré, alive and composing."

"Rather than dead and decomposing," put in Stephanie.

Jonathan shot her a withering look which didn't disturb her in the least.

"Thanks for the news, Theo. With any luck we should be able to pour Marc onto the next plane for Toronto and get ourselves to Kenya right after that. We're going on safari."

"Great idea. I'm told that one goes to East Africa for the animals and to West Africa for the people. Or is it the other way around? Let me know when you get hold of Marc. Ciao for now."

Jonathan clicked off his phone, reached forward and tapped the driver on his scrawny shoulder:

"We have a change of plans; please take us to Oshogbo."

"Ah, nice town, Oshogbo. It is where I myself, reside. You will like it very much," burbled their chauffeur, turning to smile approvingly at them and narrowly missing two water buffalo who were enjoying an afternoon nap in the middle of the road.

"Assuming we live to clap eyes on it," said Jonathan. "Stephanie, my dear, I'm told that Oshogbo is a decorator's paradise. You'll be able to write off this trip if you buy a few masks and pots and things."

"I've already written off this trip." Stephanie said grimly. "I'm just going to lie beside the hotel pool and make believe I'm in South Beach".

"You won't want to do that, Madame," broke in Salif, who was eavesdropping unabashedly. "Now is the time of the Oshun Festival. People come from the world over for it! Not to be missed!"

"Oshun? That's the name of our hotel," said Jonathan. "What *is* Oshun?"

"Oshun is the goddess of love and abundance and Oshogbo is her birthplace, where she arose out of the Oshun river."

"What do they do at this festival?" Stephanie asked.

"Ah, it's wondrous, Madame. Everyone goes to the sacred groves - there are many shrines to the gods there - marvellous to behold! There are ancient ceremonies with singing and dancing, all very beautiful."

"Let's go, Jonathan - it sounds interesting."

"What about our safari?"

"We can still do that. Marc is in Oshogbo, so we don't have to waste time searching for him and whatever buying I do won't take long. We can be in Kenya by Monday."

"All right, I could use a few days to unwind. We'll stay over the weekend in Oshogbo, I'll deal with Dupré while you take a fast look at this festival, and we'll head for Nairobi on Monday."

"What do you mean you have no rooms? My wife and I have just arrived from Canada. We are exhausted and we called ahead for a double room with private bath for tonight through Sunday." Jonathan glowered at the tall young desk clerk who spread his large hands apologetically.

"Your request for a reservation was not received, but we couldn't have filled it anyway. There isn't a hotel room available anywhere in Oshogbo because of the Oshun Festival. I'm very sorry, sir."

This was one frustration too many for Stephanie, "I don't *believe* this! You drag me half way around the world on a wild goose chase for a crazy composer. We drive three hours with a deranged Yoruban at the wheel and now we have nowhere to stay! Well, you can solve this problem with your keen legal mind and when you do, you'll find me in the bar!"

She stormed across the lobby and disappeared into the depths of the bar, only to reappear a few minutes later, happily intertwined with Angel and Marc.

"Our worries are over! Here is your wandering minstrel and the room problem is solved, too. This is Angel Zimmermann of The Hot Box Agency."

Jonathan and Angel had a nodding acquaintance and they shook hands cordially.

"Stephanie can move in with me, Jonathan," Angel said, "and you can share Marc's room."

"Good. I'll shackle him to the bedpost until I send him back to Canada."

Marc gave him a reproachful look. "Is this the way to treat your friend and client?"

"It is when the friend and client disappears leaving me high and dry with the TPO breathing down my neck."

"I meant to talk to Theo about that. I got so excited about this new project that I decided to put the recording sessions on hold and you know I have no head for details.

I forgot to tell Theo to postpone the TPO and when we arrived we started working right away. I *must* finish here, Jonathan - Theo will be able to straighten things out with Hardwicke."

"What *is* it with you artists? There isn't one of you who can be let out without a keeper. None of you has a shred of responsibility and you have all the emotional stability of a passel of hyperactive ten-year-olds."

"But you forgive us everything for the sake of our talents," beamed Marc.

"I'll consider forgiving you if you get me out of this lobby and into a room with a shower and several highly alcoholic drinks - and speaking of drinks, I think you've had more than your quota for the day."

"Nonsense," replied Marc with offended dignity, "I've only had two glasses of wine with lunch and, just now, a Zombie's Curse. I'm not counting this morning's Bloody Sunrise, that was Vitamin C."

During this discourse the rest of the group had joined them in the lobby.

"Jonathan, let me introduce my friends and fellow workers," Marc waved an arm that included the desk clerk, the bellman and several passers-by.

Brent, seeing that Marc was in no condition to differentiate between him and the closest potted palm, leaped into the breach and introduced himself and the others. During the handshaking and general pleasantries, Marc led Angel to the other side of the lobby.

"Instead of Jonathan and Stephanie having to split up, it would be far simpler if you'd move in with me and let Jonathan and Stephanie have your room," he said coaxingly.

"I can't, Marc," Angel sighed. "It's bad enough that I've broken my rule about getting involved with colleagues. I don't dare make it public knowledge."

"Of course," he agreed solemnly. "Nobody has a clue as to what's coming down with us. I'm sure Keisha swallowed that story about us working late when she caught you leaving my bedroom at 4 am."

"Keisha was returning from a little assignation of her own, so I don't think she'll be too quick to spread the story around."

"Do you know who she's seeing?"

"A number of people including that snappy little flavour of the month, Brent Lockwood."

"Brent! I thought he was gay."

"Bisexual. Brent never lets a pretty face pass him by, male *or* female."

Marc looked at Angel, eyes narrow with drunken suspicion: "You're his closest friend..."

"And that's *all* I am. Brent and I agreed long ago never to let sex of any kind come between us. We love each other too much to complicate matters."

Marc smiled with relief and put his arm around Angel's waist and his head on her shoulder.

"Let's go and celebrate with a little drink or two," he said fuzzily.

"You've already had a drink or two, possibly five," Angel replied with tolerant disapproval. She shepherded him to his room and steered him inside.

Marc dropped onto his bed and patted the space beside him invitingly.

"Lie beside me".

"I don't think so," Angel replied, "the Bernsteins could come in at any moment." But even as she spoke, Marc had reached out and pulled her down beside him.

"They're having lunch in the bar and you know how slow the service is. They'll be at least an hour." He curled around her spoon fashion and burrowed his head into the hollow of her neck.

"Anyway, we won't do anything, he crooned, "just wanna *hold* you".

Angel stifled a giggle, "I don't think you're capable of doing anything at the moment," she said.

Marc considered her statement. "Possibly not at this moment," he conceded, "but I shall rise again."

"I expect so," she replied encouragingly. "Now, why don't you have a little nap?"

"You'll stay with me, Cher?" Marc asked anxiously.

"All right, darling." Angel lay in Marc's arms, listening to his breathing slip into the quiet, shallow rhythm that signalled sleep. She could never sleep during the day unless she was ill, so she let her mind drift back to the early stages of their relationship. One night in particular was vivid in her memory, the night when she realized the depth of his dependency on alcohol and drugs.

She had been riffling through *Whatever Turns You On*, the hottest self-help book on the market. It was a cerebral little bundle of sexual fantasies designed to encourage creativity in the bedroom or, if one followed the author's advice, in the living room, dining room or the washroom in the Food Court of the Eaton Centre.

It wasn't that sex with Marc was unsatisfactory, it was so good that she felt obliged to make it even better. She had promised Marc a surprise for tonight and thumbed frantically through such pulse-quickening scenarios as *Hospital Hi Jinks* and *Truck Stop Teresa*, considering and rejecting the nurse and doctor motif and firmly renouncing Teresa and her group grope. She was getting desperate enough to re-think *Peter Pan and Tinkerbell* when she struck pay dirt:

Torment Me With Grapes…'She blindfolded him, tied him to a chair and slowly fed him one grape at a time'…hmmm…I think we can do that – and more.

After making a few notes, Angel went in search of the needed ingredients and then set to work, humming happily as she peeled green grapes, opened a jar of black olives in balsamic vinegar, filled lychees with cream cheese and assembled other exotic delicacies.

I may not be able to cook, she thought, *but I'm unbeatable at tarting up ready-mades.* When everything was arranged on a large silver tray, she slid a bottle of Taittinger Comte de Champagne into a wine cooler and put the tray, the cooler and a fluted crystal wine glass on the dining room table. She brought a comfortable, open-sided armchair with carved legs from her bedroom and placed it beside the table.

A short rummage through her bureau drawers yielded a sleep mask and four long silk scarves, all of which she rolled into tidy little cylinders and tucked neatly behind the wine cooler.

Back in the living room, she arranged clusters of candles on the mantelpiece and the tables throughout the room. She put jasmine oil in a pottery diffuser, fluffed up the vase of anemones on the coffee table and went to get ready for the evening.

After a leisurely bath, she slathered herself in Glissando body lotion and sprayed herself with *Nikki de Saint Phalle* then, seating herself at her dressing table, she spent half an hour making herself up to look as if she was wearing no make up at all.

Angel went back into her bedroom and opened the doors of her walk-in closet to search for the perfect outfit. Silk jersey lounging pyjamas...too obvious. Green cashmere sweater and matching skirt...too conservative. Discarding several other possibilities she decided on her favourite black jeans and an old shirt of soft, white linen. Quickly she slid into the jeans and tucked the shirt in tightly, leaving the top two buttons undone. She rolled the cuffs to just above her wrists, slid a black and silver

Italian leather and steel belt through the waist loops of the jeans and pulled on a pair of black and red Tony Lama boots: she was ready for action.

Angel hurried into the living room to make her final preparations. She lit the diffuser and the candles and dimmed the electric lights. Soon a subtle scent of jasmine tinted the air and the candles' glow gave the room a golden ambiance. Crossing to the wall unit that held a sophisticated sound system, she loaded the five-disc CD player with music by some of Marc's favourite performers: Tom Waits, Leonard Cohen, Randy Newman, Annie Lennox and Peter Gabriel. Pressing random play, she gave a final look around the room and, satisfied that all was in order, sat down to await her lover's arrival.

The doorbell rang and Angel's stomach tightened. Whenever she was waiting for Marc she always felt the same mixture of excitement and apprehension. How would it be this time? What kind of mood would he be in? Would he be affectionate or distant? Kind or quarrelsome? She never knew and often an evening that began with him in one frame of mind, quickly swung to another. It was nerve-wracking but it could also be enchanting.

She opened the door. Marc stood leaning against the door jamb, looking at her with wicked black eyes and a crooked smile. Her heart lurched and she held out her hands wordlessly, bringing him into the apartment.

Once she had taken his coat and settled him in the living room, she had calmed enough to make airy small talk while pouring him two fingers of Cardhu, his whiskey of choice.

They sat facing each other on the large couch in front of the gas fireplace. It was spring, but Angel had a low flame burning because Marc loved fire. He sat staring at the flames while she watched his profile, fascinated as always by the lean lines that were sometimes boyish and sometimes ancient looking.

Turning from his study of the fire, Marc looked at Angel, his eyes locked onto hers. Placing his long fingered hand gently under her chin, he turned her face slightly, first to one side then the other.

"So, Ahn-ghel, what is this little game you spoke of?"

Angel smiled as she rose from the couch. Taking him into the dining room, she sat him in the armchair and told him to close his eyes. Swiftly, she took the sleep mask from its hiding place and tied it over his eyes.

"Hey!" he exclaimed.

Angel put her hand firmly on top of his head.

"You are not to speak unless I tell you to."

Placing his hands on the arms of the chair, she took out the four scarves, tied his wrists on either side, and then tied his ankles to the chair's feet. The bonds were secure but not uncomfortably tight.

Rising from her task, Angel stood back a little and enjoyed the sight of Marc bound and sightless. He was completely in her power - hers to do with whatever she chose.

"What now?" A small smile quirked the corner of his mouth.

Angel laid her forefinger firmly against his lips. "Hush," she commanded. "Do *not* speak unless I ask you a direct question. Now - I am going to put something in your mouth but you are not to bite into it until I give you permission nor must you chew or swallow until I say so. Nod your head if you understand."

Marc nodded once, his mouth serious.

"Good," Angel took a grape from the tray. "Open your mouth."

Obediently, Marc opened his mouth widely.

“Not so wide...that’s better.” She slid the grape between the small opening so that it brushed his upper and lower lips. “Hold it in your mouth.”

What is this? A marble?

“Bite down.”

Marc’s teeth closed and a burst of flavour flooded his mouth. He longed to chew the firm, cool flesh but Angel had not yet given the word, so he sat in darkness with the grape halves rolling gelidly on his tongue.

“Now...chew.”

He concentrated all his remaining senses on the experience - the fresh scent of the fruit, its clean taste, the slight sound of the grape fragments being ground between his teeth, the feel of them turning into pulp.

Angel put her hand lightly on his throat.

“Swallow,” she said.

Silence and stillness for a while, then: “Open.”

The taste of vinegar pricked the back of his tongue. Again he was told to hold the object untouched in his mouth and again, at intervals, to bite...chew...swallow. The little pickled gherkin went the way of the grape to be leisurely followed by a cheese-filled lychee, and a marinated mushroom.

“Open,” murmured Angel. The sweet shock of her lips trickled icy champagne from her mouth into his.

And so it went - from grape to mushroom from gherkin to lychee to champagne and back again. Angel felt a heady blend of power in his helplessness and maternal love as he trustingly opened his mouth like a baby bird. Marc was turned on both by his surrender to Angel and the kaleidoscope of tastes and textures she was feeding him. Just as he was getting used to the menu, Angel introduced blackberries and raspberries dipped in clotted cream. She alternated them until the little dish was empty and then slid a climactic chocolate truffle between his lips. One final champagne-filled kiss and then she took off his blindfold, untied his legs and released his hands.

Slowly, Marc stood up, not taking his eyes off Angel, who smiled and asked, "did you like it?"

He nodded silently, hands at his sides and then, so quickly that she couldn't react, he pushed her down to the floor, tied her hands behind her, blindfolded her and after lying her none too gently on her back, knelt over her.

She lay, unseeing, heart pounding from his swift attack. Then came the unmistakable sound of a zipper. "Open," he said.

They made such abandoned love that Angel couldn't believe she was doing the things she was doing, even as she was doing them. Afterwards they lay quietly in bed, to where they had progressed in stormy stages that led from the dining room floor, to the kitchen table to the hall.

"Would you like something to drink, darling?" Angel asked as she watched her lover roll a cigarette that consisted of two parts tobacco to one part marijuana, spiked with a little crumbled hash.

"Yes. Pour me two fingers of Cardhu, no ice, in one of those square tumblers - they fit my hand better than the round ones." He lit the spliff and inhaled deeply.

Feeling uneasy, Angel said, "Do you think that's a good idea? I mean to drink while you're smoking?"

Marc looked at her steadily from wide set eyes that darkened as he spoke. "Yes, I *do* think so," he replied with mock sweetness.

Her throat felt coated with sadness. Silently she went to the liquor cabinet in the living room, and made the drink to his specifications. Coming back to the bedroom, she handed Marc the glass, which he took without a word. He tossed back the contents of the tumbler, placed it on the table beside him, took a final deep drag from his cigarette and extinguished it in the glass.

"Now," he said to Angel, "I want to crash and I don't need you dithering around me, so leave me alone."

"But - "

Marc's eyes narrowed into a spiteful gleam. "What part of 'leave me alone' don't you understand? Let's try it again. *Leave - me - alone.*"

He lay back, covered his closed eyes with his arm and fell into a deep sleep.

Angel stood beside the lean figure that lay unmoving in her bed. She looked at the mouth, which had kissed hers, at the hands that had caressed every part of her, at the body, which had brought her such pleasure.

Automatically her hand reached out and removed the glass from the bedside table. She walked into the kitchen where she threw out the cigarette butt, rinsed the glass in scalding water and put it into the dishwasher. Then she sank down onto a stool at her kitchen island, her mind clouded with pain. Fragments of thought pierced the grey mist:

He looked at me like he hated me...he was so cold...I feel so cold...so old...too old for him...old and ugly... She twisted both hands into her hair, pulling at it until her scalp ached. The tears which had been stinging the backs of her eyes, flooded down her cheeks.

Can't stand this...must walk away before he leaves me... break it off now, while it's early enough for me to get over him...

"Liar," she said aloud. "You'd never get over him."

Her stomach roiled in nausea; her throat spasmed with choked-back sobs. Burrowing her head into her folded arms she cried despairingly while her bracelets chimed and jangled, "you'll never leave him - he'll never leave you...you'll never leave him - he'll never leave you..."

Angel was so immersed in her remembrance that it took a few seconds to register that Marc was now awake and caressing her breasts while pressing against her and murmuring "Open to me."

Angel looked down at Marc as he lay sleeping, exhausted after their passionate interlude. She had slid quietly out of bed, showered, dressed and written him a note; "Gone to town with Keisha and Brent to look for indigo fabrics. See you later. Luv, A." She put the note on the pillow beside him where he'd see it upon awakening and left the room, closing the door noiselessly behind her.

Brent and Keisha were waiting for her in the lobby, Brent smoking his twentieth cigarette of the day while listening amiably to Keisha's harangue on the evils of tobacco. Spotting Angel, Brent's eyes lit up with relief.

"Hi, Angel girl. Will you get this beautiful harpy off my back?"

Angel raised a tolerant eyebrow at Keisha. "Would this be the old why-do-you-still-have-that-disgusting-habit lecture?"

"What else?" Keisha's full mouth was pursed disapprovingly but as this showed her dimples almost as much as when she smiled, the effect was less grim than she would have liked.

"Give it up, darling. Countless others of his loved ones have tried and failed."

"But he's doing terrible things to himself!" Keisha wailed.

"Have you been spying through my keyhole, you naughty girl?" Brent waggled his eyebrows à la Groucho Marx and blew an insouciant smoke ring.

"Dammit, Brent!" In spite of herself, Keisha laughed and so did Angel.

“Well, that’s it as far as I’m concerned,” Keisha said severely when she’d regained control of herself. “You can go to hell in a hand basket for all of me.”

“I’d go worse places than that for even a little part of you, my bronze beauty,” he leered affably, putting one arm around her waist and his other arm around Angel. “Our chariot awaits, miladies. To the shops!” The trio swept out of the lobby and to the jeep where Salif sat waiting.

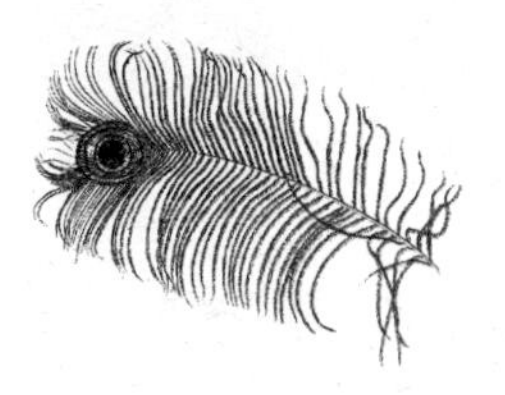

There was a tap at the door of the suite that served as the Hot Box office. Angel, Brent and Keisha were sitting at a large table, deep in discussion on their search for a model.

Keisha, who was closest to the door, leaned over and opened it to reveal a small boy with huge eyes, clutching an envelope.

"Come on in," said Angel.

"*Adunni* send me," the moppet said shyly, edging into the room.

Angel beckoned him to her side and he gave her the envelope, smudged and crinkled from his hot little fist.

Angel opened the envelope.

"Susanne Wenger has invited us to her house for five o'clock tea," she said. Fishing around in her handbag, she gave the child a coin, saying "tell *Adunni* we'll be there."

The little boy's eyes grew even larger as he looked at the tip. Grinning wordlessly, he slipped out of the room.

"That's Alix's friend, isn't it?" said Brent, "the artist who came here from Austria."

"Yes," Angel replied.

"Should be interesting," Keisha said, opening a file and taking out a sheaf of eight by ten photographs, "which is more than I can say for these." She threw the glossies onto the table and spread them out for the others to see.

"Are these the shots you took of the girls from the Lagos agency?" Angel picked up the one nearest to her. "This one is *very* beautiful, Keisha."

"And there's nothing wrong with these, either," said Brent, fanning several pictures and waving them at Keisha.

"Yes - there's nothing wrong, and that's what's wrong." Keisha replied. "All these girls are gorgeous and they're all too *NYLA*. Look at them: pert little noses, streamlined lips, straightened hair - this isn't the look of Africa."

Angel studied the picture in her hand closely, then dropped it on the table.

"You're right, K. What do you want to do?"

"The Oshun festival is in two days time and a large part of the population will be there, so let's all keep our eyes open. Any likely looking females we'll test shoot right there; better bring lots of consent forms along."

"Great idea, not to mention a terrific way to meet women."

"You always manage to mix pleasure with business."

"Never let work stand in the way of carnal knowledge."

"Spoken like a philosopher and a lech. Marc's working beside the pool this morning; we can join him out there for lunch, have a swim and leave for Susanne Wenger's with time to do a little sightseeing along the way."

The group set out just past four pm with Salif, as usual, behind the wheel. He was a one-man tourist bureau, never losing an opportunity to extol the virtues of Oshogbo. Salif was invaluable once you got used to his erratic driving and his habit of joining every conversation. As they bowled along Iwo Road he pointed out the Nike Centre, which was the only cooperative promoting sales of Oshogbo art.

"We have many artists of international fame here in Oshogbo," he said proudly: "Twins 77 ... Rufus Ogundele ... Muraina Oyelami, as well as young artists like

Shangodare Gbadegbin who makes batik fabrics; sometimes he uses as many as thirty-two colours in one cloth ... then there is Kasali Akanbi who carves the most wonderful masks of the Orisha ... there are many, many such and during the Oshun Festival you will see their works on display.

"What about Susanne Wenger's work?" Keisha asked.

They would certainly see that, he assured them. *Adunni* was not only famous for her art but venerated for her work in restoring the Oshun Groves with their magnificent shrines.

"You are most fortunate to meet her," he said reverently.

"Why does everyone call her *Adunni*?" Keisha asked.

"It means The Adored One. The people of Oshogbo gave her the title and nobody calls her by any other name. She has worked many, many years to save the shrines and it is a never-ending job, but she never gives in and never tires of rebuilding the Orisha images, even though materials are difficult to obtain and the funds she needs are so hard to raise."

When they arrived at Susanne Wenger's house, Salif parked the car with a flourish and continued his commentary. "Before we go in let us take a moment to admire her house from the outside. As you can see, it is well worth your attention."

"This is called a 'story' building."

"Why is it called that?" Angel asked, adding, "It doesn't look African."

Salif nodded: "It was built in the Brazilian style, which was brought back to Nigeria by returnees who were the descendants of former slaves. And it's called a story building because it has three floors."

The large house had a low fence running across the front, which was made of cement figures with a thick tangle of green vines growing all over the frontage. There was a verandah with sculptural chairs on either side of the door, as well as several benches for those wishing to sit near to the street.

As they came onto the verandah, the front door opened and a young girl, smiling widely ushered them inside. Salif spoke to her briefly and she gestured to a huge staircase of dark wood, which spiralled to the third floor. This was unusual, Salif pointed out, because there are no stairs in most Yoruba houses and the few that do exist are made of concrete, not wood.

The house was filled with sinuous sculptures in metal and wood and there were a few metal chairs that seemed decorative rather than utilitarian. At the back of the ground floor, Salif told them, were many shrines, all secreted behind doors.

He indicated a room on the left, "This is the studio of *Adunni*'s son, Sangodare." He led them past the closed door. "*Adunni* will receive us on the third floor."

As they climbed, Salif told them that the house was unique in many ways, including the size of the rooms which were much larger than was usual in Yoruba houses. All the windows were open, allowing a slight breeze to play throughout. The voices of children could be heard and when they reached the third floor they saw a balcony at the back where a group of youngsters played.

"Sometimes *Adunni* sits here watching the children at their games," Salif said, gesturing to a small table near the top of the stairs, "and as they pass back and forth to the balcony, she gives them a kiss or a hug."

"Where is she now?" Angel asked.

"Waiting for us in her private apartments." Salif said, gesturing to the door in front of them, which opened as he spoke.

"So, you are the goddaughter of my old friend." The woman who greeted Angel looked something like Alix,

Angel thought, and she might wear just such an indigo print caftan for home entertaining as the one Susanne Wenger was wearing.

"I'm so happy to meet you," Angel said. Shaking hands with her hostess she said, "Miss Wenger, these are my friends and associates; Keisha Adams..."

"Welcome to my house," Susanne Wenger said, smiling at Keisha who thanked her with uncharacteristic shyness.

"My partner, Brent Lockwood..."

"How do you do," Brent said in a subdued manner.

"...and Marc Dupré, who is composing the music for the Glissando campaign."

Susanne Wenger shook hands with both Brent and Marc. Inviting them all to sit down, she reclined in a low-slung African chair beside which was a large brass trestle table.

An attractive young woman entered with a tray of cups, a teapot and a plate of small cakes. She poured a fragrant amber liquid into each cup, handed them to everyone, offered the cakes around and then left, taking the empty tray with her.

"Before I forget," said Angel, putting down her cup and rummaging in her handbag, "Alix asked me to give you this little gift and this letter." She passed a small box and a thick envelope to Susanne Wenger.

"Thank you," the older woman said, putting them on the table, "I will look at them later."

She smiled at her guests: "You are all most welcome here, but you," her sharp blue gaze rested on Angel, "I especially wanted to meet. Your godmother has played such a vital part in my life and has done a great deal to help me with the preservation of the Oshun groves. Did you know that?"

"No, I didn't", Angel said. "Alix has often spoken of you over the years and shown me pictures of your work, but she didn't say anything specific."

"Without Alix my work would have been even more difficult than it is," the older woman said. "She was one of the few who encouraged me in the early days - not just with money, although she has been very generous in her financial support - but with friendship and prayer and an unshakeable faith in *Iyalode*. We often joke about the fact that I am the one who ended up as a priest of Oshun. I always thought it should have been Alix."

"Why didn't she?" Angel asked.

"She never felt the call. Alix completely opposed the idea of priesthood for herself, although she was delighted when I underwent initiation. She practises her own form of Orisha worship and is utterly faithful to Oshun who has great love for her. This love extends to you, Angel and will soon manifest itself. When it comes, open yourself to it."

Angel sat silently for a moment, filled with a mixture of skepticism and vague apprehension.

"How will it come?"

"I don't know," the older woman replied, "but it will be clear to you when it occurs."

She turned to Keisha and Brent. "Forgive me for concentrating on Angel, but it was important that she receive that message."

For the rest of their visit, Susanne Wenger was graciousness itself, answering innumerable questions about Oshogbo, its art colony, the festival and her own work. When it was time for them to leave, she walked them to the steps of her house.

"Possibly I will catch sight of you at the groves on Friday," she said, "but I will have duties to perform so there will not be time to spend together."

Back in the car, Brent turned to Angel. "What was *that* about?"

Angel shrugged. "The Oshun thing? I don't know and I can't worry about something I don't believe in. But it's easy to see why Susanne Wenger and Alix are such good friends. They have so much in common."

"Don't be so sure there's no truth in what *Adunni* said. When she shook my hand I felt the same kind of power I felt back in N'Awlins when I met Calinda, the Queen of VouDou."

Angel laughed. "You ragin' Cajuns are all alike - a mass of superstition. No," as Marc opened his mouth to speak, "I don't want to hear another word about it - from *anybody*."

Salif, who had been ready with his own opinion, sighed disappointedly.

Jonathan surveyed his surroundings, well pleased with the spacious terrace dining room where they had just finished dinner. The table gleamed with candles and a perfumed breeze murmured through the acacia trees. Huge stars were flung like glittering confetti against the blue velvet sky. Jonathan lit a cigar and inhaled with a benevolent smile for everyone in the group.

"I have to thank you for tonight, Angel."

"Yes," said Stephanie, "it's absolutely wonderful."

"I'm glad you're enjoying the evening but it's not over yet." Angel gestured to the far end of the terrace where a stage was set with many musical instruments. Musicians were wandering onto the stage, laughing and talking among themselves while they began tuning up.

Marc, who had been watching the band silently for some time, now said: "You won't *believe* the sound of this group. I've wanted to hear them live ever since I listened to their first disc."

"What is that instrument?" Stephanie asked, pointing to a rough wooden box set with comb like strips of metal.

"It's a *kalimba*, a thumb piano and it sounds like a cross between a xylophone and a music box."

"And the thing with shells strung all over it?" Brent gestured to the right hand side of the stage.

"It's called a chekeré."

Just then a conga drum struck up a soft, sustained beat and a voice came over the loud speaker system:

"Ladies and gentlemen, the Oshun Presidential Hotel is pleased to present *Babatunde Gbadeo and the Pulse of Africa*."

A stocky, middle-aged man strode briskly on to the stage, flung up his arms and smiled at the audience, which let out a joyous roar of expectation. In one supple motion Babatunde Gbadeo bowed, whirled to face his orchestra and with a downbeat, unleashed a hurricane of music.

Marc was on the edge of his chair with excitement. He recalled the term "wall of sound" which was coined to describe the music produced in the Sixties by the legendary Phil Spector. This was comparable, he thought, except that it was fluid; a tidal wave of sound, swelling, roaring to the shore, thundering on the rocks, receding and then building again to an even more massive attack.

He let the sounds wash over him, drowning happily in the liquid melody.

This kind of music would be perfect for the campaign, he thought. He remembered hearing a recording by the Baka pygmies of the Cameroon rain forest, where the women used the river as drums. He wanted to implement that technique in his composition and wondered if Gbadeo would be familiar with it. *I'd love him to work on this with me. Maybe I can talk with him later this evening.*

A burst of applause interrupted his thoughts, but Babtunde Gbadeo hardly waited for it to die down before beginning the next number.

The sound of the chekeré was heard and all the musicians stood and raised their right arms straight over their heads, chanting "*Oba Ko So*." The locals in the audience immediately responded in the same way and the tourists straggled to their feet and wondered what to do next.

The chekeré*'s* rattle was joined by the crisp clack of the clavé and again, the chant of "Oba Ko So" rang out in a call and response between the musicians and the audience. This was done six times, then the orchestra burst into a fast-tempoed number of tremendous intensity. All the percussion instruments were used, from the tiniest of gourds to the huge standing drums and the musicians sang a song, the chorus of which, "Chango, *Oba Ko So*," was taken up by the audience.

Brent's fingers dug into Keisha's shoulder: "Listen!"

"Ow! I *am* listening, idiot! Let go!!"

"No - *listen,* Keisha. They're saying 'Chango'. That's the name of the man in my dream - remember?"

Prying his fingers off, she rubbed her shoulder and listened intently.

"Yeah, they are! I wonder what else they're saying."

Brent looked around the room and caught sight of Salif standing nearby, singing enthusiastically. Brent kept his eyes on their guide and when the song finished, beckoned him over.

"Salif, what was that song about?"

"Ah - that is one of the most famous stories of our tradition," Salif said with even more exuberance than usual. "Many thousands of years ago, Chango was the King of Oyo. His two brothers were generals of Chango's army and were loyal to him, but others were jealous and told Chango that his brothers were plotting to overthrow him. Chango forced them to fight each other and when one brother killed the other, the victor was stricken with grief and Chango was overcome with sorrow. He rushed into the forest and hanged himself from an Iroko tree. The people saw his body hanging and marched, mourning, through the town chanting '*Oba Ko! Oba Ko*!'

"But tonight everyone was singing '*Oba Ko So*." Brent said.

"Very true," Salif said approvingly, "I will explain that also. When Oya, who is Chango's favourite mistress, heard that he was dead, she rushed to the Iroko tree, weeping and wailing, to take down his body and bury it, but when she got there, Chango's body was gone. She sat under the tree, crying and suddenly she heard his voice from above telling her that he was not dead but that Oluddumare, King Over All, seeing his remorse, took him to heaven where he would live forever as the God of Fire and Thunder."

"When she heard this news, Oya rushed back to the palace, shouting '*Oba Ko So*! The king is *not* dead!'

"Ever since then, when Chango's name is mentioned, his followers stand and raise their right arms to indicate how he rose to heaven. The song you just heard was written by Babatunde many years ago in praise of Chango, and it made him the most popular musician in the country."

Marc listened with interest to Salif's story. He remembered his daydream of a man whom he now knew to be a deity and he was intrigued to find out that the god had played an important part in the life of Babatunde Gbadeo.

"Salif," he said, "I would like to meet Babatunde. Would you take a message to him and ask him if he'd join us for a drink after this set?"

A short time later, Salif escorted Babatunde Gbadeo to their table. Marc jumped to his feet, introduced himself as a fan and fellow musician and made him known to the rest of the group.

"Are you here for the festival?" Babatunde asked.

"Not exactly." Angel replied, "we're shooting for an advertising campaign and getting footage from the festival will be a bonus we hadn't counted on."

"Ah - you're the people from Canada!" Babatunde exclaimed. "I saw *Adunni* earlier today and she mentioned that you had been to see her. She very much enjoyed your visit."

The affable Gbadeo charmed the Canadians with his warmth and extended an invitation to visit his home.

"I live in a small village some ten miles from Oshogbo," he told them. "It would be my pleasure to show you some of our countryside and you might find it of interest to see African life outside the major centres."

"We'd love that, thank you." Angel said.

Marc turned to Babatunde: "Is there anywhere we could speak privately?"

"How about the lounge? Everyone's out here, so it'll be empty."

Excusing himself to Angel and the others, Marc headed off with Babatunde. The rest of the group ordered more coffee and liqueurs, chatting lazily while waiting for the music to begin again.

Within fifteen minutes, Marc and Gbadeo were back. The older man waved to the group as he made his way back to the stage and Marc, visibly elated, slid back into his place beside Angel.

"He's going to do it! "I'm going to his place tomorrow to begin work with him and his band."

"That's great."

"He's invited me to a *bembé*, a religious celebration, later tonight. Do you want to go?"

Angel was reluctant: "I don't think so, darling. I'm quite tired."

"Oh." Marc was disappointed. "Do you mind if I go?"

"Of course not. You can tell me all about it in the morning." She was glad that he didn't press her further. She *was* tired, but also she didn't want to be involved in any mystical matters. Relieved, she settled back to listen to the final set.

Once the concert was over and Marc had left with Babatunde Gbadeo, the rest of the group strolled into the lobby. Keisha was thrilled to have met Gbadeo. She explained to Angel and Brent that he had been a superstar in the black music world long before he received any mainstream recognition.

"You can't imagine the influence this man and his music have had on the black Diaspora, and getting to actually work with him, it would be like you collaborating with - oh, I don't know - Shakespeare or Renoir"

Brent laughed. "I guess it's true about famous people being as star struck as anyone else."

"What do you mean?"

"Well, here you are, a household name, and you're like some schoolgirl meeting Leonardo Di Caprio."

Keisha snorted. "Apart from a few icons like Richard Avedon or Yousuf Karsh, a photographer's fame is rather restricted, so I'm hardly a household name. Besides, why shouldn't I be excited about working with a man whose music I've loved since I was a child?"

"It's just funny to see you acting like a fan, you're always supercool about everything."

"That's just my public persona, darlin' - inside I'm a seething mass of excitement."

"I remember being a seething mass of excitement inside you, myself," he whispered to her.

"Stop that sweet talk, you silver tongued devil. Besides, unless I'm very much mistaken, you've found true love."

"Stephen? It's too soon to tell. I like him a lot but I still have a huge hankering for you, Keisha, my chocolate bunny."

Keisha laughed comfortably and gave Brent a little hug.

"Tell you what, darlin'; if you're feeling lonesome when your little Meals on Wheels is off on his appointed rounds, the door to my room just might be unlocked."

She waved goodnight and headed for the elevator.

Just after sunrise, Marc Dupré let himself quietly into his room. Jonathan was sound asleep and Marc quietly readied himself for bed to avoid disturbing his roommate. His head was whirling with the experience he'd had at the *bembé*. Marc was from New Orleans and although he had never attended a Voodoo ceremony, he had grown up with various bits of knowledge about the practice.

"Still," he reflected, as he sank onto the bed, "it's one thing to have heard of these matters and quite another to see them for oneself."

Babatunde Gbadeo and three other men had been waiting for him in an old pick-up truck, which had a number of items in the back, including three drums. They drove to a spot just outside of Oshogbo, stopping at a clearing in the bush.

"This is an *igbodu*, a sacred space for dancing." Babatunde told Marc. "It is between the town and the country and is suspended between the two, like a separation of the human and spirit worlds. As the *bembé* progresses, the Orisha will be brought to the human world and the people taking part will be drawn to the Orisha until they become as one."

Large torches were stuck into the ground in a circle around the area and a bonfire was burning in the middle of the clearing. A large number of men, women and children were visible by the firelight and the children ran amongst the trees, laughing and calling to each other while the adults made preparations for the ceremony. An altar to Chango was swiftly constructed, draped in the Orisha's colours of red and white, decorated with flowers and candles and filled with offerings of fruit and other foods. Climbing down from the truck, Babatunde Gbadeo and the other men removed the instruments, carrying them to the clearing and setting them down with great reverence. Marc was intrigued by the drums, which were made of wood and curved into hourglass shapes with different sized heads at their ends.

"They are *bata* drums," Gbadeo explained. "*Batas* are always carefully made and dedicated with special ceremonies that give them the power needed to call down the Orisha."

Marc had reached to touch the largest drum but at Babatunde's words he drew back, eyeing them with nervous respect.

"They're used in groups of three," Babatunde continued, "this one," he gestured to the largest drum, "is called the *iya* - it leads the other two: the next one is known as the *itotele* and the little one is the *okonkolo*."

"I see you have a chekeré, too." Marc pointed to a large beaded rattle, much like the one that had been used earlier at the concert.

"Yes," Babatunde looked at Marc consideringly. "If you like, you can use it during the ceremony."

Marc's eyes lit up. "I'd really get off on that." He picked it up and gave it an experimental shake, enjoying the two-toned sound of the instrument which blended a sand-like swish from inside the gourd with the sharp click of the beaded net that covered it.

His companion opened a velvet pouch, which he'd taken out of his trouser pocket. He drew out a magnificent necklace of red and white beads, which he kissed and then slid over his head, settling it firmly on his shoulders. It hung in a wide collar of openworked diamond shapes with heavy tassels of beads at the end of each point and six long strands of beads that cascaded from the centre almost to his knees.

"This is an *ileke ikarun* - a priest's necklace," he explained to Marc who nodded appreciatively, admiring its beautiful workmanship.

While Gbadeo and Marc had been talking, the other men had set up the *bata* drums in front of the altar. Facing the altar, Babatunde seated himself at the iya and two of the other men settled down behind the smaller drums. The third man handed Marc the chekeré and then joined the congregation who stood in a semi-circle behind the drummers. Marc sat cross-legged on the ground, cradling the instrument which he had been instructed not to play during the oro *de igbodu*, the opening litany to the Orisha.

Then a space was cleared for dancing and the drummers moved so that they faced the crowd. The music began again but now the drummers were joined by the chants of a songmaster with the joyous voices of the congregation responding vigorously to every call.

The litany began as always with a song to Eleggua, who opens the paths to all the other deities. At a nod from Babatunde, Marc began to play the chekeré, using its husky rattle to underscore the insistent beats of the drums.

After the salute to Eleggua there were songs and dances for the other Orisha and his chekeré punctuated their steps almost without his realizing it.

There was a short pause during which everyone mingled, laughing, talking and nibbling on fruits and pastries from tables on either side of the altar. Babatunde offered Marc a cup of what looked like water and which turned out to be just that.

Laughing at the surprise on Marc's face, the older man explained: "This is a *bembé* for Chango, my friend, and Chango does not touch alcohol."

"Perhaps it's just as well," Marc replied. "I need all my wits about me tonight. This is the most amazing experience."

"Just wait," Babatunde said. "It becomes even more astonishing."

The ceremony resumed and at once Marc could see and hear the difference. The songmaster called to the Orisha in tones both demanding and cajoling and the responses of the congregation had a new urgency. The flames seemed to leap in time to the drum beats; the teeth and eyes of the congregants gleamed in the firelight and the slap of their bare feet on the dusty ground echoed the sounds of the drums.

A tall, well-built man came into the central space and began to dance with incredible athleticism and grace. He had the regal bearing of a king and with every movement he appeared to grow taller still. He faced the drummers and Marc drew in a sharp breath as he saw his face. The man was no longer in this world; his features had the rigidity of a carved mask and his eyes were unseeing and more widely open than would be possible in his normal state. He began to turn in a movement known in ballet as *fouetté*, where one leg acts as a pivot and the other lashes out, turning the body with its force. He spun thirty-six times before falling into the arms of two priests who led him away.

The dance space became a maelstrom of activity as other members of the congregation felt their Orisha mount them, too. Those who were taken by their particular spirit danced with the movements of that deity. A man being ridden by Obatala moved stiffly like an old monarch, a daughter of Oshun danced in a languorous, seductive manner while Oya's child turned in a steady whirl. Marc was fascinated. There was an Eleggua, capering jokingly amongst the crowd... an Ogun, stalking grouchily around the edge of the clearing and two Yemayas dipping and swaying in the distinctive steps of the ocean mother. Their dances completed, each of them roamed through the congregation, giving messages and advice to their supplicants.

While this was going on, the first dancer appeared back in the clearing. He was magnificently dressed in red and white; Chango's crown was on his head, the god's double-headed axe in his right hand and he wore an *ileke irun* that was even more elaborate than Babatunde's.

He danced again, leaping higher and spinning faster than before. He went to the tables of food and ate and drank enormously, swallowing fruits without chewing and pouring pitchers of water down his throat. Turning back to the clearing, he crossed the space and stood in front of Marc.

Waves of energy poured from the ebony figure. Marc was frozen with fright but he dragged his gaze up to meet distended, unblinking eyes that saw nothing of this world. Obeying an unspoken command, Marc rose to his feet and stood in front of this man who was the manifestation of the god Chango.

The commanding figure reached out with a huge hand. Long, spatulate fingers grasped Marc's chin. He forced a small pastry into Marc's mouth, which was so dry that he almost choked on the offering. A rumbling voice said: "*OMO* CHANGO," the staring eyes contemplated him briefly and then the being moved on to deal with others of the congregation.

Marc felt an arm on his shoulder: he jumped and turned to see Babatunde Gbadeo standing beside him with a broad smile: "you have been greatly honoured, my brother."

Marc coughed and swallowed, sending the last crumbs down his throat. "What *was* that?" he asked weakly.

"You have found favour with Chango and he has claimed you as his child."

Marc sank back onto the ground. His head buzzed with the vibrations he still felt from the deity's touch and he was relieved by Babatunde's suggestion that he just sit quietly for the closing ceremonies, which he could now barely recall.

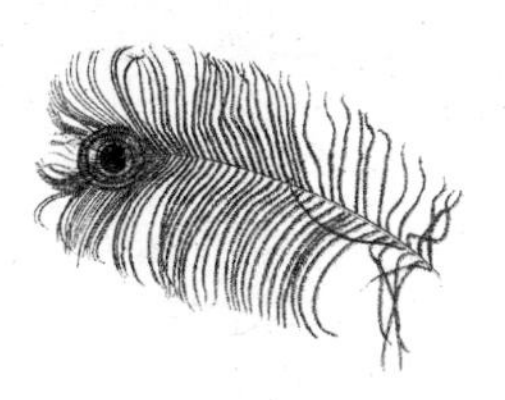

Deep in the groves Oshun began her preparations for the last day of her festival. It was well before dawn and tall torches flamed along the riverbank illuminating the water and the area of her boudoir. She bathed in the river using Yoruban black soap and then lay on one of the large, concave stepping stones known as Oshun's Dye Pots, letting the breeze dry her until there was just a slight film of moisture on her coppery skin. Making her way back to the shore where two attendants waited, Oshun stretched herself flat on the carpet-like moss. One of the women opened a large clay jar and poured a golden stream of acacia-scented honey into a shallow brass bowl held by the other.

Dipping their hands into the honey, they rubbed it over every inch of her body using a firm yet gentle circular motion, raising her limbs and turning her as needed. When they were finished, all traces of the honey had disappeared, leaving only its scent.

Oshun stood up and held her arms away from her body at shoulder height. The women placed a bowl of sparkling golden powder on a tree stump that stood between them. Each scooped some powder carefully into their cupped hands and, as Oshun turned very slowly, they gently blew the powder onto her body until her skin shimmered with tiny dazzles of light.

Beside the honey vessel were a number of long-handled brushes and small clay pots which held powders and creams of many different colours. The older woman wrapped Oshun tenderly in a sheet of pure white cotton and seated her on a moss-covered boulder. Kneeling in front of the goddess, she held a large brass mirror so that it reflected her face. The other attendant began applying the cosmetics with exquisite artistry. She dusted Oshun's face with bronze powder and then shaded coral and terracotta tones onto her beautifully curved eyelids. Next she outlined both upper and lower lids in deep brown and brushed a black kohl paste onto her eyelashes, making them even longer and thicker than they were in their natural state. Finally she took a red cream, mixed it with a few drops of honey and painted Oshun's voluptuous mouth.

Oshun inspected her ravishing face in the mirror and smiled with blinding whiteness at her attendants.

The two women changed places and the one formerly holding the mirror produced brushes, combs, a bowl filled with amber beads and a flask of mimosa oil. She poured a tiny amount of the oil into her hands, rubbed them briskly together and smoothed them over Oshun's hair, working the oil into every strand. She brushed the long, black tresses until they crackled and shone with blue lights and then, taking a two-pronged comb, lifted a small section of hair and began braiding it tightly from the crown to the end, weaving amber beads throughout its length. Her fingers flew like knitting needles and soon Oshun's head was a mass of ribbon-thin braids, studded with beads that glistened like drops of honey. The goddess shook her head playfully, causing the braids to clack like a thousand tiny castanets.

"Now, now, My Lady," said Faleeda, "if you don't keep still we will never be ready in time."

"Then everyone will just have to wait," laughed Oshun, but she quietened obediently as Faleeda fashioned the braids into an intricate fan shape that rose high above her head.

When she was finished, Faleeda produced a brass hand mirror and held it to Oshun's head at different angles so the goddess could observe herself from every side.

Oshun looked at herself very carefully and then sighed happily: "Faleeda, you've got golden fingers!" She drew Faleeda's head down and kissed her fondly on both cheeks and on her forehead. The woman was overwhelmed at this mark of Oshun's favour and to cover her delight, turned to the young woman who was holding the large mirror:

"You going to stand there gawking all day? Get *Iyalode*'s robes ready."

"They're already laid out," the younger woman replied shyly.

"And not a moment too soon," Faleeda grumbled, "In another five minutes they'd have been as wrinkled as a hippopotamus' hide."

"Malindi has done a fine job, Faleeda," said Oshun in soft reproof but Faleeda, still keeping her feelings in check, sucked her teeth in feigned criticism.

On a soft white cloth lay the wardrobe Malindi had prepared. Oshun rose to her feet and stretched her arms above her head as the women lifted the first garment, a pale yellow shift woven of such fine cotton that it was almost transparent. It floated over Oshun's body and settled softly around her ankles. Over this went a tunic of deep yellow silk, which was cut in a deep *V* at the front and slashed almost to the waist at both sides. A belt of amber nuggets with a sunflower shaped clasp was fastened on at her hipline.

Faleeda opened a large chest and took out a magnificent golden headband in the form of a butterfly set with topazes. She handed it to Oshun who placed it so that it curved around her forehead. Faleeda then held out a brass tray full of jewellery. Oshun chose a pair of large fan-shaped earrings of gold filigree with a delicate tracery of small canary diamonds. She slid five gold bangles onto each arm and then selected an exquisitely carved ring of rare red jade, which she placed on the index finger of her right hand.

She looked at herself in the large mirror held by Malindi; Faleeda stood behind Oshun holding a shimmering cloth of gold cloak which she draped over her shoulders and then folded back so that it framed Oshun's body perfectly. She handed a large circular fan made of peacock feathers to the goddess and then stood back, admiring the picture she had helped to create.

Malindi, standing at a distance, gazed adoringly at Oshun. The goddess beckoned her to her side and held out her other hand to Faleeda.

"My thanks to you both," she said warmly. "You have made me more beautiful than I have ever been."

Oshun reached into her jewel chest and drew out a topaz ring and a gold pendant in the form of a peacock. The ring she put onto Faleeda's right hand and then fastened the delicate chain around Malindi's neck.

The women knelt at either side of Oshun and kissed her outstretched hands. She raised them up, and embraced them.

"Leave me now," she told them, "soon the groves will be filled with people and I want a few minutes alone."

Faleeda and Malindi hurried to pack away toiletries, clothing and jewellery, which were then secreted in tree trunks and hollowed out stones. In short order the groves were empty of all save Oshun and her radiance filled the sacred area.

"Time to get up," Brent crooned, gazing down at the splayed-out figure.

"It's festival day, rise and sparkle," he continued, giving a gentle shake to an uncovered shoulder.

Getting no response, he produced a warm, damp face cloth and began trailing it over the sleeper's face and neck.

There was a slight stir followed by a deep sigh, "Ohhhhhh, that is *soooo* annoying."

"Just be grateful it isn't a pail of cold water. Come on, Stephen, I know you're tired after arriving so late last night and I let you sleep as long as possible, but it's time to get up."

Stephen opened one green eye and shut it again tightly. "It's pitch black for Chrissake! I don't *do* pitch black on my days off!"

Brent sighed patiently, "The festival begins at sunrise, my sweet, and we have to leave for the groves in less than an hour, so disinter your warm young body, hurl it into the shower, wash it, clothe it and bring it down to the dining room with all possible speed."

"Now I know why they say it's always darkest before the dawn."

Stephen slid from the bed and disappeared into the bathroom from where there shortly came the sound of the shower and a voice raised in song informing the world that it was only a bird in a gilded cage.

Brent headed for the dining room where Angel, Marc, Keisha, Gabriel and Stephanie sat in varying degrees of somnambulism, picking indifferently at their plates.

"Good morning, fellow festival followers," he beamed.

Five jaded pairs of eyes gazed up at him.

"Where's Jonathan?" he asked Stephanie who was pouring coffee into herself with religious intensity.

"He said he wasn't getting up in the middle of the night for anyone, not even a goddess," she replied. "He's going to spend a cozy day at the pool cuddled up with his phone."

"Is Stephen coming?" asked Keisha.

"He'll be here soon," said Brent, sitting down, pouring himself orange juice and gesturing to the waiter for coffee.

There was silence for a few minutes while coffee, eggs and toast began to have beneficial effects. Eyes brightened, mouths smiled tentatively, and by the time Stephen arrived, everyone was deep in conversation and second helpings.

"Keisha," Brent said, "I've noticed that a lot of people here don't like having their pictures taken. Are you having much trouble with that?"

Keisha shrugged. "It's the same the world over. There's a widespread belief that taking a person's picture is to take away part of their soul but when they're offered payment it usually takes away their fear."

"It doesn't always work," Angel said, "you can't pay anyone to have their picture taken in Mea Sherim, the orthodox section of Jerusalem. Those guys hide their faces with their black hats and scuttle away as fast as their spindly legs can carry them." She looked through the window at the brightening sky and said: "It's starting to get light out, we'd better get moving."

"How far is it?" asked Stephanie.

"About half an hour's walk from here. It's traditional to go on foot and I'd like to do that."

"I would, too," said Marc.

"I have to take the jeep with the equipment," Keisha said. "I could use a couple of bodies to help set up."

"We'll go with you, right, Stephen?" Brent volunteered.

“Just let me get two more gallons of coffee into my nervous system and I’ll do anything for anyone.”

“I’ll hold you to that later,” said Brent, pouring him another cup of coffee, adding cream and sugar and stirring the cup for him.

“Are you going to drink it for me, too?” Stephen asked, “all this attention is going straight to my poor, simple head.”

“Don’t come all that naive girlie stuff with me, Fiona; there’s nothing simple about you - you are fearfully and wonderfully made.”

“Yes, and I was all night long, too,” Stephen agreed, taking a demure sip of coffee and batting his eyelashes at Brent over the rim of his cup.

Keisha giggled and got up from the table, saying, “Okay, boys - meet you at the jeep in five minutes.” She swung her backpack onto her shoulders and headed out of the door.

A steadily growing stream of celebrants was passing the hotel and by the time the rest of the group left the building, there was a throng of twenty thousand on the road; an amazing mixture of people, all dressed in their finest clothes and jewellery, surging through the town, past churches and mosques. They were laughing and singing, beating drums and using other rhythm instruments and among them were Yoruba chiefs mounted on horses and shaded under the silken swaying of huge umbrellas.

Salif was waiting for Keisha with the jeep. Brent, Stephen and Salif loaded her gear into the jeep, then they jumped aboard and took a side road to avoid the throngs clogging the main street. Angel, Marc and Stephanie waved goodbye after them, stepped into the crowded street, and were swept into the tide of celebrants heading towards the groves.

Jonathan Bernstein lay moodily in a lounge chair by the hotel pool. By his side was a table that held a laptop, a bottle of spring water and his cell phone.

Everyone had gone to the Oshun festival, so Jonathan had the pool to himself. The sun was climbing and a light breeze ruffled the flowering bushes that were filled with butterflies. They fascinated him - so many shapes and sizes - such varied colours - they even had different ways of flying, some flapping their wings into blurs, some floating gently among the blossoms, others simply climbing between the leaves and languidly opening and shutting their wings.

Nice life they have, he thought, *just flying around, drinking nectar, waggling their antennae when they want a fast fuck...*

His nature-loving interlude was interrupted by the ringing of the phone.

"Hello, Africa!"

" Theo - what are you doing up? It must be four in the morning there."

"Three, actually and I haven't gone to bed yet. What's happening in beautiful downtown Oshogbo?"

"A pair of black and red butterflies are screwing each others brains out on the hibiscus bush to my left."

"Let's hope they're practising safe sex."

Jonathan reached over to the chairside table for his bottle of water, took a deep draught and asked: "To what do I owe the doubtful pleasure?"

"When you hear my news you'll regret your snide tone, my boy."

Jonathan sighed. "Theo, you are in Toronto - I am in Africa. Have you any idea of the cost involved? Speak!"

"I've settled the TPO thing."

"No way! Hardwicke was screaming lawsuit at the top of his leathery lungs when you last spoke to him."

"Yes, but something I'd heard about him kept niggling at me - I just couldn't remember what it was. Anyway, I had dinner tonight at Centro...actually, technically it was last night."

"Forget technical, just get to the point".

"The point is that I saw Hannah and Paul Fine".

"Yeah?" Jonathan's interest was piqued; Paul Fine could buy the Reichmans and the Bronfmans with the change in the pocket of his golfing trousers.

"Anyway," Theo continued, "that's when I remembered Hannah mentioning to me that Sir Trevor had been making overtures to her, if you'll pardon the pun, about being Chair of the Friends of the TPO and she wanted my advice."

"Hannah Fine asks *your* advice on her life?"

"I am her confidante, her mentor, her preceptor and her guide. We've been friends since we were kids - lived next door to each other in the old days. The woman never makes a decision without asking herself, 'What would Theo do in this situation?"

"And what *would* Theo do in this situation?"

"What Theo would do - what Theo *did* do, in point of fact, was to say 'Go for it, Hannah, my sweet. The TPO will be a finer and a better orchestra with you at the helm of the Friends. But Sir Trevor Hardwicke is an autocratic old devil and must be shown that you are not easily led. Tell them that you will consider it and then leave it to me to speak with Sir Trevor on your behalf. By the time you sweep into the boardroom to chair your first meeting, the entire committee will be trembling like so many blancmanges."

Theo paused to take a puff of his Sobranie.

"Well - what happened?"

"I called Sir Trevor and told him that at a word from me, he'd have Hannah as Chair of the TPO Friends but that I needed his guarantee that he'd drop the lawsuit against Marc and would be ready to record at such time as Marc deemed convenient."

"And he bought it?"

"Bought it and had it gift-wrapped and delivered."

"There are times, Theo - few and far between though they are - when you are an absolute genius."

"How true. And now I must leave you and catch a couple of hours' sleep before leaping into the daily fray. Give my love to Stephanie."

Jonathan put down the phone, lay back and sighed with pleasure. What a wonderful day this was: the sun was climbing ever higher and shining brighter with every step, the pool steward was asking if he could be of service and the butterflies had finished their mating ritual and were enjoying the entomological equivalent of a post-coital cigarette. Beaming on butterflies and steward alike, Jonathan made a courteous request for a car and driver to take him to the sacred groves. He would, after all, go to the festival. Humming happily, he headed for his room.

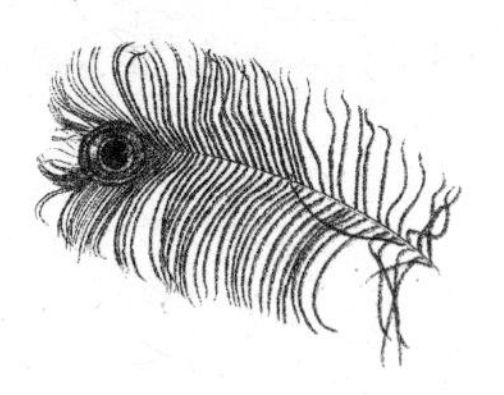

The groves overflowed. There were many tourists, here for entertainment, there were pilgrims from other countries, fulfilling their dreams of worshipping Oshun at her source, but the majority were locals, honouring the deity of the river as they did every year.

Angel, Marc and Stephanie found Salif watching for them at the entrance to the groves.

"Come," he said, "we will place ourselves near the temple. That will give us the best view and I'll be able to explain the ceremonies as they are progressing."

No sooner were they settled than he drew their attention to the gateway of the groves where a group of magnificently robed dignitaries were slowly making their way towards them.

"Here come the *Ataoja* and his chiefs."

"Who is the woman with them?" Stephanie asked.

"She is the *Iya* Osun, the High Priestess. They have been performing ritual since just after midnight. They began at the inner shrine of Gbaemu with a sacrifice to Oshun that symbolizes the clearing of the roads to Oshogbo, which allows festival visitors an easy journey. Then at five in the morning, the *Ataoja* began his procession to the holiest shrines in Oshogbo where he offered kola nuts to the Orisha and the ancestors of Oshogbo."

"All the Orisha - not only Oshun?" asked Angel.

"He requests of all the ancestors and the other Orisha, beginning with Eleggua, to ask Oshun for her acceptance of the sacrifice. Eleggua is honoured as the guardian *and* the trickster and always he must be offered gifts to avoid misfortune."

"Kind of like paying the piper in advance." Brent had joined them with Keisha and Stephen. They joined the others, settling onto the grass and listeneing intently to Salif's commentary as the pageant continued to unfold around them.

From her vantage point at the top of a tree on the highest point of the sacred groves, Oya, goddess of the wind, watched the proceedings jealously. She had to admit that the festival was impressive and in recent years it had become even more powerful as Oshun's popularity had increased in other parts of the world. Take Cuba, for instance; she was the patron saint of the whole damned country. Then there was Brazil where she was venerated as Oxun, and Haiti where she was known as Erzulie. But it was in North America that she had made her greatest strides and not only in large US cities such as New York and Los Angeles; even Canada had discovered Oshun and both Toronto and Montreal had large numbers of followers.

And what of Oya? Where was her festival? Where were her worldwide disciples? Only last week she had been complaining to Chango about playing second fiddle to Oshun. Her lover had been sweetly sympathetic:

"Don't fret, Antelope," he told his fuming mistress. "Oshun appeals to the masses, but you are like a rare wine to be savoured by the discerning. Your followers may be fewer in number, but what they lack in quantity, they make up in quality."

“So you say, my lord,” she snapped, “but I notice that you are only too happy to be one of Oshun’s many followers.”

Chango’s handsome face grew shadowed by a frown.

“Oya, you know that Oshun and I - and *you* - are tied together for all time. No one can resist her, not even you when she comes to you in friendship, but you know, too, that you are my greatest love.”

He kissed her passionately and, as usual, their argument was settled in each other’s arms.

Oya sighed as she remembered the discussion. Chango was right. In spite of their rivalry for his affections, she and Oshun had a strong relationship and were almost like two sides of the same coin.

As she observed the proceedings, her attention was taken by Keisha Adams who was perched on a large boulder at the edge of the river. Her eyes brightened as she watched the young photographer who moved with a speed that reminded Oya of herself. One minute she was stretched on tiptoe, clicking the camera and whirling simultaneously to sweep the crowd with a panoramic shot, and the next she was crouched to the ground, capturing the charm of a tiny girl playing at the water’s edge.

“Yes,” said Oya to herself, “she is indeed my daughter and before long I will make her aware of it.”

Smiling in anticipation, she settled back into the crook of the tree branch to enjoy the spectacle.

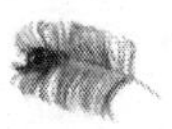

When Jonathan arrived at the groves they were so crowded that he decided not to search for the others right away. Working his way through a sea of celebrants, he managed to find a relatively quiet corner, high on a bank with a clear view of the river. He sank down onto the grass with a grateful sigh and took a drink from the thermos of water the driver had provided, while watching the people around him. There were large numbers of Brazilians and Cubans, Scandinavians and Germans, Eastern Europeans, Americans, Canadians and many Japanese tourists.

Representatives of all the tribes were everywhere; some wore modern clothing but the majority dressed in traditional robes; *dashikis* and caftans woven in time-honoured patterns and glowing with deep colours, including the indigo dye of the area. Many of the women had elaborately braided and beaded hairstyles, but an equal number wore skillfully tied *gelés*, making their heads look like brilliant butterflies. In the tradition of the Oshun Festival, there was a role exchange with some women carrying weapons such as toy guns or swords and more than a few men wearing feminine hairstyles and earrings.

Jonathan observed the people closest to him. They were a striking group with skin tones that ranged from coppery-bronze to a deep blue black. There were four couples, all young and good-looking...wait, he must have counted wrong, there were five men ...no - he was right the first time - just four. Not wanting to be caught staring, he looked away and then glanced back. Damn it - there *were* five men and four women. He squinted to concentrate his gaze and saw that the group of eight were laughing and talking among themselves, paying no attention to the fifth man who, just then, looked straight at him, gave him a huge wink and disappeared.

Before Jonathan could catch his breath, the stranger appeared again, this time on the opposite side of the group. Jonathan shook his head, squeezed his eyes shut and cupped his hands over his face.

Either I'm going crazy or I have a bad case of sunstroke. Whichever it is, I'm going to open my eyes and if he's still there I'm going to speak to him and see if he's wired for sound.

It was a reasonable idea, but when Jonathan opened his eyes and found the apparition nose to nose with him, he screamed and fell backwards, rolling down the slope and coming to rest at the edge of the bank where he lay face down with wildly staring eyes that refused to close. In his line of vision was a pair of feet with remarkably long, thin toes. Their owner stooped down, grasped Jonathan's arm with a hand as bony as his feet and pulled him firmly into a sitting position. He regarded Jonathan with amusement

"Now, my friend," said Eleggua, "it is time for you and I to become acquainted."

Jonathan gave a low moan, his eyes rolled back in his head and he slid to the ground in a deep faint. Eleggua chuckled, picked Jonathan up with no more effort than if he was handling a rag doll, and disappeared with him into the far end of the groves.

Angel and Marc were both fascinated by the festival but each absorbed the scene on different levels. Angel sat upright, watching the kaleidoscope of shapes and colours that swirled around her, her body echoing the excitement that vibrated from every part of the groves. Marc closed his eyes and let the sounds of the day wash over him - sometimes hearing them together in a sweep of harmony, sometimes zeroing in on a single chant or concentrating on a group of handclapping singers. Over all there was the constant sound of *bembé* drums, the sacred instruments of Oshun. Opening his eyes, he touched Angel's arm.

"Hmmm?" She dragged her attention from a group of young women who were dancing at the water's edge.

"Listen to the drums. They sound like the heartbeat of the groves."

"The whole place is one huge heartbeat", she said, " even those who are sitting are caught up in the rhythm. It's such a strange mixture of relaxation and excitement."

The rhythm of the drums changed to a rapid tempo and the atmosphere became even more highly charged. Women were gathering all along the riverbank, standing closely together, swaying from side to side, clapping and chanting with an intensity that filled the groves until there was no room for any other sound. Everyone was getting to their feet and, feeling the rising excitement, Angel and Marc stood, too and faced the entrance together with the rest of the crowd.

A young woman, wearing a plain yellow cotton robe, headed a large group of similarly dressed older women. On her head she balanced several brass objects and walked with slow, steady grace. Her eyes were wide open, her expression was impassive and she seemed unaware of her surroundings.

"It's the *Arugba*," Salif said. "She is a member of the royal family and she is a virgin. The women with her are priestesses of Oshun and the one who walks closest to her is one of the wives of the king."

"She looks as if she's in a trance," Angel said.

"She is. This morning, after she had been prepared by the priestesses, she was presented to the *Iya Oba*, the head of the king's household in Osun State. As is traditional, he placed two kola nuts in her mouth to prevent her from speaking of what she saw and heard at Oshun's inner shrine. That is where she made a sacrifice to Oshun and was possessed by the goddess. She will stay in her trance all day. During the long walk here she has had to carry the sacred brass symbols of Oshun on her head without tripping or stumbling even once; if she does, it will signify great disaster."

They turned their attention back to the ceremony where the *Arugba* was approaching the riverbank. The women at the water's edge increased the fervour of their chanting. Their voices pitched higher, the clapping grew faster and became more intricately patterned: some of the women ululated with piercing notes that carried high above the main chorus.

The *Arugba* reached the river. The king's wife gestured to the four women behind her, two of whom were carrying bundles of yellow cloth on their heads and two who had long bamboo poles. They drove the poles into the ground and unfurled the fabric, weaving it quickly around and over the poles to create a canopied shelter.

At another signal from the *Arugba*'s attendant, four more women came forward and removed the burdens they had been carrying. These were cushions of all sizes and shapes as well as several small, brass trays and wooden trestles. The cushions were arranged to form a long, low couch, the trays and trestles snapped together and placed on either side of the seating area.

The *Arugba* stood motionless as the king's wife removed the sacred objects from her head and placed them on the table to the right of the couch. Two women then led the *Arugba* gently her into the shelter and guided her onto the cushions. She lay quietly while the King's wife used a large peacock feather fan to cool her.

The chanting, which had quietened after the settling of the *Arugba*, grew louder again. The women were joined by a large group of men and their descant enriched the female chorus.

Once again everyone came to their feet, looking towards the entrance. The *Atoja* and his chiefs had arrived.

It was a most impressive group, robed in red and yellow with shaped, embroidered hats and many strands of beads, which as Salif explained, were all dedicated to Oshun. Their different colours and patterns indicated which of her different paths were followed by the wearer.

The *Atoja* was dressed in pure white, showing that he was a follower of Obatala. He had double the number of necklaces that the other men wore, all of milk-glass beads and crystals, and in his left hand he carried a ceremonial white horsehair whisk.

"You see that large, flat-topped stone to the right of the group?" Salif asked. "It has been sacred since Oshogbo was founded and the *Atoja* will sit there to renew the pact with Oshun which he does by feeding the fish of her river."

While this was going on, Keisha was shooting near the riverbank. She was keeping Brent and Stephen busy, too, although she was working four times as hard as the two of them combined.

"Brent - give me the *Leica* - no, that's the *Hassleblad* - the *Leica* is the small one with the zoom lens - hurry up! Stephen, hold up that reflector, I'm getting too much dazzle from the water. Higher, higher - stretch yourself, man! Damn - missed the shot! You guys are going to have to move faster than that."

"If I move any faster I'll collapse from heat exhaustion," Brent said, fanning himself with Stephen's straw hat.

"You wuss - we're not even working at half speed." Keisha was amused in spite of her annoyance over the lost shot.

Stephen was no slouch in the speed department but Keisha left him at the starting post and he was grudgingly admiring..

"Which of your parents was a whirling dervish, luv?" he asked in mock innocence.

Keisha laughed, "In my business, honey, you either move it or lose it. Come on, you two - let's get a little work done."

Her dance began again: whirl, click, stretch, click, stoop, click; accompanied with non-stop comments and commands.

"See that group of kids dancing by the water? Oh, yeah!"

Click, click, click - camera freezing the charming little bodies in motion.

"Brent - reload for me - use 100. There, over by that rock - look at the old woman telling those kids a story. She's the matriarch, honey - what a fabulous face! - Pass me that zoom, Stephen, I want to nail every wrinkle!"

Oya, watching Keisha intently from her perch in the tree, couldn't resist any longer.

"I won't take her over completely," she said to herself, "just enough so that she knows I'm there."

Gathering her robes around her, she twirled herself into an invisible whirlwind. Swooping silently down on Keisha, she spun around her, closer and closer until she melted into the young photographer's body.

Because Keisha was turning very quickly there wasn't an apparent change in her behaviour. Had Brent or Stephen looked closely at her, they would have seen that her eyes were opened abnormally wide, but she was circling too swiftly for either of them to have noticed that. It was only when Keisha became a complete blur, that the two men looked bemusedly at each other.

"Uh, Keisha?" Brent said tentatively.

No reply but the non-stop click of the camera and the spiralling force that was Keisha Adams.

"I was only joking about the whirling dervish," Stephen said.

Whiz! Click! Keisha continued to spin and shoot.

"She's going to screw herself into the ground if she keeps this up," Brent muttered fearfully.

Oya was having a marvellous time. She'd never used a camera before and now here she was, shooting as fast as Keisha's finger could press the button. All too soon she heard a final click and, rummaging inside Keisha's brain, realized that she was out of film.

"Nice to work with you, my daughter," she said and neatly released herself from Keisha, who slid to the ground and lay with unseeing eyes and a dazed smile as Brent and Stephen clustered round her, begging her to speak.

Eyes gradually focusing, her smile widened and she sat up and said, "Whooo-eee, baby - what a *ride!*" A puzzled look came over her face.

"Who was that woman who called me her daughter*?"*

Stephanie wanted to get a better look at some of the crafts that were offered for sale.

"I'm going to wander for a while," she said to the others, "I'll be back before the ceremony ends."

She strolled down the slope and passed by the grotto where Eleggua and Jonathan were secreted. Jonathan saw her walk by close enough for him to touch. He reached out but a gesture from Eleggua froze him in place. By the time Eleggua released him, she was out of sight.

"Why did you do that?" he demanded angrily. "That was my wife!"

"I know, my friend, but it is not the right time to accost her. She has much on her mind and must be left alone to think."

"How do you know what she has on her mind? What concern is it of yours anyway and why have you brought me here?"

"Because it was time for our paths to cross."

"I don't want our paths to cross," Jonathan replied icily. "I came here to see the festival. You start flickering in and out of view like a demented jack-in-the-box, knock me unconscious and abduct me and you have the unmitigated gall to tell me that you did this because it is time for our paths to cross? I'd sooner cross paths with a dyspeptic tiger."

"This is Africa, my friend - no tigers. For that you must go to India."

"God, I wish I *was* in India," Jonathan said fervently, "at least there I wouldn't be incarcerated with a deranged gremlin."

It was now Eleggua's turn to be offended and he spared no expense: "Deranged? You call me deranged? I, EsuEleggua, the Messenger...Interceder for the Orisha...Guardian of the Crossroads...Keeper of the Keys..." He shimmered and changed size with every phrase; now becoming as tall as the tallest acacia tree; now shrinking in size until he danced on the tree's smallest leaf.

Jonathan had clients whose tantrums made Eleggua's outburst seem like a vicar's hiccup, so in spite of the deity's waxing and waning, this was familiar territory. He sat bolt upright, narrowed his eyes and spoke in a tone that had quailed entire rock groups.

"Listen, you African Alice In Wonderland, settle on one size and do it *right now*. I don't care whether it's seven foot ten or three inches; choose a height and then we'll talk."

Eleggua had been executing a rapid up and down size change that until now had never failed to cow his opponents. He was so surprised that he stopped in mid bounce which left him at his regular height. It also made him dizzy enough that he had to sit down rather suddenly, which put him and Jonathan at eye level.

"That's better," Jonathan said affably. "Now - who, or what, are you and what do you want with me?"

Eyeing his opponent with a wary respect, Eleggua pulled his dignity around him and said, "I am that I am."

"We already have one of those where I come from. Let's try again, starting with your name."

"I am Esu, also known as Eleggua. As I said, I am the messenger, the guardian and," he grinned wickedly, "the trickster. Oluddumare, who created all the Orisha, beginning with Obatala, chose me as the deity to whom all must pay tribute before speaking with their personal Orisha. I intercede for them and see that their prayers are heard."

"So, if someone wanted to speak with the Goddess Oshun, for instance, they would first have to ask you?"

"That is correct."

"Sounds something like my line of work."

"It is not dissimilar."

"I have not asked for your intercession with any of your deities and yet you chose to intercept me. Why?"

"Your path is such that you must be guided by me."

"That is the second time you've mentioned paths. What do you mean?"

"My friend, we all have the choice of many paths at any given time in our lives. I have just told you, I am the guardian of paths, the keeper of the crossroads and you are at a very important crossroads in your life. It was no mere chance that brought you to Oshogbo - and no accident that you are now with me. It will soon be time for you to find your path and I will help you to do that."

"I already have my path, thank you very much. It's a nice, rewarding path which I found for myself and I intend to keep it just the way it is."

"You only *think* you found it yourself. Nothing is done without the aid of your Orisha - and for you, that is me."

Jonathan gave a heartfelt moan, which Eleggua ignored.

"Furthermore, what is high can soon turn low. Should that happen, you will need a different road."

Jonathan opened his mouth to answer and just then saw Stephanie returning from the river. She was walking slowly, observing all that was around her and at one point she stared directly at Jonathan.

"Stephanie!" he shouted.

She looked right through him and walked by.

"*Stephanie!*"

Eleggua touched his arm. "She cannot see you, my friend, nor can she hear you. She is on her own path and it no longer meets with yours."

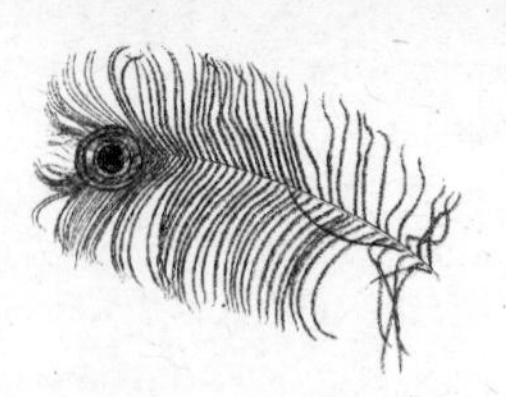

Oshun sat beside the river, emotions flowing through her like the water that flowed between the soft green banks. The festival was over and as always, she felt a touch of sadness mixed with pleasure. She loved mingling with her followers whether invisibly or in human form and, unlike like the other Orisha, Oshun regularly assumed mortal shape. This was partly because she herself was once human, but that wasn't the only reason or Chango would also become earthly more frequently. Being the goddess of love - that most wanted attribute - it was only natural that she would often appear as a human willed into being, as it were, by the prayers of her supplicants.

This year, Oshun had decided at the last moment to show herself as an ancient crone. This was one of her lesser known personas and perhaps because of that it was one of her most powerful; it enabled her to bring messages of love as the ancient mother and it also freaked everyone out, which she enjoyed.

Just before the festival came to an end, when all were gathered at the river's edge, Oshun appeared; not as a beautiful woman rising dramatically from the centre of the waters and gliding over the stepping stones to the bank, but thrashing through the tangled sprays of the Honey Money Bush and scrambling to the shore. Many willing hands reached out to help a poor old woman and when she was on the ground, she touched each person in blessing. Her helpers experienced profound ecstasy and recognized her, surrounding her and shouting her name in exultation. Their excitement spread throughout the crowds who realized that the old woman was indeed 'The Oshun' and their voices rang out in a praise song to this ancient incarnation of the deity.

Oshun stood on the bank of the river, a stooped, frail figure in a hooded robe of coarse hopsacking. A snaggle-toothed grin showed her pleasure in this outpouring of love, but after the tenth verse and chorus, she raised her wrinkled hands and gestured for silence.

"Thank you, my beloved people," she said benignly. The crowd kept on going and Oshun waved again, more strongly this time. "Thank you, my children," she croaked, but the worshippers were really into it and were halfway through verse fifteen before the object of their affection drew a breath that lifted her off the ground a few inches as she bellowed, "ENOUGH!"

An obedient silence followed. "That's better," she wheezed, leaning on a tree trunk to catch her breath.

"Now, I'm not going to drone on in an endless state of the State address. I'm just going to walk amongst you, accept petitions, offer predictions, and do a little laying on of hands. Don't crowd me - I know who needs what and I'll get to you all in turn." So saying, she began to totter through the throng, accompanied by two stalwart attendants who had appeared at her side.

Marc, who was watching with Angel from their spot near the shrine, was fascinated by the old woman. "It's hard to believe that she's really Oshun, isn't it?" he said.

"She's just some crazy old crone who's brainwashed everyone," Angel scoffed, "it's mass hysteria."

"Don't be too sure," Marc said. "Oshun can take on many disguises."

"How do you know about Oshun?"

"Everyone in N'Awlins knows Mama Oshun, she's a great power there - she even has her own parade at Mardi Gras."

Angel scowled disbelievingly but she never took her eyes from the bent figure as it weaved through the petitioners, listening intently to one, bestowing a blessing on another and eventually working her way near to where Angel and Marc sat. The closer Oshun came, the more nervous Angel became and when the crone beckoned her, she went cold with fright."

"She's calling me - what should I do?"

"Go and see what she wants," Marc said. "She can't bite you - there's hardly a tooth in her head."

Unwillingly, Angel rose to her feet. Her legs, which didn't seem to belong to her, carried her over to the ancient figure who took Angel's hand and drew the younger woman to her.

"You don't believe in me, do you, Alix Morton's Godchild?" Oshun asked in a cracked voice.

The blood drained from Angel's face as she tried to answer, "H-h-how d-did you k-n-now...."

Oshun cut her off with a brief cackle, then she said: "I know who and what you are and what you will be."

With a dismissive gesture, Oshun turned to speak to a mother with a young child in her arms, leaving Angel to stumble back to Marc who was waiting with a concerned expression.

"What did she say to you? You look stunned."

Angel decided to make light of her encounter.

"Nothing that made any sense - she's just a harmless old soul who's a few sandwiches short of a picnic."

"Like I said, don't be too sure." Marc said.

"You and your Cajun beliefs." Angel gave his neatly tied ponytail a gentle tug. " Keisha and the boys are packing up. I'll tell Salif that we're ready to leave. It's been a long day and we could all do with a little down time before dinner." She kissed him on the cheek and went in search of their driver.

Now, as Oshun sat waiting for Chango, she thought about the day's events. All had gone smoothly: the *Arugba* had made her journey without a false step, the feeding of the fishes had been spectacular and she had been particularly pleased with her appearance as the crone. Faleeda was annoyed that the work she and Malindi had done had gone for nothing but Oshun had assured her it wasn't wasted - that Chango would more than appreciate their efforts later. Besides, she said with a mischievous grin, it was such a rush to make the reverse transition and see the reappearance of her radiant beauty. Faleeda shook her head in resignation. It was useless to fight her mistress' whims.

Every year, after the end of the festival, Oshun and Chango spent the night together. It was an iron bound tradition and not even Oya would interfere with it. She had tried once, and Oshun, taking her warrior path, had fought the goddess of the whirlwind and won.

While waiting for her lover, she thought of other post-festival nights. One in particular was as vivid as yesterday; it had been a night just such as this - warm and soft as a river mist in summer.

She had lain on a brass couch with amber satin cushions that echoed the copper glow of her skin. The walls of her chamber were lined in ancient mirrors stippled with flakes of gold leaf and they reflected her image over and over.

She wore a length of sheer yellow cotton that covered her body like spun sugar. Her ravishing face had been painted in gleaming tones of copper and amber with deep brown kohl shadowing her eyes. Metallic gold cloth was wrapped into a tight turban around her beautifully shaped head, completely covering her hair. A wide band of beaten gold circled her left upper arm and every finger of both hands wore rings of citrine and tiger's eye.

She had told Chango that she had something special planned for this night and asked that he comply with all her arrangements. Chango was intrigued and agreed. Now she signalled to her attendants that she was ready to receive her lover.

The doors to her chamber opened and Chango entered. There was Oshun looking as delectable as a chocolate cream cake. Chango wanted to swallow her in a single bite, but she had told him that all overtures must come from her and, with difficulty, he restrained himself.

"Give you greeting, my Lord," Oshun's honey-toned voice murmured like the river gliding softly over its bed. "Are you ready for what this night will bring?"

"I am," he replied.

She signalled two male attendants who removed Chango's garments, leaving him dressed only in a white loincloth. A third man brought fabrics that were identical to the ones Oshun was wearing and the three servants swiftly wound them around Chango, the soft cotton draped toga-like around his body and the gold tissue twisted into a turban. It was the first time he had ever worn anything other than his customary colours of red and white and he felt curiously vulnerable. It was not an unpleasant sensation.

Oshun's personal attendant brought a tray of cosmetics and brushes and, using the same techniques and colours as she had done for her mistress, painted Chango's face into a mask of exquisite androgyny.

Dismissing the servants, Oshun drew Chango to her. She placed a gold bangle on his upper right arm and rings on both his hands. They stood together, gazing into the mirror and seeing the double image of their immortal beauty.

They turned and looked into each other's delineated eyes. Painted mouth touched painted mouth, softly, softly, cool as the glass that reflected them. Jewelled fingers stroked hair and eyelids, sketching neck muscles, outlining breast and shoulder. He brushed his lips against her throat and she traced the hollow of his with her tongue.

He stroked her cheek tenderly and she lay the palm of her hand on his. They each cupped the other's face and kissed until their mouths were bruised.

The walls mirrored their kisses over and over. They caressed and the mirrors endlessly repeated each touch.

Sinking to the floor, they inched their way through their draperies to the bodies that burned beneath. He covered her and their reflections undulated and shivered. They made love until they drowned in the wetness of their juices. They made love until they were drained dry. They made love until they blazed into flame.

The mirrors flung their images back and forth in a frenzy until they appeared to shatter into a million shards, each sliver containing the microscopic image of Oshun and Chango, locked together as they crashed their way to an endless orgasm.

"What are the thoughts that bring such a blissful smile to those lips?" Chango's voice broke into her remembrance. She looked up to see him towering over her and her smile widened as she leaned back onto the cushioning moss.

"You are early, my Lord."

"Too early?" He leaned down and lightly kissed her mouth.

"Never. Come, sit beside me and we will watch the sun set while you try a new drink I have prepared for you."

An attendant appeared with two goblets of amber glass, which were filled with a foamy golden liquid.

Oshun took them from the tray and handed one to her lover, raising her glass in a salute to him, which he echoed before tasting the beverage.

"It's wonderful - what is it?" Chango asked.

"Puréed mango, cream of coconut and honey, beaten with a whisk made of cinnamon sticks. I call it 'Golden Sunset'."

"That is just what you look like tonight, my love, as if the setting sun had reached out and wrapped you in its rays."

Oshun inclined her lovely head in thanks and thought: *That will make Faleeda happy.*

"Beyond delicious!" Chango said, draining his goblet and holding it out for a refill.

Oshun smiled complacently. This was an area where she far outshone Oya who, although an excellent cook, didn't have Oshun's passion for fine food. Chango was a challenge to cook for because he was no connoisseur of haute cuisine. He liked familiar foods, highly spiced and Oshun always served his favourites, ringing a few subtle changes on each dish. For tonight's meal she had prepared a savoury goat curry but instead of serving it with the usual cornmeal mush, she had made polenta, cooled into a solid mass, then cut into fanciful shapes and fried in palm oil until the little stars, moons and suns were crisply browned on the outsides and creamy inside. Chango would love it. He would also love what came after. So would she.

Angel sat on the bank of the Oshun River watching the sunrise. It was the day after the festival and she had awakened while it was still dark with an urgent need to be in the groves. Her back against a large boulder, she listened to the water eddy around the rocks with a seductive murmur that sent ripples of pleasure through her, similar to the feelings that Mark's voice aroused.

Everything reminded her of Marc. She'd forgotten how all-consuming romantic relationships can be and it was with both annoyance and delight that she found herself thinking of him constantly...how he looked at her, the feel of his skin, the touch of his clever musician's hands, the things he whispered to her when they were alone in the night.

At the beginning, she had been afraid that this was a romance of circumstance for him but she knew now that it was more and that was her concern. Angel wasn't a pushover but neither was she a coy virgin. She had had several affairs of varying degrees of commitment but had never considered living with a man. Now she found herself wondering if they could share her hi-tech, high-rise apartment or if she would move into the sprawling loft where he lived and worked. She was a vegetarian - he was a dedicated carnivore; he listened to music from his huge library of CDs and tapes; she was addicted to radio and TV, surfing channels and stations with a fervour usually reserved for the male of the species. She loved the theatre, art galleries and musuems while he lived for jam sessions, raves and all-night parties with hordes of friends.

She laughed at herself for even considering living with Marc. *It's the last thing I should be thinking of"* she told her reflection. *The questions are: What are we going to call this youth lotion - how are we going to present it and shall I wear my white dress for dinner with Marc tonight?*

She threw up her hands in disgust with herself and then gave in to her fancies, lying full length on her stomach at the river's edge and gazing dreamily into the water.

Angel had come back to the sacred groves hoping they would give her inspiration. Salif, who was Yoruban and worshipped the Orisha, had driven her there and told her more about Oshun while they were on their way.

"She is beautiful beyond description," he rhapsodized, "and her charm is irresistible. She has great powers, Miss Angel, and is generous in answering prayers. If you want love, Oshun can assure that you get it. Women pray to her to give them children and you can bring money problems to her, as well, for she also rules over gold. *But*," his face became serious and he waved a finger in emphasis, "never take her lightly, never offend her or forget to offer thanks for the wishes she grants, for this can make her very angry. She is the youngest of the gods but she has great powers and she can be whimsy-whamsy." At Angel's blank look, he elaborated, "you know - sometimeish."

Angel nodded: "She's capricious."

"Ah - a good word that - capricious - yes, that is how *Iyalode* can be - capricious." Chuckling, he waved and left, repeating "capricious" with the determination of committing it to memory.

Angel was fascinated by all she had heard both from Salif and Susanne Wenger and promised herself that she'd delve into these legends while she was here at the source. Stretching out her hand, she gently stroked a leaf of the Honey Money Bush, the essence of Alix's miracle lotion. It really *did* look like a little gold coin. Gold! That was it! They'd call it *Oshun's Gold* and build the campaign around the goddess of love and beauty, the mysterious African deity whose gift to the world was this magic fluid that restored youth. They'd put it in capsules made like coins and pack them into miniature treasure chests.

Angel's excitement grew until she couldn't contain it any longer. She stood up and twirled around, chanting

"*Oshun's Gold*! *Oshun's Gold*! *Oshun's Gold*!" Becoming dizzy, she dropped back on to the riverbank and when a large golden fish leapt out of the river and spouted water at her, it didn't register.

The fish did this several more times, still unnoticed and finally swam over to Angel.

Putting its head out of the water it said indignantly, "Five times I've jumped for you. "*Five times!* Do you know what that means?"

Angel's mouth fell open, she gasped for breath and her eyes bulged out of her head lending her more than a passing resemblance to the fish who gave a 'tut' of impatience:

"Young woman - I'm asking you again - don't you know the meaning of this?"

Angel closed her mouth, squeezed her eyes shut, opened them again and said:

"I *think* it means that I've totally lost my mind."

The fish gave her a pitying look: "Haven't you heard the legends of this place?"

"A few."

"Obviously you need to learn a few more. For instance, the important thing to know right now is that when a fish jumps out of this river and squirts an arc of water at you thusly," he shot a perfect, sparkling bow of water that sprinkled Angel's face, "it means that you will be blessed by a visit from Oshun."

"The *goddess*?"

"None other. You have found favour with the great and glorious Oshun and she is about to bestow her presence on you."

"B-b-b-but...w-w-hat will I do...w-w-w-hat will I say?"

"What you do or say is of no importance. Just pull yourself together and try to show a modicum of intelligence." With that, he turned in the water and began to swim out to the centre of the river.

"Wait! *Please* wait!" called Angel.

The fish sighed: "What now?"

"Tell me what to say. I don't want to offend her."

"She's completely charming and very easy to talk to. Just be sure to tell her how beautiful she is. She likes that."

"She didn't look beautiful yesterday, if that was her." Angel said dubiously.

"It was indeed she; yesterday was yesterday and today is today," the fish said primly. "Beauty is in the eye of the beholder and beauty is as beauty does. And now - goodbye."

He turned again, gave her a wave of his tail and dived deep into the river.

Angel stared at the spot where he'd been, then turned away in disbelief.

"I must have imagined it," she murmured. "Fish can't talk."

"Mine can," said a voice behind her.

Angel's heart clattered against her teeth and her spine dissolved. Her back was to an acacia tree, she slid down its trunk and sat, mute. There was a roaring in her ears, which was suddenly pierced by a ringing laugh. Angel's hand flew to her throat and her bracelets jingled loudly.

"Ah! You're wearing my gift. Stand up and turn around so I can see you properly. Come on, girlfriend, no need to fear Oshun. Show me your sweet face."

The voice was liquid honey pouring from a golden spoon. Pulling together a few fragments of spine, Angel stood up, clutching the tree for support. She turned and saw a yellow haze that shimmered and danced on the water. As she watched, the haze gathered itself together in a glowing mass that became slimmer, taller and denser until it coalesced into a human form.

In front of Angel stood the most ravishing creature she had ever seen. It was the woman from her dream but she was even more magnificent than Angel remembered.

"How beautiful you are," she whispered, entirely unprompted by the advice of the fish, "how incredibly beautiful".

Oshun smiled complacently, and gave her yellow robes a little shake. "It's my job," she said. "I'm the goddess of love and abundance and one of my main responsibilities is to look like this. At least, on this particular path - I have a number of them, you know," she said confidingly, "different attributes - various persona; you saw one of the others yesterday - but this is my primary path and, I must admit, it's my favourite."

"I can see why," Angel murmured.

Oshun ignored the interruption and carried on, ticking off her credentials one by one on her slim fingers as she spoke:

"My mandate includes the power to bestow success in romance and business. I am also an expert in divination and I am the deity one prays to for fertility. In short, girl, I have the solution to almost every problem and whatever you want or need I can give you. But right now the important thing is that we have met and that we are going to do wonderful things together."

"We are?"

"Didn't you say you are going to name your youth potion after me?"

"Yes - *Oshun's Gold.*'

"How perfect! My name on the most exciting beauty product in history!'

Oshun perched herself on a nearby rock, pulled a brass comb and a long-handled mirror out of the air and combed her hair, humming softly to herself and gazing with pleasure at her reflection.

Angel was touched by Oshun's innocent, almost childlike appreciation of her own beauty.. And why *shouldn't* she love the way she looked? False modesty had no place in the perfection of this creature. The whole *world* should see her. A thought struck Angel with the power of a lightning bolt. The whole world *would* see her!

"Er - you said you could give me anything I want," she said hesitantly.

"That is so." Oshun tugged her comb through a recalcitrant lock of hair and complacently patted it into place.

"I want *you.*" Angel blurted, startling Oshun who stopped in mid-comb and looked quizzically at her. She blushed a fiery red.

"No, no - not like that! I want you as the model for *Oshun's Gold*"

Oshun opened her mouth to speak, but Angel rushed on.

"There isn't a model anywhere who could compare to you - you will be the most famous person in the world".

Oshun pulled a peacock feather fan out of the air and wafted it lazily.

"I'm a goddess, not a person."

"Oh," Angel faltered, "I didn't m-mean to offend you..."

"That's all right. In any case, I'd have to assume human form if I did this."

She stood up and paced back and forth absent-mindedly, hovering about a foot above the river.

"I have only twenty million followers throughout the world but with my name on this product I'd be famous everywhere."

Hardly able to breathe for excitement, Angel nodded in agreement.

"It would mean leaving Oshogbo? Travelling afar?"

"Yes. We'd begin work here but we'd have to return to Canada for final production and there'll be personal appearances everywhere: London, Paris, Rome, New York...."

"We-e-l-l," the goddess hesitated prettily.

"Private jets...luxury hotels...haute couture fashions... fabulous jewellery..."

Oshun floated gracefully to the riverbank and enfolded Angel in a perfumed embrace.

"Well, girlfriend, I said I could do anything for you, but it looks as if you can do a great deal for me, too. There's just one thing - if I am making this venture, you also have to do something courageous."

Angel was mystified. "What do you want me to do?"

"Stop hiding your relationship with that young man."

"I'm not ready!"

"You love him, don't you?"

"Yes, but -"

"No 'buts'," Oshun said decisively, "it's time you acknowledged your love openly."

Angel sat in thought, turning the bracelets on her arm. They jingled gently, saying "do it, do it, do it."

"Right!" said Angel, jumping to her feet. "Marc has been at me forever about this. We fight about it all the time.. I'll tell him tonight."

"And I will make a grand announcement to all the Orisha that I'm to be the figurehead for Glissando Beauté. What an adventure it will be!"

The two women hugged each other in an ecstasy of excitement, both talking at once. Oshun was so elated that she spiralled them high into the air. Only when Salif, who had returned at the appointed time, screamed and fainted at the sight of them entwined twenty feet above the ground did they regain their composure and drift back down to earth.

Angel raised his head and splashed water on his face while Oshun plied her fan. Salif moaned and opened his eyes, shutting them again tightly at the sight of the goddess and began praying rapidly.

Oshun addressed him soothingly : "Have no fear, my son. It is I, Oshun. I will not harm you."

Her voice had a calming effect on Salif, who stopped babbling to every deity in the pantheon, gazed at the wondrous beauty of the goddess and smiled in tremulous rapture.

Angel eyed him speculatively: "Salif...how would you like to do a little travelling?"

Back at the hotel, Angel found the rest of the group having breakfast in the dining room. Keisha spotted her in the doorway.

"Hey, Angel," she called, "we thought you'd lost yourself. Where've you been?"

"I - I went back to the sacred groves." Angel said.

Keisha pulled out a chair beside her and Angel sank into it gratefully.

"And how were they on the morning after the day before?"

"What? Sorry, Brent, I was miles away. What did you say?

"I was asking you about your time at the groves

"Oh. it was fine. In fact, it was more than fine. If I were to tell you how more than fine it was, you'd never believe me."

"Try us," said Marc, eyeing her in puzzlement.

Angel looked at them as warily as a doe approaching a hunting lodge. She drew a long, deep breath and spoke on the exhale:

“I met Oshun and she’s going to be our model.”

There was a stunned silence, which was broken by Brent.

“Sunstroke. Angel, sweetie, you just come up to your room and lie down while we put out an APB for a doctor.”

“I know it sounds crazy, but I’m telling the truth. Oshun appeared at the riverbank. *Better not mention the talking fish, no point in gilding the water lily.*

“I’d just thought of calling the product *Oshun’s Gold* - and when she came she told me how pleased she was about that and then I asked her if she’d be the model and she said ‘yes’, and then Salif came back for me and he saw her and fainted and...and...there you are,” she finished lamely.

“*Oshun’s Gold* - great name,” said Brent.

There was a chorus of approbation from the others.

“And where is Salif now?” asked Keisha.

“He’s lying down. I drove us back from the groves because he was still a bit shaky.”

“Sunstroke can do that,” said Keisha sympathetically.

“Now, listen to me,” Angel said in a steely voice. “I understand that this news is a little difficult to swallow but I assure you that neither I nor Salif are suffering from sun- stroke, that we *did* see and speak with the goddess Oshun and that she has agreed to be the model for the campaign.”

“And I can’t wait to get started,” said the vision in yellow standing in the doorway.

It seemed as if nobody breathed while Oshun wafted her way to their table. The goddess smiled radiantly at them and Keisha turned to Angel.

“I don’t know where you found her, darlin’, but I promise you she’ll set the world on fire. Will you *look* at that!”

She rose, took Oshun’s chin in her hand and turned

her face from side, to front, up and down and to the opposite side, purring with pleasure.

"She hasn't a bad angle anywhere. Turn around for me, sweetheart. Let's see if that body is as photo perfect as the face."

"*Keisha*!" Angel exclaimed but Oshun gave her an imperceptible "keep quiet" gesture and followed Keisha's instructions.

"Lord, lord - she moves like she's on ball bearings," Keisha marveled.

The others, speechless until now, all began to talk at once.

"Where did you *find* her?"

"I've never seen anything so ravishing in my life"

"Wait 'til Alix sees her."

"Wait 'til *everybody* sees her."

"What's her name?"

"I've *told* you where I found her and who she is, but you obviously need to hear it one more time. She is the Goddess Oshun and I met her at the sacred groves."

Brent reached over and put his arm on her shoulder: "You've been working too hard, sweetie."

Angel opened her mouth to retort and then closed it with an audible little snap of her teeth. She surveyed the room and said:

"Take a look around the room."

Heads swiveled to every corner.

"What's the problem? Everyone's minding their own business," said Brent.

"Exactly. If they could see Oshun, every eye would be riveted to this table."

They stared at Oshun, who gazed benignly back at them.

"You're right," Brent said in a choked voice.

"Nobody sees her," said Keisha, "nobody except us."

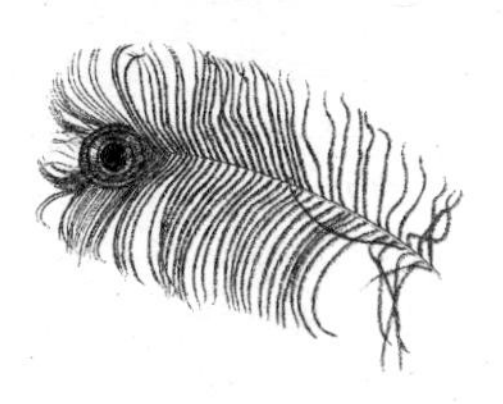

"I'm getting too much shine off her forehead. Powder her down, please Faleeda." Keisha put down her camera and sat under a tree, taking several swallows from a bottle of Evian water.

Angel laughed wryly as Oshun's senior attendant dusted a large brush over her mistress' face. Here they were in Africa, a group of highly-seasoned professionals working with a Yoruba goddess and her acolytes. Who would believe it? How was she going to cope with the deity when they returned to Canada? And how would she manage Alix ? They'd need a stun gun to control her enthusiasm.

"Let's take it one step at a time," she said to herself. "The concept is working superbly and Oshun is a dream come true, so don't borrow trouble."

As if reading Angel's thoughts, which she probably was, Oshun turned and blew her a kiss before settling back into position. Today they were shooting on the river, using the stepping stones known as Oshun's Dye Pots to pose her among a variety of finely wrought clay vessels. The jars were in different shades of yellow, orange and red and painted with intricate, rhythmic lines and dots that Marc swore could be set to music.

Oshun was in the middle of the river on the largest stepping stone. She was framed by branches of Honey Money Bush and was wearing the leaves in a spiral that twisted around her body, with delicate tendrils of the plant twined through her hair. At a cue from Angel, Faleeda and Malindi trotted onto the stepping stones, hopping their way to Oshun while carrying large spray bottles with which they spritzed her, and the branches, all over. They had been doing this several times an hour for most of the day, but they were as thorough with this last misting as they were with the first.

Keisha took a dozen more shots and then shouted to Angel:

"The light will be gone soon and I've shot everything on the storyboards. Is there anything else you need before we strike it?"

"I don't think so. It looked great from here - can't wait to see the proofs."

"I'll have them for you in the morning."

"All right, everybody, that's it for today," Angel called out: "Brent, would you have the crew pack up the jars and make sure they're put in the right boxes."

"O-o-o-kay, Angel." Brent said cheerfully, gesturing to the three young Oshogbons who had been pressed into service and were fascinated by the proceedings.

Angel was eager to get back to the hotel and see how Marc had progressed in the makeshift studio that he'd set up in the living room of his suite. Marc's accommodations were his own again as Jonathan and Stephanie had gone off to Kenya for their safari.

Angel went up to Oshun who had been carefully tended by Faleeda and was now dressed in a yellow muslin robe with a matching *gelé*.

"Are you coming with us?"

"No. I will miss my groves very much and I will spend my time here until we leave for your country."

She kissed Angel softly on the cheek and disappeared.

"Damn it, I'll never get used to all this vanishing," complained Brent, who had come up behind Angel.

"When I think of the problems I've had with bulimic and anorexic models who are blitzed on cocaine, who have the most insane love lives imaginable, who spend every day and night in varying states of hysteria, I'm happy to have one who does nothing more startling than disappear every so often."

"So far."

"Brent, you croak like the raven of doom. What was it Keisha called you?"

"Cassandra."

" That's your name from now on."

"Mark my croaking, Angel - we're going to have trouble, trouble, trouble before we're through with this venture. A little raven told me".

"Come on, Cassandra. Let's get back to the hotel and after a shower and a rest I'll buy you the finest dinner we can find in Oshogbo."

Marc closed his eyes, muttered a short prayer and clutched his guitar case as Salif, with an ear-shattering clash of gears, set off on the journey to the home of Babatunde Gbadeo.

It wasn't that Salif was a bad driver, Marc reflected, he just refused to believe that anyone else had a right to be on the road. *Actually*, he thought, *Salif doesn't realize that anyone else is* on *the road.*

Just then Salif bolstered Marc's theory by steering the car straight at an ox-driven wagon carrying a family of four generations and all their possessions. All four generations yelled at Salif, who continued to be oblivious of their existence. Marc prayed bilingually to *le Bon Dieu en ciel* and God in Heaven and the driver of the cart dropped the reins and buried his face in his hands. At the last millisecond the ox, showing great presence of mind, dived into the ditch, spilling the entire contents of the wagon in its muddy depths. The family shook its collective fist after Salif and then philosophically gathered themselves and their household goods together while the ox took a few self-congratulatory mouthfuls of grass.

Marc gazed at his driver in disbelief tinged with unwilling admiration.

"Salif," he said through white lips, "I have driven in a Paris taxi around the Arc de Triomphe at the height of rush hour, I have ridden a scooter in Rome on the wrong side of the Via Veneto, I have been taken from the Golan Heights to Tel Aviv by an off-duty jet pilot who thought he was in his Sabre rather than behind the wheel of a Mercedes, but I think it's safe to say that never have I experienced the quality of driving that I have found here with you."

"Thank you, Mr. Marc," Salif beamed, showing his appreciation by driving between two oncoming vehicles whose drivers were ambling along side by side at 30 miles an hour while conducting a discussion on the poor crop yield.

Marc crossed himself, closed his eyes again and thought of the upcoming meeting. He was excited about working with Babatunde Gbadeo. The musician had a profound knowledge of the Yoruban religion and had written many praise songs to the Orisha. Marc knew that this experience would be of great help and he spent the rest of the trip listing questions for the meeting, ranging from how many *bembé* drums could be used to who would be the best female vocalist to be the voice of Oshun.

At the village, a group of children were playing at the side of the road. Salif stuck his head out of the window.

"*Eh, omo - ibo je naa ile ti* Babatunde Gbadeo?"

The children swarmed on to the hood, roof and fenders of the car, pointing the way and shouting and laughing as Salif drove slowly to the large, low tin-roofed house a few hundred yards down the road. Drumbeats could be heard through the low wall surrounding the building.

Waving goodbye to the children, Marc and Salif went through a gate in the wall and found themselves in an enormous courtyard. Ranged along one side was a group of laughing musicians playing drums of every shape and size with a joy and verve that Marc had never experienced.

He leaned against a tree and let the rhythms wash over him. This was definitely the sound he wanted and he would ask Babatunde if they could incorporate the water drumming technique of the *Baka* as well. He was so absorbed in his thoughts that it took him a moment to realize that the music had stopped and that the figure standing before him was that of his host.

"Welcome, my friend. Are you ready to make a little music?"

Three hours later, Babatunde had dismissed the rest of the musicians with instructions to regroup the following morning. He and Marc sat in the shade of an acacia tree, each with a tall, frosty glass of fruit punch. Marc took an appreciative sip while rolling a large joint of his finest sensemilla. After a preliminary toke, he raised an inquiring eyebrow at Babtunde, who smiled and shook his head.

"Later, perhaps."

Marc nodded amiably, took another puff and extinguished the joint, putting it into a small silver case, which he carried in his shirt pocket.

“That was a great session,” Marc said. “I wasn’t sure I’d fit in but I felt right at home after the first few bars.”

Babatunde nodded, “I knew there would be no problem - not for a son of Chango, which I am sure you are.”

“That’s what you said the other night at the *bembé* - and what the possessed man said. And it’s also the person I saw -” Marc broke off suddenly and took another sip of punch.

“What were you going to say?” the other man asked. Seeing Marc’s discomfort he added, “I won’t laugh at anything you tell me, I promise you.”

Marc told Babatunde of his daydream where Chango had appeared in the fire. The older man listened silently and when Marc had finished he said,

“I believe that Chango *is* your spiritual father, as he is mine. I am a *babaolawo*, a priest, and I can use divination to find out if this is indeed so.”

Marc was intrigued: “Let’s do it.” he said.

Babatunde went into the house and re-emerged shortly wearing his beaded collar. On one hand he balanced a round wooden board with a wide border that had symbolic figures carved in high relief all around it. It had a large, flat centre filled with a fine white powder and a wooden pointer in the shape of a male figure rested on it. On the rim of the board was a ball of white chalk and a smooth black stone. In his other hand he carried a red velvet pouch embroidered with white beads.

Babatunde set the board down, sat cross-legged on the ground in front of it and gestured to Marc to sit on the opposite side. Taking the bag, he murmured a quiet prayer, touched the pouch to his forehead and heart, then leaned over and touched it to Marc’s forehead and either side of his shoulders. Next he opened the pouch and poured out the contents.

"These are *ikin*, sacred palm nuts", he explained to Marc. "For more everyday matters, we use the *opele*, which is a divining chain of eight half nut shells but *ikin* are used for divination in serious matters, such as the verification of one's Orisha."

Marc opened his mouth to ask a question, but Babatunde silenced him with a shake of his head.

"There will be time for questions after. Right now, you must sit quietly and follow instructions. Here," he handed the chalk and stone to Marc, "put one in each hand and close your hands around them."

Marc did so, feeling the slightly gritty warmth of the chalk ball and the cool smoothness of the stone in his palms.

Babatunde leaned forward and scooped the palm nuts into his hand. Two nuts were left on the ground in front of them and he took up the pointer and wrote the number '1' in the powder on the divining tray.

"Open your right hand." he said to Marc and nodded when he saw the black stone.

Casting the *ikin* back to the ground, he again grasped a handful of them; this time three nuts remained and nothing was marked down. Babatunde threw the nuts and swept them up again. One was left and the figure '11' was inscribed.

"Change the items in your hands back and forth a few times and then open your right hand again." he instructed Marc; this time the chalk ball was revealed.

The procedure was repeated many times until there were eight sets of marks on the divining tray. Babatunde studied the two columns of figures, pursing his lips and nodding wisely.

"The message here is that you must work hard and not be afraid of your new project as fear could block your success."

He looked searchingly at Marc. "What is it you are fearing in your work?"

Mark spoke haltingly: "I've always been fascinated by African music. As soon as I began working on this project I knew I wanted to compose a symphony based on the Orisha but I'm afraid it's presumptuous for me to attempt an interpretation of the Yoruba gods. I know so little of the culture - I'm so ignorant of the history..." his voice trailed off.

Babatunde smiled. "You are *meant* to do this. In the writing will come the knowledge and the voices of the Orisha will speak through your music."

He took both of Marc's hands and covered them with his own.

"It is as I had thought," he declared, "you are indeed a son of Chango and I welcome you as my spiritual brother."

Marc thanked the older man gravely and Babatunde poured them both another glass of punch. Marc fished the joint out of his pocket, relit it and after a preliminary toke, offered it to his friend, who accepted it gravely, inhaled deeply and returned it to Marc.

"I will make you an *ileke* which, as a child of Chango, you should always wear." Babatunde told Marc.

Marc looked doubtful as he eyed Babatunde's beads. "I don't think I could wear anything like that, wonderful though it is," he said.

Babatunde laughed. "Only a priest wears an *ileke* like this," he explained. "Yours will be a single strand of six red beads and six white ones, strung alternately, six being the number of Chango."

"I will be proud to wear it and I will never remove it." He smiled fuzzily at Gbadeo who said,

"That is very good, my friend, except there are some moments at which the *ileke* must not be worn. I refer," he said delicately, "to the times of love."

"You surprise me," Marc replied, "one might have thought that the wearing of one's *ileke* at such a time would spur one on to greater heights, or possibly depths."

Babatunde gave this statement serious consideration.

"That is a theory which is not without merit but, sadly, it is one which we cannot put to the test."

Marc nodded. "It shall be as you say, my brother. No balling with beads on."

The two men sat in contented silence while they finished the joint. Marc rolled another, larger than the first and when they were halfway through it, he asked,

"Could we use water drumming in the music for *Oshun's Gold*?"

"That would be good. Fatunbi, the bass player, has a cousin who recorded with the *Bakas* and I will ask him to work with us."

"Great! said Marc. "It will be the perfect sound for the theme." He took another deep drag and started to pass the joint over, but experienced technical difficulties.

"Do you think," he asked Babatunde politely, "that you could keep still long enough for me to hand this to you? You're shimmering like an *ouled naill* dancer."

"What," asked Babatunde, "is an *ouled naill* dancer?"

"I'm not exactly sure, but I know shimmering enters into it somewhere."

"That being the case," Babatunde said, "I must tell you, my friend, that you're doing considerable shimmering yourself."

Marc looked down at himself, squinting with one eye down the length of his body.

"So I am," he said with mild surprise.

"It's probably caused by dehydration," Babatunde said wisely, "in which case the only thing to do is have a little more punch."

"I bow to your superior knowledge," Marc replied, holding out his glass which Babatunde managed to fill without spilling more than half the contents of the jug on the ground.

Raising his glass to his host, Marc splashed most of it over his head but got a couple of mouthfuls inside himself. Babatunde abandoned the idea of filling his own glass and drank straight from the jug.

Smiling beatifically, Marc took one last toke from the roach, fell backwards and drifted into oblivion.

Babatunde stayed awake a little longer but eventually he lay on his side, pillowed his cheek on his hand and soon he, too, was unconscious.

When Salif arrived to take Marc back to the hotel, he found both men sound asleep. He shook his head tolerantly and picked Marc up. Leaving Babatunde under the acacia tree, Salif carried Marc to the car, laid him gently on the back seat and headed back to Oshogbo.

Meanwhile, back at the hotel, Brent was doing a little drinking of his own. Stephen was flying the friendly skies of British Airways and he wouldn't be seeing him until he was back in Canada. They'd made arrangements to meet in Toronto at the earliest opportunity but no actual date had been set. Brent had only known Stephen for a few weeks but a deep bond had been formed and he felt a sense of loss. He tried to tell himself that it was only a passing fancy, like all the others in his hectic life - that if he were in Toronto where he could choose from a hundred desirable bodies, he wouldn't be giving another thought to the beautiful young Englishman with the face of a wicked angel. And yet...and yet...

"And yet," said a disembodied voice near his ear "you know you're telling yourself a donkey load of lies."

Brent looked wildly around for the source of the voice, which chuckled lazily and said: "Have a drink, Brother."

The voice sounded disturbingly familiar. More to brace himself for whatever might follow than to obey the unseen's instructions, Brent reached for his glass, started to wave off what he thought was a fly on the olive and almost sent his drink crashing to the floor. He gripped the table with both hands as he peered at the tiny being bobbing on the surface of his Martini.

"It's you, isn't it?" he said with hollow resignation. "You're the one I dreamed about that first night at Caprice."

"Indeed yes, that was I," beamed the miniature Orisha "EsuEleggua, Messenger, Trickster, Guardian of the Crossroads, all present and accounted for."

"Why?"

"Why?" Eleggua was disappointed at Brent's palpable lack of enthusiasm.

"Yes, *why*? I didn't ask for your presence and I don't *want* you to be accounted for. One deity at a time is all I can handle and I'm still trying to deal with the Oshun factor."

"Now there is where you are mistaken. More than one Orisha is a blessing earnestly to be wished for. In numbering there is safety, many hands make lightness of the work..."

"And too many cooks are spoiling the broth," Brent finished. "Now, if you would kindly get the hell out of there..."

"All in good time, my brother, all in good time. I am a god with a mission."

"And that mission would be", he asked, knowing he didn't want to hear the answer.

"You! As I promised in your dream, I am here in your foremost interests."

Eleggua kicked his feet briskly to propel himself around the glass, ignoring Brent's cry of protest. After a few circuits, he came to a halt directly in front of Brent and lay full length on the olive, propping himself on one elbow and trailing the fingers of the other hand languidly in the gin.

"What is it that this drink is named?" he asked.

"It's a Martini," Brent replied frigidly, "and now that you're frolicking in it I wouldn't touch it with a ten foot tongue. It's all yours."

Eleggua removed his fingers from the liquid and popped them one at a time into his mouth, sucking each thoughtfully, his expression changing from critical to delighted.

"It is a fine thing, this Martini," he pronounced. "I am highly pleased with it and to show my appreciating, I am going to take you on a wondrous journey."

"Journey? What kind of journey?"

"To your path. You are a child of EsuEleggua and it is my incumbenation to help you choose your way in life. What better time could there be than now?"

Brent could think of many better times, preferably far into the future, but he could tell that when Eleggua made up his mind to do something, he would not be deterred. Clambering out of the Martini glass, the Orisha shook himself like a dog after a bath, and scrambled up Brent's arm to perch on his left shoulder.

"You're soaking my shirt." Brent grumbled.

"It will dry," Eleggua said breezily. "Now, my friend, let us be departing from this place."

Brent left the bar with Eleggua riding snugly on his shoulder, invisible to all except his carrier. Through the lobby they went and out onto the street with Brent turning left or right as his passenger dictated. In a short time they were out of the city and onto a dust-filled country road.

"Now what?" Brent was hot, irritable and apprehensive.

"We will continue to ambulate this way." Eleggua was so cheerful it made Brent even more snappish.

"*We*?" The only pair of legs I see moving around here belong to me."

"It is a figurement of speech."

"Well, while you're figurementing try this one on for size: *Quo* bloody *Vadis?*"

"This is meaning?"

"Where the fuck are we going?"

"To the crossroads. It is not far from here."

"I don't suppose it's occurred to you, but if you made yourself into your large economy size and carried *me* we'd get there much faster."

"Getting there fast is not of the urgency," Eleggua said. "It is important that you make the journey using your own legs - even though they may not be as long as you'd like," he added slyly.

"That," gritted Brent, "is really hitting below the belt, if you'll pardon the pun."

"I have not been saying this to be unkindly, my brother, but to help you stand up to this matter of height which I know is the cause of much grieving to you."

"I know it seems like vanity," Brent said, "but you're right - it bothers me terribly - it has ever since high school. Before then I was taller than a lot of the other guys, but in ninth grade they all started to shoot up. One day I was talking to them eye to eye and the next I was chatting to their belt buckles."

Eleggua laughed sympathetically. "And what were you doing to cope with this obstruction?"

"I tried every remedy known to a desperate adolescent; swallowed every patent medicine, no matter how vile the taste and sent away for every piece of stretching apparatus advertised in the back of body-building magazines. None of it worked so all I could do was become the impossibly good-looking, charming, brilliant and talented fellow on whose shoulder you are riding at this very moment."

"Do you know how tall I am, my friend?" Eleggua asked.

"You don't have any one height. You stretch and shrink until it makes a person dizzy."

"True, but when I am staying at one size I am no taller than you."

There was silence for a moment then Brent said: "Why do you choose that height when you can be as tall as you want?"

"That *is* as tall as I want," Eleggua replied. "When a man is very short he is often using the pushiness to make up for his lack of inches and when he's very tall, he can be the object of unwelcome attention. By taking an unobtrusive height, I can accomplish a great deal without drawing notice when I don't want it. Now, in your case, your 'impossible good looks' are bringing you more attention than any ten men need but other men are looking at you and saying to themselves, 'Oh, well, I'm taller than he is' and they are not having the resentiment of you as they would if you were tall. This is another reason why you are liked by men as well as women."

"I never thought of that, but you're right. Most men, straight or gay, are comfortable with me.

He laughed and shook his head. "Well, I can't say I don't still want to be taller, but you've certainly made it easier to tolerate the situation – funny - Angel always says I'd be overwhelming if I was a six-footer."

Eleggua knew that Brent had something on his mind more pressing than the matter of height. He knew what it was, too, but waited until Brent felt able to unburden himself. The moment came:

"Erm, Eleggua?"

"Yes, my friend?"

"Oh, nothing." Brent sank back into his pool of contemplation only to resurface seconds later.

"Eleggua…"

"My ears are still belonging to you, my brother."

"Good...good. Uhhh, it's a delicate matter, but here goes; you know that I am what is called bisexual?"

"I have noticed that you are more than friendly with members of either persuading."

"Exactly," Brent replied. "Been that way ever since I was knee-high to Ru Paul. But lately I find that I'm torn between the two. More and more I have the feeling that I want to be one or the other - I'm just not sure which it is."

Eleggua nodded thoughtfully: "Soon, I think, you will be clarificated."

"That would be good," Brent said and continued along the road at a brisk pace. He was still apprehensive, but he was also looking forward a little to the experience at hand. Soon they were at the crossroads and Eleggua swung himself down to Brent's left hand.

"Put me down in the middle of the path," he said.

Brent deposited him carefully in the centre of the crossroads. As soon as his feet touched the ground, Eleggua shot up to Brent's height and then kept on going. Up and up he stretched, stopping only when he was so high that Brent had to lean far back to see the deity's face.

Eleggua spoke and Brent had to listen carefully to understand what was being said, so deep was Eleggua's voice and so long did each rumbled syllable take to reach Brent's ears.

"CLLIIIMMMB ONNTTOO MYYY HAAANNND." The deity's words thundered around Brent's head. He leaned down from his enormous height, resting his hand, palm up, on the road in front of Brent.

Eleggua's palm looked like a road map and when Brent stepped onto it, he found himself faced with a profusion of roadways, some as narrow as country lanes, others as wide as a highway.

Eleggua raised his hand until Brent was on a level with his eyes. They were as large and deep as a pair of lakes, fringed with lashes as long as willow branches; every blink caused a gust that made Brent cling to the massive pillars of Eleggua's fingers.

"NNOOWW, MY BRROTHHERR..."

Brent bent double and clutched himself around his middle, trying to block the vibrations that surged through him.

"Eleggua," he gasped, "*please*...turn down the volume!"

The god lowered his voice to a tone which Brent could tolerate.

"Sorry," he whispered. "I forget sometimes the glorious power that blooms within me."

Brent waved a weak gesture of forgiveness.

"Now," Eleggua said briskly, "take nine steps backwards, then look down."

Gingerly sliding his feet backwards, Brent took nine cautious steps and then stood still, lowering his eyes to the area beneath his feet. Three ribbons of light stretched from Brent's feet into infinity. As he watched, the glow coalesced into shapes that stood out against the background luminosity. Brent looked closer still and saw on the right hand path, Keisha beckoning laughingly to him: the middle path held people of both sexes, also making inviting gestures but on the left there was only one figure and as it came into focus, Brent saw that it was Stephen. Unlike the others, Stephen made no move, but stood perfectly still, looking lovingly at him.

Eleggua spoke softly. "There are your paths, my friend. Make your choice."

Brent fought the sense of panic that was rising into his throat. "How do I know which is the right one?"

"I am not saying that one is right and the others wrong. I am saying that you must be moving in one direction or the other."

Eleggua's enormous eyes regarded him with unusual seriousness. Turning back, Brent gave a dismissive glance to the path of many people. He gazed at Keisha for a long moment and then shrugged ruefully. She smiled and nodded in understanding. Brent blew her a kiss and stepped firmly onto the path at his left.

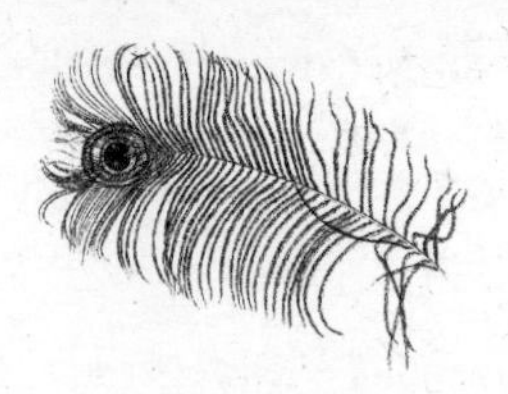

The entrance to Oshun's palace was hidden by the rushes at the river's edge. Only by parting the reeds at a certain spot could you find the opening of the long, deep tunnel, which led under the river and ended in the courtyard of the building on the opposite riverbank.

Oshun was giving a party. The palace glowed with the light of a hundred beeswax pillars, huge sunflowers bloomed everywhere, thousands of butterflies flittered among the trees, and flocks of peacocks paraded through the grounds, fanning their magnificent tail feathers.

Oshun had hinted that this was a special celebration and now revelation time was here. All the Orisha were gathered in the courtyard and Oshun was in her element. She greeted each in turn beginning, as was proper, with Obatala, seeing that the musicians played every deity's praise song and making sure that each one received their favourite foods and drink.

Oya and Obba, Chango's wife, stood together in a quiet corner of the room. The two were bitter rivals but tonight they were united in their envy of Oshun, and a tentative truce prevailed.

"Look at that brazen creature," sniffed Obba, "she has all the men slavering like a pack of hungry hyenas."

Oya listened to the litany of complaints from Chango's unhappy wife, her eye roving around the gathering. How jaw-achingly boring they all were: Obatala, sipping milk and puffing on one of his little cigars. Yemaya, feeding him morsels of *igbin*, the giant land snails that he loved and pretending to slap his hands away when they strayed towards her billowing bosom: Oggun the blacksmith and his brother, Ochosi the hunter. Sparkling repartee was unknown to those two; If they weren't discussing the merits of the macheté versus the sword, they were arguing about the superiority of pheasant over grouse.

"And another thing about that hussy," Oya guiltily dragged her attention back to Obba.

"I'll never forgive her for the trouble she caused between me and Chango."

Discomfort clouded Oya's face.

"In all fairness, Obba, I was more to blame for that than Oshun."

"No. True, you tricked me cruelly when I came to you for advice on how to hold Chango's love, but if she hadn't been stealing him from me *and* you, none of it would have happened."

Both women cast their minds back to that far gone time. Oya had been by the river, scouring her cooking pots when Obba had approached her.

"Give you greeting, Oya."

"Greetings, Obba. Why so sad on this beautiful morning?"

Obba sighed. "Chango is having guests to dinner tomorrow and I am to prepare the food. My cooking is dreadful and you are such a good cook - please give me your secret."

"There is no secret. I choose the best ingredients. I pray to my knives to cut sharp and clean. I ask the fire to burn evenly. I sing to my spoons to stir smoothly and, as I cook, I visualize the pleasure my dishes will bring. Then I line the bowls with beautiful leaves and decorate them with flowers so that they delight the eye as well as please the mouth."

Obba's own mouth turned down skeptically.

“I can’t believe that is all there is to it. You don’t want to share your secrets because you’re afraid that Chango will pay more attention to me than to you.”

Oya had a terrible temper and it flared high at this unjust accusation but she hid her anger and sat silently for a moment as if in deep thought, then

“All right, Obba,” she said, “I will tell you but you must promise never to reveal what I say.”

Trembling with eagerness, Obba agreed.

“You see how I wear my *gelé* low on my head?”

“I don’t give the pop of a flea about the style of your headdress.” Obba exclaimed impatiently. “ I want to know your cooking secrets.”

“And so you shall, Obba, dear,” Oya purred soothingly, laughing to herself at how easy this was going to be.

“Listen closely, now. When I want a dish to be especially delicious, I cut off a tiny piece of my ear and add it to the pot. It gives a richness of flavour that Chango can’t get enough of and,” she winked slyly, “he can’t get enough of other things, too, when he’s eaten one of my special offerings.”

Wide eyed and mouth agape, Obba reached out to lift Oya’s *gelé* but Oya grasped her wrist,

“Never seek to look at my ears”, she hissed, “and remember your promise.”

“Oh, I will, I will!” Babbling thanks and vowing everlasting gratitude, Obba scrambled to her feet and hurried off to begin her preparations for Chango’s feast.

She had agonized for days over the menu, choosing first one recipe, then another, discarding them in favour of something else that sounded even more delicious and then starting the entire process over again. Now, with Oya’s secret, she felt equal to any challenge.

She would begin the banquet with *Akara* balls followed by *Egusi*, the classic Nigerian soup with bold, fiery flavours that burst upon the tongue like the flames that leaped from Chango's mouth. It was one of his favourite dishes and perhaps it would warm his feelings towards her; "After all," she thought, "they say the way to a man's heart is through his stomach. I'm just aiming a little lower,"...and hadn't Oya said that a piece of ear made Chango eager for a piece of something else?

She blushed at her thoughts but they kept her in a frenzy of carnality.

Once she had chosen *Egusi* as the starter, the rest of the menu fell into place easily: *Hkatenkwan*, a spicy chicken and groundnut stew with the stinging snap of ginger root and chilies, *Masamba* greens and for dessert, Mango Snow.

Oya had told her to add the slice of ear just when the cooking was complete. Obba decided to give her first course the benefit of the magic ingredient; she felt it would set the tone for the dishes to follow.

She had chosen her ingredients with care: lean beef and scarlet crayfish for the *Egusi*, two fat, snow-white hens for the groundnut stew, slender green beans, plump pods of okra, crisply ruffled kale, black-eyed peas and ripely perfumed mangoes.

She plucked and cleaned the chickens, causing a snowstorm of feathers to swirl around her. Next she chopped the vegetables and put them, together with the cut up beef and crayfish, into the soup kettle.

Her cooking fire had gone out as usual - she could never keep it at the steady glow Oya always achieved - but she managed to rekindle it without burning herself more than twice. She fanned the fire to a high roar and soon the contents of the pot were rolling around in a galloping boil, crashing into each other and bruising their flavours.

Obba turned her attention to the black-eyed peas which had been soaking in cold water. Plunging her hands into the bowl, she rubbed the peas between her palms until the skins loosened and floated to the top; she skimmed them off and discarded them, then drained the peas and mashed them to a rather lumpy pulp.

She mixed the peas with eggs, chopped onions and spices, beat the mixture vigorously and dropped spoonfuls of it into an oil filled skillet to fry until they turned into crisp, golden balls. The oil wasn't hot enough and the *Akara* became sodden, lying sullenly at the bottom of the skillet. Annoyed, Obba fished them out of the pan and flung them at a group of Vervet monkeys who had been watching the proceedings with deep interest. The monkeys sniffed the balls and then threw them at each other until they disintegrated. Sighing, Obba mentally crossed the *Akara* off the menu.

Meanwhile, back at the soup, the meat had flaked into shreds and the vegetables were boiled beyond recognition while the crayfish bobbed disconsolately among the bubbles. It smelled all right, though, so she left it to its own devices while she peeled, chopped, stirred, and simmered. When everything was ready she stood beside the soup pot and grasped her sharpest knife. Reasoning that if a tiny bit of ear was good, more was better, Obba breathed a silent prayer for courage and quickly severed her left ear. Stanching her wound with leaves, she wrapped her headdress low and tight "*à la* Oya," she thought grimly. The pain was so bad that she was unable to chop the ear finely, as she'd intended, and she dropped it whole into the soup.

Obba bravely bit back her tears, loaded the stacked dishes onto her head and staggered to the compound where Chango and his guests were seated, waiting for the feast to begin. The cooking had taken so long that she had had no time to bathe and change and her dishevelled appearance displeased Chango.

“I hope, my dear wife, that your food tastes better than you look,” he said, sweeping her from head to foot with a disdainful glare.

Obba was in such pain that all she could do was pray not to collapse in front of the assemblage. She hung her throbbing head and made no reply, meekly ladling soup into bowls which servants placed in front of each guest. Obba waited hopefully for the sounds of appreciation that would signal success.

Chango dipped a spoon into his soup, took a large mouthful and choked, dropping the spoon back into the bowl with a splash.

“What is this?” he spluttered, gazing in revulsion at the ear floating in his bowl. The guests at his left and right slid under the table in a dead faint.

Obba burst into tears. Chango lunged at her, gripping her shoulders and forcing her to look at him. The action caused her *gelé* to slip, disclosing the bloodstained leaves beneath.

“What have you done, you stupid creature?”

“I wanted my food to please you and was told that adding my ear to the cooking would make everything taste wonderful,” his poor wife sobbed miserably.

“Who told you such a wicked thing?” Still holding Obba, he shook her until she was in such pain that she forgot her promise.

“It was Oya!” she screamed. “She adds pieces of her ears to the food she makes for you.”

Chango released his hold on her and she fell to the ground, moaning in agony.

Summoning Oya, Chango tore off her headdress and pushed back her hair to disclose two small, perfect ears.

“Foolish woman,” he said to Obba. “You are my wife but you will remain so in name only for never again will I come near you. Get to your house and treat your wounds.”

Obba crawled to her feet and shuffled out of the courtyard. Although she was in agony, her heart suffered still more for she knew that never again would she find favour with Chango.

Ironically, she became obsessed with cooking and night or day could be seen slicing and chopping, stirring and frying, adding a pinch of this and a dash of that. Obba turned into a master chef and everyone praised her cuisine except for Chango, who never again touched anything prepared by his unfortunate wife.

The noise of the party brought Oya and Obba back to the present but the memory of that time disturbed the armistice. Obba nodded stiffly to Oya and walked away to the farthest part of the room where a group of her friends were waving to her.

"What were you and Obba so deep in conversation about?"

Chango leaned over her with a quizzical look.

Oya smiled mirthlessly. "We were discussing times past."

"Was she dragging up that old grievance again?"

"Yes."

"Forget about her - everyone else does."

"Certainly you do, my lord."

"Surely that is as much to your benefit as mine."

"I suppose so, but I can't help feeling sorry for her."

"Who would think that the fiery Oya has such a soft spot? Your many dimensions never cease to amaze me, Antelope. It's one of the things I love best about you."

"But you do not love me alone."

Chango gestured impatiently.

"You know how it is with me, Oya. I will always have other women - it is burned into my nature - but there is no one I love as much as I do you."

"Not even Oshun?"

Chango paused before answering. It was déjà vu all over again and, just as he had done in his confrontation with Oshun, he decided that it was time for the truth and, again, the relative safety of a party was as good a place as any to deal with the situation.

"Oshun and I have a different relationship to yours and mine. It is full of passion and there is love between us, but she knows that the depth of my soul belongs to you."

Oya's sadness at his words was mixed with relief. He loved her best! Though it pained her to share him with Oshun, her great love gave her the strength to accept the situation. The other women meant nothing to him and so were equally unimportant to her. She nodded resignedly.

Relieved by her unexpected compliance, Chango held out an olive branch bursting with fruit.

"I feel the need of change and I was thinking of taking a little holiday. Will you come with me, Antelope?"

"Where will we go?"

"I don't know. Perhaps we can discuss it later tonight." He smiled wickedly and wrapped his arm tightly around her waist.

At that point the *bembé* drums struck an urgent tempo ending with a sharp tattoo. Everyone looked up towards the stage where Oshun stood, ready to speak.

"Good evening, friends. I hope you are enjoying yourselves. This is a very special night for me and I wanted to share it with all of you.

"There is a group of Canadian advertising people who are doing work for a cosmetics company here in Oshogbo. They have a miraculous product, which will restore youth, and they have named it after me. Soon they will return to Canada to bring this discovery to the world and I will be going with them as the face and figure of *Oshun's Gold*, as it will be called.

There was a wild buzz of reaction to Oshun's news and she clapped her hands to regain silence but before she could speak, a voice called out: "This is very exciting for you, Oshun, but what will happen to your duties? How will you answer the prayers of your petitioners? How will you watch over your temple and guide your followers?"

It was Ogun, the god of iron. He was a misanthropic deity, living like a hermit deep in the woods. Everyone was surprised that he'd come to the party, but Oshun knew he nursed a secret longing for her - *much good may it do him* - she thought, smiling patronizingly at him.

"An Orisha can work anywhere, Ogun. Don't we all travel to ceremonies as far afield as Cuba, Haiti, New York - indeed, anywhere that Yoruba or Santeria is practiced? Is there a day that passes without one of us taking possession of acolytes at tambours that are happening simultaneously in different countries?"

She watched the reactions carefully. Those who had been nodding at Ogun's self-righteous words, were now nodding even more emphatically at her reply.

Yemaya's voice was heard over the hubbub:

"There is something else to consider, my friends. By Oshun being made visible in every sense of the word," she paused to chuckle appreciatively at her own wit, "we will gain fame for all the Orisha."

"You are right, Ocean Mother," Obatala nodded approvingly. "There will be many new followers, new folk tales and praise songs. People will learn that African religion is not the mumbo-jumbo they have seen in bad Hollywood films. It will be the dawning of an exciting era for us. You will bring us great honour, Oshun. Go with our blessing."

He rose, walked over to Oshun and embraced her fondly as the gathering applauded, whispering to her, "a quiet word with you?"

"Certainly, my father."

Oshun swept aside a golden curtain and opened the door behind it, gesturing to Obatala to precede her.

"This is my meditation chamber."

Obatala looked around the little room with interest. The walls were hung with yellow silk and there was one circular window, which looked out on the river. Large cushions of yellow and red silk were placed around the room and the only furniture was a low round brass table that held an incense burner, a bowl of sunflowers and a huge beeswax candle.

Oshun sank gracefully onto one of the cushions, inviting Obatala to sit opposite her. He eased himself down gradually. "Damned knee joints!" he muttered with a grimace. Once comfortably settled, he smiled paternally at Oshun and took her hand.

"Let me say again how proud and happy I am at your news."

"Thank you, my father."

"I know that this venture will offer many opportunities, but there is one caution I must give you."

He gazed at Oshun solemnly, lowering his chin and puffing out his cheeks which made him look like a stuffed bullfrog. Oshun was amused but, not wanting to offend Obatala whom she loved and respected, she pretended to be looking out of the window, while biting the insides of *her* cheeks to control herself.

"Yes, my father?"

Her voice trembled with laughter, which she hoped would sound like emotion. Evidently it did, because Obatala patted her hand benignly as he continued:

"You know that we Orisha can make ourselves visible to humans in order to counsel them, to possess them ceremonially and even to share love with them."

"Yes."

"And you also know that you have to take on human form in order to be photographed or filmed or recorded, for that matter - something to do with light bands and frequency waves. I never *did* understand the technicalities of it."

"Oshun wrinkled her lovely brow, "is there a problem with that, my father?"

"Not an insurmountable problem - dear me, no. You just have to be sure that for every hour you spend in human form you spend an equal amount of time in the normal way."

He patted her hand again and rose stiffly from his cushion.

"But what happens if I forget?"

"Your powers fade and it takes a long time to recharge them. Ask Eleggua to work it out for you, he knows all about these things."

Giving her a paternal kiss on the cheek he said: "Shall we rejoin the celebration, my dear?"

The guests, meanwhile, had been talking of nothing else but Oshun's news. Canada! The United States! Probably even Europe!

"Well, now we know where to go."

Puzzled by Eleggua's words, Oya looked at Chango who shrugged helplessly.

"We?" Oya raised a grimly inquiring eyebrow.

"Why not? I, too, feel the need for change."

"Knowing you, you'll cause more change than we have need of," Oya said waspishly.

Eleggua put a long finger under Oya's chin. "I will cause no more change than necessary, my dear sister. And I promise you this, I'll not interfere with you and Chango."

Oya looked at him searchingly and could see that he was sincere. "So it will be," she said, "but what do you mean, 'now we know where to go'?"

"Why, to Canada, of course. Oshun is going to be a big celebrity and will want the support of her fellow deities. Besides - it'll be one hell of an adventure and we can do lots of shoppings."

Chango and Oya mulled this over. The Orisha loved to shop and as their interpretation ran to simply taking what they wanted, they indulged themselves at every opportunity.

"There is another, more important reason for us to go to Canada," Eleggua said. "The child of Oshun, Angel Zimmermann, has friends who belong to us and, unlike so many in the western world who never know their spiritual mother or father, these people must be made aware. *Oshun's Gold* is going to be a huge success and they'll need our assistings."

"And why should we care if it's successful?" Oya snapped. "I, for one, hope it fails miserably."

"And that's where you are shortsighted, my dear Oya," Eleggua answered. "All that dust you blow around clouds your vision. Remember what Obatala said - the success of *Oshun's Gold* will bring fame to us all."

"Eleggua is right, Antelope." Chango said and Oya nodded grudgingly.

Chango put his left arm around Oya's slim shoulders. The three deities raised their right arms and clasped hands, saying, "To *Oshun's Gold* - may it take us far!"

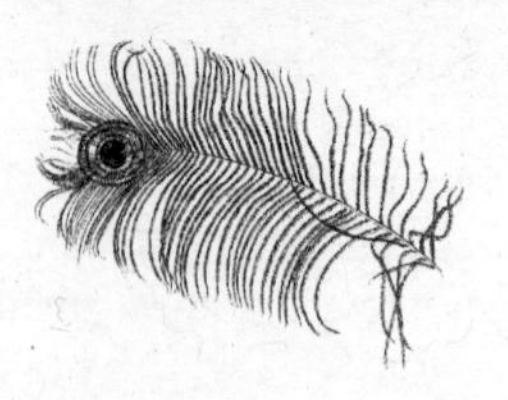

Angel was scanning Keisha's photos when Brent appeared in the doorway.

"You wanted to see me?"

"It's about Oshun. We leave for Canada soon and she has no passport, visa, or identification papers of any kind."

"What self-respecting deity does?"

"Well, this one will have to. I've spoken with the Minister of Trade and Commerce and told him that we've discovered a new model who's going to put his country on the map, fashion wise. He seemed co-operative, but you know what officials are like. They give you vague promises and you spend the next six months getting the royal run-around from one department to another. We haven't got time for that, so I want you to go to his office, take him out for the best lunch in Lagos, offer him anything and everything and stick to him like Blu Tac until he gives you the go. I'd do it, but I've got to get these edited down for Keisha."

"Why bother with passports? Let Oshun travel in her usual way. She won't even have to worry about lost luggage."

"Uh, *uh*" Angel shook her head firmly. "She has to have a proper identity and arrive like a human being. It'll prove useful once the media start nosing around for background stories on her."

"I guess you're right."

"Salif will drive you to the city but you'd better start right away. It'll take you nearly three hours to get there."

"Consider me gone," and, with a wave, he was.

Smiling, Angel turned back to her work and her smile deepened as she inspected the photos again. They were astounding; Keisha's work enshrined Oshun's astonishing beauty and the personalities of both women shone through in every shot.

The Hot Box group was checking out of the Oshun Presidential Hotel and the hotel lobby was a maelstrom of madness. Suitcases, cameras, lights and recording equipment littered the floor, making everyone pick their way gingerly through the obstacle course.

Brent was distributing plane tickets, passports and visas. "Angel - here you are, seat 18. Where's Marc?"

"He's having a phone conference with Babatunde - I'll take his stuff."

"Thanks . . .Keisha, where are you?"

"Over here," a hand waved from behind a pile of cameras and tripods.

"Here you go - ticket - passport - visa. Don't lose them."

"Right.... Brent, wait just a minute, would you?"

Catching the uneasy tone in her voice Brent stopped in mid-turn and looked at Keisha with concerned curiosity. "What's up, K?"

Keisha was discomfited: "I meant to say this before but the moment never seemed to arise and I don't want to go back to Toronto without telling you how I feel."

Oh, Christ, Brent thought, *I* knew *I should have told her last night after dinner but we were having such a good time that I didn't want to spoil the mood.*

"How you feel about what?" he asked apprehensively.

"You - me - us."

"Ah - yes, well..." he stammered.

"Listen, baby. I love you dearly and we've had some fun-filled days and nights but fun is all it was, darlin'."

Laughing with relief, Brent scooped Keisha into his arms and gave her an enormous hug.

"Keisha, my nut brown maiden, you don't know how happy those words make me. I love you, too, but my heart belongs to Stephen and I'm going to ask him to settle down in with me in a rose-covered cottage - well, actually in my condo, but you get the picture."

Keisha beamed with delight. Giving him a huge kiss on each cheek, she said, "I'll dance at your wedding until my feet fall off, but right now, I've got a little work to do."

She returned to the job of checking her equipment and Brent dashed off light-heartedly to distribute the rest of the tickets and documents.

Having secured everything, Keisha fished out her Nikon digital camera and began photographing every mad moment of departure, especially Salif who was giving orders to everyone and getting matters more confused than they already were.

"Where's Oshun?" Brent clutched the precious documents that would give the goddess her new identity.

"In the loo."

"Fish her out of there. I have to go over these papers with her."

In the women's room, Angel found Oshun inspecting herself from every angle in the full-length mirrors that lined the walls.

"What in the name of all that's unholy have you *done* to yourself?"

"I decided to take a little off my behind and my bust and add five inches to my height. How do you like it?"

"I don't. You were perfect as you were."

"But the women in the fashion magazines are so tall and slim -"

"You are not those women. First of all, you are more beautiful than any of them could ever hope to be."

"This is true," Oshun never committed the sin of false modesty.

Angel ignored the interruption: "Secondly, people will relate to you far better as a woman with breasts and a behind - not some tower of bones whose legs begin at the neck. Now, for pity's sake, put yourself back the way you were and come with me."

Taking a last wistful look at her giraffe-like reflection, Oshun jangled her bracelets, murmured an incantation and shrank in height while simultaneously filling out in other directions.

"What mortal women would give to be able to do things like that," said Angel. "Come on, girlfriend - the world awaits you, heaven help it!"

Brent gave a sigh of relief when he saw Angel approaching with Oshun in tow.

"OK - here's everything you need: passport, visa, birth certificate and your plane ticket. I've written down that biography we created for you. Please have it memorized and destroy the paper before we land in Toronto."

Nodding obediently, Oshun took the material from Brent and opened her passport at the picture page.

"This is supposed to be me? It's terrible! I look like *Iku* - like death!"

Angel laughed. "Nobody is allowed to look good in a passport picture, it's an law of the Department of Immigration."

"Never mind your picture, just concentrate on having the facts of your life straight." Brent was a little edgy at the prospect of Oshun's arrival in Canada.

"Don't worry, she'll be fine."

"Let's just pray that we don't get clapped into jail for importing an Orisha."

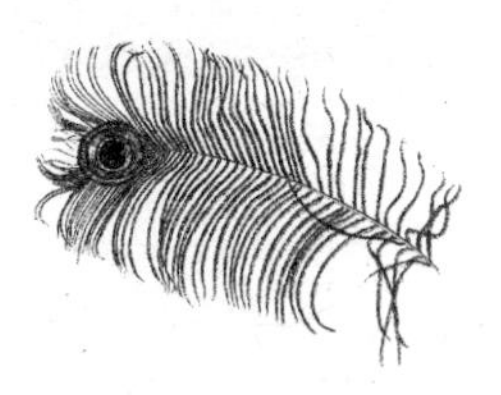

"Alix - how wonderful to see you," Stephanie kissed the older woman in Parisian style, left cheek, right cheek and once more to the left.

"For God's sake, Stephanie, you'll knock me off balance." Alix grumbled good-naturedly. She was fond of Jonathan's wife and felt rather sorry for her, married to a man whose every word was law.

"An army of bulldozers couldn't knock you off balance, you misanthropic old madam." Jonathan arrived in the hall, beaming widely.

"Always a pleasure to see you, too, you legal buzzard," Alix replied cordially.

They stared beadily at each other for a moment before dissolving into mutual cackles of delight.

Stephanie took Alix's arm: "Everyone's here already and *dying* to see you: Marcia Allensby..."

"Lord - I haven't seen Marcia since she took over the editorship of *She Who Must Be In Fashion.*

"Yaacov Kreizler..."

"Is his protégé with him, that fiddle-playing floozy - what's her name - Nafka Courveh?"

"That's 'Navra Dourva', Alix. '*Nafka*' and '*courveh*' are very uncomplimentary words in Yiddish, as you know." Stephanie said sternly.

"Don't be silly, darling. Where would an old WASP like me come to Yiddish?"

"From your many Jewish friends and associates."

"Amazing what can seep into one's subconscious. But enough psychological chitchat. Who else is here?"

"Belinda Bardon with that new designer, Craig LaFortune, Joan and Russell Mendelssohn, our next door neighbours and Theo Slotkin."

"All right, lead me on to the slaughter. Lord, I get talked into anything these days. It's either softening of the brain or hardening of the arteries."

"Possibly both," suggested Jonathan, offering Alix his arm and escorting her into the living room where the assemblage fell on her with glad cries.

"Yaacov - how was your tour?" Alix gave her hand to the renowned violinist, who bowed over it with portly grace.

"It was a triumph but the journey - a nightmare beyond belief! I felt like the woman in the old joke on a round the world trip who was going somewhere else next time." He laughed heartily as he always did at his own jokes: "but, of course", his arm circled the waist of the young woman at his side, "I had the comfort of my darling Navra."

"Ah, yes - the world tour with the world wh - wunderkind," Alix finished smoothly. "How are you, Miss Dourva? Still fiddling your way into the hearts of all mankind?"

Being thicker than the proverbial brick, Alix's jibes passed right over Navra Dourva's bleached blonde head and before she could open her over-rouged mouth in reply, Alix had already whirled on.

"Marcia - how *lovely* to see you after all this time. I absolutely *devoured* the last issue of your splendid magazine. The cover story on retro fashion was *beyond* brilliant."

Marcia Allensby fluffed her green hair and flashed a brilliant smile made even more dazzling by the large diamond set into her left front tooth.

"Thank you, darling. I was worried that it might be a *tad* over the top using Baby Geoffrey in a Molyneux ball gown, but the issue had more legs than a centipede and it *galloped* off every magazine rack in town."

"Not only that, it revived Baby's career overnight," said Theo, who had materialized at Marcia's elbow.

"You must have been grateful for that," Alix said. "I'm sure you haven't enjoyed having a 300 pound hermaphrodite languishing in your stable for the past two years."

"He's a cross-dresser, Alix, not a hermaphrodite," Theo said mildly.

"Whatever."

"Anyway, his new single is number one with a bullet and he's got eighteen more tracks laid down for a double disc with a Christmas release date."

"Marvy!" said Marcia, flashing her 3-carat smile. After her graduation from a third-rate journalism school, Marcia had spent a year in England and returned to Canada more British than the late Hermione Gingold. Everything was "marvy," "ghastly," "brill" (short for "brilliant"), or "perfectly foul," rather like the magazine she spearheaded, which was a fashion macédoine of the good the bad and the ugly and which, like Marcia herself, was too influential to be ignored.

"It never ceases to amaze me," Alix had once said to Angel, "how Marcia Allensby became editor in chief of Canada's leading fashion magazine. I suppose it's a case of mediocrity rising to the top."

"Or sleeping its way there," Angel had replied.

After bouts of greetings to the other guests, Alix glanced into the next room and noticed the back of a familiar figure.

"Do these tired old eyes deceive me or is that Christopher huddled in the corner?"

A thin, slightly stooped man came forward and took her hand: "I'm supposed to be a surprise," he said with a quiet smile.

"And indeed you are, my darling." She kissed him on the cheek. "How are you?" she asked gently.

"Very well. It's grand to see you."

"I thought you weren't coming until next week," Alix said, squeezing his hand.

"I wasn't supposed to, but I missed you."

"Dinner is served," said Stephanie. She slipped an arm through each of theirs and escorted them to the dining room.

"May I be of assistance, madame?"

"It's me, Henry." Angel peeked out the limousine window and lifted her large dark glasses briefly, while crouching under the wide brim of a battered straw hat.

"Miss Zimmermann! Welcome back. How was your trip?"

"Great, but I can't talk right now. Unlock the door to the freight elevator and don't let anyone see you."

As the long standing, long suffering doorman of Angel's Avenue Road condominium, Henry had learned to fill residents' requests swiftly and Angel's was less strange than many he could mention.

He stuck his head into the office of the concierge: "René."

"*Oui*?"

"Keep an eye on the front door for me, would you?"

"*Certainement, mon vieux*," replied the amiable René, swivelling his chair to face the entryway.

Henry was a large, placid man but he could move quickly when the occasion required. He wasted no time in reaching the back of the building and securing the freight elevator. A limousine pulled up and the driver got out swiftly, opened the back car door and extracted Angel and an unknown female.

Henry helped the driver to unload the luggage and gave him his fare and an enormous tip. The limousine sped off, blending in with the traffic that zipped along Avenue Road.

"Henry, get this luggage up to my apartment without anyone seeing you. The building will be crawling with media any minute now. You haven't seen me and you haven't seen anyone else, either."

"Yes, Miss Zimmermann. It's still good to have you back - or not, as the case may be."

"Thanks." Angel and her companion stepped into the freight elevator and were gone.

When the elevator returned, Henry nimbly loaded the suitcases on, delivered them to Angel, then took the residents' elevator down.

Arriving back in the foyer, he found René holding off television camera crews as well as reporters and photographers from the major dailies. Angel's building was often subjected to media blitzes, being home base for many celebrities and Henry was no stranger to the ladies and gentlemen of the press.

"What's all this, then?" he boomed. Henry was a former London policeman and used the time-honoured inquiry of the British bobby to defuse many tricky situations.

"Is Angel Zimmermann at home, Henry?"

"Did you see the new supermodel?"

"Phone up and see if she'll give us a statement for *Primetime*."

"Miss Zimmermann is not here." Henry announced calmly.

"Yeah, right. We followed her car from the airport but we lost her at the Bloor intersection."

"Pity. Still, she's not here, I don't know anything about any supermodel and the interests of the other residents, who will not appreciate you cluttering up the premises, I suggest that you push off."

Such was the strength of Henry's personality that, after a few grumbling comments, they did just that.

"*Henri*, my old *chou-fleur*, you certainly have a way of handling the rabble."

"It's something one learns over the years, René, my little Brussels sprout"

He gave René a small wink and picked up the house phone.

"Miss Zimmermann? Henry here. They've gone but they'll be back sooner or later, so be careful. If I see or hear anything, I'll let you know."

Good. I'm expecting Miss Morton, Ms Lane Mr. Lockwood, Miss Adams and Mr.Dupré at eight o'clock, closely followed by a delivery from *Dinner Is Served.* See that everyone gets up here without a hassle, and ask René to bring the food up himself. I don't want any strangers at the door."

"Consider it done."

"Thanks, Henry. You are a prince among doormen."

Angel hung up the house phone and turned to Oshun who was walking towards the window, attracted by the city lights.

"Don't go near the window," Angel said, "the Paps are out there with zoom lenses at the ready".

"What are Paps?"

"Paparazzi: ratty little photogs who shove their cameras in where they're not wanted."

"Oh," Oshun looked wistfully towards the window, "But the lights look so *beautiful*. I want to see it all!"

"And you will, my dear deity. But until we unveil you at the media conference, you *must* stay out of sight."

"I'll go crazy - I'm not used to being confined."

"My darling Oshun, I'd like nothing more than to show you off to the world, but the media hell hounds have caught scent and are baying at our heels."

"How did they find out? I thought we were being so careful?"

"At every airport in every city in the world there is someone ready, eager and more than willing to let the media know who of interest is on their passenger list."

"Well," Oshun said reasonably, "if they know I'm here, what's the point in staying hidden?"

"Because so far, we're still ahead of the game. The beauty industry, which is the ugliest business possible, has spies everywhere and we don't want anyone catching a glimpse of your fabulous face until we're ready to unveil you. I promise you the time will pass quickly. We have to put a wardrobe together for you and we'll do that tomorrow morning. In the afternoon we'll have sessions with the hairstylist and the makeup artist and the evening will be spent with the head of Glissando's PR department who will coach you for the conference. Once the news breaks, you'll be famous beyond your wildest imaginings."

Oshun pouted and a small storm cloud gathered on her lovely forehead. "But what will we do *tonight*? It's my first night in Canada and I want to celebrate."

Angel patted her hand soothingly. "And so we shall. Alix and the others will be here later and we'll have a small but select dinner party."

The goddess brightened. "I am *very* much looking forward to meeting Alix Morton. We've never talked face to face."

"Yes, it should be interesting, to put it mildly." Angel breathed a small sigh of relief - another crisis averted. "Now," she continued briskly, "there's no food in the place - not that there ever is - so tell me what appeals to you and we'll order it."

Oshun rubbed her cheek thoughtfully, "I've never tried lobster and I've always wanted to."

"Lobster it is, with champagne; they go so well together and I have several bottles on hand. One can live without many things, but *never* without a good supply of champagne; on the rare occasions I indulge, it's with *Dom Perignon*."

"I don't have it very often." Oshun said, "my followers usually give me rum and honey, which I like, but I l-o-o-v-e champagne."

"Well, you'll be able to drink it whenever you want from now on," Angel told her. "People will ply you with champagne at every given opportunity."

"That will be lovely." Oshun took out her golden comb and, standing in front of the mirror over the mantelpiece, began to comb her luxuriant hair as Angel watched in fascination.

"You do that a lot, don't you?" she said to the goddess who smiled complacently.

"It is important to keep my hair beautiful at all times," she said, "I am so often in the water that it gets easily tangled." She looked sharply at Angel. "You are always occupied with your hair, too."

"No-o-o.," Angel said doubtfully. "I only comb it once or twice a day."

"You're always handling it," Oshun said, "running your hands through it when you're stressed...twisting it around your fingers and sometimes you even chew on a strand."

Angel was taken aback. "You're right!" she laughed, "Brent's forever telling me to get my hair out of my mouth."

"You see," Oshun laughed, "my children are all obsessed with their hair."

"Mine's a mop." Angel said, pushing her hands through it and shaking out the curls. "I often wish that I had wonderful straight, blue-black hair like yours instead of this red Medusa mass."

"Be happy with your hair, Angel, it's a colour of great power and it suits you perfectly."

"Well," Angel said practically, "I couldn't bear the amount of time I'd have to spend at a salon getting it straightened and coloured every few weeks, so I guess I have no choice."

So saying, she left Oshun to her rhythmic hair combing and went to order dinner and set the table.

Brent and Keisha walked to Angel's from his townhouse, which was on nearby Oriole Parkway. As they went in, Alix's limousine purred up the drive. The press had re-convened and there was a loud spate of questions accompanied by the popping of flashbulbs and whirring of video cameras.

Keisha and Brent waved good-naturedly but said nothing and Alix stared through the gaggle of reporters as if they were made of glass.

Henry, delighted to see so many of his favourite visitors at once, ushered them in with a deep bow and René, equally tickled, whisked them into a waiting elevator and up to the top floor.

" 'Ere are your guests, M'zelle Zeemmermann," he said, as proudly as if he'd produced them from beneath a magician's cloth.

"Thank you, René," said Angel, "Alix - I'm so glad to see you!" Alix wrapped her in a hug and then held her at arm's length for inspection.

"You're too thin and paler than you should be after a month in Africa."

"Aren't you the one who lectures on the evils of life without sunblock?"

"Yes, but a *hint* of colour wouldn't go amiss."

Angel laughed, kissed Alix's cheek and then said, "Hi, Brent, Hello, K. Go ahead in, Marc's already here."

She turned back to Alix: "I have the face of Oshun's Gold waiting to meet you. Come"

She led Alix to her bedroom, where Oshun was sitting looking out of the window. She turned and rose to meet the older woman.

Alix stared at the goddess, shaking her head from side to side almost imperceptibly.

"I've spent all my life in the beauty industry but never have I ever seen a sight to equal you, *Iyalode*."

Oshun smiled gently and took both of Alix's hands in hers, "It's good to see you, Alix Morton."

Shaken from her customary composure, Alix turned to Angel: "But –what…where…why…?"

Angel laughed. "You sound like the five Ws of journalism - 'who, what, why, where, when.' Give me ten minutes and I'll explain everything."

"Ten minutes? It'd take ten *years* to come up with a sane explanation."

"I didn't say it was going to be sane, Alix. It started at the Oshun Festival..."

Angel outlined the events in a crisp, accurate fashion - her honours degree in journalism had been well earned. When she finished, Alix patted her hand maternally.

"You're right," she said cheerfully, "sanity doesn't even begin to enter into it." She looked at Oshun shrewdly. "Could the Honey Money Bush be part of your reason for accepting Angel's offer?"

"It crossed my mind." The goddess said archly.

It was Angel's turn to be baffled. "What are you talking about?"

"You saw the film," Alix said. "the harvesting of the Honey Money Bush and the negotiations with the High Priestess to use the extract for *Oshun's Gold*."

"Yes," Angel replied.

"Well, it didn't happen *quite* that way. A long time ago I petitioned Oshun for permission to use her plant, which she granted, but we could never use the real story ..."

"You mean that the dealings with the priestess and all of that was a setup?" Angel asked.

"No," Alix answered. "We still had to win the trust of all those involved, but having Oshun's approval made that easier, too."

"And what about Oshun agreeing to be the model. Was that a setup as well?"

Alix laughed. "No - that was a little twist I'd never have envisioned."

Angel left Alix and Oshun to have a few moments together and joined the others in the living room. A few minutes later the door phone rang to announce the arrival of dinner.

Angel's round black lacquer dining table was piled with platters of enormous boiled lobsters, Caesar salad, giant stuffed potatoes, asparagus Polonaise and a magnum of chilled *Dom Perignon* which Marc opened silently with just a wisp of smoke escaping the lip of the bottle.

"You didn't pop the cork!" Keisha said disappointedly.

"It's bad for the champagne - kills the bubbles," he explained.

Everyone busied themselves in passing platters to each other.

"No lobster, Angel?" Keisha asked, when Angel refused the plate," I know several vegetarians who eat fish and seafood."

"I don't eat anything with a face."

"A lobster doesn't have *much* of a face - just eyes on stalks," Brent mused, peering at the one he was dissecting.

"An oyster doesn't have a face at all," Keisha said thoughtfully.

"Let's just say I don't eat anything that has a mother and father." Angel said good-naturedly.

Oshun was fascinated by the anatomy of the crustacean and under Marc's instructions, she ate her way methodically through a huge hen lobster; beginning with the claws, ending with the delectable slivers of meat nestled like pipe cleaners in the straw-thin legs and missing nothing in between.

"Those are the best parts," Marc said, gesturing to clumps of bright red eggs and the virulently green liver. "Don't let the look of tomalley put you off. It is absolutely exquisite."

After one cautious taste, Oshun was in ecstasy and went around the table stealing coral and tomalley from everyone's plate.

A thought suddenly struck Alix. "Angel - what happened to that fellow you said you were bringing back with you?"

"Salif? He's here and he's already been very useful. When we cleared customs and came out into the reception area, there was a mob of his friends and relatives on hand and, of course, the non-welcoming committee - two reporters and a shutterbug who had been tipped off that we were coming back with a fabulous new face. Oshun was swathed in a scarf and the biggest shades this side of Hollywood and Vine and Salif plunged us into the depths of his family who swept us out of the airport and into a limousine before the gentlemen of the press realized we'd left the building. The last I saw of

Salif, he was being borne off in triumph, shouting that he'd call me tomorrow."

"I must meet this treasure." Alix said.

During dessert, a miraculously light lemon tiramisu with raspberry coulis, talk turned to a discussion on the progress of *Vegging Out,* which was taking place in mid-November. Angel had been concerned that it would clash with the launch of *Oshun's Gold* but in fact, the times meshed well. The launch was being held the week before and, as Brent pointed out, much of the work for the food fair had been done months before.

Angel had told Oshun about *Vegging Out* during their flight home. She was very impressed, especially since most of the proceeds were going to aid hunger victims in Africa.

"I want to go to this party," she said now to Angel.

"Actually, I'd like you to be one of our celebrity chefs," Angel said.

"I would *love* that. Can I wear one of those big white hats?"

"Absolutely."

Oshun gave a little wriggle of pleasure, "and do I get to cook what I want?"

"I'd like you to work with Matthew McCall, he's the hottest chef in town", Angel told her. "We're having a meeting next Wednesday to co-ordinate what everyone is making, so you can discuss it with him then but I'm sure there won't be a problem; Matthew's always up for something new."

"That Matthew is one dishy little chef," Keisha mused. "I'd like to have him served on a platter with a tactful parsley garnish."

By the time dinner was over, it was almost midnight. Everyone was tired and Angel waved them out of the door with hugs and kisses all around, including a couple of extras for Marc.

"Can I not stay the night, Cher'?" he murmured, biting her ear gently.

She deftly extracted her ear lobe from between his teeth, "No, darling, I need to sleep. I'll see you tomorrow."

"Eh, bien. Have a good night." He blew a wistful kiss and headed home to a cold shower and sleeplessness. When was he going to get up the courage to suggest that they live together?

Angel closed her front door and leaned against it, half-wishing she'd let him stay.

"How much longer are you going to keep him dangling?"

"I can't decide what to do. I'd like to suggest that we move in together, but I've never lived with a man. What if I hate it? What if *he* hates it?

"Then you stop living together. But you'll never know unless you try it out."

"All I want to try out right now is my bed." But once in bed, Angel was wide-awake. She missed Marc's body against hers…the feel of his skin...the sound of his breathing. After several hours of restless tossing, she drifted into an uneasy sleep.

Jonathan and Theo sat in Jonathan's office with a stack of contracts and a large ashtray, brimming over with cigar and cigarette butts. It was five-thirty and Jonathan opened the credenza behind his desk and extracted a bottle of Glenlivet Single Malt and two squat tumblers of heavy crystal.

He waved a glass at Theo. "Drink?"

“Absolutely gagging for one,” replied Theo, lighting another cigarette and relaxing into the deep recesses of the antique porter’s chair.

“How about you and Stephanie joining me for dinner tonight? I thought we’d take a look in at North 44 - I haven’t been there for a while.”

Jonathan looked uncomfortable. “I don’t think so, Stephanie is away visiting family - some problem with her cousin, Rita.”

Theo eyed Jonathan speculatively. He’d not been himself over the past few days; more short-tempered than usual and not dressing with his usual exuberance.

“Stephanie - on a *family* matter? There isn’t a member of her family that she’s spoken to in the last ten years. Would you like to tell me what’s going on?”

Jonathan glared at the diminutive agent for a moment and then sagged like a strand of overcooked fettucine.

“She’s left me.” He looked at Theo who gazed imperturbably back at him. “You don’t seem surprised.”

“That would be because I’m not. Stephanie and I had lunch a while back and I could see that she was desperately unhappy. She didn’t want to say anything but you know what a past master I am at getting people to open up.”

“Not even the sphinx could stay mum around you. So - what did my dear wife have to say?”

“She talked about the problems of twenty years of a marriage that’s been mostly in name only. A partnership with a man to whom the term partnership is seen only in legal terms. The union of a pair of mismated souls; wedlock in deadlock with the emphasis on dead.”

“And what did you say?”

“What *could* I say, Jonathan? She’s right. You’re familiar with the saying ‘the law is a cruel mistress’. Well, that doesn’t apply to you because you’re *married* to the law and she’s a very demanding wife.”

“Look who’s talking, you’re as wedded to your work as I am to mine.”

“True, my boy, but there are a couple of very important differences. One, outside office hours I have other things to talk of than contracts and clients and two, I’m not married. I’m the quintessential social butterfly, fluttering from one little flower to the next, loving all and hurting none.”

“Pretty empty life if you ask me.”

“While yours is a bursting cornucopia.”

“At least when I came home, I had someone there.”

“But she didn’t.”

“Is that what she said?’

“In considerably more words than that, yes.”

Jonathan rubbed his forehead and eyes. His face looked even more worn than usual and Theo, whose worldwise exterior hid a marshmallow heart, asked gently: “What did she say to *you*?”

“Nothing she hasn’t said before: we have nothing in common, no mutual interests, no shared goals; the same old litany and I didn’t think it meant anything more than it had in the past.” He took a large swallow of his single malt and continued, “except she told me that the trip to Africa made her realize that she couldn’t go on like this.”

“If it will help, she told me that she loves you.”

“Yeah, she told me that, too, but she said it’s not enough. She wants companionship, someone to laugh with - she says we never laugh together. Who am I supposed to be – Robin Williams?”

“Theo took a thoughtful puff of his cigarette. “What can I say, Jonathan? It’s always sad to see a marriage crumble. All you can do is accept her decision and hope that she’ll change her mind.”

“Do you think she will?”

“She may have the bad judgment to do so.”

Jonathan smiled wryly. “And what do I do in the meantime?”

“What you’ve always done - work! We have fresh rows to hoe, new worlds to conquer.”

Theo pulled himself out of the depths of the porter’s chair and instead of his usual double handshake, he gave his friend a bear hug and said, “Let’s have dinner tomorrow night and in the meantime, if you need to talk, call me - no matter what time it is.”

Jonathan nodded and gave him a wave before turning back to the pile of papers on his desk.

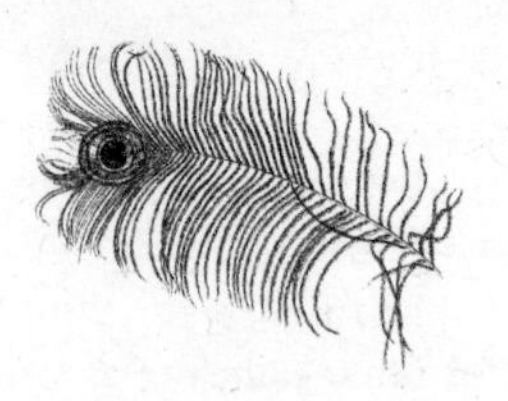

"No, no, *no*, Biba! Get that bilious rag off her. It looks like something left over from *The Mummy's Curse*!"

Silently, the chic young woman in black peeled an ecru gown of shredded chiffon from Oshun's pliant body while fashion stylist Avery Winslow fell back dramatically onto a convenient couch and clapped a failing hand to his forehead.

Oshun exchanged a bemused glance with Angel. Avery hauled himself upright and wandered over to the rack of clothes, petulantly twitching each hanger and eyeing the garments with disgust. His fluff of dyed blonde hair and sharply beaked nose gave him the look of a dyspeptic chicken and his jerky motions added to the resemblance.

"Avery - would you like some coffee?" Angel asked.

"Coffee...*coffee*? We have to pull together a drop dead wardrobe for Miss World Sensation in about thirty nano-seconds and you're offering me *coffee*?" he squawked.

He even sounds like a chicken, Angel thought.

"Well, *I'd* like some," Oshun said, stepping off the low platform where she'd been posed for the last two hours. Picking her way through the litter of discarded dresses that covered the floor, she took a proffered cup from Angel and sank into a chair. "Ah, that feels good," she said gratefully. "This is hard work."

Biba looked at her curiously, "But you must be used to fittings, being a model in Africa."

"It's different there," Angel said hastily. "African garments don't require the meticulous fittings that are called for in western fashion."

"Oh," Biba nodded wisely and poured herself some coffee, adding four spoons of sugar.

"And where's *mine*?" Avery demanded.

"You said you didn't want any".

"Well, if everyone else is going to sit around swilling coffee all day, what *else* can I do?"

Angel gave Avery a mug of coffee and offered him a plate of assorted bagels. He took one and pecked at it irritably, scattering sesame seeds everywhere.

Wandering over to the clothes rack, Angel fingered a silky length of jersey.

"This is lovely," she pulled it off the rack and waved it invitingly.

"It's a Jean Muir ," Avery said, "no one but *no one* does silk jersey like dear Jean." He brushed sesame seeds off his black cashmere sweater, took the gown from Angel and held it in front of Oshun.

"It's a dream; try it on, darling."

"It's the wrong colour," Oshun said.

"It's pure scarlet - perfect for you," Avery clucked.

"I have tried on gowns in every colour of the rainbow. They don't feel right and they hurt my eyes. I will only wear yellow or gold." Oshun sat down, folded her arms and frowned mutinously.

Here we go, thought Angel, *back on the whim wagon..* But even as she had the thought, she realized that Oshun was right. The theme of *Oshun's Gold* should be reflected in every garment the goddess wore.

"It's true, Avery," Angel said contritely to the little stylist. "They really *are* the only colours for her. I should have thought of it before."

Shrewish though he was, Avery had a genuine fondness for Angel. He gave a long-suffering sigh and said to Biba, "Get Jean Paul Giroux on the phone. He's got the most *ravishing* yellow ball gown in his new collection and I *think* I can talk him into letting us use it."

Four hours and ten outfits later, Angel waved Avery and Biba out the door and sank into a chair. Oshun lay full-length on the couch, stretching her arms and legs and wriggling her fingers and toes.

"If I'd had to try on one more dress or stand there for one more minute while those scrawny creatures stuck me with pins, I'd have turned them both into dung beetles."

"You didn't make it any easier by changing height on them," Angel reminded her.

"I only did it twice - well, three times," Oshun said, "and it was just a couple of inches."

"Enough to send Avery into a hissyfit," Angel said severely, "I thought he was going to choke Biba when she pinned that hem line in so many different lengths that it looked like a scalloped edge: *'Can't you even keep a straight line, you cross-eyed tart!'* Poor girl - she was in a terrible state and it was all your fault."

"But it *was* funny, wasn't it?" Oshun giggled.

"Hilarious. You've been hanging out with Eleggua too long, Oshun; you simply *can't* keep playing these tricks. We have a lot to do and very little time to do it."

Oshun gave her a hug, "All right, girlfriend," she cooed. "I'm sorry. Don't be angry."

Angel hugged her back, "Nobody could stay angry with you, but I never know what's going to happen next. You have so many different moods, and you switch from one to another so quickly that nobody can keep up."

Oshun laughed, "That's how I am. We Orisha live within you humans; we couldn't exist without you and we reflect human behaviour, but on a very large scale. Because I am the goddess of love, I'm more changeable than the others and because of my many paths, I have many different characters."

“The others have different paths too, don’t they?”

“Y-e-e-s,” Oshun said slowly. “But not as diverse as mine and although I enjoy my different persona, there are times when I wish I was a little more settled, like Oya.”

“*Oya*? She can go from benign to ballistic in the flick off an eyelash.”

“ But she’s predictable – either really happy or ready to tear the world apart.”

“Still, she’s not as fascinating as you, deity of delight. Now - get ready for the second onslaught. The hair and makeup team will be in our midst in five minutes.”

“Maybe this time I’ll have my nose grow...or perhaps I’ll make my eyes and ears change places.”

“Oshun,” Angel said warningly.

“Joking - just having my little laugh!”

The house phone rang. “Henry here, Miss Zimmermann. Your people have arrived.”

“One moment, please, Henry.”

Covering the mouthpiece of the receiver she turned to Oshun, “I want your sworn promise that at all times you’ll be wearing one full head of hair, two symmetrical eyes, one on each side of your regulation length nose, which will surmount one normal mouth plus a pair of perfectly placed, impeccably proportioned ears. Got it?”

“Got it,” Oshun replied.

“Good,” said Angel. She spoke into the phone, “Send them up.”

Oshun and Angel breathed sighs of relief as the door closed behind the makeup and hair stylists who had spent four hours creating a variety of exotic looks while they twittered over Oshun’s fabulous beauty.

But no sooner had they collapsed into armchairs when the door opened again and Brent bounded into the room.

"I just passed the slap and crimp team in the hall. They said the new model makes Kate look like an old slag. Goddess of my heart, you are the most ravishing creature in this or any other universe...and you're not too bad either, Oshun."

Oshun giggled.

"Cut out your nonsense." Angel said, "I wish Henry would stop letting you slide in here unannounced."

Brent was unperturbed. "He knows you're always thrilled to see me. Is there a bottle of gin in the house? It's time for a Martinus."

"In the usual place in the liquor cabinet - and that's 'martini.'"

"If I wanted two I'd have asked for them," Brent replied.

"And *that*," Angel said, "is an old Wayne and Shuster joke."

"Yeah-*The Julius Caesar Caper* - remember..? 'I told him, Julie - don't go...' "

Angel handed him the gin bottle. "Here - you do a better Martini than an impression."

"Am I drinking alone? I know you won't want anything stronger than Ty Nânt, Angel girl, but what is your pleasure, Lady Oshun?"

"I am in desperate need of rum with the Coca-Cola." Oshun said

"Sounds as if you've had a busy day." Brent rummaged around for rum, while Angel brought a coke and ice from the kitchen.

"I haven't been so exhausted since the preparations for my wedding."

"You're *married*?" Angel was surprised and curious.

"I was, many centuries ago."

"Just let me get these constructed and then tell us all about it." Brent said, mixing madly. He gave Oshun her highball and poured his drink into an oversized Martini glass.

"When I was very young, I lived with my mother, Yemaya, Goddess of the Ocean. We had a beautiful little house made of seashells and pebbles that stood where the river meets the sea.

"My mother and I were happy and lived a simple life. I was considered a jewel beyond price and Yemaya knew that as I grew to marriageable age there would be countless suitors for my hand. She took great pains to conceal my identity, and when prospective husbands began to present themselves, she made sure that none knew my name, saying that the man who could guess it was the man who would win her daughter's hand.

"To every aspiring lover she gave five guesses but each time the swain failed to find the name and departed, heartbroken. One day, three brothers, princes of a foreign land, arrived at the house of Yemaya. The legend of my beauty had spread far and they were determined that one of them would have me as his wife. The eldest brother was the first to approach the redoubtable Yemaya who greeted him with reserved courtesy.

" 'I have come,' he said portentously, 'to win the hand of your daughter, for I hear she is fairer than a flamingo in flight - more graceful than a palm tree in the wind and lovelier than a lotus bloom drifting on the water.'

" 'She is all these things and she is also one hell of a good cook,' replied Yemaya, who is of a practical nature.

" 'I claim her as my bride,' said he, with a confident smile.

" 'Name her, my boy, and she is yours,' replied Yemaya, smiling back at him with equal assurance.

“The eldest son thought long and hard. She was as beautiful as the dawn... ‘Is her name Ojumi?’

“ ‘No.’

“Her voice was like a melody…Orin Didun?’

“Yemaya shook her head.

“The eldest son knit his brow: Wait - she was as graceful as the breeze, ‘Is she called Kawi?’

“ ‘No.’

“His last two guesses were also unsuccessful and he left in disappointment.

“The next day it was the turn of the middle brother but he was not noted for his imagination and could only come up with names of the African equivalents of Janet, Helen and the like and he struck out as badly as his elder brother had done.

“The youngest son was the brightest and most beautiful of the three. He was called the Little Prince and was greatly loved by all. That evening, while his brothers sat in their tent after dinner, drinking wine and lamenting their ill fortune, he went for a walk in the cool night air. Following the river path to the sea, he reached Yemaya’s house where he hid in a tree, which grew outside the kitchen window. Yemaya and I were clearing away after dinner, laughing and talking about the failure of the two princes and scoffing at the chances of the third brother for the next day. To tell the truth, I had fallen in love with him at first sight, but it wouldn’t do to let Yemaya know that. I happened to look outside and saw him sitting on a high branch; right away I knew what to do. I picked up a stack of bowls, balanced them on my head and began to dance.

“ ‘Be careful, my daughter,’ warned Yemaya, but I just laughed and continued to sway and twirl. At one point I executed a pirouette, and pretended to be overcome with dizziness. I took a step backwards, tripped over a stool and sat down abruptly on the floor; the bowls shattering around me like so many eggshells.

" 'Oshun - you foolish girl - look what you've done!' Yemaya scolded.

"I hung my head in assumed repentance but when Yemaya sent me to get the broom, I peeked through the window to see the jubilant Little Prince slide quietly down from the tree and run back to his camp, whispering my name every step of the way.

"In the morning the Little Prince shook hands with his two elder brothers who solemnly wished him luck as he set off for the house of Yemaya.

" 'Give you greeting, my mother,' he called to Yemaya, who sat in the courtyard, pounding yams.

" 'I am not your mother, nor will I ever be,' she replied tartly.

" 'How sad that you should think so,' he said in mock sorrow, 'when I am so sure that your daughter, Oshun, will be mine.'

"Yemaya dropped her pestle, scattering the yams on the ground as she clapped her hands to her face in amazement.

" 'How did you discover my child's name?'

"The Little Prince smiled as he picked up the pestle and brushed the soil from the yams, returning them to the bowl.

" 'The trees told me,' he replied gently.

"Yemaya gazed into his eyes, saw the beauty of his soul and knew that this was the man for me. And so he was and so we wed and the Little Prince and I lived together for many happy years."

"What a great story," said Angel. "It's like *Rumpelstiltskin*."

"Most legends have their equivalent in all cultures," Oshun replied.

"It's all part of the collective consciousness," Brent said airily. "You know - how every culture has similar customs and superstitions and all."

"How erudite!" Angel raised a eyebrow in mock surprise.

"You know me - just *Jung* at heart."

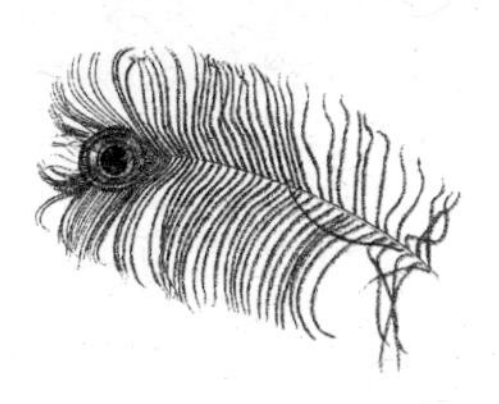

Alix stood inspecting her image in the full length mirror in her office dressing room, silver grey silk jersey dress with matching coat; sheer hose and high heeled pumps in gun-metal grey; small, pewter toned handbag; grey pearl and diamond earrings, matching necklace – all present, all perfect.. She slid on two rings, an enormous star sapphire and one of paved diamonds, edged in carved crystal, adjusted the drape of her sleeve and moved the diamond clasp of her pearl necklace a fraction of an inch downwards. After a final check, she stepped into her private elevator and headed for the top floor.

Glissando's penthouse suite didn't have an angle anywhere, just a seamless sweep of creamy marble pouring from floor to ceiling. Instead of the usual expanse of plate glass there were, at different levels, round windows set into the walls like jewels, containing magnificent views of the city. Interspersed were arched niches displaying Alix's famed collection of ivory carvings. A mammoth chandelier of Millefiori crystal holding fifty vanilla coloured beeswax candles glittered overhead.

The penthouse was staffed with an army of ravishing creatures; models, actors and dancers 'resting' from their chosen occupations. These jobs were highly coveted, not only because Glissando was a great place to work, but also for the influential visitors of the inner sanctum. It was common practice for casting directors to drop by the Glissando hospitality suite to case the talent and many future stars had been plucked from behind the reception desk or out of the dining room.

When Alix stepped into the foyer, she was greeted by an enchanting, mopheaded girl whose curves echoed her surroundings.

"Good evening, Miss Morton. Miss Zimmermann and the others are waiting for you."

"Thank you, Bettina."

Nodding to the statuesque brunette behind the telephone console and to the blond Apollo who opened the glass doors to the inner area, Alix entered the great hall, which was set up for the media reception that would introduce Oshun to the world.

Serving stations stood against the near wall. Tables of hors d'oeuvres alternated with bars stocked with vintage French and California champagnes and each table was manned by several Glissando Glams as the staff was known.

The central part of the room had a number of seating areas, ranging from large couches and coffee tables to smaller armchair groupings for more private conversations. Towards the far end of the room, nestling against the curvature of the walls, were rows of low-backed banquettes in graduated heights. They were moved by hidden wheels that locked into place and gave unimpeded stadium seating views. Every seat had a microphone, a small side table with computer and phone lines and a beautifully boxed media kit.

"You look wonderful."

Angel hugged Alix and gave her a kiss on the cheek.

"So do you, dear heart," Alix inspected Angel, nodding with approval at her pink organdy suit, teamed with an orange silk blouse shell. On her lapel was an antique cameo brooch of carved coral that Alix had given her for her 25th birthday.

Keisha was checking her display of African landscape photographs mounted on black velvet screens running down the centre of the room

"What a marvellous outfit, Keisha." Alix said, admiring the long, formfitting dress in an Oshogbo indigo print. It cut away deeply at the neck and shoulders highlighting Keisha's beautifully toned shoulders and arms; with it she wore a matching *gelé*.

"Decided to go back to my roots," Keisha said nonchalantly.

"Well, Alix, are you ready to give the world the greatest invention since penicillin?" Brent swooped to her side, fizzing with excitement.

Alix laughed and straightened his tie.

"Stop whizzing around like a demented humming bird and get me some champagne, elf."

She settled herself on a couch. "Angel, would you give us the programme line up?"

Marc, hindered by Salif who insisted on lending a hand, was balancing the music coming softly from hidden speakers; songs that he'd recorded in Oshogbo. Seeing that Angel was about to speak, he turned the volume down and joined the others.

"It's almost five o'clock now and the media will arrive at 5:15. We'll give them half an hour for champagne and chitchat, then I'll do the official welcome and introduce Alix. We'll roll the tape at her cue."

"When do we bring in Oshun?"

"After the film. She'll be unveiled over there," Angel gestured to a small stage at the end of the room, curtained by yellow satin.

"Everything seems to be in order up to that point," Alix said, "after that it's in the hands of the goddess. Where is she?"

"In the back cloakroom - security is good there." Angel answered, " she's finished with the hairstylist and is ready for makeup, after which Avery and Biba will dress her."

"If she's wearing that micro monokini from the photographs we'll have a riot on our hands the minute the rabble claps a camera lens on her."

"She'll be in Jean-Paul Giroux's show-stopper; a yellow chiffon ball gown with a matching taffeta cape."

"It sounds divine."

"Almost as divine as its wearer."

"They've started to arrive - shall I let them in?" Brent was wearing his official worrier look.

Angel raised an inquiring eyebrow at Alix, who nodded.

"Okay, " Angel said, " let the mayhem begin."

"It's too quiet around here," Chango sat under his favourite palm tree, idly rattling a pair of thunderstones.

Eleggua lay at his side, sipping rum and coconut water.

"I thought you'd be glad of a rest after Oshun's farewell party, my brother. You danced yourself into such a frenzy that the floor was churned into ashes."

"That was days ago. I'm noted for my regenerative powers."

"If I had a penny for every little token of those powers, I'd be a very rich god."

Chango turned a disapproving eye on his friend, who rolled on the grass whooping with mirth. He tried to remain straight faced but Eleggua's glee was infectious and soon they were both roaring with laughter as they reminisced about their amorous experiences.

"This is all very well, brother," said Chango at length, "but it doesn't change the basic situation."

"Which is?"

"I'm bored beyond belief."

"What about our holiday plans?"

Chango groaned. "May my double-headed axe cut out my tongue! It was in a weak moment that I promised Oya I'd take her to Canada. I love Oya and Oshun dearly, but the last thing I want is to deal with them at the same time, especially in a foreign country!"

"Don't take on so. We'll have a perfectly splendificant time and you'll make all sorts of new conquests."

"With Oya watching me like a chameleon eyes a bluebottle? With Oshun wrapping herself around me like a vine around a baobab tree?"

"I think you'll find that the ladies in question will have many diversions to occupy them."

Chango looked at his friend speculatively. Of all the Orisha, Eleggua was the only one who knew past, present and future without having to resort to divination. Being Eleggua, however, he never shared his knowledge outright, preferring to dole it out in tantalizing little morsels that never completely satisfied one's curiosity. But it was useless to question him, so Chango just laughed and clapped Eleggua on the shoulder: "Right, my friend. Let's dig Oya out of whatever mischief she's getting up to and head for adventure."

They found the goddess of the whirlwind sitting in her courtyard, stirring the breezes into tiny tornadoes that spun around the yard, bouncing off each other and ruffling the feathers of the chickens who were scratching up a desultory lunch of driver ants.

"Greetings, Oya"

"Greetings, my Lord."

Give you good day, Oya."

"Good day to you, Eleggua," Oya replied coolly. Eleggua was too all-knowing for her comfort and the fact that he and Oshun were such close friends kept her on guard.

"What brings the two of you here?"

"It's time to discuss our travels," Chango said.

"I thought you'd forgotten about that," Oya replied, with studied indifference.

"Would I forget?" said Chango expansively.

Ignoring the obvious response, she said: "I have spoken with Yemaya and she will be happy to take over my responsibilities as keeper of the graveyard."

Well, she certainly has experience with that," Eleggua smiled maliciously.

He was referring to the old history of Oya and Yemaya, when Oya was in charge of the ocean and Yemaya of the graveyard. Finding the waters too cold for her liking, Oya tricked Yemaya into trading places with her and there was a dreadful fight. But that was thousands of years ago. Yemaya came to love her ocean kingdom and being a kind-hearted creature, had forgiven Oya long ago, as Eleggua well knew. He just couldn't resist stirring up trouble.

Oya shot him a swift look of dislike. He laughed and extended his hand. "Peace, sister. This is to be a pleasure-filled time, so let us be in harmony with each other."

Oya eyed the offered hand as if there was a scorpion in his palm, but finally gave his bony fingers a brief shake.

Chango smiled approvingly: "that's what I like to see. Come, Oya, my love and help me to choose my wardrobe. We're heading into the world of fashion and I must be even more dazzling than usual."

They left Eleggua to make his own preparations. He was more concerned about packing the proper ingredients for his spells and potions than about his clothing, and by the time he was finished he had sufficient materials to enchant the entire population of Canada with enough left over for the eastern seaboard of the United States.

Alix stood at the microphone, revelling in the uproar she had unleashed. "Ladies and gentlemen, I'm afraid that's all the time we have for general questions. Your media kits have all the information and Brent Lockwood is available to arrange interviews...Brent - would you show yourself?"

Brent rose from his chair and gave an amiable wave.

"Treat him gently, please, he's precious to me. Now we come to the part you've been waiting breathlessly for," continued Alix. "The star of Africa; Glissando's face of the future - please welcome the divine Oshun."

The lights dimmed, the scent of amber incense filled the air and *bembé* drums played the opening beats of Marc's praise song to Oshun as the curtains parted silently.

Swathed in a hooded cape of gold taffeta, Oshun stood on the stage against a backdrop of green vines and giant sunflowers. A pair of magnificent peacocks perched on marble columns on either side of her and her head was bowed, completely hiding her face. The music built and the peacocks fanned their tails as she slowly raised her head. The hood fell back to her shoulders and she allowed the cape to slide off gracefully, revealing an exquisite gown of yellow chiffon cut into multilayered petals. With a radiant smile, she bowed left and right, then floated to a throne at the centre of the stage; as she seated herself, the peacocks flew from the columns to the arms of Oshun's chair, where they perched with their tails sweeping the ground.

Bedlam ensued.. Camera crews climbed over each other and reporters screamed questions that went unheard in the general uproar. Angel, who stood at the microphone ready to mediate the question period, called in vain for quiet and the peacocks not only boosted the noise factor with ear shattering screeches but flew over the crowd and dropped a few calling cards which caused several photographers to lose their footing.

"Dammit," said Brent, "I *knew* we should have given those birds an enema."

At the back of the room Keisha was busy recording the melée and Alix, dissolved into tears of laughter.

"This won't do, Alix. It won't do at all," Brent said disapprovingly.

Alix mopped her eyes with a scrap of Valenciennes lace and pulled herself together with a visible effort, "You're right," she said. "Do something, Elf."

Striding firmly up to the stage, Brent brushed aside all in his path, including a small but determined video operator, who kept shooting even as he was trampled underfoot.

Brent beckoned to Oshun who came to the edge of the stage, listened, nodded and clapped her hands three times. There was instant quiet. Angel, still at the microphone, took a deep breath and said, "Ladies and gentlemen, Oshun will now take your questions - one at a time."

Angel and Oshun were curled up in the comfort of Angel's living room. They'd relived every moment of the conference and were now onto more personal matters, namely the pros and cons of Angel's affair with Marc.

"I'm not sure how long this will last," Angel said. "Sometimes I'm not even sure if I *want* it to last." She took a strand of hair and nibbled on the ends of it until Oshun fished it out of her mouth. She took Angel's hands in her own.

"Listen carefully to me, my child." Her voice held a profound gravity that Angel had not heard before and a finger of trepidation touched her spine. She gazed at the beautiful deity and for the first time felt Oshun's true power.

"Marc Dupré will be in your life forever," the goddess stated. "You are the moth and the flame; sometimes you are the flame and Marc is the moth, sometimes it is the other way around, but whichever way, it is a deep and true love for both of you'

Angel sighed, torn between the relief of knowing that Marc loved her as she did him and the dismay of contemplating further turbulence.

"When are you seeing him again?"

"Saturday night."

"You should make dinner for him."

"Cooking isn't my thing. "I can make instant coffee, Kraft Dinner and when pressed, I can scramble eggs; anything more complex than that is beyond my capabilities."

"I can teach you and believe me, sweet thing, there's nothing more rewarding than cooking for someone you love."

"But Marc is a wonderful cook. I could never make anything that would measure up."

"People are always afraid to cook for an expert, but those who know how much effort goes into a dish are the ones who most appreciate it and I will show you how to make food that will sing in the mouth."

Angel looked skeptical, "I thought you were the goddess of love, not the kitchen."

Oshun laughed. "When it's made with love, food is part of romance."

Remembering the Night of The Grapes, Angel's misgivings lessened

"All right, let's give it a try."

Oshun rummaged briskly through the kitchen, clucking disapprovingly at the barren cupboards and empty refrigerator.

"You have wonderful cooking pots, but nothing to put in them; marvellous knives and not even a radish to cut with them; beautiful plates with nothing to serve on them."

Angel looked shamefaced, "My designer put in a completely furnished kitchen as part of the accessories."

Oshun snorted, "Accessories! We need *ingredients*. First thing tomorrow morning, we go shopping."

"Not until I've read the morning papers." Angel protested. "They'll all be carrying stories on Glissando and you."

Oshun smiled widely, "I suppose we can wait until after that."

The next morning, after gloating over all the front page stories, Angel and Oshun headed off to Kensington market. Two hours later they returned, loaded with kitchen staples, a cornucopia of fruits and vegetables and many herbs and spices. Oshun surveyed the produce with a pleased smile, then turned to Angel:

"Fetch that big red candle from the living room."

Puzzled, Angel did as asked. Oshun rubbed the candle with a little olive oil, sprinkled it with a pinch of cinnamon and lit it, releasing a spicy fragrance.

"A red candle stands for passion and preparing food must always be done with fire of more than one kind. Now, we're going to make *Ye'atakilt alich'a*, which is a wonderful dish of cabbage, potatoes, onions and carrots."

"It sounds like Irish stew," Angel said, wrinkling her nose disdainfully.

"It's a little different, not that there's anything wrong with a good Irish stew. Now - why don't you peel the potatoes while I do the onions and while we work I'll tell you how I granted eternal safety to Oshogbo."

Oshun chose a large purple onion and began her story.

"It is not my best known image," she said as she removed the papery magenta coloured skin, "but one of my paths is that of the warrior. When Oshogbo was being settled, the site chosen was on the banks of my river, which was not acceptable to me. I caused the peaceful waters to become stormy and lash the shore with crashing waves and, when they were at their worst, I rose from the river and told the settlers that my groves were sacred and must be kept intact. Woe betide them if they built their town on the riverbank. 'However,' I said, 'if you build in the hills above the river, I promise that Oshogbo will never be taken by enemies.' The newcomers obeyed me and I kept my word to them. To this day, Oshogbo has never been conquered in battle."

Oshun cut the onion in half and then into translucently thin slices while continuing her story.

"In the early days of settlement, an army of Fulani troops marched against Oshogbo. They had conquered many villages and the townspeople were gravely concerned for the safety of their town. Eleggua, who knows all, warned me that the Fulani would be there by evening but Chango was fighting a battle in the north and Oya, as was her custom, was at his side, so I was on my own."

"Weren't you afraid?" asked Angel, pausing in her potato peeling.

Oshun gestured to her to carry on working as she answered. "No, I knew what I had to do."

"What *did* you do?"

"Exactly what we are doing now? I peeled potatoes, sliced onions, chopped cabbage and made a delectable stew."

"Why would you do that?"

Oshun took the cabbage, peeled off the outer leaves and with one stroke of her chef's knife, sliced the head in two. "The better to cut them down, my dear."

Laughing at Angel's confused look, she chopped the cabbage into a meticulous pile of cube shaped pieces while carrying on with her tale.

"While the stew simmered, I took a leisurely bath in the river and sprayed myself with honey scented coconut oil. I combed my hair until it streamed like a black waterfall. I painted my mouth into a provocative smile. I wrapped a long yellow cloth of finest muslin around my hips and put on many strands of tiny amber beads, which allowed my breasts to peek through as I moved. Then I placed the enormous pot of stew onto a flat basket, lifted the basket to my head and walked to where the Fulani army had made their camp a few miles down river - if you've finished the potatoes, peel the carrots."

"Oh, *screw* the carrots," said Angel, who nevertheless took up a vegetable peeler and attacked them vigorously. "I want to know what happened."

"All in good time," Oshun said serenely. "When I arrived at the camp, the soldiers had put up their tents and were resting on the bank, drinking palm wine and boasting about their forthcoming victory against Oshogbo."

She broke off her narrative to open several spice jars. "Here comes the most exciting part," she said, sniffing the contents of each jar.

"In the story or the cooking?" asked Angel, smelling the jars in turn and sneezing from the unaccustomed aromas.

"Both. Now, let's see...paprika, chili powder, piménton, saffron and just a *touch* of asafoetida." Oshun put pinches of each spice into a brass mortar.

"What a wonderful mortar and pestle," she remarked, scrutinizing it closely. "It looks very old."

"It belonged to my great-great grandmother," Angel said. "She brought it with her from Russia. It's always handed down to the eldest child in the family but I've never used it."

"You will now." Oshun slid the mortar in front of Angel and handed her the pestle. "Grind the spices together."

Angel did so, saying " We could have done without the asafoetida - it smells *dreadful*!"

Oshun laughed, "That's why it has that name, but the smell will disappear as the spices blend and it adds depth to the finished dish."

She took a tiny frying pan, put it on the gas range and after lighting the burner and turning the flame down low, had Angel pour the spices into the pan.

"There's nothing else in the pan," Angel said. "Won't the spices burn?"

"The pan has to be dry," Oshun explained as she stirred the mixture. "Roasting the spices gives them a rich flavour that you don't get when you use them straight from the jar, but to avoid burning them you have to keep stirring and take them off the heat as soon as they release their fragrance - like right now."

She whisked the pan off the element and turned off the gas. "Now, we'll let them rest while we continue. Where was I?"

"At the army camp."

"Ah, yes. The men spotted me and fell silent as I came towards them. One man, a big, burly fellow, bolder than the rest, grasped my arm and bellowed, 'Look what we have here. A delicious-smelling stew brought by the most luscious dish I've ever seen. Which should we try first?'

"The rest of the men began to shout and jostle each other, fighting to get next to me."

"What did you do?" Angel was so fascinated by Oshun's story that she had whittled the last carrot into a thin stick. She shrugged and bit into it as Oshun continued.

"Nothing. The officer in charge, who had been resting in his tent, was disturbed by the noise and came out to see what was going on. The uproar immediately ceased.

" 'What is going on here?' he barked. As he spoke, his eyes travelled up and down my body, growing wider with every sweep.

" 'Sir - this woman appeared suddenly,' began my captor, whose huge hand still gripped my arm.

" 'Let go of her,' snapped his leader. The big fool dropped my arm as if it was red hot. I stood imperturbably, my eyes fixed on the officer with a cool smile on my lips.

" 'Now, my dear, why have you come here?' asked the handsome young man.

"In one smooth motion I knelt at his feet, removing the basket from my head and placing it in front of him. 'My lord,' I said, 'in Oshogbo we have heard of the many victories of your army and ask that you will be merciful to our town. I have been sent by the elders to tell you that we do not want bloodshed and, as a token of peace, I have prepared this for your evening meal.'

"The young officer was ecstatic. Victory without lifting a spear, plus a delicious meal which, he was confident, would be followed by a night's dalliance with me. Caution was swept from his brain.

" 'And you will feed me with your own beautiful hands?' It was more of an order than a question.

“ ‘Gladly, my lord,’ I replied, giving him a languishing look from beneath my eyelashes.

“He gave orders for the stew to be heated and the men to be given their rations after his portion had been brought to him, then putting his arm around my waist, he took me into his tent.

“Once inside, I forestalled his advances by asking him to have his servant bring water so I could bathe him before he ate. Nothing could have pleased him more and a large vat of water arrived with a calabash of stew kept hot in a basket filled with straw.

“I lavished his body with the cool water from my river, trickling it over his arms and legs, pouring it slowly onto his back and sprinkling it on his chest. He lay back, eyes closed in bliss, and I dried him with a soft cloth and massaged his body with the honey-scented oil I had in a little flask tied around my waist. By the time I brought the stew over to him he was as relaxed as a sleepy kitten.

“ ‘Open your mouth,’ I whispered, and he did, just like a baby bird waiting to be fed by its mother. I slid in a generous spoonful of the fragrant stew and he chewed and swallowed docilely, making appreciative noises in his throat.

“ ‘Open.’ Again the little bird opened its beak and the process was repeated until the stew was finished.

Through the tent flap I could see the soldiers eating enthusiastically, ‘I think your men like the stew as much as you did, my lord,’ I said to the young leader.

‘But they won’t be enjoying what I have saved the rest of my appetite for,’ he replied, pulling me towards him.

“I went pliantly into his arms, but instead of folding them around me, he clutched his stomach, letting out a tremendous roar of pain.

“I feigned concern. ‘What is wrong, my lord?

"He made no reply but rolled around the floor in agony. From the screams outside I knew that his men were in equal distress. I stood up and looked at the miserable man convulsing at my feet. His face was ashen and contorted with pain and his body streamed with cold sweat.

" 'Do not fret, foolish man,' I cooed, 'you will not die, although you and your troops will have a few miserable days. When you are able to walk, return home with your army and tell your ruler that no one conquers that which is under the protection of the Goddess Oshun.'

"Even in the midst of his pain, a shock of recognition crossed his face. I laughed, patted him on the head and, stepping over his twitching body, left the tent.

"I wandered between the littered bodies of his troops, enjoying the sight of their suffering; then I picked up the empty stew pot, placed it back into the basket and on my head and made my way back to Oshogbo to tell the people that their town was safe."

Angel sat open-mouthed, the carrot stick still in her hand.

"So you see, girlfriend, Oya is not the only female warrior Orisha," Oshun laughed. "I can be formidable too, when necessary."

They surveyed the neat piles of vegetables. The cabbage lay in a mound of ice green cubes next to a heap of coin cut carrots. Crescent moon slices of purple onion and pearly cloves of garlic nestled beside tiny yellow potatoes and a few slivers of Scotch Bonnet peppers added bright red exclamation marks.

"It looks beautiful," Angel said, "like a still life by Caravaggio."

"That's why artists paint food so often - because it is so beautiful. Now - pour enough olive oil into that pot to cover the bottom and then heat it slowly until the oil makes little ripples."

While Angel was doing this, Oshun minced the garlic cloves until they were as fine as grains of sand.

"Is the oil ready yet?" she asked Angel, who peered doubtfully into the pot: "I'm not sure."

Oshun looked over Angel's shoulder. "Yes, it is. See - it quivers as if it's excited to cook the good things we have waiting."

She swept the onions into the pot, gave them a stir with a big wooden spoon and then handed the spoon to Angel saying, "stir these every so often and don't let them brown; they must be soft and translucent."

While Angel stirred the onions, Oshun gathered up the minced garlic and added it to the pot.

"Recipes usually say to sauté onions and garlic together but garlic burns so easily that it's better to give the onions a tiny head start - now we'll add the garlic – good…and the spices... that's right, mix them in well.'

"What goes in next?" Angel asked, stirring madly.

"Tomato paste," replied Oshun. "Blend it thoroughly. Now, just watch them and give them a stir once in a while: when the onions are tender we'll put in the potatoes and the peppers, then after about fifteen minutes, we'll add the carrots and cabbage and cook everything slowly for about half an hour."

"Do I still stir it?"

"Every so often, *very* gently so the vegetables don't get squashed We want them to keep their shape."

"Ummmmm," Angel said, breathing in the savoury aroma, "it smells wonderful."

"It'll taste wonderful, too," Oshun replied, "and it'll come to perfection tomorrow. Many dishes are better when they're left for a day to let the flavours blend."

"Is that like sex being better the second time?" Angel teased.

"Very like," Oshun answered with a wicked smile. "When one has learned the secret tastes and textures of one's lover, making love is far more satisfying."

"But what happens when you both know every ingredient by heart?"

"For a good cook there is always a change to be rung - a different spice, perhaps, or a new sauce," She broke off to taste the stew.

"Try it." Oshun held the spoon out to Angel.

"It's divine! Marc will *love* it! Thank you, Oshun."

"You're welcome, girlfriend. Just make sure you're ready for the after dinner activity. I put a little extra something into the pot.

Angel's eyes widened. "What? "

"A little of my magic honey: you may notice I didn't suggest making anything for dessert?"

Angel nodded.

"That's because dessert, sweet child, will be you."

The stew had been a huge hit with Marc and Angel was almost as proud of her maiden culinary foray as she had been when she won her first major account. Later – *much* later - she lay on the couch with her legs across Marc's lap and he massaged her feet while they watched *Entertainment!*, a weekly round-up of top show business and fashion news. Tonight's lead story was on the Glissando conference and Angel crowed over the coverage.

"Look at that," she gloated, gesturing to the screen where, variously pictured were: Oshun, in several different but equally dazzling poses, Alix at the podium, footage of the Honey Money Bush harvest, herself conferring with Keisha and Marc being interviewed by the host of *Music, Music, Music.*

"Too bad Oshun isn't here to see the sensation she's causing," Marc said.

"Oshun is at Mirabelle with Waterfall and I guarantee you she's getting more attention than Herbie, Harry and Charley all rolled into one."

"Are you sorry we didn't join them?"

"Not in the least. I've been to too many rock parties and I'd far rather stay here alone with you." Angel smiled. "I promised Jonathan Bernstein we'd meet him later at *Imogene's* - something he wants to discuss about Oshun's contract - but we have hours to ourselves before then."

Marc nodded distractedly. He ceased his ministrations to Angel's feet and sat upright, looking troubled.

"Ahn-ghel -" he said hesitantly.

"Yes, darling?"

"I can't help feeling that you're still not comfortable when we're in public together."

"No, I've stopped worrying about the age thing."

"But the last two times we were out, you made an excuse and left."

Angel bit her lower lip: "I was waiting for a more appropriate time, but now that it's come up we'd better deal with it. What you say is true, but not for the reason you think."

"Then what is it?"

"It's so difficult ..."

"Just say it." Marc fished a Galouise out of his pocket and Angel slid a small crystal dish in front of him. He lit the cigarette and inhaled deeply. Angel took a deep breath, too.

"When we're with your friends there's a lot of drinking and drugging going on and you do more than your share. When you're high, you become a person I don't like very much. You laugh too loudly, make cutting remarks and eye every woman who walks by."

"You're jealous!" Marc was elated. "Ahn-ghel - none of it means anything. I'll stop seeing those people, I'll quit drinking and dope - I'll -"

"Hush," Angel said gently, "let me finish. I *am* concerned, Marc, but I'm not jealous - I'm angry, not with you but with myself for being in an inhospitable environment. You have every right to be with your friends. As for drinking and drugs – of course I'd be delighted if you quit but you have to do that for yourself, not for me. And as far as other women are concerned - you're a free agent, and if you want to wander, so be it. You don't owe me any explanations.

"It took me a while to realize that the best way to handle the matter is not to handle it at all, so from now on, if we're in that kind of situation and I leave, don't get upset. I'm just going back to my own space and leaving you in yours. You'll know where to find me."

Marc paced up and down, saying nothing. Angel watched him fondly. They were ill-matched in so many ways, yet she loved him beyond reason.

I guess the old saying is true, she thought wryly, - *you can't choose who you love.*

Her musings were interrupted by Marc who wrapped her in his arms, laid his cheek against hers and said, "Ahn-ghel - I love you so much. I make so many mistakes, but I am trying to learn. Please don't give up on me and promise me that whenever you decide to cut out of an evening, ask me if I'm coming, too. Most of the time, the answer will be 'yes'."

"I promise," she said softly.

Picking up the remote control, Marc clicked off the set without a sound of protest from Angel who gave him a toe curling kiss that would have led to other things if

Chango, Oya and Eleggua hadn't chosen that moment to materialize.

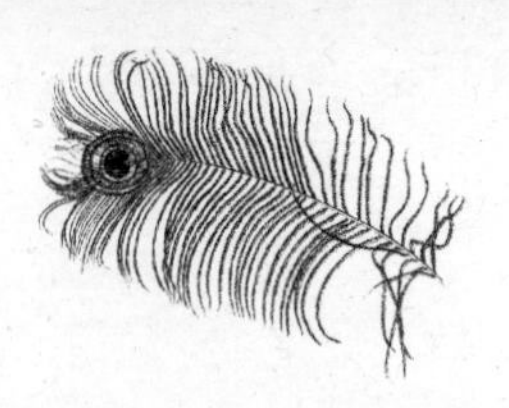

Keisha, Theo and a trio of bodyguards had escorted Oshun to Mirabelle, where Waterfall were throwing a traditional English tea party to celebrate last night's concert success. Theo was as busy as a bushel of beavers, making sure that the right people met Oshun while the muscle squad kept the paparazzi at bay. Keisha cruised the scene in her whirlwind fashion, catching up with friends and acquaintances, cup and saucer in hand, miniature camera on a jewelled chain nestled in her cleavage.

"Keisha, you luscious lollipop - I saw the Glissando item on *TopNews* - what a story!"

"Hey, Glenn - how's my favourite VJ?"

"Spinnin' like a top, baby. I'm told that the new supermodel is here - where do I check her out?"

"Just go where the crowd is thickest and take a number - they're lined up twenty deep."

"They don't call me Buzz-Saw Bailey for nothing, honey. I'll cut through that mob like a hot knife through a snowball. Ciao!"

"'Bye." Keisha gave him a little wave. She caught sight of a group of friends and was making her way over to them, when:

"Keisha, Keisha, Keeeeisha!!! What hath you wrought?" Keisha found herself enveloped in a mass of shocking pink egret plumes.

"I'm in awe," squawked the feathers, "I'm filled with admiration... with adulation... with ... "

"With feathers, Belinda," Keisha gazed with ill-concealed amusement into the parrot-like face of Belinda Barden, social chronicler of *The Toronto Times.*

Makes you want to offer her a cracker, she thought, accepting a double-barrelled kiss.

"Darling," gushed Belinda, "The 'Glissando' coup is just too riveting for *words*...the *genius* of The Hot Box group...the *power* of your photographs and that *divine* creature, Ocean."

"Oshun."

"Yes, Ocean."

Keisha gave up and smiled mutely at Belinda while casting around in her mind for an excuse to remove herself.

Theo appeared just then and Keisha threw an arm around his neck:

"Theo, I believe you know Belinda Bardon?"

"Who doesn't?" He grasped her raddled claw, kissing the air above it.

Belinda gave a simper that was terrible to behold, "And do you have entrée to that glorious creature, Ocean, you naughty boy?"

"I do indeed, and will give myself the inestimable pleasure of introducing you to her." Drawing Belinda's stick of an arm through his, Theo grimaced secretly at Keisha, who blew him a grateful kiss, and whisked Belinda away.

Teatime segued into the cocktail hour and Darjeeling and Earl Grey were set aside in favour of Stollys and Gibsons. The soft sounds of Loreena McKennit's harp were replaced with the hard-edged guitar riffs of Waterfall's new single, *Rev My Motor*; guests began dancing and a group of A and R's started a food fight with leftover cream scones.

Throughout the room, conversations were being shouted and whispered by concentric circles of the in, inner and innermost members of fashion/music/advertising who made up the guest list.

"Have you ever *seen* anything like Oshun? She makes Linda and Naomi look like last year's leftovers..."

"So I told Herbie that his next disc should go light on rock and heavy on rap..."

"Did you hear that Angel Zimmermann and Marc Dupré are an item?"

"What do you mean hemlines will be down next season? At the Paris shows the models were wearing skirts no bigger than bandaids."

"Oh, man, just lemme *near* Oshun, just close enough to ask her out to dinner."

"In your dreams, homeboy. She's guarded like the crown jewels."

Music fought with conversation: having exhausted the scones, the A and Rs, soldiered on with cucumber sandwiches and everyone scrambled to meet Oshun, who revelled in the clamour.

At that point, Angel and Marc arrived with Chango, Oya and Eleggua in tow.

All action ceased as every eye swivelled towards the newcomers. Oya was dazzling in a long purple skirt and matching blouse that dipped dangerously off her shoulders. Her hair was braided with flashing multicoloured stones and a fringed rainbow scarf swathed her slim hips.

As always, Chango wore red and white, but in a nod to Western culture this took the form of a faultlessly tailored white linen suit and a red silk shirt. A ruby stud sparkled in his left ear and his smoothly shaved head glowed like the finest mahogany.

Eleggụa had also opted for North American fashion. Like the other two deities, he wore his colours, cutting a slightly sinister figure in a black and white chalk striped, double-breasted suit that emphasized his elegant thinness.

His shirt was black damask with a red, white and black rep tie. In his lapel he sported his emblem, a red parrot feather, his head was its usual mass of dreadlocks and he was barefoot.

"These outlandish garments make an intriguing change from my customary garb," he told Angel, who had tried to coax him into a pair of black and white Italian spectator shoes, "but my feet must feel the ground."

Oshun, holding court in the middle of the room, caught sight of her fellow Orisha, and hurled herself into Chango's arms while simultaneously hugging Oya and Eleggua. The crowd buzzed wildly. Who were the new arrivals? Was the black Adonis Oshun's husband? Did the striking siren in purple belong with the skinny devil at her side?

"I've certainly never seen any of them before," Belinda said to all and sundry. She plowed her way through the surrounding mob, determined to discover all.

"Angel, my dear - *lovely* to see you! I was just asking Keisha where you were...and Marc - how *nice*!"

"Hello, Belinda," Angel said with hastily assumed pleasure. "You look...colourful," she finished lamely, in a desperate attempt to cope with the juxtaposition of feathers and face.

"Aren't you going to introduce me to your friends, sweetie?"

"Yes, of *course!* Belinda Bardon, this is Chango, King of Oyo; his consort, Oya and EsuEleggua, the Prime Minister."

"Quick thinking," Marc breathed admiringly. The deities graciously acknowledged the introduction, triple-talked their way through a brief interview and allowed pictures to be taken for the lead item in Belinda's column.

"We must be going," said Angel, "I promised Jonathan Bernstein that we'd meet him at *Imogene's* and we're already late."

With some difficulty, she and Marc shepherded their charges away from the party. Oshun wended her way slowly to the door, bestowing smiles all around. Oya glided out with quiet dignity, Chango inspected every likely-looking female in his path and Eleggua, walking backwards, scattered triumphant little waves with both hands.

Once outside, a waiting limousine whisked them off to *Imogene's*, Toronto's chicest private club, where Jonathan was waiting. He had been at Waterfall's party, but left early to drop in at two other functions before ending up at *Imogene's*; consequently, he had no idea of the new arrivals.

"What a surprise this is going to be for Jonathan," laughed Eleggua. "I am picturing the bafflementation on his little face when he sees us."

"It's not a pretty thought," said Angel, grimly. "Whatever possessed all of you to show up here?"

"It's we who do the possessing," replied Eleggua, nudging her with a sharply pointed elbow. "We felt the need of a holiday and, as our sister was already here, what would be more natural than we should follow to look after her well-being?"

"What, indeed," she replied dryly, giving him a suspicious look at which he grinned disarmingly.

The car pulled up at the grey stone mansion on a discreet side street off King and its passengers were ushered into *Imogene's* darkly elegant foyer.

Gregoire, the maitre d' and, it was rumoured, a deposed Russian count, gave them a deep bow and a gold-toothed smile: "Miss Zimmermann, Mr. Dupré, and Madame Oshun!!! What an honour."

He ushered them smoothly through the main dining room.

"Mr. Bernstein is at a quiet table in the back."

"Thank you, Gregoire," said Angel, resigned to the knowledge that, in order to get to the coveted quietness, they had to parade past every guest in the place.

Imogene's clientele was too well-bred to actually stand on the tables for a better view, but necks craned, heads swivelled to the point of whiplash and the buzz of conversation, normally soft and sibilant, was raised to an muted roar.

"Here we are," bubbled Gregoire, "Mr. Bernstein, I have brought your guests."

"Hi," Angel said with false brightness, "sorry we're late."

Jonathan, who had been on the phone with his back to the rest of the table, hung up and turned around to greet his guests.

"Oh, my *God*!"

"Exactly," beamed Eleggua.

"I don't want to go to *Imogene's* tonight, Keisha," Brent put on an exaggeratedly tired face that unfortunately couldn't be seen over the phone, "It's too hot, I'm exhausted beyond belief and -"

"- and you're brooding because Stephen is on the Australian run and you haven't seen him for two weeks. Get a grip, Brent, it's bad enough you missed the Waterfall bash - "

"How was it?"

"An absolute blood bath. You never saw such slashing and clawing and that was just at the tea tables.

The mob scene around Oshun defies description and when Angel and Marc showed up with thc others -"

"What others?"

"Of course, how could you know - Chango, Eleggua and Oya are in our midst."

Brent sat bolt upright on his bed, "Are you serious?"

"Never more so."

"What are they doing here?"

"They wanted a holiday."

"Where are they?"

"At *Imogene's.*"

"Give me ten minutes to throw on something calculated to make everyone swoon in envy and I'll meet you downstairs."

Brent hung up the phone, leaped off the bed and flung open the doors of his walk-in closet. Humming the chorus from *Turning Japanese*, he chose an Issey Miyake shirt in bleached lawn and a pair of black, stone-washed silk slacks by Yohi Yamomoto. Rejecting an Alpaca jacket, he donned a waistcoat in silver grey antique brocade and a long black linen coat. He slipped his bare feet into a pair of black ostrich skin loafers, put on two silver rings and three lapel pins from his collection of Art Nouveau jewellery, dabbed a touch of gel onto his slicked back hair and set off.

The Bernstein group was still the cynosure of all eyes and when Keisha and Brent were escorted in by Gregoire, clucking like a goose leading the golden goslings, there was a fresh frisson of whispering and head swivelling.

"I knew this outfit was sensational, but I didn't think it would cause *quite* such a stir," Brent grinned, "or could it be the Out Of Africa contingent that's creating all this havoc?"

They reached the table in a flurry of greetings

"It's good to see you again, my friend," said Eleggua, leaning over and clasping Brent's hand.

“Welcome to Canada,” said Keisha, smiling warmly at all three deities.

Oya drew Keisha’s head down and kissed her on both cheeks. “You are one of the reasons I am here, my dear. We have things to accomplish.”

Keisha smiled again, this time a little apprehensively.

“Hello, all - mind if I join you?”

Jonathan raised his eyes to the ceiling, “Theo - it only needed you.” He turned to a passing server, “shoehorn a chair in here for Mr. Slotkin, would you?”

Theo slid his slight frame deftly into the micro space between Jonathan and Oya.

“I saw you only from afar at the Waterfall bash,” he addressed the newcomers, “so let me welcome you to Toronto and if there is anything I can do for you at any time, just say the word.”

“And what word might that be, my friend?” asked Eleggua

“It’s just an expression,” snapped Oya, “he means he’ll grant your wishes.”

“That is *our* job,” Eleggua said indignantly. “If there are wishes to be granted, people are applicating to us - not the other way around.”

Theo nudged Jonathan, “What’s he talking about?”

“He means that in his country, people bring their requests to their kings and prime ministers.”

“Ahh, I see. Well, Your Majesty -”

“No - *he* is Your Majesty,” said Eleggua, gesturing to Chango. “*I* am Prime Minister. You go through me to get to him. In fact, you go through me to get to any of the deities.”

“Deities?”

“He means kings,” put in Jonathan hastily, “bit of a language problem.”

“Yes, of course.” Theo looked warily at Eleggua who smiled expansively back.

Just then a movie magnate at the next table violated *Imogene's* no smoking rule by lighting a huge Havana cigar. A server politely requested that he extinguish it, but was ignored. Gregoire was called into action and was given a storm of abuse. The host, an impoverished earl who was hoping that his guest was going to buy his ancestral home in Kent, closed his eyes and prayed for the earth to engulf him.

Chango stood up, sauntered over to the earl's table, plucked the cigar out of the titan's beefy face, put it in his own mouth, lighted end first and swallowed it with enjoyment. Then he placed one hand on top of the man's head and the other under his chin, closed his gaping mouth with a teeth-rattling click, bowed gravely and went back to his own table.

The awed silence was broken by Brent, "how did you *do* that?"

Chango gave a deprecating shrug: "a little trick."

"Can you teach it to me?"

"Let's order, shall we?" said Jonathan hastily.

"No doubt, Jonathan, in your own sweet time, you'll tell me who the hell these people are and from which weird corner of your world they've sprung?" Theo murmured from behind the shelter of his menu.

"Believe me, you don't want to know."

"Oh but I *do.* My life won't be complete until I discover how the ebony emperor accomplished his cigar trick and why his companion confuses 'deities' and 'kings'."

"It's a long, involved story, Theo."

"And I want to hear every convoluted twist and turn of it. Shall we say breakfast tomorrow at The Studio Café?"

"Seven am,," Jonathan said resignedly.

"I can't wait." Theo turned to the newcomers, "*Imogene's* is noted for its kitchen and if you don't find what you want on the menu, they're happy to do a special order."

Chango ordered three alarm chili, a specialty of the house. Eleggua asked for opossum, which was unavailable but he was content to have smoked salmon, which was an equal favourite of his. *Aubergine a la Indien du Nord* was on the menu and, as the eggplant is Oya's particular food, she was pleased, too.

Oshun studied the menu but couldn't settle on anything. The server suggested several dishes but nothing seemed right.

"Can you make me an omelet with shrimps and watercress."

"Certainly, Madame."

"Please serve it inside a hollowed-out pumpkin."

The server didn't turn a hair: "We don't have pumpkin this evening, Madame, but we do have acorn squash. Will that do?"

Oshun nodded regally.

She explained to Angel: "I have ordered *Ochinchin.* It's a favourite dish of mine and I haven't had it for ages."

When Chango's chili arrived he tasted it critically and said, "This is food for a baby - there is no fire in it.."

A bottle of hot pepper sauce was produced, Chango poured the entire contents over the chili, tried it again and pronounced it good.

By the time they were ready for dessert and coffee, everyone was feeling fine. There was one dicey moment when both Oshun and Oya pointed at the same chocolate eclair on the sweet trolley, but the server brought forth a duplicate, which made them both happy.

The lights dimmed, the house band struck up a fanfare and Imogene took the floor: "Good evening, members and guests and welcome to just another Smashing Saturday. As always, there are many celebrities here but I simply must single out a table, which has everyone in a total tizzy. Here, on an unofficial visit is Chango, King of Oyo...his beautiful consort, Oya and his Prime Minister, the Right Honourable EsuEleggua.

A spotlight swung to the table where the deities sat and, on instructions from Theo, they stood and waved in acknowledgment of the tumultuous applause.

Imogene carried on, “and, the fabulous new face of Glissando Beauté, the phenomenal Oshun!”

The room went wild as Oshun rose like a Phoenix and turned in all directions, kissing both hands in response to the thunderous approval that roared around the room. It was a full five minutes before Imogene could restore calm.

“And now,” she bellowed, “the hottest Canadian troupe since Cirque de Soleil - just back from a triumphant European tour - please welcome First Nations Fantasy!”

The room was plunged into total darkness as a single drum tapped softly. Gradually, the sound become more insistent and, as it increased, the stage grew golden with the flare of torches that lit one by one to form a semicircle of fire. As each torch sprang alight, another drummer joined in until twelve of them sat between the torches, beating intricate rhythms in a kaleidoscope of sound that pulsated throughout the room. The drums reached a crescendo and stopped so abruptly that echoes hung in the air.

Lines of men entered from both sides of the stage, each holding two long, thick poles of wood which they alternately clicked together, then pounded on the floor as they strode in patterns across the stage, interweaving themselves and the sticks in intricate designs.

The drums began again, counterpointing the sound of the sticks and women’s voices were heard softly. The singers came into view, inching across the stage in a serpentine line, their bodies joined front to back, moving as one, voices ululating. When they reached the front of the stage they sat cross-legged on the floor in front of the drummers.

The men's marching turned into dancing; they leaped and spun, using their sticks to vault high into the air, jumping over and diving under them at incredible speeds. The tempo accelerated until the movements became a blur of motion and the sound a constant *click, crack* that urged the dancers on.

Neither the audience nor First Nations Fantasy was prepared for what happened next. Unable to resist the rhythm, Chango tore off his jacket, shirt, and shoes, leaped onto the stage, grabbed the closest drum and, standing on one leg and drumming furiously, spun like Elvis Stoiko going for gold.

The audience, thinking that this was part of the show, applauded like crazy. The performers, after a moment's blank amazement, realized that here was a talent to be reckoned with and carried on with even greater vigour. Chango danced and played like a god possessed, which, let's face it, he was. He ran up and down the line of drummers using the instruments like a giant xylophone. He vaulted almost to the ceiling without benefit of poles. He twirled like a whole tribe of whirling dervishes and, as the *piece de résistance*, added his soaring tenor to the singers' chorus. The audience went berserk.

Theo had been watching this astonishing performance with ever- increasing excitement. He bounced up and down in his seat, smashing the table with his fist, then he clutched Jonathan's jacket by the lapels:

"I don't care if this guy is King of Oyo or Lieutenant Governor of the UN," he shouted, "I'm signing him up. Get a contract ready, Jonathan. I'm going to make him the biggest star in the immediate universe!"

"Theo - listen - there are some things you don't understand."

"What's to understand? The guy sings like Seal, dances like Gene Kelly and plays drums like Gene Krupa. He's better looking than Harry Belafonte and Denzel Washington rolled together and he's going to be *huge!*"

"Okay. Just believe me when I tell you that you don't know what we're letting ourselves in for."

Theo was used to Jonathan's dire warnings, which were standard issue with every new contract.

"I don't have to worry, sweetheart, that's your department. Grab Chango and let's get him to your office where we can explain the facts of life to him."

Knee deep in a sea of admirers, Chango was reluctant to leave but Theo promised him a party at the First Nations' hotel suite, and whisked him away from his disappointed fans.

In the meantime, Jonathan rounded up the rest of the group and deposited them at the First Nations party,. Taking a deep breath, he plunged back into the limousine and headed for his rendezvous with Chango and Theo.

Chango was fascinated by Jonathan's office. He sat behind the desk, happily swivelling the ergonomic chair and pushing every button on the console. As the biggest entertainment law firm in the country, Jonathan's office worked round the clock, seven days a week, dealing with the endless emergencies of show business. Thus at one am there was a full staff on duty and Chango was keeping them on the move. Every button he pushed brought instant response from secretaries, clerks and junior lawyers. Chango's enthusiasm increased with every new arrival and when Jonathan arrived, he walked into an impromptu party.

Hustling everyone back to work, Jonathan took to his desk. Theo sat in an armchair and gestured to Chango to take the porter's chair.

"Now," said Jonathan to Chango, "it's like this..."

An hour later Chango was installed as the newest light in Theo's glittering stable of talent. Theo had painted a colourful picture of instant stardom, Jonathan had outlined the necessary legalities and Chango had signed everything in triplicate. The three men shook hands after which Theo suggested that it was time for bed.

"It's very late," he said, "or, more accurately, very early."

"It's the weekend," Jonathan said airily. "We can sleep in."

"Chango can," Theo said. "You and I have a seven o'clock at The Studio Café."

"Wonderful," Jonathan replied bitterly. "That will give me an entire three hours sleep."

"That's all Winston Churchill ever had." Theo said.

"He had Field Marshal Montgomery."

"And you have me," Theo smiled complacently.

"Don't remind me. See you at seven."

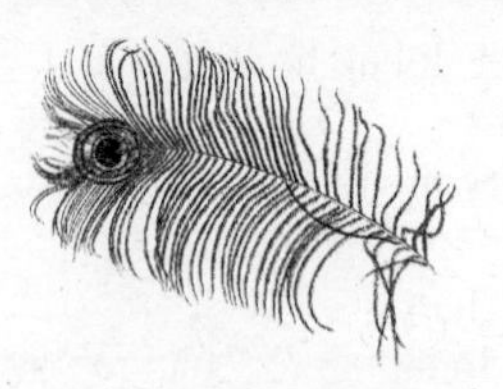

"That's the funniest thing I've ever heard," Theo leaned back in his chair, wiping tears of laughter from his eyes. "Those incredible people aren't just the hottest supermodel of the century, an African king, his consort and his Prime Minister - *no!* They're gods - supreme beings - what did you call them, 'O'Reilly'?"

"*Orisha,*" Jonathan hissed. "For Chrissake keep your voice down, Theo. This isn't exactly public knowledge, nor do I want it to be."

"Jonathan - you are *priceless!* If I didn't know better, I'd swear you were serious. You're getting back at me for sending that Nicole Kidman look-alike to see you about her divorce from Tom Cruise. Right?"

"Wrong."

Theo looked closely at his friend. Man and boy he had known Jonathan Bernstein and he knew when he was lying; this wasn't one of those times.

"Jonathan," he said carefully, "I sense that you're telling me the truth as you know it, but you'll forgive me if I find it a tad difficult to believe."

"You don't have to believe it, you'll find out for yourself eventually. Just go along with me on this, Theo, it's much simpler that way."

"I'll do anything that'll get us back to work," Theo replied obligingly. "Just let me make sure I know what you're talking about: Oshun is a goddess in the guise of a supermodel?"

"Yes."

"And Chango, Eleggua and Oya are deities, too?"

Jonathan nodded heavily.

"And I've signed one of them, to wit, Chango, as the newest star in my galaxy."

"I tried to warn you, Theo."

"You know I never listen to you."

"Maybe now you will."

"Why spoil a perfect record? Okay: we have a goddess who is the model for the world's first youth potion, and need I point out, both the goddess and the cosmetics company are clients of yours *and* of mine. We also have a god who is going to be the megastar of the century - likewise a front runner in each of our stables, plus an additional pair of deities as a bonus - so what in *hell* are you moaning about?"

Jonathan looked at his friend pityingly. "Only an idiot would call Eleggua and Oya a bonus. Eleggua is never happy unless he's playing tricks in seven different locations at once, and Oya has a fuse so short that you couldn't pick it up with tweezers. Between them they can cause more trouble than Bin Laden's commandos at a bar mitzvah."

"And your point would be?"

"They're going to make us completely *crazy*!"

"*All* our clients make us completely crazy. Take Waterfall,"

"*Please!*""

Theo ignored the interruption, "Crazy behaviour is standard issue for talent and we handle it with the delicacy of a pair of snake-charmers knee-deep in a pit of gaboon vipers; I deal with impossible requests and irresponsible behaviour and you forge ironclad contracts that can undulate like slinky toys. He paused to take a swallow of his now lukewarm coffee and would have continued but Jonathan cut him off.

"You've forgotten one thing: Yes, our assorted actors, models and musicians get up to more merry pranks than Ken Keysey and his mob ever dreamed of - *but* - they're only human beings. They don't appear and disappear at will. They don't grow larger and smaller or take over people's bodies whenever they get the urge. They can't inhabit several different time zones at once. *They aren't super fucking natural!*"

Jonathan had been leaning forward intensely, now he fell back in his chair, mopping his forehead with a Ferragamo handkerchief. Even in the midst of his concern for Jonathan's sanity, Theo couldn't help but admire his friend's fashion sense. Jonathan might forget to get his hair cut and his shoes went without seeing polish for weeks at a time, but the shoes were by Lobb of London and his barber was top of the line.

Theo, who often referred to Jonathan as 'Rumpled Of the Bailey,' knew that Jonathan's dishevelled look gave him great appeal for clients. They slipped their little hands into his, instinctively trusting this man whose attention to their affairs outweighed his sartorial concerns.

Theo himself had innate good taste. Even as a struggling young promoter he wore only the best: he had just two suits, both black, which he rotated on a daily basis, wearing them with French-cuffed shirts of the finest white broadcloth. When he became successful, he stuck to his black and white colour scheme and his clothes cupboard was part of his legend, holding a battalion of black suits in wools, silks and linens, together with countless white shirts, rows of beautifully polished black lace up shoes - none of your naff slip-ons for Theodore Slotkin - and an enviable collection of black and white patterned ties. He looked like a fashionable penguin.

Bringing himself back to the discussion, Theo began a soothing answer, but Jonathan said, "There's no use talking about this any more. We're stuck with the situation and I hope we can live with the consequences. Just promise me one thing. Watch them at all times."

"We always keep a sharp eye on our clients."

"You'll need more eyes than a swarm of houseflies with this little mob." Taking a final swallow of coffee, he pushed back his chair.

"I've got to get to the office. I'll give you a lift if you're heading that way."

"No thanks," Theo said. "I'm meeting Danielle Fressange here in half an hour, so I'll order some more coffee and make a few phone calls while I'm waiting."

"I didn't know Danielle was in town. How long will she be here?"

"Not sure. David Rubenstein wants her for his new show and it depends on how long the negotiations take."

"Well, send the proposal over to me before she signs anything and ask her if she's free for lunch tomorrow."

"Will do. I'm seeing Marcia Allensby later for drinks at *Black and Blue* - she wants to do a major fashion spread with Oshun and Chango. Care to join us?"

Jonathan shuddered. "I'd sooner stick my willy in a wasps' nest."

He left at his usual brisk lope and Theo ordered more coffee but his cell phone lay untouched on the table while he pondered Jonathan's bombshell. Had his old friend flipped out? Jonathan seemed as sane as ever except for this sudden belief in African deities, but what if he started thinking he was Richard The Third?

I'll worry about it if he calls for a horse, Theo decided.

Hello, Canada! is the country's top morning show. Guests are scheduled months in advance, agents clamour to get a slot for their clients; still, Theo wasn't surprised to get a request for Chango to appear that week; he would have been amazed if the call hadn't come. There was an early morning message from an assistant producer which Theo left languishing in voice mail limbo, quickly followed by a plea from the producer. This was also ignored and shortly after, Theo heard from the hosts themselves, Hal and Helen Harper.

The Harpers were often referred to as Canada's *Richard and Judy* and fancied themselves as a modern version of *Burns and Allen.* They came off a poor second on both counts, but they swung a fair amount of weight in Toronto.

They placed a three-way call, speaking to Theo in tandem on their cell phones as they were driven home from the Canadian Television Corporation in their twin white Corniches; Hal and Helen never travelled together in case of an accident.

"Theo, baby! How goes?" Hal's rasping voice was the perfect foil for Helen's sugarcoated whine:

"Theodore, my angel - it's been *forever* since we saw you!"

"Goes good, Hal - yes, it must be at least a week, Helen," Theo said cheerfully.

"Helen and I caught your boy's act at *Imogene's* the other night and we thought you might like a little exposure for him," Hal wheezed through his cigar smoke.

"The '*boy'*, is a king, Hal," Theo said.

"King, shming, do you want him on the show or what?"

"Shut *UP*, Hal! Theo, sweet, we'd be *so* honoured if His Majesty would appear."

"I'll consider it, Helen and get back to you."

"Top billing, Theo," Hal croaked morosely.

"Wouldn't accept anything less, Hal." Theo replied lightly. He clicked off his phone and charged off to rearrange his day and prepare Chango for his first appearance on national TV.

Chango, Eleggua and Oya arrived at the CTC studios dutifully shepherded by Theo who'd given his word to Jonathan to keep an eye on the group at all times.

While Chango was whisked off to makeup, Theo guided Oya and Eleggua to the VIP lounge to watch the final rehearsal, after which they were seated in the studio for the show where they would be introduced from the audience.

Chango's début was an overwhelming success. He captivated his hosts, electrified the studio audience and caused the CTC switchboard to overload. By the time the final credits rolled, he was on his way to stardom.

Eleggua and Oya were restless after having been cooped up all morning in the studio, Theo was dropping Chango off at Marc's studio and wanted to explore the city.

"Theodore, will you take Oya and me to the little village where everyone sits in the street?" Eleggua smiled ingratiatingly at the agent.

"You want to go to Yorkville?"

"With the wonderful shops." said Oya.

" Sorry, Madame Oya, I don't have time to go shopping with you."

"Why can't we go on our own?" There was a dangerous edge to Oya's voice and her eyes became razor-thin slits.

Eleggua intervened.

"My dear old boy, we have serious shoppings to do and there would be no point in you escorting us, even if you could. Let me give you a demonstrating: Now you see me." He stood at Theo's left and vanished, "now you don't." Grinning widely, he reappeared on Theo's right

Theo was in shock. Taking a shaky breath, he pinched the bridge of his nose as if trying to ward off a headache.

"So it's true," he said. "Jonathan *isn't* crazy. You're,"- he couldn't bring himself to say 'supernatural' - "you're not human."

Eleggua shrugged: "We are the Orisha. You had to know sooner or later, my friend."

"Later would have been better. Much, much better. Never would have been best of all." Theo straightened up and looked at Eleggua and Oya with wary respect. "So - what do we do now?"

"We go to the wonderful shops," Oya said firmly.

Theo was resigned: "Come along, then, I'll drop you off on the way to Marc's studio, or perhaps you'd rather go via Orisha Air?"

"Oh, *no*," Eleggua said, "it's much jollier to travel in your limousine. I like the bar in the back and the small-small television."

"And everyone stops and stares when we get out," added Oya. "They think I'm someone famous - which I *am*, back in Africa," she added truculently.

"You are here, too, Antelope," Chango said soothingly, "your picture has been in every paper."

"Yes - as one of your entourage," she said bitterly, "Pictured dancing the night away at *Imogene's*. New sensation, Chango and his consort, Aya'. They didn't even get my name right!"

Chango looked at her helplessly. When Oya was in this mood you couldn't argue with her. Helping her into the limousine, he slid in beside her while Eleggua and Theo sat facing them. A short time later, the huge black Rolls pulled up at the corner of Bloor and Avenue Road.

Jonathan drew a little map with the streets and lanes of Yorkville clearly marked and gave it to Eleggua, saying:

"This will get you anywhere you want to go and you can easily walk back to your apartment from here. Happy shopping."

Eleggua and Oya slid out of the limousine and promptly dived into the ultra-chic depths of Hazelton Lanes while Theo and Chango watched them go.

"They'll steal everything that's not under lock and key and half of what is." Chango said.

"It'll be justifiable theft," Theo replied as they sped off to Marc's loft, "those shops have been robbing their customers blind for years."

"Listen to this," Marc flipped a switch and the room filled with the sound of the *Baka* women's water drumming.

Chango listened intently to the rhythmic splashing. Picking up a small conga drum, he played a counterpoint that began delicately and built to a bubbling crescendo.

At the end of the song he turned to Marc; "It is interesting, is it not, my friend; those drums are water and my drum is fire. Water can extinguish fire, but the flame of my playing makes the water boil." Gesturing to Marc to repeat the tape, he took up his drum again, this time using a sharper beat with an increase in the tempo

Marc nodded in approval, "We're going to use water drumming for *Oshun's Gold* - Babatunde's laying down a track for it...he'll send it next week and we'll sample it in the studio."

"It will blend well," Chango agreed, "just as I, God of Fire and Lightning, entwine in passion with Oya or Oshun - although there's been very little entwining these days, with them or anyone else for that matter." He kicked gloomily at a nearby cymbal.

"Everyone's busy," Marc said soothingly: "Once things quieten down you'll be entwining all over the place."

"Let it be soon. A day without at least six entwinements is no day at all."

Marc stared at him in disbelief. "Six?" he said, in a voice tinged with considerable envy.

"Only on a slow day," Chango assured him. "When things are going well, ten, twelve, fourteen entwinements are the usual."

"*Dieu en Ciel*! Where do you find time for anything else?"

"Time is nothing to me I can stretch it or compress it and divide it as I please. For instance, right now I am working with you but I'm also dancing at a *bembé* in Bahia, and meeting with Obatala in Ile Ife"

"How can you do that all at once?"

"It is as I said. I can bend time so that it's yesterday or a quarter to four a week from Thursday. Different planes, my dear fellow...simultaneous levels of existence...I'm sure it's all written up as some scientific theory or another. I can't explain it - I just do it."

"Well, it's too complex for me. Now, if you don't mind, Lord of Fire and Thunder - can we make a little music?"

"I am ready. Please give to me a little more reverb on the intro."

"You certainly picked up the techno-talk quickly."

"We deities are very fast on the uptake."

"Is that what you call omniscience?"

"Om...?"

"The gift of all knowledge. Isn't it standard equipment?"

"Ah! No - we have many abilities in common, such as casting spells, but we also have our own special attributes and om - what you said - belongs to Eleggua."

Chango broke off and looked around to make sure they weren't being overheard. He continued in a conspiratorial tone; "as a matter of fact, he drives everyone *crazy* with it, and I've often thought that particular gift would be better off in the hands of someone who wasn't quite such a, such a..."

"Joker?"

"I was going to say sodding troublemaker, but that'll do."

He moved to a tall, narrow drum and gave it an experimental tap. Nodding approvingly, he gestured to Marc who struck a fluid, opening chord on the keyboard.

While Oya and Eleggua made the rounds of Hazelton Lanes, Oshun was also on the premises. She wafted through the halls, fascinated by the fabulous shops which displayed the newest styles, the most glittering jewellery, the most amazing shoes and hats - everything, in short, that a fashion-conscious Orisha could want. *Make that three fashion-conscious Orisha,* she said to herself as she caught sight of Oya and Eleggua in a boutique that sold nothing but belts. Oya was holding a gold, jewel-studded chain in her left hand while her right hand grasped a wide sash of soft purple suede and Eleggua had five belts looped around various sections of his toothpick torso. Having made their choices, Eleggua sent the salesclerk to sleep with a single pass of his bony fingers, while Oya crammed all seven belts into her voluminous handbag. Giggling wildly, they turned to leave and bumped into

Oshun who stood with folded arms and tapping foot, blocking the exit.

"Haven't you forgotten something?" she asked sweetly.

"Forgotten...?" Eleggua gazed at her in wide-eyed innocence while Oya struggled to close her overstuffed bag.

Oshun unfolded her arms and held her hand out, "you'll find it much easier to close your bag once you give me what's inside it."

Oya glared at her, "Get your own, girlfriend. These belong to us."

"Did you pay for them?"

"Not exactly."

"Then they're not yours. Put them back."

Oya looked at Eleggua who gave a resigned shrug: "Do what she says or we'll never hear the end of it."

Oya took the belts out of her bag, hurled them to the floor and flounced out of the shop with Eleggua following.

"You're not quite finished."

He turned around impatiently, "Now what?"

Oshun indicated the salesclerk who was frozen bolt upright and unconscious: "Put her back as well."

Eleggua gestured briefly and the clerk opened her eyes and called after their departing backs, "Have a nice day and do come again."

"She doesn't know what she's asking," Oshun said. "Now, could you restrain yourselves to just looking or to the more conventional way of shopping - namely, paying for the merchandise."

"At home if we see something we want, the owner is happy to give it.", Oya said.

"Yes," agreed Eleggua, "it's an honour to have a deity claim an item."

"You're not at home, nobody knows we're deities and they won't take kindly to us helping ourselves to whatever strikes our fancy."

"A strange way to live, if you ask me," sniffed Oya.

Oshun suddenly realized that she,felt the same way. She too, was tired of stifling her immortality. She was being wined, dined and feted as the world's hottest new supermodel, but the elements of awe and worship were lacking. Nobody bowed down in her presence, no candles were lit, no offerings were made - she hadn't smelled a stick of incense in *weeks*. Oya was right. What was the point of being a deity if you couldn't do what you wanted?

"You know," she said musingly, "that yellow belt with the gold coins was absolutely made for me."

Eleggua and Oya beamed delightedly and all three, moving as one well-oiled piece of machinery, turned around and swung back into the boutique. The salesclerk, poor creature, smiled.

After the other deities arrived in Toronto, Angel had found accommodations for them all at a chic apartment hotel in the Bloor/Avenue Road area.

"Is the staff discreet?" Alix asked, "we can't have anything leaked."

"Don't worry. Madonna stayed there for a month while she was recording her last album and not even her next door neighbour knew."

The discretion of the establishment more than lived up to its reputation and the deities came and went at all hours of the day and night without incident.

Now, they had returned home from the great Yorkville heist loaded down with their ill-gotten gains.

Oshun and Eleggua were in great good humour, giggling over the massive amounts of merchandise they'd liberated but Oya, although having scooped in everything she wanted and more, wasn't happy. Oshun was still the epicentre of attention. This had been bad enough in Oshogbo but at least there she was treated with the awe that her position deserved. Here she was just a member of Oshun's retinue and it infuriated her, especially since Chango was also in the limelight: between making guest appearances on every talk show in town and working with Marc, he had hardly any time for her. Some holiday this was turning out to be.

She had to do something to discredit Oshun and turn Chango's attention back to herself, and after a short period of fuming and thinking, she found the perfect solution.

Eleggua had brought with him every possible spell-casting ingredient including the dreadfate root, an insignificant looking little plant that, in the right hands, could bring about any results the user wished - providing they were negative. With just a tiny piece, she could make a powder so potent that a single pinch dissolved in a vat of *Oshun's Gold* would cause cataclysmic results. This would involve stealing some of the root from Eleggua but Oya wasn't averse to a little light-fingered activity; after all, long ago she'd filched the secret of fire and lightning from Chango.

They had had a terrible argument over his continuing affair with Oshun and Oya was determined to be revenged on him. There was a room that he always kept locked, telling her that it contained state secrets that not even she could be privy to. Instinctively, she knew she'd find what she needed there. The locked door posed no problem for the goddess, who blew it in as easily as the wolf had blown down the first little pig's house of straw.

Stepping over the splintered wood, she saw a table on which sat Chango's mortar and pestle and a gourd full of thick, dark paste with a strong aroma of spices and herbs. Dipping a cautious finger into the mixture she tasted it and choked on a burning sensation that felt like molten lava. She blew out air, trying to cool her scorched tongue and was terrified when flames shot out of her mouth.

Oya blew again and again, but only succeeded in causing an inferno. She was beside herself with fright, but soon realized that, not only was her mouth *not* burning, but that she could control the flames. With a little experimentation, she mastered the fire completely and was able to send flames shooting from her mouth or her nostrils, hitting her target with deadly accuracy every time. She discovered, too, that she could turn off the fire whenever she chose, simply by willing it away. This was something like! Now she could control not only the wind but fire and this brought her closer to equality with Chango.

Next she turned her attention to the mortar and pestle. She had several of her own for grinding everything from corn to cinnamon, but what would Chango use a mortar for? The man couldn't so much as boil a simple egg, so it certainly wasn't used for cooking.

Idly, she ground the pestle into the bottom of the mortar. A flash of lightning lit up the room and Oya dropped the pestle with a thud as electricity ran through her. Her hair stood out all over her head, tiny blue sparks flying from its ends and her body prickled with a sharp, not unpleasant tingle.

"*Eeepah*, girl, you've got it now!" she crowed and she plunged the pestle back into the mortar, laughing triumphantly at the resultant crash of thunder and slash of the bolt as it ricocheted around the room.

As quickly as she'd learned to control the fire, she mastered the art of throwing lightning. Now she had all

Chango's secrets and, once he got over his initial anger he'd be glad to have her fighting by his side. Together they'd be truly invincible.

And so it proved. Chango was furious and hunted her down, uprooting her from her hiding place underneath a palm tree. A terrible fight ensued with each of them hurling lightning bolts and throwing flames. Being immortal, no serious damage was done to either of them and finally, singed and exhausted, they fell, laughing, into each other's arms.

Gently brushing a smudge of soot from Oya's forehead, Chango ran his hand into her hair, tangling his fingers through her wild mass of braids and bringing her close enough to kiss. Oya twined her tongue around his, sucking it deeply into her mouth. Their arms tightened around each other. Oya curled her legs around Chango's ankles and pressed against him as if she would dissolve into his body. She made small movements to the right and slowly, he began to turn. Oya's motions became stronger and Chango turned faster until they rose into the air, twirling as they went. Their clothes were blown apart by the whirlwind Oya had generated and their naked bodies clung together. Oya wrapped her legs around Chango's waist and he put his hands under her buttocks, sliding into her like a pestle into its mortar. She gripped him inside and out and spun their interlocked bodies in an upward spiral, howling with passion until the wind blended its voice with her cries. Chango pulsed into her, thunderbolts crashing with every thrust as he ground the seeds of his passion inside her.

At the moment of climax, thunder, lightning and wind reached a frenzied crescendo and then slowly died as the two deities, still coiled together, circled lazily back to earth where they lay upon the ground.

Chango gasped for breath while Oya exulted: "When the whirlwind blows while lightning blazes and thunder crashes, the people will say 'Chango and Oya are making love.' "

And so it was.

Oya sighed with remembrance, then, giving herself a brisk little shake, she slid quietly into Eleggua's bedroom, safe in the knowledge that he was splashing happily in his bath. His chest of ingredients was beside the bed and it was but the work of a moment for her to find the dreadfate root and pinch off a small piece.

Returning to her own room with the pilfered treasure she placed it in a little copper bowl and blew a thin stream of fire onto it until it turned to charcoal which she crumbled into a fine dust. This she poured into a tiny pouch, which she tucked into her décolletage, then, twirling herself into a miniature tornado, she swept out of the window and over the rooftops to the Glissando building.

Making herself invisible, Oya went past the security guard's desk, scanned the directory for the location of the laboratories and made her way there to find a white-coated scientist working alone in a small room off the main lab. Beside her was a flask labelled *Oshun's Gold* and small vials marked with the names of Alix, Angel, Brent and Keisha. At that moment, the phone rang in the lab and she went to answer it, leaving the field clear for Oya to do her tampering.

Oya laughed silently as she dropped a pinch of powdered dreadfate into the flask. Murmuring a short but potent incantation, she stirred it until it dissolved, leaving no trace in the clear, amber fluid.

"What a stroke of luck! Not only was the formula waiting for me on a silver platter, it will be used by people I know, so I'll see *exactly* how well this works." Twisting herself happily into a tight little whirlwind, she spun out of the nearest window.

Returning from her phone call, the young scientist carefully poured equal measures of the *Oshun's Gold* formula into the vials, sealed them and set them aside for delivery.

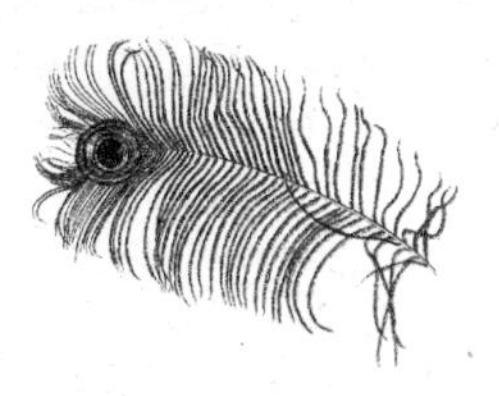

Angel awakened with an inexplicable feeling of excitement. Then she remembered; this was the day of the *Oshun's Gold* trial. Alix had offered the Hot Box group a preview sample and they'd accepted eagerly, agreeing that they'd each use it the next morning and compare results.

She vaulted out of bed and made short work out of brushing her teeth and showering. Now she stood in front of her bathroom mirror, vial in hand. Following the instructions, she applied a few drops of the liquid to her face and neck. It felt cool and pleasant with a slight tingle and immediately vanished into the skin, leaving no trace.

Alix had told them that, although it would take several days before the full effects of *Oshun's Gold* would take hold, they would see some results immediately. Peering eagerly into the mirror, Angel saw that the faint crows' feet at the corners of her eyes were quickly fading. It took a few seconds for her to realize that, as the wrinkles began to disappear, so did her hair and by the time the information kicked in, her head was as bald as Sinead O'Connor's. Her agonized scream was not unlike one of Ms O'Connor's top notes.

Brent shaved with an ultra-magnifying mirror with a built-in light. This morning he was even more thorough than usual, gliding his straight razor meticulously over every little nook and cranny. He sang as he worked and his tuneful baritone reverberated through the bathroom. “Look at that face, just look at it, look at that fabulous face of yours...”

Carefully applying the elixir, he continued to warble:

“I knew, first glance I took at it, this was the face that the world adored.” Halfway through the line his voice suddenly sounded like one of the Chipmunks.

Brent snapped his mouth shut so quickly he almost bit his tongue in two, “What was that!” he squeaked at 45 rpm, “What’s happening?” He reeled out of the bathroom, clutching his throat in wordless panic.

Just out of the shower, Keisha was spreading her vial of *Oshun’s Gold* over her entire body, “We want to be perfect all over, don’t we, girl?” she said to her reflection, which nodded in agreement.

Wrapping herself in a bath sheet, she proceeded to her closet with a feeling that she was being followed and on looking behind her, she found that the follower was none other than herself. Her rear end had grown to the point where it looked as if several people were hidden under her towel, all fighting to get out. She dropped the towel, backed up to a mirror and gazed at her expanded backside in horror, “I can’t believe it,” she moaned. “I’ve spent my life working my ass off and this is how it repays me!”

Angel sat numbly gazing at her shiny-skulled reflection. The phone rang and her hand automatically reached for the receiver.

"Angel?" The voice sounded as if it was speaking through a filter. "Angel - are you there?"

"Is that you, Alix?" she faltered.

"What's wrong?"

"Oh, Alix - I've l-l-l-ost all my h-h-h-hair!" Angel burst into tears.

"Oh, my dear girl!"

"It's my worst n-n-nightmare come true," she sobbed.

"Stay where you are, I'll be right over."

"Stay where I am? I'll never leave this apartment again!"

Fifteen minutes later Alix was knocking at the door. Wrapping a towel around her head, Angel opened the door just wide enough for Alix to slip inside. She gazed at her godmother in misery tinged with stupefaction:

"Why are you wearing that?"

"That" was a black hat with a veil so thick it totally obscured Alix's face.

"You're not the only one with a problem, dear heart; brace yourself."

Whipping off her headgear, Alix faced Angel who gave a stifled scream.

"I know," Alix honked dismally. "I make Cyrano de Bergerac look like Sally Fields."

It was all too true. Alix's nose, formerly thin and aristocratic, had grown almost to her chin and acquired a sinister bend to the left.

"My mother always talked about the Odie nose - the Odies were cousins on my mother's side of the family - and my greatest fear was that I'd end up with a proboscis like Great Aunt Odie's. Well, I have - only ten times worse! And why it should happen so suddenly is beyond me!"

Angel gasped: "Your secret fear? Mine was always of losing my hair the way my friend Mary Beth's mother did. I always loved Mrs. McAllister's hair. It was thick and shiny and the colour of butterscotch. Then she got Graves disease and started to lose her hair. The cure was radioactive iodine, which made her lose even more hair and although it grew back eventually, it was never as beautiful again."

Alix sat down in the nearest armchair and took off her hat, "If you and I have had our worst dreams come true, it's a safe bet that similar things have happened to Keisha and Brent as well."

They looked at each other in silence, then Angel picked up the phone and dialed Brent's number.

Half an hour later the four guinea pigs sat in Angel's living room trying to come to grips with the situation.

Oya, who had transported herself to Angel's, perched unseen on a window ledge, enjoying herself hugely.

Alix took charge of the discussion and after a few minutes of group wailing, she summed things up succinctly:

"There are three factors at work here:

1. We all used *Oshun's Gold* this morning.

2. We've all experienced disastrous side effects.

3. Those side effects are the realization of our worst fears regarding physical characters: for instance, Brent was afraid that he'd grow up to have a squeaky voice like his Uncle Albert, right?"

Brent nodded. He was damned if he'd say another word after all of them, even Angel, had cracked up while he was telling his story. Oh, they'd *apologized* - but still!

"And you, Keisha, dreaded the possibility of inheriting your family failing?"

"Most of the women in my family have behinds you could balance a full place setting on."

Brent was unable to resist: "Well, you could set a banquet for twenty-four on yours."

"Why, you helium-sucking little cretin..."

"Insulting each other isn't going to solve this mess," Alix said severely.

"What is?" answered Keisha gloomily. "None of us is in any shape to go out in public, except for Angel."

"ME?!?!!"

"Sure. Shaved heads for women have become quite commonplace. Nobody'll look twice at you."

"Perhaps you'd like me to sport a nose ring and pierce my tongue as well?"

"Clients wouldn't like it." Brent said briefly.

"Thank you, my little squeaky toy." Angel replied caustically.

"Stop it, all of you - we have to think," Alix paced the floor, head bent as if pulled forward by the unfamiliar weight of her nose. "The formula must have been tampered with. But by whom – and why?"

"That is something you will never know."

Eleggua, perched on the dining room table, grinned at the four misfortunates.

"I wish you gods would strike a gong or something when you're about to materialize," Alix said testily, "these sudden appearances make me dizzy!"

"But then, dear lady, we'd miss the fun of startling people."

"You call it fun to scare people out of their skins?" Alix sniffed.

"Of course. But then, I find most things in life to be fun which, as I'm immortal, is just as well. Imagine being bored throughout eternity."

"I'd settle for a few years of boredom; right now I have more excitement than I can handle."

"Don't we all." Angel turned to Eleggua:

"Do you know who did this?"

"Of course, I know everything."

At this point Oya decided to leave before Eleggua noticed her. She'd seen enough anyway.

"Who?
"Why?"
They crowded around Eleggua who fended them off laughingly, shaking his head.
"No, no, - I cannot tell you."
"Why not?"
"You can't mean to leave us in this situation!"
"You *must* help us!"
Eleggua gazed soberly at them until they quietened.
"Certainly I mean to help you, my friends, but I must handle this in my own way and it will take a little while."
"In one hour I have a meeting with the head of CTC to discuss a TV special on *Oshun's Gold,* " Angel cried : "I can't possibly cancel it!"
"Wear a wig," Alix suggested. "We have all kinds of them in our makeup department and there's bound to be one that matches your hair. I'll call and have them deliver several right away."
"Thanks, Alix."
"That solves it for you, but what do I do with *this?"* Keisha gestured at her nether regions with disgust.
Brent was suddenly inspired: "Get a wheelchair, tape up your leg with a tensor bandage and say you've sprained your ankle. If you keep a blanket over your lower half, nobody will know."
"That's brilliant!" Keisha lumbered over to Brent and gave him a hug before hurrying to call a medical equipment rental company.
"You can pretend to have laryngitis," Angel said to Brent, "but what will you do, Alix? You can't go around looking like the Merry Widow in purdah."
"This is the perfect excuse for a day off: I intend to order in lunch and spend the day here with your collection of old films "
Half an hour later the house phone rang:
"M'zelle Zeemermann?"

"Yes, René."

"I have in my possession several parcels and a wheeled chair."

"Bring them right up, please."

"But of course. Is it that you have injured yourself?"

"Not I, René. Miss Adams, who is visiting me, has wrenched her ankle."

"*Dommage*! I will shortly be at your door."

Brent answered the door, mutely smiled his thanks and wheeled in the chair and wig boxes, barely getting out of the way before Angel and Keisha fell upon the supplies.

Instructing the four unfortunates to meet him back at Angel's at five pm, Eleggua left them busily equipping themselves and went to find a few answers. He knew it was Oya who had tampered with the formula and he was sure she had used the dreadfate root. Sure enough, on checking his supplies, he discovered that a tiny piece of it was missing.

"Olokun take the woman!" he swore, half angry and half amused. He rummaged through the chest, picking out the powders and elixirs that would be needed to counteract the spell. Working swiftly, he concocted a potion that bubbled and foamed before settling to a clear liquid over which he murmured an incantation, making delicate motions with his long fingers. The finished product had to be buried in earth for several hours to complete the spell. Remembered the potted palm that stood beside his favourite table in the Four Seasons lounge, he went there for a in pre-prandial cocktail. Deftly tucking the flask into the soil around the palm tree, he sat very much at his ease in a large armchair, glass in hand.

Once he'd discovered the dry Martini, Eleggua had fallen in love with it, almost as much for the elegant glass as for the contents. Now he was halfway through a triple classic made with Bombay Blue gin. Having several hours yet to kill, he gestured to the server to do it again - might as well spend the time here where the chairs were comfortable and the Martinis dry as desert sand.

By mid afternoon he had gone through three more triples, a club sandwich and all the daily papers. There was one more hour to go. Just then, he heard a voice saying, "For God's sake, Lex, watch what you're doing with that wheelchair."

Looking up, he saw Keisha being steered through the maze of cocktail tables by an impossibly good looking young man with an identical version walking beside the chair.

Keisha didn't notice Eleggua, who was sunk deep into his armchair and he decided to observe the trio for a while before making his presence known.

The twins made a huge fuss over settling Keisha who sat with her back to Eleggua, while they placed themselves across from her. After giving their drinks order with elaborate instructions to the waiter, Thing One, as Eleggua mentally dubbed the man to Keisha's left, turned to her with a pout that enhanced his cherubic mouth.

"Keisha," he said in a petulant whine, "we've been waiting for the past three weeks."

"Yes," Thing Two chimed in, with an identical sullen *moué*, "you said that *Cosmo* is going to use

us for their centrefold but we haven't heard anything and we've checked with Theo every day."

"Twice a day," added Thing One.

Keisha took a sip of her Kir Royale, then reached over and patted two clean-cut cheekbones.

"Don't worry your beautiful little heads," she smiled. "Of course '*Cosmopolitan*' is going to use you - they went wild for the test shots."

"You see, Rex," Thing One said smugly, "I told you Keisha wouldn't let us down."

"*You*!" his brother said indignantly, "*I* told you -"

"Don't argue, children. It doesn't matter who said what. The important thing is that you're going to be the centrefold for next July as well as being featured in a major article on twins, which is a perfect tie-in and we're shooting it in Bora-Bora - how great is that?"

The twins fell into an absolute tizzy of delight, hugging first Keisha and then each other before settling down to a deep discussion on whether they should wear posing pouches or rely on teasingly placed hands for the centre spread. Rex, who fondly believed he was the better endowed of the two, wanted to use gold lamé pouches while Lex opted for the hands on approach.

"What's the matter, bro'?" Rex sniped "afraid the public will discover that we're not completely identical?"

"Get a grip on yourself," Lex snarled.

"I'll leave that to you, you do it so well," his brother replied sweetly.

While Lex rooted around in his dimly lit mind for a comeback, Eleggua appeared at the table and Keisha hailed him with unconcealed relief. The twins stopped squabbling and waited expectantly for Keisha to introduce the stranger.

"EsuEleggua, may I present Lex and Rex Middlesex. Gentlemen, I would like you to meet EsuEleggua, Prime Minister of Oyo."

Forgetting her supposed injury, Keisha gave her companions a kick on the shins with both feet at once, nudging them into rising. The twins were so in awe of the exotic newcomer that they didn't notice her mistake. Eleggua acknowledged them graciously, and on their stammered invitation, joined their group.

"How fortunate to find you here, my dear Keisha I was going to meet you at Angel's for our five o'clock appointment but now we can go together."

"What appointment?" Lex and Rex were as curious as a pair of magpies.

"You know that I'm doing the photography for *Oshun's Gold.*" Keisha said.

Lex and Rex sighed in unison.

"Yes - and what we wouldn't give to be part of it... can't you just see us on either side of that *divine* Oshun."

"Nice thought, boys, but it's not going to happen," Keisha replied briskly. "Finish up those drinks and wheel me out of here. The First Minister and I have to get going."

Signalling for the bill which Lex and Rex insisted on picking up, they made their way out of the lounge and into the street where Rex flagged down a taxi.

Keisha and the twins gave each other the usual triple-sided air kisses and Eleggua shook hands with them: "Twins are venerated in my country where they are known as the *Ibeji*," he told them. "They have great powers and nothing is refused them."

Lex and Rex were all of a twitter over this information. They would have been less impressed had they heard Eleggua's next words to Keisha when they were safely inside their taxi.

"Those two could bring the whole *Ibeji* power structure down in no time. I've never seen such a pair of idiots."

Keisha laughed in agreement, then said, "Were you sucessful? Do you have the antidote?"

Eleggua grinned and tapped the breast pocket of his jacket. "Close to my heart, loveliest lady."

Keisha breathed a deep sigh of relief. "I can't tell you how happy that makes me. It's hell having to literally cover my rear and I have new respect for people in wheelchairs."

The cab pulled up at Angel's building and the driver, smitten by Keisha, actually got out of the car to help her into her wheelchair. Eleggua paid him, adding a generous tip. Nodding to Henry who held the entrance door wide open, he trundled Keisha through the lobby and into a waiting elevator.

The cab driver stood looking after them and shaking his head: "It's a fine thing for a woman to got back" he mused, "but that poor girl got more back than a mama elephant."

Eleggua smiled benignly at the afflicted group whom he had seated, one in each corner of the room.

"This will not take long, my friends."

"Will it hurt?" Angel voiced a shared fear.

"Not in the least," he assured her. "You will just close your eyes, give concentrations to the afflicted area, and you'll feel nothing but a pleasant warmthness overall."

"Can I think of it as less than it was?" Keisha asked hopefully.

"Or deeper?" squeaked Brent.

"No." Eleggua replied firmly. "This spell has been customated to restore you to your former selves; there is no clause for changings."

"Just asking." Keisha said with unusual meekness.

Eleggua busied himself with preparations for the spell-breaking ceremony. He removed his suit, shirt, tie and footwear. Besides a love of Martinis, Eleggua had developed a passion for fashion, including male lingerie. He had underwear in every possible style, colour and pattern, ranging from Joe Boxer shorts stamped with heavily lipsticked mouth prints to silk thongs in neon tones. Today he wore a pair of tiny briefs, checkerboarded in red and black, which he thought very fetching.

Brent leaned towards Keisha, gesturing towards Eleggua with a small movement of his head:

"Quel basket case," he whispered in a mouse's squeak and Keisha nodded in awestruck agreement. They sat in furtive admiration until Eleggua looked up at them from under his eyebrows and grinned wickedly. Embarrassed, they looked away.

Eleggua placed a small leather pouch on the floor in front of him. Sitting on his heels, he opened the pouch and took out so many jars and packages that it was like watching a stream of clowns piling out of a circus car. As he removed each object, he touched it first to his forehead, then his heart and placed it in one of five groups, chanting in an inaudible whisper. When he was finished there was one large group of ingredients directly in front of him and four small vials, two on each side of the centre pile.

Reaching into the pouch again, he withdrew a bundle of dried herbs, a fan made of peacock feathers, a bowl of fine sand, a leafy branch and a calabash of water. He placed them around the mound of items and murmured further unintelligible phrases. Then he picked up the bundle of herbs with his right hand and rose effortlessly to his feet. He snapped the fingers of his left hand and a small flame sprang between his fingers and thumb. Lighting the herbs, he quickly snuffed out the flame, leaving the bundle smouldering with a fragrant green smoke.

Turning to his left, Eleggua walked to the corner where Alix sat. He motioned to her to rise and circled her slowly, moving the smouldering herbs in a spiral that began at her feet and ended above her head. All the while, he made a steady humming sound in which words could barely be discerned. Continuing in a circle to his left, he performed the same movements on Angel and then on Brent and Keisha.

He returned to the centre of the room, extinguished the herbs and placed them back in the pouch. Next, he took the bowl of sand and, beginning again with Alix, poured a steady stream of sand in spiral formation around her feet. As before, the same motions were performed on the others.

The next implement to be used was the fan and with this Eleggua used both hands, waving it up, down and around as each person in turn revolved slowly from left to right.

He took the branch in his left hand and the calabash in his right. Moving again to Alix, he dipped the branch in the water and shook it all over her, starting at the top of her head and ending by brushing the leaves over her feet and again, the ritual was executed for the other three in turn.

Eleggua's humming chant continued throughout the entire procedure.

Once again the Orisha returned to the middle of the room. This time he sat cross-legged on the floor in front of the items he'd first removed from his pouch. He opened every jar and took pinches of the contents, dropping them into a wooden bowl and blending them by rubbing them between his long fingers. Lastly, he opened a small glass vial that pulsated with light. He poured the contents of the bowl into the bottle, tightly recorked it and shook it vigorously while he whirled in a tight circle, first crouching low to the ground and gradually straightening until he was turning on the tips of his toes. The humming sound increased until it vibrated through everyone, beginning at their feet and spiralling upwards into their heads where it floated into every part of their minds, sweeping thought away and leaving a tranquillity usually only achieved by deep meditation.

Eleggua slowed in his spin, stooping lower, ever lower until he was sitting on the ground again. He opened the four bottles each of which was half filled with a different coloured liquid and topped them up with the contents of the vial, corking each one in turn and shaking it into a frothy blend.

"Now, my friends, close your eyes and think of yourselves as being back to usualness."

Taking all the bottles in his left hand, he went over to Alix. Eleggua uncorked a bottle filled with a golden liquid and, gently opening Alix's mouth, he poured in the contents. Next he went to Angel and administered a green coloured potion. For Brent, the liquid was blue and the content of Keisha's bottle was deep red.

The ritual was complete. Standing in the doorway so he could face all four of his patients, he ceased his humming. Their eyes opened and they looked dazedly first at Eleggua and then at each other.

"It worked," Brent shouted to Angel, "you have your hair back… and I have my voice!"

Angel's hands flew to her head and her fingers performed a joyous dance among the luxuriant strands. "Oh, thank you, Eleggua - thank you!" she said, rushing over to hug him.

"I've lost that behemoth of a behind!" Keisha said exuberantly. She gave Eleggua a big kiss on the cheek and boogied around the room, shaking her neatly restored hips.

"And my nose is back where it belongs," said Alix, taking one of Eleggua's hands in both of hers and shaking it warmly.

Brent clapped the Orisha on the back and said "I'm buying you the biggest, coldest Martini in town."

Eleggua and Brent headed off to the *Park Plaza*, Alix's car arrived to whisk her back to her waterfront pied-à-terre and Angel and Keisha settled down to tea and a recap of the day's harrowing events.

Eventually Keisha stretched her arms and rotated her shoulders; she felt stiff after sitting over a teacup for the past two hours.

"I must get going," she yawned. "I've still got tons of work to do."

But she made no move to leave. Angel knew she had something on her mind, so she poured them each another cup of Jane Austen blend and waited for her friend to speak.

"What do you think of Eleggua?" Keisha asked with elaborate casualness.

Angel eyed her friend suspiciously: "*What* are you doing with Eleggua?"

"Nothing… yet."

"What do you *intend* to do - no - I don't want to know. I've suffered through too many affairs with you, K. There was the one with the acrobat from *Cirque de Soleil* ...there was the grand passion for your hairstylist that ended when he wanted to trim your pubes into a heart shape -"

"So naff," Keisha interjected.

"Then there were those dreadful twins who don't have a brain cell between them."

"Lex and Rex were only once, Angel, purely out of curiosity - besides, they're so *bee-ootiful*."

"And those interludes with Brent."

"Oh, - we were both lonely. I wasn't involved with anyone of interest when we were at Caprice and then in Africa, Stephen was off on a flight and Brent needed someone to cuddle. We're really like brother and sister most of the time."

"Great - mock incest! But Eleggua would be a different ball game, if you'll pardon the pun."

"Well, we've just been circling around each other to this point. A little look here, a little wink there. But when he finished setting things to rights, he whispered that he'll come to me late tonight. I gotta tell you, girl, I'm looking forward to it - he may be on the skinny side, but you must have noticed that he stretched those briefs to the point of no return."

"Keisha!" Angel giggled unwillingly, followed by a resigned sigh.

"What can I say? Nothing can stop you once you've made up your mind. You charge ahead, sweeping everything out of your way, just like Oya."

Keisha smiled wryly, "Well, as she says herself, I am her child.. But -" she rose from the couch, and picked up her shoulder bag, "Lovely as this is, I've got to get to the studio and put out whatever fires are burning." At the door she draped her arms over Angel's shoulders:

"Don't be fooled by my wicked mouth, honey - it's not just Eleggua's godly bones I'm interested in. He has a fascinating quality beneath all that deviltry and he could be what I've been looking for all my life."

"Keisha - Eleggua isn't just another man to be conquered; he's immortal and you can't *imagine* what might happen."

"Yeah, I know. You read mythology in university, Angel, so you know there are precedents for human/divine relationships. Don't worry - I'll take all the necessary precautions so I don't end up with a little half divinity."

Flashing her brilliant smile, she whirled on her heel and charged off down the hall to the elevator.

Shaking her head, Angel closed the door and went to take a shower.

Back in the seclusion of the apartment, Oshun disappeared for one of her marathon bubble baths while Chango settled himself comfortably in front of the wall-screen TV with a large coke in one hand and the remote control in the other.

"It is a wonderful thing, this television and its changer," he had proclaimed after first using it. "Much like ourselves, it can be in so many different places at the same time."

Seeing him now, happily immersed in a round robin of *CNN*, an old James Bond movie and the comedy channel, Oya gave a wordless exclamation of chagrin and would have flounced off to her room, but Eleggua, who had just returned from his cocktail hour with Brent, barred her way.

"I wonder, sweet sister, if I could have a moment of your time," he said silkily.

"What do you want, Eleggua? I am tired."

"I shall not keep you long - I'd just like to clear up the little matter of your malicious game with *Oshun's Gold*."

"I don't know what you're talking about," Oya cast a furtive glance at Chango, but he was immersed in his programmes.

"Don't worry - he'll not hear us as long as that screen is alight," Eleggua said, "and don't even try to deny that it was you, my dear Oya, who stole my dreadfate root and used it to such good effect. It was a masterful touch to bring each person's secret fear to life, but you must have known I'd suspect you of intervenings."

"That's intervention, you semi-literate fool," snapped Oya, "and I really didn't care about arousing your suspicion. I wanted to shake things up and I did."

"And now you will stop," Eleggua said, unperturbed by Oya's insults. "I said I wouldn't meddle with you and Chango and I've kept that promise, but any more trouble and I'll cause considerable grief for you."

Oya opened her mouth to reply but Eleggua cut her off with a single gesture. "I don't want to hear anything; it is finished and we will go on as if it never happened. Good night, my dear sister."

He gave a mocking bow and vanished, leaving Oya to fume, which she had to do quietly, not wanting Chango to know that anything was wrong. Retiring to her room she found a slight relief in kicking around the pillows from her bed, but she really needed to break something. Crashes and clatters figured largely in Oya's expressions of anger; without them, a temper tantrum wasn't worth the effort.

After a few more kicks that sent feathers flying around the room, she calmed down and sat on the edge of her bed, drumming her fingers. Chango showed no signs of leaving his beloved television; Oshun, before disappearing into the bathroom, had announced her intention of having a rare quiet night at home and Eleggua was off doing Oluddumare knows what - not that she'd choose to spend an evening with him.

But wait! She had been promising herself to visit Keisha and introduce her spiritual child to her path. What better time than now? Humming happily to herself, she retied her *gelé* at a jauntier angle, sprayed herself with perfume and shook out her robes. Pirouetting forcefully in one spot, she spun herself into a blur, disappeared from her bedroom and reappeared instantly in Keisha's studio.

The young photographer was studying enlargements of shots she had taken of Oshun when they were working on *Oshun's Gold.* These pictures were not for the campaign but for a future book of photographic essays. Although Oya felt a stab of jealousy as she watched

Keisha smiling over the pictures, she had to admit that they were superb.

Sensing that she was not alone, Keisha looked up and saw Oya. Keisha had quickly become inured to the sudden appearances of the Orisha, so she smiled and rose from her chair, saying:

"Give you greeting, my mother."

"Give you greeting, my child."

Keisha took Oya's hands in hers and touched them to her forehead in an instinctive gesture of respect. Oya was moved but covered her emotion by picking up a picture of Oshun. She looked at it briefly and then tossed it back into Keisha's desk, saying sniffily:

"Why does everyone make such a fuss over that creature? Back in Oshogbo there are those who prefer my looks over hers."

Keisha was aware of the rivalry between the two deities. She smiled at Oya:

"You are a woman of great beauty and I have been wanting to ask if you'd pose for me.

Feigning reluctance, Oya said, "Well...I'm not sure..."

"Oh, please, my mother," Keisha looked beseechingly at the goddess.

Oya nodded graciously: "It shall be as you wish."

"Wonderful!" Keisha said. "Stand right here." She placed Oya in front of a scrim of seamless paper.. Working swiftly, she moved T-bars and adjusted lights until she had the goddess properly lit. Squinting through the viewfinder, she drew in her breath sharply:

"*Just* what I want. Now - do that whirling thing, but v-e-r-y slowly at first, all right?"

"All right," Oya said doubtfully. She began to revolve and Keisha started clicking her camera.

"That's it - that's good - stay in the same place and just turn...turn...turn. Great! Now, keep turning but move slowly to your left, just a little - watch my hand - move that way - okay?"

"Okay." Oya was beginning to enjoy herself.

"Keep going." *Click... click... click.*

"A little faster..." Keisha began travelling with Oya turning in the opposite direction to the goddess, firing off a shot each time the two faced each other.

"Stay in that spot but turn faster ... faster..."

Oya's robes flew out around her and Keisha increased her movements to match those of the goddess.

"*Faster*!" Oya became a blur, Keisha whirled into her orbit and the clicks became a steady tattoo as both women twirled in a double eddy.

"Now - gradually...start to slow down"

The turning slowed, the snick of the shutter lessened its tempo until Oya and Keisha stood unmoving, facing each other with wide smiles.

Keisha bowed in gratitude: "Thank you, my mother. Now - if you want to see what we have done, we'll develop these right now."

Oya could hardly wait to see the results. She followed Keisha into the darkroom and was bewildered by the blackness.

"What can you do in here where you can see nothing?"

"The darkness protects the film," Keisha explained, working as she talked. "First I remove it from the camera and wind it onto a spool. Then it's put into a container and I put a funnel in to block the light and make it ready for the next step."

She took Oya back into the main room where she went to the sink and began the developing process.

Oya watched intently as Keisha put the film through the various baths and washes.

"This is the fun part." Keisha cut the strips of film into individual shots. Working at speed, she enlarged the shots, made test strips and then put the shots of her choice into the developer trays.

Oya was fascinated to see the pictures appear as if by magic. There she was at many different angles, frozen in mid-whirl, robes flying, head flung back in ecstasy.

Keisha placed the pictures into a cold water bath, agitating them gently while deep in thought. At the end of the process, she removed the prints, turned to Oya and said:

"Why did you honour me with this visit?"

Oya looked at her with solemn respect.

"I had come to show you your path but I see there is no need. You have already found your way and we are melded together as mother and child."

Keisha stripped off her rubber gloves and came to Oya's side. She and the Orisha looked into each other's eyes and embraced warmly.

"I have never felt so strong in my life as at this moment," Keisha said.

"That is my gift to you," Oya replied. "The strength to work and the courage to live. They will never desert you."

Deep into the night Keisha lay wide awake, her heart thudding, her ears attuned to every little noise. Time ticked by and traffic noises lessened, signalling the lateness of the hour. Just before three am Keisha gave up her vigil and drifted disappointedly into an unquiet sleep.

"Keisha...*Keisha.*"

Her whispered name floated through the room.

"Ke-e-i-sh-a-a!. The name rumbled inside her head, waking her from a fitful dream in which Eleggua was playing hide and seek with her among the leaves of the Honey Money Bush.

She sat up in bed

"K-e-e-i-sha-a-a!.

She looked around the darkened room. No one was in sight.

"Eleggua?" she whispered. "Is that you?"

A deep laugh sounded close by her left ear and she turned swiftly, thinking to find him beside her. Nothing.

She leaned over and switched on her bedside lamp.

The laugh echoed around her again.

" Eleggua, where *are* you?"

"Closer than you think."

"But I can't see you."

"Look in the mirror."

Keisha got out of bed and padded over to her dressing table. Gazing into the mirror, at first she saw only herself and then, swinging out of her ear and onto her shoulder came a tiny figure.

"What were you doing in there?" she demanded.

"Exploring."

"Well, if you've finished why don't you bring yourself back to normal size."

Eleggua laughed, "This size is as normal for me as any other, lovely one, but anything to oblige. Go back to the bed."

Keisha went back to her bedside and lowered herself gingerly to the mattress.

Suddenly he was lying beside her, his eyes gazing into hers.

"I have thought of this ever since I first saw you, beautiful Keisha," he said, running a long forefinger gently over her mouth.

Keisha shivered with excitement. She was never shy when it came to sex but this was different and she couldn't begin to imagine what would happen.

Eleggua took her chin in his hand and lightly outlined her mouth with his tongue before kissing her deeply. Marvelling at the softness of his lips, she slid her hands into the mass of his dreadlocked hair, which smelled of sandalwood and held his mouth to hers.

He flicked his tongue inside her ear, swirling it around the little whorl where he'd hidden himself, then nibbled his way down her neck and to her breasts where he drew first the left breast and then the right completely inside his widely opened mouth. It was an amazing sensation, but Keisha had barely time to enjoy it when he was off again, moving lower and lower down her body, tracing every outline with kisses. When he reached the point where her thighs met, he suddenly disappeared.

"Eleggua - where *are* you - *what* are you....Oooooooooo!"

She had never felt anything like this in her life. Shrinking back to micro size, Eleggua had slipped inside her vaginal cave and was using her clitoris as a ski slope.

"Oooooooooooo," went Keisha, "OOOoooOOOoooo OOOOoooOO!" as Eleggua rode up and down the quivering pink mound, pausing each time he reached the summit to give special attention to the sensitive tip.

Keisha felt herself building to an orgasm but just before the moment of explosion, Eleggua returned to full size and plunged himself into her. As she felt him within her, she climaxed with a rolling wave of contractions that shook her body convulsively. Eleggua pinned her firmly to the bed, which concentrated her movements into tight little ripples of almost unbearable delight.

She was, in effect, turned into a life-sized vibrator which not only had made her come three more times, but brought Eleggua to a vastly satisfying orgasm as well. At that point, he bit off her eyelashes but she was so much a part of him at that moment, that she saw nothing strange in his action. Later on, while inspecting the stubbly rims around her eyes she asked him why he had done it and he said in Africa it was an expression of great passion.

A lesser woman might have been angry but Keisha considered the loss of her eyelashes more than a fair exchange for the incredible pleasure he had given her.

"Try to control your ecstasy from now on," she said, examining the stubble on her eyelids. "I'll have to wear falsies until my own lashes grow back."

"No need," Eleggua said airily, passing a fingertip across Keisha's eyes, "this will bring them back in the twinkling of a toenail."

"The expression is 'twinkling of an eye'," Keisha said, examining hers in her dresser mirror, "hmm, you made them longer than they were - how lovely!"

"I like twinkling of a toenail better than an eye," Eleggua mused. "It is a more pleasing sound to the ear."

"You do that a lot," Keisha observed, "You take words and phrases and use them however. It's like being with Humpty Dumpty in *Alice in Wonderland*."

"What is this Dumtee? Who is this Alice? Jonathan talked about her, too, when he first met me."

Keisha laughed, "Humpty Dumpty is a character in a children's nursery rhyme. He's a huge egg." She recited the poem to Eleggua who nodded thoughtfully.

"And what about the Alice?"

Keisha settled herself cross-legged on the bed: "*Alice In Wonderland* is one of the most famous books ever written. Actually, there are two books, the first is *Alice in Wonderland* and the second is *Alice Through the Looking Glass*. In *Alice in Wonderland*, a little girl sees a white rabbit all dressed up and hurrying along the riverbank, scolding himself for being late.

Alice is intrigued to find a talking rabbit, so she follows him and falls down the rabbit hole. She ends up in Wonderland where she has all kinds of adventures, including finding foods that make her smaller or larger."

Eleggua sniffed disdainfully. "I need no potions to change *my* size. It is my *ashé* that gives me my miraculating abilities."

Keisha had learned enough from the Orisha to know that *ashé* means power. Patting Eleggua's hand soothingly, she said, "I know that and so does everyone who has experienced your amazing faculties."

Mollified, Eleggua put his arm around Keisha and hugged her to him.

"And what of the Dumtee and his words which are like mine?"

"Alice meets Humpty Dumpty in *Through the Looking Glass* – wait a minute - I still have the book and I'll read that part to you if you'd like."

"That would be very pleasure making," Eleggua lay back on the bed as Keisha went to find the volume.

"This is a children's book," she told Eleggua, as she thumbed through the well-used pages, "but it's one of my all time favourites and throughout the years I've read it over and over again... ah - here we are. Now - listen to this..."

Eleggua was enthralled as Keisha read the Humpty Dumpty episode and when she came to the part where Humpty Dumpty says: *When* I *use a word it means just what I choose it to mean - neither more nor less.,* the Orisha bounced bolt upright, shouting:

"Yes! Yes!! that is the exacticality of my belief. This is a fine story - like the patakis of Africa."

Keisha looked at him affectionately. EsuEleggua, the most powerful of the Orisha – was as excited as a child over a child's story. Then she remembered Alix telling them that Eleggua is a child in one of his paths.

She closed the book and tucked it into Eleggua's hand. "I'd like you to have this," she said gently. "It's a fitting gift, for you have taken me into my own wonderland and my life will never be the same."

Eleggua opened the book carefully, turning pages at random and smoothing the paper with his palm. After a few minutes, he closed the book and said:

"People give me gifts all the time, when asking favours or when I have granted their prayers but no one has ever given me a present for no reason. I am in gratefulness to you, dearest Keisha."

He held out his arms and she went into them, curling herself against him. He gave a throaty gurgle and disappeared but, just as Keisha gave a little moan of disappointment, she heard his voice:

"I have not left you, lovely one. I just have the desire to sleep between your beautiful breasts."

Looking down, she saw a tiny Eleggua snuggled into the cleft of her bosom. Sighing contentedly, she reached up and turned out the light.

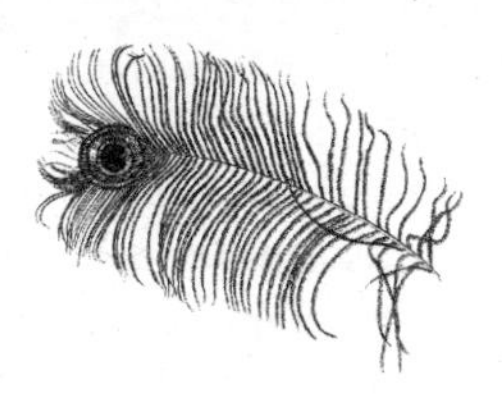

"This'll be the hottest dance craze since the *Twist*, Jonathan!"

Jonathan turned down the volume on his phone, wishing that he could control Theo's enthusiasm in the same way.

Theo continued at a muted decibel. "Remember the *Achy Breaky*? - not even lukewarm. Remember the *Macarena*? - No contest. Remember - "

"Theo - much as I'd love to continue this little dance down memory lane with you, my meter is running."

"Oh, right. Well," Theo continued briskly, "Marc's song is finished and it is unfuckingbelievable! Sara Vigneault is directing the video - she's *only* the best in the business - and we're starting to cast tomorrow so I'll need a batch of standard contracts right away."

"No problem."

"Would you like to come to the auditions?"

"I don't have time for that nonsense." Jonathan rattled some papers to emphasize his point.

"That little Chicana dancer will be there...."

"The one who can wrap both legs behind her neck?"

"That's the one - The Steel Pretzel."

"Well," Jonathan said with unconvincing nonchalance, "maybe I could stop by for a few minutes."

"Marvin's Rehearsal Halls at ten am Ciao for now."

After a week of crazed activity during which it seemed that every Afro-Cuban singer and dancer in the country was auditioned, casting was complete. Chango wanted Oshun, Oya and Eleggua play themselves, but Sara Vigneault was reluctant.

"Mon cher Chango," she purred, "We need people who will personify the power and excitement of the African gods. Oshun is a model and knows how to move and project a mood but the other two are not singers or dancers. Granted they *look* the part, but..."

Chango's face grew thunderous and Theo deftly cut in.

"Could I have a teensy word, Sara, darling?"

Theo walked the young director to a quiet corner, offered her one of his Black Russian cigarettes, took one himself and lit both.

Sara took a deep drag and spoke on the exhale: "Theo - this happens time after time: the star surrounds himself with his friends who tell him how wonderful he is; in return he gives them a bit part so that they can impress *their* friends and it becomes a production nightmare that takes three times as long to complete."

Theo patted her hand sympathetically. "I know, darling. There's nothing worse than star struck amateurs, but let them audition. Hell - we're trying out every singer and dancer this side of LA - what's two more?"

"*Eh bien*, - but I'm warning you - they don't get any extra consideration."

But all Sara's doubts were swept away when she saw them in action, and the deities were delighted to perform, especially Oya, who had become dazzled by the glamour of showbiz.

"It's the most exciting thing I've ever attempted." Marc took his hands from the keyboard where he'd just played the opening melody of his new opus. "A symphony on the Orisha! I was nervous about it – but Babatunde said it is given to me to do this. I'm calling it *Pathways* and the central theme will be *Orisha Dance*.

"It'll be marvelous", Angel said, hugging him in pride and relief. In the last few weeks Marc had a new lease on life for which both he and Angel were grateful. His drug and alcohol abuse had been out of control, but help had come through the intervention of Chango.

He and Marc had been working flat out on *Orisha Dance* and he saw very quickly that Marc couldn't function without a little help from his friends. First it was a shot of Cardhu here and a few tokes there, but soon intake was mounting and output decreasing in quantity *and* quality. The day he rhymed "June" with "moon", Chango knew something was terribly wrong.

"My brother," he said to Marc who was listlessly tapping the same note on the piano over and over while he drew on his third spliff of the morning; "We must have a discussion."

Marc eyed him disinterestedly. "About what?" He took another puff, but Chango caught his hand.

"About this," he said, "and this," he gestured to an empty glass perched on the piano's lid.

"What about it?" Marc twisted his wrist in an attempt to break Chango's grasp but the Orisha held him as effortlessly as if he was a baby. Plucking the spliff from Marc's helpless fingers, Chango put it into his mouth and swallowed it.

"Hey!" Marc barked, "that was the best stuff I've found in months."

Chango pulled a wry face. "I'd hate to taste the worst."

"Who told you to taste it in the first place?"

"Nobody is the telling me, my brother. It is I who am telling you and if you value your future, you will listen with your ears and your heart. To now I have said nothing of your drugs and drinking, because I know it is usual in your culture and I, who neither drink nor smoke, do not wish to impose my beliefs on others."

"Very large of you, dude." Marc said sarcastically.

Chango ignored the interruption: "But with you there is too much smoking, too much drinking. It is harming your work, it is damaging your health and it is hurting the woman who loves you."

Marc glared at the god of fire who looked at him with such compassion that Marc's eyes filled with tears.

"Success came easily to you," Chango said, "but now you have to surpass your early victories and the most difficult opponent is yourself. You're trying to escape yourself by the use of liquor and dope and all that is doing is to cause more problems."

Chango was not noted for his intellect and what he said was simplistic but his sincerity was so powerful that Marc was shaken. He left the piano and circled the huge room, pausing at the kitchen counter to twirl one of the stools, moving on to the pool table where he rolled a few balls into the mesh pockets and ending up at the couches by the fireplace. He slumped on the soft leather cushions and sighed.

"What should I do?"

Chango joined Marc at the fireplace. Snapping his fingers, he caused the fireplace to burst into flame. "You do not mind?" he asked, "I think better in the presence of fire."

With his eyes fixed on the fireplace, Chango spoke: "I am going to take you on a journey - the most important one you will ever undertake. It is a journey of the soul, and although you will not move from this spot, you will travel far."

He rose from the couch and stood behind Marc. "Look into the fire. I am going to take you within yourself and we will travel through your body and your mind."

"How can I go through my own body," Marc burst out, "I'm already *in* it!"

"With the Orisha, my brother, all things are possible." Chango put his huge hands on top of Marc's head, twisting the palms in opposite directions, much like the Chinese burn that children give each other, but instead of causing pain, the movements created a warm, expansive feeling. The crown of his head seemed to ripple and Marc swayed to the calming rhythm.

The ripples became the spiral of a slow-moving whirlpool; Marc felt himself moving in wide circles whose speed increased as their size diminished. The smaller the circles grew, the faster Marc went, funnelling downward, deeper and deeper until he came to an abrupt stop on a surface that gave slightly beneath his feet. As his eyes grew accustomed to the dim light, he saw that he was standing on a shiny pinkish hill. Other hills stretched as far as he could see in every direction, divided by deep convolutions that curved around themselves. It was a strange landscape, made stranger by sparks that flew between the different ridges, some at a steady rate, others in a more erratic fashion.

"Do you know where we are?" Chango's voice boomed in Marc's ear, causing him to lose his footing and slip down into the next ridge.

"Sorry," said Chango, extending a hand and hauling Marc back up beside him. They surveyed the scene and the more Marc looked at it the more familiar it seemed.

"Is this my brain?"

"Yes." replied Chango. "We're in your memory centre and if you put pressure on an area, you will relive past experiences."

"No shit," Marc said.

He knelt down and pressed his right hand firmly onto the surface. Suddenly he was in his kindergarten class. The teacher was giving out tambourines and triangles to most of the children and Marc desperately wanted the only drum. It went to his best friend, Greg, and Marc felt sick with disappointment. He looked around; everyone else had instruments and he was left with nothing. His eyes filled with tears and his heart thudded sickly in his ears.

The teacher stood there, holding a thin wooden stick. She was speaking, but Marc was so upset he didn't hear what she was saying. Greg poked him. "Miss MacKenzie is calling you."

Marc stumbled up to the front of the class and his teacher handed him the stick, saying, "You will be the conductor."

He wasn't happy about that - it sounded boring - but at least he was part of the band. Miss MacKenzie seated herself at the piano:

"Now, children, I'm going to play a tune and you will accompany me on your instruments. Watch Marc carefully and follow his directions.. You'll know by the way he waves the baton - that's what the stick is called. If he waves it quickly, you play faster. If he waves it slowly, you play slowly, too. Are you ready? And..."

Miss MacKenzie struck up a spirited version of *Pop Goes The Weasel*, Marc raised his baton and they were off. They had hardly begun when he realized he'd never had so much fun in his life...no, it wasn't fun - it went way beyond that. Just by pointing his stick and waving it at his classmates he could make them speed up until they sounded like galloping horses, or he could make them slow down until they were like the ticking of the grandfather clock in the front hall at home. He was giddy with the thrill of making music - of moulding the movements of the band to his desires. By the time the song was ended, he knew what he wanted to do with his life. Marc Dupré, aged five, was going to be a musician.

Marc lifted his hand from the pressure point and was back with Chango on the landscape of his brain. He looked at his companion in disbelief:

"I was back in kindergarten," he said, "I was with my teacher, Miss MacKenzie and my best friend, Greg and I...and ..." He broke off and ran further down the ridge, choosing another place and pressing down with the ball of his foot. This time he found himself in the middle of a quarrel between his mother and father. His mother was crying and telling his father that if he came home drunk once more, she was leaving and taking Marc with her. Marc quickly removed his foot - this was one memory he'd rather not remember. He roved over the surface of his brain, choosing spots at random in the channels of his memory and reliving fragments of his life. At length he returned to where Chango was waiting.

"That was awesome," he told the deity. "I can't believe I'd forgotten so much - so many people who were important to me…most of them have disappeared from my life."

"Do you want them back?" Chango asked.

"Some of them," Marc replied, "but they might not want to come. I kind of lost them."

"Like Greg?"

"Yeah," Marc said regretfully. "We were friends all through school and he was part of my first band, but he never dug the rock scene and he quit just before my first hit single. I've often wanted to call him, but I never quite knew what I'd say."

" 'Hello, how are you?' is always a good start," said Chango.

"And then there's Angel," Marc said. "I'm afraid I might lose her. I just replayed the day we met...I'd forgotten how she knocked me out...still does, come to think."

Chango regarded the young musician levelly, then he said: "Have you noticed the sparks all around?

"Yes."

"Do you know what they are?"

"Electrical impulses, I guess."

"Yes, but they're more than that. Each spark is a movement or idea. The steady ones are automatic responses like breathing or blinking and the others represent memory, thought, decision making, all the things that create your intellect and personality."

He led Marc to an area where sparks were trying to leap a valley to connect with a ridge on the other side. They were weak and instead of crossing to their connection, they fizzled and faded in mid-air.

Chango put his hand on Marc's arm. "This is what I brought you to see. It's a broken connection. These can happen for many reasons - aging, illness...."

"...or drug and alcohol abuse," Marc finished. "I think it's called synapse failure."

"Look around you," Chango said, "there are many like that. Let's see that one over there."

Holding onto Marc's shoulder, the Orisha steered him to a shallow ridge that was some distance away. The spark, which had been fairly bright when Marc began heading towards it, was growing dimmer each time it ignited and as they watched, it gave a faint crackle and went out.

"We'll go down here," Chango said, indicating the crevice that the spark had been trying to cross. Chango and Marc slipped into the narrow opening, coasted downwards and found themselves in a large room filled with people. Some were elderly or infirm, several were sitting by themselves, rocking in a rhythm only they could hear, while others drifted in aimless circles. A few used walkers, some were in wheelchairs and two of the oldest were tied into what looked like children's high chairs. Male and female nurses were dotted around the room and in one corner was an old upright piano where a young woman sat, playing a simple tune. The music caught the attention of a few people who went over to the piano.

"Hello, Harry...Hi, Sylvia...how are you Gerald?..." The woman greeted each person by name as she continued playing. "Is there anything special you'd like to hear today?"

The woman called Sylvia had wispy white hair, which stuck out at crazy angles; her pink scalp gleamed through the sparse strands. Her eyes, once dark brown, were faded to a tan colour and the skin of her face and hands was wrinkled and blotched with the marks of age. She plucked at the pianist's sleeve and mumbled something.

"What was that, Sylvia?" the young woman asked, "I didn't quite hear you."

Sylvia took a deep breath and tried again "Alice.... Gown."

"You always ask for that. Isn't there anything else you'd like to hear?"

Sylvia shook her head and said again, more firmly this time, "Alice... Gown."

"I tell you what. I'll play it if you'll sing it with me. Will you do that?"

Nodding happily, the old woman looked at the two men who were sitting quietly.

"Alice...Gown," she announced importantly.

The pianist's tinkling drifted into the opening notes of the song and she began to sing: "In my sweet little Alice blue gown, as I first wandered down through the town...come on, Sylvia - you promised to sing, too. Let's start over."

She played the introduction again and sang the first line. This time Sylvia joined in; she was several beats behind and sang only the last few words of each line, but her eyes shone and her fragile hands swayed to the music.

One of the men who had been wandering around the room was captured by the sound and he lumbered over to the piano. He was a thickset man whose dulled eyes indicated heavy medication. He stood, hunched over, gazing at the floor until the song ended, then he sat on the edge of the piano bench, nudging the young woman beside him, who smiled at him and said: "And what would you like to hear?"

His only response was to move further up the bench, pushing the pianist along until she had to either stand or end up on the floor. She got up and stood beside the piano, eyeing him cautiously. A male nurse came over to them but the pianist shook her head slightly, indicating that he should do nothing and he stood silently behind the figure slouched over the keyboard.

"Want to play." The voice was thick as if his tongue was too large for his mouth. He raised his hands which were as bloated as his body, and crashed them onto the keyboard.

"Want to play…want to *play*...WANT TO PLAY!!!" The splayed hands repeatedly smashed the keys.

Harry and Gerald had wheeled their chairs away at the first sign of trouble but Sylvia sat frozen; hands clasped over her ears and eyes tightly shut while her thin screams counterpointed the thunderous discord.

The nurse leaned over and clamped his arms around the seated figure who roared with rage, twisting from side to side as he tried to shake off his attacker while still pounding the keyboard. His attendant held on grimly while two more nurses ran to help and the patient was soon subdued and taken from the room. The young woman returned to the piano and began to play a quiet melody as calm was restored.

Marc turned to Chango. "That was quite a performance."

"Not one of your better ones, my brother," Chango replied.

"What do you mean - that wasn't … that isn't..."

Chango cocked a quizzical eyebrow, "Not you? I'm afraid it was...or will be."

Marc turned ashen. "But that man was nothing like me. He was fat and clumsy and his hands were useless. His hair was thin and his eyes were dead...that wasn't *me*, I tell you. It can't be...it *won't* be me."

"Come," Chango said, "it's time to go back." He touched his forefinger to Marc's forehead; there was a moment's blackness and then they were back at Marc's loft, staring into the fire. They sat in silence for a while, then Marc said:

"I get the picture. If I don't want to short out altogether, I'd better clean up my act."

Chango nodded kindly. "I knew you would understand."

Marc gave a grim smile. "It's one thing to understand and another to act upon the understanding. A few guys manage to kick it, but I've seen too many who failed over and over. Every time they swear they're finished and every time they go back to the scene. Some of them aren't around any more and those that are - well..." His voice trailed off.

"There's one thing you have that they didn't," Chango told him. "You have me."

Marc looked hopeful, "You mean you can say a few magic words and I'll be cured? No more drink - no more dope?"

"Not quite," Chango said carefully. "To do that that would take away your free will and I don't want to do that. What I can do is to remove the physical cravings - the emotional need will have to be overcome by you."

Marc grasped Chango's hands. "If you do, I *swear* I can handle the rest." he said fervently. "I've been so scared by not being able to write because I'm smashed - or stoned - or both and I've been taking it out on everyone - especially Angel. Let's do it - right now."

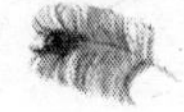

A week later Marc began to feel alive again. He'd been wrapped in a cocoon of drugs and alcohol that smothered his creativity and bred negative feelings about everything in his life. Now, with his physical being in good shape, he was finding the emotional strength needed to overcome his addictions. True to his word, Chango had healed Marc's body, sweeping away all traces of damage and leaving every muscle and organ in perfect order. He took huge pride in his work and kept demonstrating how he'd accomplished the job until Marc begged him to stop:

"It isn't that I'm not grateful, but there's a limit to how often I can watch you re-create the cleansing of my circulatory system."

"Then let us look at the purging of your kidneys."

"We did that yesterday."

"And the lung regeneration?"

"I found the left side even more fascinating than the right. We have also toured my liver several times and revisited every intestine I own, not to mention making a major reconnaissance of my head. I know myself in a way that no other human being can claim and I thank you for making such self-enlightenment possible."

Chango nodded resignedly. It was a new experience for him to perform miracles of the kind that he'd wrought on Marc; battles and entwinings were more his usual line of work, and he had been surprised to discover that he enjoyed operating on a higher plane. His thoughts brightened; just because he was a warrior god didn't mean that he couldn't also have a healing path; maybe he'd have a talk with Obatala about expanding his responsibilities.

The video for *Orisha Dance* was finished and the wrap party was in full swing, held in the studio where the video had been shot. Everyone involved with the production was there and to add to the buzz, Roger Tallant, the CEO of Worldtempo Records, had been brought by Theo, who was in acute party mode.

"Sara, you Gallic enchantress, give me a huge kiss!"

"Theo, *mon petit chou* - I will give you two kisses because I can't decide which side of your face is cuter."

"What's the difference? He talks out of both sides at once."

"Jonathan! You are just in time." Sara gave him a quick hug then climbed onto a chair and waved her arms: "*Attendez, mes amis*. Please give your attention for *Orisha Dance*".

The lights dimmed, the giant screen flashed countdown numbers and then dissolved into swirling ribbons of red, blue, yellow, orange, purple and green. Drums, clavés and chekerés played soft, insistent beats against the sound of plashing water. The colours twisted into the double helix of the DNA spiral, then spread into a magnificent rainbow arcing over a wide river.

On the riverbank was a group of drummers and singers. Three women had their hands plunged into the river, beating the water in a variety of liquid rhythms.

In front of the drummers, Eleggua sat cross-legged on the ground. The tempo of the drums increased and the singers began the Yoruba chant for the god of the crossroads. Eleggua rose in one motion, growing in height until he towered over the scene.

"Sing to Eleggua," chanted the leader.

"Praise for Eleggua," responded the chorus.

This was repeated three times and with each repetition, Eleggua alternately shrank to the size of a mouse and stretched tall again.

The tempo changed and Oya appeared. She began to spin, gradually moved faster and faster until she was a blur, while the singers offered a praise verse in her name.

The drums' voices deepened, the singers called for the god of fire and Chango filled the screen, breathing flames and throwing his thunder stones while he performed a set of thirty-six *fouettés* that Baryshnikov would have envied.

A peacock feather fan filled the screen, waving lazily then folding to reveal the ravishing face of Oshun in extreme close-up. The camera pulled back to a full shot of the dazzling goddess who undulated like the river, wafting the fan to and fro in time to the singers' voices.

The last verse praised all the deities and the song was repeated as the Orisha danced together and then climbed the rainbow, which faded slowly together with the song

Roger Tallant was beside himself. "It's a bloody marvel," he enthused: "this is going to be the hottest number ever!!"

"Just what I've been saying," beamed Theo.

"Congratulations to all of you," Tallant shook hands all around. When he came to Marc, he said: "I hear you have further work planned along this line, Dupré. I'd like to talk to you about it."

"Any time," Marc said, doing internal cartwheels.

"Theo," Angel grabbed the diminutive agent by the arm. "Can we have *Orisha Dance* performed live at

Vegging Out? The video will have been aired by then and it will be the perfect headline act."

"I don't see why not," he replied. "Of course, Chango and the rest will have to agree to perform..."

Angel laughed derisively. "*Agree* to perform? They practically weld themselves to any camera in sight."

"Coming up we have *Orisha Dance*, and with us to talk about the amazing success of his composition is Marc Dupré...Marc, thank you for getting up so early for *the Kevin and Cecily Show*."

"It is my pleasure, Cecily - who could resist Toronto's leading morning programme?"

"You're too kind." She smiled coyly at Marc while mentally calculating the possibility of a fast one with him after the programme. Cecily Michaels was a notorious starfucker. Her co-host, recognizing that measuring look, dived into the conversation.

"Marc, we've been getting more requests for *Orisha Dance* than for all other new releases put together and I know the same thing is happening on other stations, not to mention all the downloads. What do you think is the reason?"

"Well, Kevin, it's a combination of things. First of all, we have the tremendous talent of Chango as the lead singer plus Babatunde Gbadeo's band."

"For those listeners who may not know," Kevin added, "Babatunde Gbadeo is the most famous musician in West Africa"

"He was amazing to work with." Marc said

"And Chango?" Cecily asked. "He is the most be-yoo-tiful man I've ever seen in my life."

"He's a cool looking dude," agreed Marc.

"Getting back to *Orisha Dance*," Kevin cut in, "the lyrics are in African as well as English, right?"

"They're Yoruban and they're catchy and easy to remember, as are the dance steps."

"And it's a line dance which is always such fun," Cecily added.

"The information says that this is a 'Praise Song'. What does that mean, exactly?" Kevin asked.

"The African gods, who are called Orisha, have songs written specifically for them. Each deity has unique powers, and these are acknowledged by separate tunes and drum tempos. The gods have their own numbers as well, so in *Orisha Dance* we have three sets of calls and responses for Eleggua, five for Oshun, six for Chango and nine for Oya. The dance steps are adaptations of the traditional movements that are used in ceremonies to call the Orisha down to earth."

"People say that they feel wonderful when they listen to *Orisha Dance*, and all of us at the station experience a tremendous sense of well-being whenever we hear it."

"That's interesting, Cecily." Marc said, "because the Yoruba tradition says that the more one praises the Orisha in song and dance, the happier one is."

"Now, about the performers," said Kevin. "Everyone knows that Oshun is the hottest model since Kate Moss, and Chango is making a huge name for himself as a singer and dancer, but the other two - Eleggua and Oya - are an unknown quantity."

"Is it a coincidence that all of them have the same names as the gods and goddesses they represent in the video," Cecily cut in, "or are they stage names?"

"Those are their actual names," Marc replied. "It's not unusual for Yorubans to be named after their deities. We do the same thing in the western world. Look at all the Marys and Josephs and in Spanish speaking cultures, Jesus is a very common name."

"That's true," said Kevin.

Marc continued: "As for Eleggua and Oya being untried talent - they're not well-known in Canada, but they're famous in Africa and are highly accomplished dancers, as you'll see when the video premières Thursday night on *Music! Music! Music!*"

"At ten pm," said Kevin.

"We can't wait to see it," Cecily burbled.

"Before we went on air you mentioned that you're composing a symphony based on the Yoruban deities," Kevin said.

"Yes. It's called *Pathways* and I hope to have it completed by the end of next year."

"We'll look forward to it. Marc, thank you for being with us this morning"

"Thank you, Kevin. Thanks, Cecily."

"That was Marc Dupré, composer of *Orisha Dance* and now let's hear the song nobody can get enough of."

Kevin Anderson switched off the mike, pushed back his chair and grinned at Marc as the sounds of *Orisha Dance* filled the studio.

"Great interview, Marc.

"Thanks, I enjoyed it."

"Do you have time for coffee after the show?"

"Sorry, Cecily. I have an appointment across town in half an hour so I'd better make a move."

"Too bad you can't make yours," Kevin whispered to his co-host who gave him a black look and flounced out of the studio.

"These early morning shows will be the death of me!" Three interviews later, Marc had returned to Angel's apartment, He sank into a kitchen chair, gesturing desperately for coffee. Angel gave him a large mug of café au lait into which Marc shovelled three heaping spoons of coffee sugar crystals. Emptying the mug in one draught, he refilled it, took a piece of toast and ate it quickly, saying between bites, I have to get to the studio."

"And I have a meeting with Alix to finalize the launch plans."

"Do we have anything on tonight?"

"A vernissage at The Old Paint gallery, the opening of a Chai house on Queen West and Belinda Bardon's annual Oyster Quadrille."

"Can we can skip them? I want to go to The King Cole Room. Brian Browne is playing and I don't often get a chance to hear him."

"We can forget the first two, but we *must* show our faces at Belinda's." Angel shuddered delicately, "How anyone can even *look* at an oyster let alone swallow one of the glutinous little globs is beyond me."

Marc laughed at her squeamishness. "Oysters are the supreme taste sensation. We'll go for just half an hour, I'll take you to Jamie Kennedy's for dinner and *then* we'll go hear Brian, OK?"

"You got it." She gave him a quick kiss, grabbed her briefcase and said "do me a favour darling - clear away and turn on the dishwasher - I'm way behind schedule.. See you later."

Orisha Dance was an overnight sensation; radio stations were playing it every hour, which hadn't happened since The Beatles' *"Sergeant Pepper,"* and Eleggua and Oya had become hot news. Eleggua took it all in stride but Oya turned into a diva on a grand scale and alternated between signing autographs at the drop of a pen or haughtily waving fans away.

The long awaited video was having its premiere on *Music! Music! Music!* at ten pm complete with a personal appearance by the four stars, and excitement was almost as high among the TV staff as it was for the waiting fans. The difference was that the fans weren't running around self-importantly or crashing into each other with lengths of cable.

An enormous screen faced the window and sound was piped outside so that sidewalk viewers would see and hear as well as the audience inside.

The perky but vacuous Ulrika Dee was conducting the interview. Ulrika had an enormous following because of her infectious giggle and hip-hop wardrobe, but she wasn't noted for her ability to think on her feet; nor, said a jealous colleague, on her back.

Ulrika was in her element. Her black and blonde hair was done in her trademark dreads and she was wearing a mix of Volcom and Tommy Hilfiger. The bleachers were filled to capacity and there was an enormous crowd outside. The air inside and out was thick with excitement and Ulrika was bouncing off the walls as she introduced the Orisha, mispronouncing their names and tittering hysterically over every mangled syllable.

The Orisha had been smuggled into the building through the basement but when the mob outside saw them on the giant screen, all hell broke loose. Those in front were in danger of being pushed through the glass walls but Eleggua came to the window and began to play his flute. The soft little tune immediately calmed the crowd, enabling security to move more staff into the area.

The audience was so wired by being in the same space as the Orisha that they shouted and cheered until the studio vibrated. As the excitement grew, the interview crumbled. Ulrika was mouthing questions that couldn't be heard and the Orisha were unable to respond. Wisely, the director gave up and instructed the cameramen to pan the audience and then dissolve to the video.

The colours swirled, the percussion tapped the introduction and the audience clapped in time to the drums. The singing began and everyone, inside and out, joined in the call and response choruses. When the dancing began, the crowd mirrored every move as if they'd practised for months. At the close, the producer signalled for the video to play again; this time the cameras cut back and forth between the video and the audience. At the second ending, the cameras were full on the audience which was how the world first saw the amazing effect of *Orisha Dance*, with everyone hugging friends and strangers alike, laughing and calling praises to the Orisha. It was magical and the deities were deeply moved.

"This is even more respect than we get at home," Chango said to Eleggua, while they smiled and waved at the crowd.

"At home we're family," replied the levelheaded Eleggua. "Here we're new and exotic. Just enjoy it and don't get carried away."

Oshun and Oya blew kisses to all and sundry while Theo worried about getting his charges out of the building before the excitement got out of control.

In a seedy pub not far from the studios, a group of motor cycle thugs known as Hitler's Heroes had been watching the programme on the giant screen. It would be hard to find a more unappealing bunch outside of World War Two; some were overweight gonzos and others were scrawny little weasels. Many wore shaved heads and some had masses of unkempt hair. Two of them were women and they were even more frightening than the men.

"Look at that choice chunk of dark meat, Darlene," said the tall redhead named Susie. Her hot, mean eyes were riveted to Chango's image, "He's got more muscles than the Mr. Harley-Davidson winner."

"I saw him on the tube the other day," Darlene, a doughy blonde, replied. "He moves like a greased eel sliding down a firehouse pole."

"Maybe we should put him through a few of those moves." The leader of the group, a malodorous mountain named Ozzie the Ogre had joined the conversation, "And while we're at it, we can play with the rest of them, particularly those little chocolate dolls." He put his huge, dirty thumb on the part of the screen that showed Oshun and Oya.

Turning back to the bar, he tossed back a boilermaker and clapped his Nazi helmet on his head.

"Come on, you lot," he growled, "it's party time."

They knocked back their drinks and filed out in a loud yet orderly fashion.

A few minutes later, the Orisha, shepherded by Theo, slipped out the back door of the studio. Salif and the limousine were waiting but also on hand were Hitler's Heroes, lounging on their motorcycles, replete with knives, maces and other exotic weaponry. They were kitted out in black leather with spiked metal armbands and heavy chains In addition to the ubiquitous swastikas, many had huge skull and crossbones pendants around their necks. Chango froze in horror at the sight of the skulls and Oshun, Oya and Eleggua shielded him while Theo closed his eyes and prayed as he had not done since his bar mitzvah.

The gang had surrounded the limousine and were amiably terrorizing Salif who sat, ashen-faced behind the wheel. Catching sight of the Orisha, the riders pulled their cycles up in a closed circle around the car.

Ozzie the Ogre dismounted and lumbered over to the group.

"It's about time you came out - we've been waiting to meet you, ain't we?" His cohorts made subhuman noises of agreement.

"We been hearin' a lot about you," he continued, especially the big guy hidin' behind the others. Whaz your name - Changoo?"

The god of fire, eyes closed against the sight of the skulls, spoke with cold fury.

"My name is Chango, you festering moron. Remove yourselves from our path or it will be the worse for you."

Ozzie rolled his eyes in mock terror and again addressed his followers:

"D' you hear that? He's threat'nin' us - us who only wants an autograph but they probably can't write, like all them jungle bunnies. Hey - Changoo - look at me when I'm talkin' to ya, y' black bugger."

The other Orisha had remained silent. They were in human form and in physical danger. Imperceptibly, Eleggua signalled Oya and Oshun to move closer to Chango while he drew aside.

"Where d'y' think you're goin', bone bag?" Darlene grabbed Eleggua's arm with her dirt-encrusted talons.

Smiling disdainfully, he removed her fingers from his arm by bending them backwards one by one. She screeched in pain and Ozzie the Ogre lunged at Eleggua who sidestepped deftly and imperceptibly switched back to his metaphysical form.

"Grab them," Ozzie bellowed to his followers. "After we deal with the dudes we'll have a few giggles with the two black beauties."

Still obeying Eleggua's unspoken order, Chango, Oya and Oshun offered no resistance to the group that surrounded them. Salif, locked inside the Rolls, watched in terror. He was safe for the time being - until one of the horrible animals decided to break a window, he said glumly to himself. Theo resigned himself to the knowledge that they'd all be dead within the next ten minutes and launched into the *Shemah*, the prayer that Jews recite at the time of death. In the midst of his terror he felt absurdly proud of himself for remembering it.

Strolling up to Eleggua who was being held by two of the Heroes' finest, Ozzie the Ogre took hold of a fistful of the god's dreadlocks and brought Eleggua nose to nose with his own revolting face.

"Y'know what's the matter with you, dude? You're black - black as the inside of a coal cellar at midnight and black is a colour of which I'm not fond."

Eleggua smiled coolly: "For someone who doesn't like black, you wear a lot of it."

"That's just my clothes, innit? My skin is white like the skins of all right-thinkin' folks."

"But how monotonous, my dear fellow. Think how much more interesting you would be if you were, perhaps, purple."

Suddenly Ozzie was the colour of a California raisin.

"Ooooooooo!" went his followers.

"Aaaarrrggh!!!!" said Ozzie seeing himself reflected in various pairs of mirrored sunglasses.

"And for you, madame," Eleggua addressed Susie the Floozy: "let's try this. I call it 'Lawsy, Miz' Scarlett!"

Susie turned redder than a radish patch at sunset.

Eleggua warmed to his work as he focused his attention on the two goons who had been holding him: narrowing his eyes artistically, he crooned:

"It's not easy being green..."

They became as emerald skinned as a couple of Kermits.

Swiftly, Eleggua went around the group, transforming them into a living rainbow. One he tinted buttercup yellow, another orange, a tall, thin Hero became puce and chartreuse - and he turned Darlene an exquisite shade of sky blue. By the time he was finished the gang was colourful in the truest sense of the word. He then addressed the motorcycle thugs whom he had prudently frozen in place when he began his painting spree.

"I have given you new colours to show you that, no matter what shade your skins are, you all remain the same inside. You," he tweaked Ozzie the Ogre's beard, "are just as repulsive with purple skin as you were when you were white and green skin doesn't make you two any better or worse than you were a few moments ago. The same goes for the rest of you - red, white or blue, you're just colourful blotches on the face of humanity."

Ozzie and company struggled to free themselves but were held fast.

Eleggua opened the back doors of the limousine and Theo guided the other deities inside. Once they were seated, Eleggua turned back to the gang who were alternately cursing him and begging him to restore them to their former selves. He held up a long, bony hand and there was instant silence.

"When we have gone, movement will be restored to you and you can go your way."

"Like this??!!!??" Ozzie turned, if possible, even more purple. "What are you going to do about this?" He gestured wildly with his head, his only movable part, to indicate himself and the others.

"I've done quite enough already," Eleggua replied: "The rest is up to you."

"Whaddya mean?"

"If you learn to live decent, law-abiding lives; if you practise tolerance and acceptance of others; and *if* - and this is stretching credibility - you begin to help your fellow beings, eventually your natural skin tones will be restored. If not..." He shrugged, smiled and dived into the car which swooped away, leaving the multi-hued mob to recover the use of their bodies.

Under cover of night, the gang rode away to their country hideout where most of them spent the rest of their lives, a source of wonder to the neighbouring cattle and the few neighbouring farmers with whom they occasionally had contact. Strangely enough, Ozzie the Ogre did rehabilitate himself and regained his normal colour within two years. He became a settlement house worker in one of Toronto's worst areas and performed minor miracles of interracial harmony with his young charges.

Susie was a different story. She loathed the country and, after a week of misery, took her share of the Heroes' ill-gotten gains, covered herself from head to toe and went back to Toronto. She booked a consultation with one of the city's leading plastic surgeons and at the appointed time was in the waiting room swathed in concealing garments. Dr. Hubert Oldfield was a discreet practitioner so there were no other clients to wonder at her sinister appearance but she gave the receptionist a bit of a jolt. Once in the consultation room, Susie squatted on her chair like a malevolent crow and when Dr. Oldfield entered he was almost as taken aback as his staff had been. However, he was a consummate professional, and masked his unease while offering his hand to Susie's gloved claw.

"How may I help you, Miss Smith?"

"I have a problem, Doctor."

“Everyone who comes to see me has a problem.”

“Not like this,” Susie’s grim voice gave him a frisson of foreboding.

“Perhaps if you removed some of your outer garments?”

She clutched her coat more tightly around her: “You promise not to sneer?”

Visions of John Merrick danced in his head:

“Miss Smith - I’m a cosmetic surgeon. Whatever is the matter, I can assure you that you will be treated with the greatest sympathy.”

Susie shrugged off her coat, removed her hat, scarves and sunglasses and stood, glowing ruddily in front of him.

He gazed at her mutely for a moment, then cleared his throat:

“Is it only your face and hands that are affected, or....”

“All of me,” she said briefly.

“Have you had this condition from birth?”

“Since last week.”

“How did it happen?”

“You don’t want to know.”

“If I am to help you, I *have* to know.”

“You won’t laugh?”

“Laughter is the furthest thing from my mind.”

To himself he added: *wild, screeching hysteria, perhaps, but not laughter.*

Susie gave Doctor Oldfield an expurgated version of the encounter with the Orisha. She and her friends were fans who had been waiting to see these hot new stars as they left the studio.

“They came out, we asked them for autographs and the next thing I knew, I was as you see me.”

“And your friends?”

“Every colour you can think of.”

Doctor Oldfield sat, his hands steepled with fingertips touching, deep in thought. The woman was obviously mentally unbalanced but, equally obviously, she *was* red from head to foot.

"Miss Smith, we'll have to run some tests. I'm going to book you into my clinic right away. You'll have complete privacy and it won't take more than a day or so to determine the extent of the damage."

Two days later Susie and Doctor Oldfield were back in his consultation room staring gloomily at each other.

"So, you're telling me there's nothing you can do?"

"Nothing. I'm sorry, Miss Smith, the pigmentation runs so deeply through your skin that nothing can remove it. Sadly, you are, for all time, a painted lady."

Susie stood up, engulfed herself in her coat, hat, scarves and sunglasses and left with Dr. Oldfield's words ringing in her ears. She took a taxi straight to Toronto's most exclusive house of pleasure and, after the madame, a friend of Susie's, overcame her first shock at seeing her old acquaintance completely in the red, she listened with interest to Susie's proposition that she take up residence, billed as *The Scarlet Woman.*

"You could be the most popular piece in the house, Suze," she mused. "My Johns like novelty and rubescence would mean tumescence for a lot of them."

So it proved. Susie became the star of the Novello Bordello and spent many lucrative years there as a whore with a heart of ruby.

"And so, gentlemen...and ladies," Dr. Oldfield gave a hasty nod to the two women present: "It behooves the Canadian Association of Cosmetic Surgery to take a very sober look at the claims being made by. If this *Oshun's*

Gold does even half of what Alix Morton says it does, we could be in serious difficulty."

"Hubert - sorry I'm tardy... got back late last night from the Galapagos. Had a great time but it sounds like all hell has been breaking loose around here. Are you saying that Glissando Beauté is claiming to have bottled the fountain of youth?"

Dr. Oldfield turned a long-suffering eye towards the speaker who had just entered the room, coffee and a bagel in hand. "What I am saying, Stanley, is that this lotion supposedly has the power to remove wrinkles and lines *and* to restore lost muscle tone. If that's true, it means adieu to breast boosting, farewell to fanny-lifts and bye-bye to blephs."

Stanley Loudon, a cheerful, portly man who enjoyed considerable popularity among his peers, lifted an inquiring eyebrow at his colleague:

"Are penile implants also a thing of the past or do I still have my little joysticks to fiddle with?"

"This is no laughing matter, Stanley. I'm telling you...*all* of you...that we'd better start thinking of a way out of this situation."

Loudon's normally good-humoured expression hardened. He took a thoughtful bite of his bagel, chewing and swallowing soberly before addressing his colleagues:

"We've gone through a number of changes in the industry over the past few years: First there was phenol followed by retin A and its counterparts and next it was glycolic acid and then botox. We weren't able to do anything about them and we won't be able to do anything about *Oshun's Gold* either. But as I see it, the bottom line is that bottoms and other parts will still need lifting surgically. No little genie in a bottle can cure those problems."

"Hear, hear!"

"Right on, Stan!"

Louden's colleagues were loud in their endorsement of his opinion and Hubert Oldfield threw his hands up in exasperation and slapped them down on the table with such force that he caused himself considerable pain.

"What can I say in the face of such overwhelming complacency? I declare this meeting closed."

Driving home, Hubert Oldfield mentally reviewed what he knew about *Oshun's Gold* and the people involved. He was aware of Oshun - as the plastic surgeon of choice for many celebrities it was his business to keep abreast of show business news.- and had long known Alix Morton and grudgingly admired her, though he knew she had little use for him. She had, in fact, called him pompous and humourless to his face.

Now he found himself thinking of Susie and her ludicrous story of magical powers. He didn't believe it, but if the story could be doctored - he snickered to himself at his clever play on words - who *said* he had no sense of humour - and backed up by his test results on Susie's skin, it could go a long way towards helping to discredit the product that threatened his way of life. People could be made to believe that this would happen to them if they used *Oshun's Gold.* The first step was to locate Susie.

It didn't take long. A few judicious inquiries by a highly efficient private investigator and Dr. Oldfield and Susie were once more face to face, this time at her office.

"You're looking very well, my dear." He gazed intently at the rubicund figure in front of him.

She smiled sardonically but said nothing. Always an attractive if hard looking woman, Susie had made the most of her affliction and was stunning in a radishy kind of way. Her naturally red hair had been tinted to the exact shade of her skin and her eyebrows and lashes were in a darker tone, as were her lips and nails. She wore a long, sheer chiffon slip dress with drifting layers of vermilion, crimson and carmine and the overall effect was to make Dr. Oldfield not unpleasantly warm himself.

"Miss Smith - Susie - I have a proposition to put to you."

"Most men do."

"No - mine's different."

"That's what they all say. Well, what is it? Do you want to be tickled with ostrich feathers while handcuffed to a bed?..."

"No - I..."

"Would you like to be dressed in latex tights packed with ice cubes...?"

"No ..."

"Shall I dip your unmentionables in melted Toblerone and roll them in cocoa powder?"

"No...er... Toblerone - cocoa?" he said weakly.

"It's the ultimate chocolate experience, Doctor."

She slid off the couch, slithered over to Dr. Oldfield and began making businesslike movements that were both arousing and terrifying to him. With an effort he removed her hands, which had been rummaging intently in his nether regions.

"This is *not* why I'm here!"

"It isn't?" She rolled a skeptical eye at him.

"No!" He sat upright and rearranged his clothing with the air of an offended virgin.

"Oh, come on Doc, you sidle in here acting all coy and talking about propositions - what's a girl to think?"

"Well, you completely misconstrued the matter." he replied stiffly. Remembering that he needed this woman's goodwill, he unbent a little and gave her a prim smile:

"Susie - how would you like to earn a lot of money."

"I do," she replied, "there isn't a day in the week when I don't pull down at least five hundred dollars - tax free, of course."

"Of course," Dr. Oldfield agreed cordially, "But I'm talking about a huge amount of money - a lump sum which would allow you to live in comfort for the rest of your life."

"I'm pretty comfortable now...money rolling in....food, rent and all other expenses looked after..."

"That's now. What about when you're a little past it for this kind of life?"

"I'll never be past it - not with this new *Oshun's Gold.* I hear it works like a charm."

"What a coincidence that you should mention *Oshun's Gold*...that's just what I want to talk to you about."

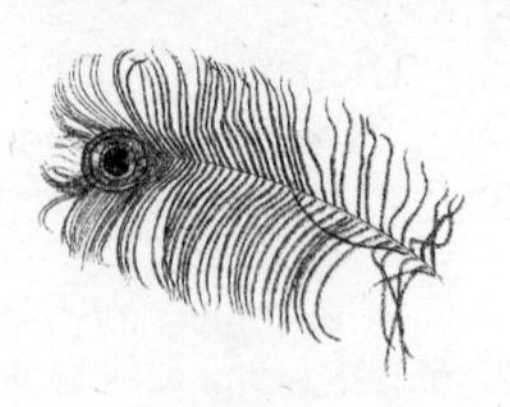

The launch day for *Oshun's Gold* had arrived. New products were usually unveiled simultaneously at the cosmetics departments of prestigious shops such as Holt Renfrew, Bloomingdale's and Harrod's, but *Oshun's Gold* was having a more exclusive debut. Glissando Beauté had booked the entire ballroom floor of the Royal York Hotel and people began lining up the day before, complete with chairs, sleeping bags and other camping out comforts. It was like the scene for an upcoming rock concert, except that the majority of the crowd were middle-aged women.

Beverley Morgan, Glissando's head of sales, deployed her staff with the skill of a MacArthur. All was in place. The focal point, a cordoned-off area filled with pyramids of *Oshun's Gold* boxes, was where Oshun would make her appearance.

Ms. Morgan adjusted her lapel microphone and smiled austerely at the throng:

"Good afternoon, ladies and gentlemen and welcome to the launch of *Oshun's Gold,* the only product in history to deliver the promise it makes – beauty, lasting youth and glowing health…

The ensuing roar of excitement made further speech impossible, so above the cacophony Beverly shouted: "And now - the inspiration for this amazing elixir - the legendary Oshun!"

A concealed door opened and the goddess glided out. Dazzling in a simple golden robe with a multi-stranded necklace of topaz beads, she exuded African mystique and the audience was struck dumb. Smiling benevolently, Oshun touched her fingertips to her lips and blew a kiss to the crowd which unleashed a storm of applause punctuated with tears and screams.

"Thank you," she cooed in her honeyed contralto: "Your wonderful reception makes me very happy and I am delighted to see such interest in *Oshun's Gold* which will astonish you with its results. I know you are eager to have this elixir for your own, and it is now time to begin your voyage into recaptured youth."

What happened next wasn't pretty. Everyone on the Glissando staff was prepared for a buying frenzy. Many extra salespeople had been hired, security guards were on hand and the St. John's Ambulance was there to administer to victims of over-excitement. But even the best-laid plans can crumble into ruins. A trio of sixty-something women all wanting to be the first to purchase *Oshun's Gold.* fought their way to the front, each trying to hold back the others and fell in a tangled heap of bleached blonde hair and jangling jewellery. Before they collapsed, they had stepped on so many toes, elbowed so many ribs and infuriated so many other customers that what began as minor pushing and shoving, blossomed into a full-scale free for all.

A well-padded matron emerged from the melée with half her clothes clawed off, her glasses looped around one ear and her left arm hanging useless. Her right hand clutched a box of *Oshun's Gold*, which she had snatched from a countertop display and a Visa card was wedged firmly between her teeth. Reaching the salesclerk, she genteelly spat the card onto the counter, smiled triumphantly at all around her and slid to the floor, unconscious but holding firm to her prize.

It was at this moment, while attention was focused on the comatose woman that Susie made her move.

"Remember," Hubert Oldfield had instructed her: "Make sure nobody notices you until you're ready, then drop your cloak, hold out the empty vial and scream. Everyone will look at you and that's when you launch into a hysterical tirade of what this lotion has done."

"Where are you going to get a vial of *Oshun's Gold*?"

He laughed indulgently. "I'm not – it will be up to you to get a vial."

"What?"

"Don't play coy with me, my girl," the benevolent pose was gone. "I know you've done a little lifting more than once and it'll be child's play for you to take a box off the counter in all the excitement.

"We-ell, okay." Susie acquiesced reluctantly.

"That's better," Oldfield said crisply. "You're being given a lot of money for this little bit of work - make sure it runs smoothly."

The time was at hand. Susie stood close to the front of the crowd, which was so dense that it was almost impossible to move. From under her cape, she took a small steel rod with pincers on one end of it and a push button on the other. Sliding it deftly between the two rows of people ahead and up to the display counter, she positioned the pincers over a box of *Oshun's Gold.* Susie pressed the button and the pincers opened; one more click and they snapped shut around the box, which she swiftly drew back to her. Putting the box in her pocket she retracted the rod, concealing it again within the folds of her cape.

Susie headed to the washroom where she went into a cubicle, removed the little vial from its packaging and threw the box into the garbage bin. Pointless to waste the contents, she thought, snapping open the vial, and rubbing the golden liquid all over her face, neck and arms. She tucked the empty container into the deep pocket of her cape and paused briefly to check her appearance in the mirror. Was it her imagination or were the frown lines at the bridge of her nose already a little fainter? Making a mental note to lift a few more boxes of *Oshun's Gold*, she left the washroom.

Threading her way back to the ballroom, Susie stood off to the side and watched the frenzied sales activity for a few moments then, taking a deep breath, she grasped the vial, dropped her cloak and opened her mouth to scream. In that moment, Eleggua, who had been watching her closely from behind a pillar, changed her back.

"If I ever have to go through anything like that again I'll be back in Oshogbo before you can blink." Oshun was not a happy goddess. She warmed to her theme: "What a madhouse! What a bunch of maniacs! What a..."

"What a triumph! What a sensation! "Alix burst into the room where Angel and Oshun had collapsed: "Have you any *idea* what happened here today?"

"Seventeen cases of hysteria, a broken arm, two sprained ankles and more cuts, bruises and contusions than at the running of the bulls at Pamplona," replied Angel.

Alix waved a dismissive hand: "Our insurance will cover everything and each of the victims has received five complimentary boxes of *Oshun's Gold.*

" I just hope this madness will die down soon."

"It will. When people realize that there's enough product for everyone they'll stop battling their way to the counters."

"I suppose you're right. In the meantime we've got to get out of here without attracting the attention of that mob."

“The car is at the back entrance with the Dreadnaughts. They’ll get us safely home.”

The Dreadnoughts were Alix’s name for the squad of bodyguards that accompanied Oshun everywhere.

“Do I have to stay cooped up? Oshun said plaintively. “I’m used to adoring crowds, but at home they worship me from afar; here they rip my clothes off for souvenirs.”

“I know, dear,” Alix patted Oshun’s hand: “But this is how celebrities are treated by their adoring public; they don’t know you’re a goddess.”

“If they knew that, they’d be even harder to control,” Angel said.

“I’m tired of pretending to be a mortal and I want to come out of the cupboard.”

“Closet,” Angel corrected absently.

“Whatever. I want to be a goddess again.”

“You can’t. All hell would break loose”

“ It’s my job and I miss doing it.”

Angel threw up her hands in despair: “Alix - *you* talk to her!”

Alix put a sympathetic arm around Oshun: “Angel’s right. If people knew the truth, they’d be hounding you night and day, begging you to perform miracles, promising you undying devotion, showering you with tributes...”

“And the problem with that is…?”

Alix looked up to the ceiling, praying for strength and then turned back to talk to the discontented Orisha.

“Oshun, you simply *must* ...Oshun...Oshun, where are you?”

A faint tinkle of laughter was the only answer.

Can you *imagine* what will happen if she blows her cover?” Angel paced the room, twisting her hair with both hands.

"Yes. We'd get more publicity than the Second Coming. Well, we can't do anything about her right now. Come on, I'll take you to Cibo and we'll worry down a little lunch."

Contrary to their fears, Oshun was back at the apartment, lying in an enormous marble bathtub filled with amber scented bubbles. Sandalwood incense smoked in a peacock-shaped cloisonné holder and a crystal flute of champagne stood at her right hand. She flicked idly at the bath's foam while thinking about recent events.

"What should I do? Stay here...? Go back to Oshogbo? Juggle both lives and deal with the fahionistas who worship at the shrine of Oshun Supermodel *and* the faithful followers of the Goddess Oshun? Too bad I can't use my powers of prophecy for myself."

She closed her eyes, leaned back, and sank deeper into the scented bath. Her mind went back to the time when she received the gift of divination.

It had been a glorious day - and as Oshun walked on the bank of her beloved river, she revelled in the sunlit sky and gold-spangled water. Suddenly, there came a loud splashing and a frantic cry:

"Stop! Stop, you thieving devil!"

A figure ran past her so quickly that all she saw was a blur but from the wild cackle of laughter she knew it was Eleggua.

Turning to the river, she found Obatala, crouching in the water and bellowing at the top of his lungs:

"Obatala, my father, what has happened?"

"I came to the river for a cooling swim and Eleggua stole my clothes! I know he likes to play practical jokes, but this is the outside of enough! I have to meet Yemaya in an hour and I'm stuck in this river like a hippopotamus in a mud wallow!"

Oshun eyed him speculatively:

"If I get your clothes back, what will you do for me?"

"I'll grant any wish you want. Just get my robes back quickly. Yemaya gets angry when I'm late and I don't need the aggravation."

Oshun had long craved to own the art of divination, but Obatala had always refused to teach her. Now was her chance.

"I want to learn divination."

"Very well! Bring me back my clothes and I promise to teach you."

Oshun was overjoyed: "I'll be back with them before you know it."

Leaving Obatala huddled in the water, Oshun hurried to her brass palace where she sprayed herself with her magic honey, painted and perfumed herself, changed into a magnificent yellow silk gown and went to Eleggua's house where she found the mischievous god sitting at his front door enjoying a pre-dinner cigar. Beside him, in a neat little pile, were Obatala's clothes and from time to time he looked at them and chuckled happily. Oshun watched him covertly for a while and then stepped forward:

"Give you good evening, Eleggua."

"Ah, good evening, Most Beautiful! To what do I owe the pleasure of your radiant presence?"

"To these," she replied, gesturing to Obatala's clothes with one hand and fending off Eleggua's encircling arm with the other.

"It's just my little joke, Loveliest of the Lovely," Eleggua said coaxingly, "come, give me one tiny kiss."

"Not even a handshake, you miserable creature. It's one thing to steal Obatala's clothes as a joke, but to take them away and leave him in the river is truly unkind. I'm disgusted with you!"

Eleggua traced circles in the dust with his bony toes. He looked up at Oshun plaintively.

"If I give them to you, will you give me a kiss?"

"Yes."

"Here you are, then," and he scooped up the clothes and gave them to Oshun, reaching for her at the same time. She took the robes, twirled laughingly out of his reach, blew him a kiss and flew back to the riverbank. She gave Obatala back his robes and reminded him of his promise, which he willingly kept, teaching her how to divine through all the methods: cowry shells, the coconut, the *opelé* chain and kola nuts. In return, however, Oshun had to agree to teach divination to any of the Orisha who wished to learn it. Most of them did, but, because self-divination isn't allowed in the Pantheon, the deities still had to consult each other regarding their own concerns, except for Eleggua, who knows everything.

"I *could* ask Eleggua," Oshun mused, running a little more hot water, "but he's such a troublemaker he'd probably give me the wrong advice just for the sheer joy of it. There's no point in asking Chango - he's too wrapped up in his new career. And Oluddumare knows I can't consult Oya." Sighing, she stepped out of the bathtub, wrapped herself in a towel and sat in front of her dressing table, comforting herself by combing her beautiful long hair.

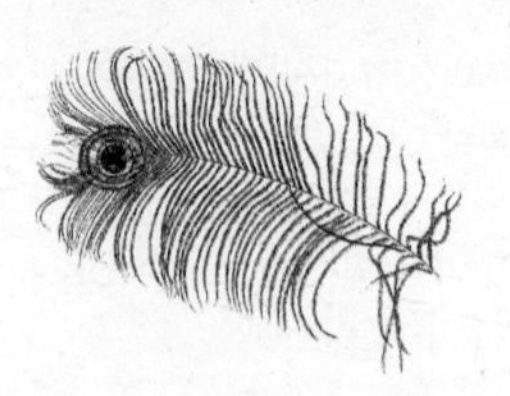

"I'm excited about tomorrow," Oshun said to Angel, "but it's too bad that I can't wear any of my wonderful new clothes." As she spoke, she slid clothes hangers along the rod, eyeing each one with longing: Yellow silk jersey dress with an ostrich feather hemline…gold metallic mesh jump suit...a floor length slip of honey coloured lace to be worn over a citrine body stocking...the inventory was endless but none was appropriate for her celebrity chef appearance at *Vegging Out.*

"So, I'll wear robes and a *gelé*," Oshun made a moué of distaste.

"No matter what you wear you'll be the most beautiful creature there." Angel said soothingly.

"I always *am*! Sometimes it's more fun to be ugly - like when I'm the Crone."

"It's only fun when you know it's not permanent. I've done ugly and it's no picnic."

"You, Angel? But you're lovely!"

"When I was young I had a forehead approximately an inch high, a large, bony nose, terminal freckles, a lazy eye and an overbite that let me to eat an apple from across the road. It took an army of orthadontists, ophthalmologists and dermatologists to turn me into something from which nobody ran screaming in terror. Later on came the nose job, the chin implant, the electrolysis-created hairline and a host of other enhancers, all of which turned me into the passably good-looking woman you see today."

"And what do *you* see?"

" I can see an attractive woman in the mirror, but on the inside I still feel like that skinny, ugly little freckled creature. Being beautiful from birth gives you a confidence that no amount of cosmetology can buy."

"That may be, but beauty is a double-edged sword. People love you because you are beautiful and you accept that but at the same time you despise them *because* they love you for your beauty. And often, beauty doesn't get you the love you really want."

"But you are the *goddess* of love and beauty."

Oshun gave a mirthless little laugh:

"Not even gods and goddesses have all their desires fulfilled, girlfriend. I suppose that's so we can relate to human suffering. Every man wants me, but the one I love will never be entirely mine."

"If you mean Chango, he loves you dearly."

"But he loves Oya more. So you see, not even the goddess of love can have her true love. Still, I suppose it's a small price to pay for all I do have."

She laughed again and said:

"That's enough moping for both of us. *Oshun's Gold* is causing a revolution, *Orisha Dance* is the biggest hit in history and your wonderful food fair is going to raise bushels of money; you should be happier than ever."

"I know." Angel twisted a lock of hair around her forefinger. "I should be over the moon - but...." she bit her lip and sighed deeply.

"Marc?"

"Yes. I'm worried about him. Last month he was on a non-stop bender of spliff and shooters and now he's given it all up and is into a cleansing binge... nothing but water, juices, meditation and Tai Chi. Every time he quits it lasts for a few days or weeks, and then he's back on the D and A track heavier than ever. I know everyone in the business does some stuff and, crazy as it sounds, I'd rather Marc indulged within reason, instead of making these wild swings from one extreme to the other."

Oshun said nothing; obviously Marc hadn't told Angel about Chango's help which meant that either he wasn't confident of success or that he wanted Angel to think he'd quit on his own - or perhaps both.

"On the other hand," Angel continued, "he's writing the most brilliant material for *Pathways,* so he must be doing something right."

Oshun seated herself and gestured to Angel to sit beside her.

"Do you remember what I said to you a while ago - that you and Marc are the moth and the flame and that you are always together?"

"Yes."

"It goes beyond that. You have always been together and always will be, in every life you've already had and every one that is yet to come."

"I'm not sure I believe in reincarnation, but if our relationships are always this stormy, I don't know whether to be glad or sorry."

Oshun laughed softly. "They are and you will be both glad and sorry, just as you are in this life."

Angel took a deep breath and smoothed her hair back from her face: "Well, I'd better get on with this particular life. I'm going down to the hotel to check the set-up."

Jonathan stopped riffling through the stack of files on his desk and looked at his watch. He had promised Angel that he'd make an appearance at *Vegging Out.*

I won't stay long, he thought - *Just a fast drink, a few handshakes and back to work.*

"But if you don't stay, my friend, you won't meet a charming woman who will find you of interest" came a voice from the depths of the porter's chair, which swivelled itself to face Jonathan, revealing Eleggua tucked, cross-legged in its depths.

Jonathan eyed him frigidly. "Eleggua, I've learned to put up with you barging in and out of my life whenever the fancy takes you - but this galloping around in my mind has *got* to stop. There isn't a thought I can call my own any more. Anyway - I don't *want* to meet a charming woman; I've had it with *all* women."

Eleggua smiled tolerantly at the frazzled lawyer. "Jonathan, my friend, you must learn to relax and go with the flowing. I have been all day at the Vegetaranian party and will return tonight for the performancing, but I have come to you for a special reason. It is time for me to reveal your path and the charming woman is a part of that."

"How often do I have to tell you - I don't want you to show me my path. Leave me *alone*, Eleggua, I'm perfectly happy as I am."

"Ah, yes? Well, let us look at 'as you are.' 'As you are' is working eighteen hours a day, seven days a week. 'As you are' is never seeing your friends and not taking any time for recreation. 'As you are' is an out of shape, miserable bundle of nerves that is well on the way to a heart attack or a stroke. All these things are 'as you are' and none of them is as you should be. Now-" Eleggua fixed Jonathan with a commanding stare: "Every other time I have *suggested* that I show you your path. But today, no more Mr. Nice God, I'm *taking* you there, like it or not."

Jonathan threw up his hands. "Okay - let's get it over with. What do we do?"

"I ride you."

"You *what*?"

"I take possession of you. Don't worry, - it doesn't hurt and you won't remember anything."

"Oh, no. No, no, no, no, *no*! If I have to do this, I insist on total recall." Jonathan folded his arms and regarded Eleggua challengingly across the expanse of his desk.

The Orisha sighed. "We're not negotiating a legal contract here, my friend but because of the affection I hold for you, I'll allow remembrance. Now, I'll just slip inside you…" suddenly Eleggua was no longer in the porter's chair.

Jonathan looked wildly around the room. Eleggua, where *are* you?"

"Here." The voice came from inside Jonathan, who ran his hands all over his skull as if he was trying to feel Eleggua with his fingertips.

"If you were any stiffer, your spine would snap like an Acacia twig. Loosen yourself, please and deeply breathing."

"It's really easy to relax with you running amok in my guts." Jonathan said bitterly. Making a supreme effort, he breathed from his diaphragm and let his arms and legs go limp.

"Much better. Now - I'm going to get you up from your chair..." Involuntarily, Jonathan rose to his feet with a startled exclamation which Eleggua ignored, "...and we're going to do a little dance that will set your spirit free."

The music came faintly at first, a whisper of flute and a tiny drum tick. Gradually it grew louder, filling his brain and flowing slowly through his body until it reached his hands and feet.

"Stretch out your arms," Eleggua said and Jonathan's arms stretched until he felt as if they could touch the opposite walls of his office.

"Now, turn, brother, around and around."

Slowly, Jonathan began to spin. The music accelerated and Jonathan moved in time with it. Inside him, Eleggua spun, too. Sometimes he stood high on his toes and sometimes he swooped low. Whichever position he took, Jonathan did the same, spinning wildly around the room.

The walls melted and the floor dissolved. Jonathan spun on air, head thrown back, wheeling and laughing with a happiness that he hadn't felt since he was a child. The music played on with brilliant splashes of colour exploding like silent fireworks and Jonathan whirled until his heart became as light as his head. Ribbons of light played around him, coiling at his feet and then streaming out into the distance.

"It is time to choose your path." Eleggua's voice echoed around him.

Jonathan looked down; wide bands of light lay all around him, stretching out towards an invisible horizon.

"But - how do I know which path is mine?"

"Listen to the music...as it slows, so will you. When you stop you will know which path is yours."

The music softened and lessened its tempo. Jonathan's twirling became a lazy circle and his arms gradually lowered until they rested at his sides. The drums gave a cascade of sharp little taps that faded into silence and all that was left was the quiet, questioning note of the flute.

Three roads stood before Jonathan, a path to the left that ran straight as a ruler, ahead; a track in front of him that zigzagged its way along and, on his right, a lane that meandered in a series of unhurried curves.

Without hesitation, Jonathan stepped onto the right hand trail; as he did so, the flute sang out a note of triumph and the road glowed warmly beneath his feet. He set off on his path and deep inside him, Eleggua chuckled with satisfaction.

"How was your journey, my brother?"

Jonathan was back at his desk, leaning back in his chair, feet propped up on the shining mahogany.

"I don't want to talk about it while you're ferreted away inside me."

"Ah - what foolishness of me. I was so comfortable that I forgot for a moment my surroundings... I'll just... I'll just..." his voice trailed off into a murmur.

"What are you doing in there?"

The murmur changed to a confused mumble. Jonathan sat upright.

"Eleggua? What's going on in there? Come out!"

"This is sincerely what I'm trying to do," came the exasperated voice.

"*Trying* to - are you telling me you *can't*?"

Eleggua gave an hysterical giggle: "at the moment, it seems not, but shortly I shall be in your midst."

"You're in my midst now," Jonathan pointed out acidly. "I want you out of it and on the other side of this desk."

"Nobody wants that more than I, my friend. I have gone all over the parts of your body searching for an escapement but so far to no avail."

"Where are you, precisely?" Jonathan asked with morbid curiosity.

"I have just gone through both your *koropons* and at present I am near the end of your *oko*: I had intended expellation through the tip but I now appear to be stuck."

" Listen up" Jonathan said grimly. - if there is even the least damage to my *oko*, to say nothing of my *koropons*, when you get out of there I will take *your* miserable *koropons*, stretch them to the length of your overactive *oko* and weave all three into a tasteful braid."

"These imprecationings are not worthy of a man who has found his path," Eleggua said prissily.

"You'd hate to hear what I would have said *before* finding my path. How come you're stuck in there anyway? I thought you could nip in and out of anything and anyone."

"I can," Eleggua said with considerable chagrin, "but what we have here is precisely what I've been warning the others about. There is a specific dividing of human/divine incarnation which must be observed by all deities. For every hour spent in human shape, an equal amount of time must be spent in divine form. Failure to do so results in loss of *ashé* - power - and the time must immediately be made up so that *ashé* can be restored. Usually we spend our divine time when we sleep so that we can assume human form whenever we like but lately I've been pushing the envelope, as it is said, and this is the result."

"So how much longer will you be jammed inside me like an oversized kidney stone?"

"Let's see; I didn't go to bed until three am and only slept until ten this morning..." Eleggua did a few silent calculations and then announced, "I'm missing two hours. That's not so bad."

"You mean I've got to spend the next two hours with you sequestered in my privates?"

"It won't be difficult," Eleggua assured him. "We can go to the fair this way and when the time has passed I'll be popping out most stealthfully and I will still be in time for the performancing of *Orisha Dance.*"

"I think we'd better stay here," Jonathan said. "I can get some work done while we're waiting."

"And what am I supposed to do?"

"You can just hang loose." Jonathan snorted appreciatively at his own wit.

"I think not."

There was a certain inflexible note in Elggua's voice that made Jonathan apprehensive. "I have enough power left to *make* you go to the party and a fine sight it will be - you marching in there, pointing the way, as it were."

Jonathan closed his eyes and shuddered at the thought.

"Okay. But no funny stuff while you're still inside me. No disembodied voices, no making me do weird things."

"You have my word as a gentleman and an Orisha. Just make sure you are drinking enough for the two of us."

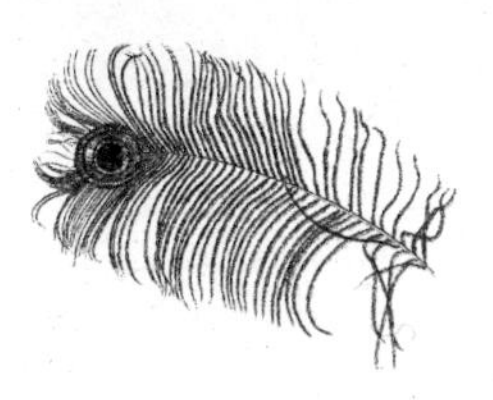

"Oshun! This way!"

"Give us a smile, Oshun!"

"Chango! Hey, Chango!"

"Over here, Oya!"

"Where's Eleggua?"

"Oshun, is it true you've signed a ten million dollar contract with Glissando?"

One of the first things Theo had taught the Orisha was, that when dealing with the press - walk while you talk. Smiling and giving brief, non-committal answers to the shouted questions, the deities moved unhurriedly but steadily towards the hotel.

Earlier they had discussed the merits of taking human versus deity forms for the event.. There was no visible difference but they couldn't be photographed in Orisha incarnation, so they had always adopted human status for public appearances.

"Don't forget," Eleggua had cautioned, "we have a whole day and evening to get through and we can only be mortal for a few hours at a time. We've been in human shape a great deal lately and if we stay that way too long we'll lose our powers."

"But we only have to spend the same number of hours in Orisha form as we do in human shape," Oya said impatiently.

"That is true. But since we've been here, we've been spending many hours in human shape and, as you know, each time we become earthly, it takes less time to lose the changing over power and longer to regain it. Eventually, we would be unable at all to switch back and forth; it would take months to regain it and if we get stuck in our human bodies we'd be in big trouble."

"But what happens when the photographers want to take our pictures," asked Oya. "They never leave us alone."

"And wouldn't you be sorry if they did," Oshun said. Oya's constant posing got on her nerves.

Oya gave her a smug grin. "What's the matter, girlfriend - can't stand the competition?"

"*Competition*! Why, you -"

"Both of you stop it," Chango stepped between them. "Eleggua is right. We can't risk diminishing our potency any more than we already have."

"That certainly would be hazardous for you, my Lord," snapped Oya.

Chango began a retort but Eleggua stilled them all with a sharp clap of his hands.

"Enough - I beg of you! We stay in Orisha form for the evening. Now - I have a few matters to look after, so I'll meet you later in the evening at the hotel. I'll be there in plenty of time for our performancing."

Now in the hall outside the main ballroom, Oshun, Chango and Oya smiled for the cameras, that had their operators known it, were clicking madly away at empty air. The only other person who got equal lens time was Dolores Monahan who, in the spirit of the event, was dressed in a micro bikini of artichoke leaves. She told the transfixed *CNN* reporter that she had been inspired by the photographs of Oshun in garlands of the Honey Money Bush, but she'd improved the concept by using edible leaves. As a finishing touch, she sported a choice of vinaigrette or hollandaise sauce, a flask of each nestled on her svelte hips in jewelled holsters.

“I’m offering people a leaf at a hundred bucks each and I’m giving the money to *Vegging Out*,” she burbled. “Great idea, huh?”

Resisting the urge to point out that, given the brevity of her costume, she wasn’t likely to raise much except temperatures, the commentator thanked Dolores weakly and left her plying her wares. Her most enthusiastic customer was her husband whose repeat business soon had her down to a few strategically placed petals, which she sported happily for the rest of the night.

By the time the three deities arrived, all the serious party goers were on hand, from the local movers and shakers to the Euroglitz celebrities whose main function was to see and be seen and seen and seen.

“If that buzzard, Belinda Barden, squawks in my ear even once, I’ll garrote her with her own feather boa,” Oya said grimly to Oshun who giggled appreciatively while avoiding eye contact with the columnist who was waving madly at her.

This was Oshun’s second appearance of the day; she had been there at noon as a celebrity chef working with the renowned Jaimie McCall. They had made *Ye’atakilt alich’a*, the stew that Oshun had taught Angel to cook and the audience got to taste the results. The demand for the recipe was so overwhelming that new copies had to be printed every few minutes. Oshun was swamped with requests for autographs and didn’t escape until well after three. Still, she’d had time to change from her working robe and *gelé*, take one of her leisurely baths and lavish hours on her hair and makeup.

The results were more than worth it. Her robe was cloth of gold overlaid with peacock feathers. She had pulled her hair sleekly into an intricate chignon at the nape of her neck, and she wore a huge corona of peacock feathers on her head. Apart from her trademark gold bangles she wore no jewellery other than a superb canary diamond ring and she carried a gold filigree fan set with fire opals.

Oya had taken great trouble with her toilette and was very pleased with what she saw in her full-length mirror. She wore a caftan of violet silk, studded with glowing stones that flashed iridescent light. Her *gelé* was made up of seven scarves, one in each colour of the rainbow, woven together and twisted around her head into a braided spiral. Oya carried her insignia, a fly whisk of black horsehair in a copper holder that was set with cabochon gems in all colours of the spectrum. She had a many-jewelled collar around her neck and her earrings were fringes of fine amethyst and ruby strands that moved constantly as if stirred by breezes. She looked spectacular but when she saw Oshun, she heaved a dispirited sigh and muttered, "Why do I even bother?"

Brent had been leaning up against the wall, watching for the deities. He was in a black Gauthier suit, a lilac silk shirt and a satin tie, hand painted with purple and silver swirls. As soon as he saw the Orisha he swept Oshun and Oya into a double-armed hug while giving Chango a welcoming grin.

"Come with me, you divine bundles of enchantment," he burbled, as he scooped two bottles of champagne into each hand from a nearby bar. Propelling the Orisha smoothly through the crowd, he nodded and smiled to everyone en route while talking non-stop:

"Angel is making her appointed rounds, Keisha is in a secluded alcove, guarding our table and I've been commissioned to round everyone up after which we'll get blind on this organic champagne and dance our little tushes into the ground."

Brent carefully deposited the three deities and the champagne at their table, all of which were met with glad cries from Keisha and Theo, who had materialized out of nowhere, a trick he performed almost as well as the Orisha.

"Isn't Eleggua with you?" Keisha asked.

"He said he'll meet us here later," Chango replied.

Keisha took a relieved swallow of champagne. She looked sensational in a form-fitting cashmere dress that was a checkerboard of black and red squares. It was low-cut and ankle length with side slits up to the thigh, displaying stunning legs in sheer black hose and red and black Manolo Blahnik shoes.

Brent set off on a second search and in a remarkably short time was back with Alix, Marc and Stephen, who was just back from Prague.

"Good evening, all," said Theo. "Where's Christopher, Alix?"

"At home." Alix replied, settling herself comfortably in her chair and smoothing out the folds of her silver Donna Karan dinner gown. "He couldn't face the madness but I'd never miss Angel's big party. Besides, I promised Clive Stanton-Dean that I'd give him a personal introduction to Oshun. He's a horrible little man, but he's one of our biggest customers in the common market and he came over from London especially for the launch. Sorry, dear heart," she said ruefully to Oshun, "I hate to inflict Clive on you but he drove me mental until I promised he could meet you."

Oshun nodded. She didn't mind spending a few minutes charming an important client, no matter how noxious, if it made Alix happy.

She stood up: "Let's see him now - then we can relax and enjoy the rest of the evening"

Alix and Oshun made their way to the ringside table where Clive Stanton-Dean sat alone. There were many reasons for his solitude, all having to do with his unfortunate appearance and unpleasant personality. He was short, lumpish and looked as if he had been pumped full of air. He had a porcine nose and wisps of dun coloured hair clung damply to his pink, glistening skull. Oshun smiled pleasantly when they were introduced but inwardly she shuddered with dislike and after shaking his pudgy hand, she surreptitiously wiped her palm on her robe.

"So, this is the famous Oshun." His goatish smile revealed an unattractive assortment of stained teeth. "Come and sit beside me, beautiful lady, and let us get to know each other."

For Clive, getting to know someone meant groping as much as traffic would bear. Oshun tried to keep a healthy distance between them but every time she edged away, he followed as closely as a sticking plaster. Sitting on his other side, Alix winked at Oshun, trying to indicate that they wouldn't stay long; this brought an over-solicitous inquiry from Clive asking if Alix had something in her eye.

"I think my contact lens is slipping," she replied smoothly, "Oshun, my dear, would you accompany me to the Ladies Room and see if we can adjust the pesky little object...no, Clive, don't get up, we'll see you later." She whisked Oshun away, leaving a chagrined Clive alone and frustrated.

Angel had briefly joined the group in the alcove.. She could never relax during the food fair but roved from the food booths to guest speakers to the bazaar and back again. It was important that she spoke to every participant and also, although they had a sterling volunteer staff, there were always problems that only she could deal with. During the day like all the other workers, she had been wearing jeans and a *Vegging Out* T-shirt, but now she was dressed for the evening in a jade green tunic and palazzo pants in a fine silk jersey that moved beautifully.

"I'm off on my last walkabout," she said. She headed for the food hall where fifty of Toronto's top restaurants were serving every imaginable type of vegetarian cuisine, from Asian to Zambian. The food hall had been open from ten that morning but even though it almost nine pm, every booth still looked as fresh as at opening time. The chefs were beaming as they filled plates with such delicacies as chili con mole on blue cornbread and jerk tofu with dirty rice.

The Green Bazaar, which was in a separate hall, looked like a Middle Eastern souk and displayed an amazing variety of environmentally friendly products. A booth selling natural fibre clothing coloured with vegetable dyes offered garments for all ages and sexes. The crafts area was a popular highlight, featuring artisans working in their respective disciplines and there were also health and beauty products as well as organic fruits, vegetables, herbs and spices

Smaller rooms, which earlier in the day were venues for lectures and workshops, were now being used for tastings of organic wines, oils, vinegars and honeys, while in a spacious demonstration area were a range of services that included feng shui for home and workspace, reflexology, aromatherapy and tarot readings.

All of these activities were now winding down, preparatory to the evening entertainment. People poured into the main room, searching for empty tables or sussing out friends who could squeeze in one or two more.

Jonathan hove into view, looking dispiritedly for the Hot Box table. Hearing his name called, he acknowledged the group in the alcove with a morose nod and slouched over.

"Come and sit," Theo said. "There's lots of room."

"No, thanks," Jonathan said. "I'm going to get some air. I'll see you later."

Leaving the party room, he consulted his watch. "Forty five minutes to go" he groaned silently and entered a side room where the dessert carts were waiting to be wheeled out. A tall, dark haired woman was putting the finishing touches to a tower of croquembouche. He watched silently, fascinated by the dexterity with which she twirled a cloud of spun sugar around the base of the pastry. She looked up, surprised.

"Oh – I didn't know I had an audience." She was attractive, with narrow green eyes that almost closed when she smiled.

"I hope I'm not disturbing you."

"Not at all." She dotted the cream puffs with crystallized violets, gave a satisfied nod and moved on to a display of exotic fruits, arranged like a head by Arcimboldo. She wove a wreath of mint leaves around the edge of the platter and pronounced it finished. "Any more than that would be overkill."

Jonathan nodded in agreement and sat on a nearby chair, delighted to watch this talented woman who worked her way steadily through the maze of confectionary, adding a garnish of cream here, a posy of edible flowers there, until the entire presentation was completed.

"It's fantastic." Jonathan said, rising to his feet. "You're amazing."

"Thank you – but this was the easy part- and the most fun."

"Did you make all this?"

"I and my staff. Hi – I'm Rosie Budd."

"Oh – I've heard of you." Rosie Budd was the top pastry chef in the country – author of a dozen cookbooks and star of "Sweet Talk", the hot new television series.

She held out her hand. "I've heard of you too, Mr. Bernstein - lawyer to the stars."

"Jonathan, please." He shook her cool, smooth hand.

"Well – time to get these out to the ravenous hordes. Nice to have met you." She turned to leave.

"Ask the lovely lady to have a drink with you." Eleggua's voice rumbled quietly in his ear."

"Don't be silly." Jonathan felt as shy as a schoolboy.

"Do it – or I will be doing it for you."

Rosie Budd paused, intrigued by the sight of a man having an argument with himself and losing."

"Sorry," Jonathan said embarrassedly, "I talk to myself sometimes."

"Ahhh," said Rosie, starting to leave again.

"DO IT!" said Eleggua.

"ROSIE!", Jonathan bellowed

Startled, Rosie turned around..

"I was wondering", he mumbled, " if you'd perhaps like to have a drink or maybe a late supper…" His voice trailed off.

She stared at him silently for a moment, then her green eyes disappeared again in that enchanting smile. " Just give me fifteen minutes to change and I'll meet you at the front entrance."

The anticipation Jonathan felt was almost overwhelming but then he remembered the business at hand. He looked at his watch it was two minutes to ejection time. Heading for the men's room, he went into one of the stalls, put down the lid and seated himself.

"Okay, Eleggua," he whispered tensely, "it's time. Come out!"

Before he could blink, there was the god of the crossroads, perched on his lap.

"Get off," Jonathan hissed.

"Easier said than done, my brother," Eleggua replied cheerfully, "there isn't much room in this little hut."

Unfolding his wiry legs, he slid off Jonathan and slithered under the door as if dancing the limbo. Jonathan pushed the door open and came out into the washroom just as Eleggua stood up. Five men, three of whom Jonathan knew, stood staring, open-mouthed. Two of

Jonathan's acquaintances turned to the sinks and madly washed their hands. The third, a tax lawyer with whom he had gone through law school, grinned at Jonathan who shrugged helplessly and said, "Harry, if I tried to explain, you'd never believe it."

He turned to Eleggua who calmly ignored the other men while he arranged his robes in front of the mirrored door. "Now that you've completely ruined my reputation," Jonathan gritted from between clenched teeth, "perhaps you'd like to get the hell out of the way so that I can leave the scene of the ostensible crime."

Tucking a fold of his outer robe more securely into the wide sash that circled his hips, Eleggua leaned towards the mirror and peered critically at the fringe of his headdress while he murmured, "Do not agitate yourself, my brother. All will be well."

Straightening up, he smiled brightly at the men who seemed unable to leave the room. Pointing the long, thin index finger of his right hand, Eleggua slowly turned in a circle, fixing each of the men in turn with his piercing gaze:

"You will remember nothing that happened in the last five minutes," he said.

The men turned away from Eleggua and Jonathan and went about the business of using the urinals, combing their hair or straightening their ties, never noticing when the deity and the long-suffering lawyer left the room.

Out in the hallway Jonathan turned to Eleggua and opened his mouth to speak but the Orisha held up a forestalling hand:

"No time for discussion now, my brother. Remember that the lovely lady is waiting for you."

Jonathan contented himself with a glare that spoke volumes and then charged off to the front entrance where Rosie awaited him. Her face lit up when she saw him and he felt an answering glow of pleasure as he took her arm..

The party progressed: the drinks got stronger and the music hotter. It was close to midnight when Kevin Anderson, the celebrity Master of Ceremonies, took the microphone and called the crowd to order.

"Ladies and gentlemen, it's time for a very special treat - a live performance of the dance craze of the century. Big it up for the stars of *Orisha Dance* - Chango, Oya, Eleggua and the fabulous Oshun!"

Applause erupted as the deities took their positions on the circular dance floor; Chango had Bata drums at his waist, Oya held a chekeré, Eleggua carried a pair of clavés and Oshun had small brass bells on her fingers. Rainbow mists of colour swirled around the room as Eleggua clicked the clavés softly together. The "ting" of Oshun's bells showered gold sparkles onto the dance floor, the chekeré rustled quietly and then came the punctuating rap of the drums. The orchestra began to play the melody of *Orisha Dance* and with the first notes the audience erupted in a frenzy of excitement.

Inspired by the energies around them, the Orisha performed as never before and each call and response carried everyone to new heights. The deities danced with all those who managed to fight their way to them, which was how Oshun found herself dancing with Clive Stanton-Dean. She would have sooner partnered a crazed tarantula but made the best of it until Clive ground his flabby pelvis into hers and, at the same moment, pinched her bottom.

Oshun is a good-natured goddess, but when her dignity is offended, she becomes more terrible than Oya in one of her worst rages. She uttered a ringing cry that paralyzed the hapless Clive and brought everything to a halt. Pouring a stream of Yoruba invective at her cringing victim, she rose up until she was floating high above the heads of the crowd. Oya, incensed on Oshun's behalf, twirled herself into a tornado and roared around Stanton-Dean, buffeting him from one side of the dance floor to the other.

Infuriated that this miserable little man had dared to touch his lover, Chango breathed a stream of fire that neatly removed Stanton-Dean's eyebrows, eyelashes and the few greasy strands that garnished his head, then Eleggua shot up and down in size, cackling gleefully as he careened all over the room, dragging the hapless Clive behind him.

At first the audience thought it was part of the show and applauded wildly but they soon realized that it wasn't special effects. Pandemonium ensued as people tried to escape. Reporters and cameramen kept their cool enough to shoot footage of the mayhem and get comments from the few guests who were still coherent, but when films were developed and videos replayed, the Orisha were nowhere to be seen or heard.

It was far too early in the morning after the night before when Angel's phone startled her out of a fitful sleep:

"Sorry to awaken you, dear heart, but we need a meeting right away. Can you get the others together for eight-thirty at the office?"

Angel looked at her bedside clock: six forty-five. "Yes, Alix, of course."

"We'll meet in the small boardroom. I'll have breakfast brought in. "

Hanging up, Angel turned to find Marc awake and lighting his first cigarette of the day.

"Command performance time?" he grinned.

"Got it in one."

"There go my plans for a little early morning performance of our own."

"I'll take a rain check. Get yourself into the shower while I phone the others."

The round marble table stood empty, high backed swivel chairs tucked neatly under its edges, while mini conferences took place in different parts of the room.

The Orisha sat on two curved couches that formed a circle of privacy.

"What's done is done and there's no use weeping into our Martinis," Eleggua said briskly. "We've had a grandiferous time but these complicatings make staying on very difficult."

"You're right," Oshun said. "I thought once it was known I am a goddess they would give me the reverence I receive at home, but these people are maniacs. When I left the hotel last night that terrible mob was shouting and tearing at my robes - that's no way to treat a deity!"

"I went through a similar experience with screaming girls chasing me," Chango said. "Whaa! it was as terrifying as the time Oya had me surrounded by skeletons! I can't wait to get back home."

"And what of you, Oya," Eleggua asked, "are you also ready to return?"

The wind goddess nodded emphatically: "I will be well content to leave. It's been exciting, but I miss my land and the peace of the graveyard."

"Once again we are in agreeance - I can't believe it!" Eleggua shook his head in amazement.

Oya laughed in spite of herself: "I think we've both learned something about getting along together, Eleggua."

At the opposite side of the room, Alix and Angel talked quietly. Marc, Brent and Keisha were stationed at the bar where Brent was busying himself with the Espresso machine while Marc concocted mimosas. Keisha unwrapped baskets of rolls and pastries and put them on the table together with jars of jam, pots of butter and a large cheese platter.

While Marc was passing the mimosas around, Keisha said to Brent:

"I need to talk to you."

"What's up?" Brent looked up from his task of grinding coffee beans.

"You remember just before we started work on *Oshun's Gold* I said I was planning a book?"

"Yes." He took the ground beans and tamped them firmly onto the brewing disc.

"Well, I'm ready to begin and it's going to be the most important thing I've ever done. I'm calling it *Women Of The World.*

"That's great, K." Brent suspended his ministrations to the Espresso machine, giving his full attention to Keisha whose words practically tumbled over each other in her excitement.

"My first subjects will be the women of Africa. I've got a jump on that with all the pictures I took in Nigeria. I want to start in East Africa this time, so I'll fly to Kenya and travel around the continent from there. I've made enough to fund the project for at least a year and when it runs low I'll come back and work to finance the next part."

"It'll take a lot of work - and a shitload of cash."

"I know. But I'll do it on a *very* thin shoestring and that's what I wanted to talk to you about. Stephen can get special prices on air fares, right?"

"Yes," Brent said, "but I don't know anything about the mechanics involved and Stephen's away until Friday. I'll set up dinner for Sunday evening and you can discuss it with him then."

"You are a *wonderful* friend." Keisha gave Brent a huge hug, then scooped up the food platters and put them on the table. Brent turned back to the machine and continued pushing buttons and pulling levers.

When the frothy demi-tasses of double espresso were ready, everyone seated themselves at the table. Alix opened a little jar of honey. She scooped out a portion of the golden liquid with a tiny spoon, dipped her little finger into it and tasted it, stirred the honey into a cup of coffee and passed it to Oshun, who smiled her thanks.

"Why did you do that?" Brent asked.

"Honey given to Oshun must first be tasted to show that it isn't poisoned."

"Say *what*?"

"It's true," the goddess nodded, "someone gave me poisoned honey once and a nasty time I had of it, let me tell you; it was five hundred years ago and I remember the agony as if it was five minutes ago, but why dwell on unpleasant things?"

"Why indeed?" Alix said briskly, "particularly since we have such good news in our midst. Keisha, I think you have something to tell us."

Keisha looked startled and Alix laughed: "A little bird whispered something to me."

Keisha glared at Brent, who gave a sheepish grin.

She outlined her plans to the group who applauded loudly but Alix's voice cut through the congratulatory buzz:

"Now I have good news for you" she said. "I will sponsor your book and the grant will come from the profits on *Oshun's Gold.* It's the perfect tie-in - the beauty of women of all countries...all races...all colours..."

Keisha looked down at her hands, which were tightly clasped on the table.

"Alix," she said chokingly, "It's a wonderful offer - but I can't accept it."

"Can't accept it? Nonsense!" A frosty eyed CEO drew herself up and stared across the table at the miserable Keisha.

"You see," Keisha faltered, "this won't be a book on just beauty ...I'll be photographing women in all walks of life and all situations...giving birth...working in the fields...lying in illness...even dying..."

Alix leaned across the table towards Keisha: "Listen to me, my girl; I've spent many years in the beauty industry and the most gratifying part isn't about enhancing the looks of the few who are born into beauty but in helping the so-called average woman to feel good about herself.

"*Oshun's Gold* will do much towards restoring youthful looks but it won't be everyone's choice. Many will be content to let old age write its lines on them; they will be admired for who they are and what they have achieved, and they'll have a beauty of their own.

"On my first trip to China I saw a ninety-five year old woman whose skin was as lined and fragile as a cobweb. She had yellow-grey hair that barely covered her scalp, and her eyes were sunk deep with age. She sat in a corner of her grandson's courtyard, watching his children play. The sunlight washed over her, and she laughed with the joy of being with her great grandchildren and in that moment she was the loveliest woman I ever saw."

"That's who I'm looking for," Keisha said, "and her daughters and her daughters' daughters."

"They'll be waiting for you," Alix said, "in Africa and every other country; women of every race and every age. You'll take pictures of them giving birth, working, playing, celebrating and dying and you will give them immortal beauty. Your book will be an epic work of art worthy of Glissando sponsorship."

Keisha took a deep breath: "Alix - again I thank you for your generosity and I know it must seem crazy, but this book is something I *have* to do on my own. It can't have any other presence, not even one as illustrious as Glissando. Please, *please* understand."

Alix looked at Keisha for a long moment, mouth tight with disapproval.

"Oh, I *understand*, Keisha. I'm quite familiar with the 'I did-it-on-my-own' syndrome which affects today's' young geniuses. In my day there was nothing wrong with having a benefactor but I'm obviously out of step with the times. I'll say no more about it except to wish you success.

"Now for *my* good news:

She turned to Oshun: "My darling deity - I haven't forgotten that you promised me my greatest fame in my old age and now that it's come I can fulfill two vows I made to myself a long time ago. One was to enable complete restoration of the Oshun Groves and to maintain them in perpetuity. *Oshun's Gold* is already doing so well that I can make arrangements for that right away. The other vow was to retire while I could still put one foot in front of the other. So - at last I'll have a life of my own - Christopher and I will travel, I'll write my memoirs...I'll - why are you shaking your head?" she asked Oshun. " Aren't you pleased about the groves...?"

"Of course I am, Alix," the goddess replied. "But it's no more than I expected of you. Whatever I have given you, you have always repaid with great generosity. I thank you with all my heart and I know *Adunni* will be ecstatic."

"Then what's the matter?" Alix demanded. "You look as if you're about to tell me I have six months to live."

"The world won't see the end of you for a long while, Alix Morton; I was just wondering how to break the news that your retirement is a long way off."

Alix narrowed her eyes in a way that unnerved everyone from underlings to bank presidents. but Oshun merely pulled her mirror and comb out of the air and began grooming herself.

"Don't you comb your hair at me. What do you *mean* 'a long way off'?"

Oshun gave a few more strokes of the comb and then threw it and the mirror into the air where they vanished neatly.

"I mean," she said evenly, "that your work isn't over."

"My dear Oshun, you are talking through what would be your hat if you were wearing one."

"Is it so? Well I have a little hat for you to try on - if it will fit your enlarged head." Alix gasped in indignation but Oshun continued:

"I gave you the secret of the Honey Money Bush to do with as you wished. You developed *Oshun's Gold* and it's an enormous success but that's hardly surprising. Most people will pay anything for youth and beauty and you have given them a genie in a capsule."

"You were happy to have that genie named after you *and* to be the image for *Oshun's Gold*."

"I don't deny that," Oshun said. "I have my frivolous side, as everyone knows, but I am not on that path today." As she spoke, she browsed among a tray of pastries, and selected a flaky cherry strudel.

Taking an appreciative bite, followed by a sip of espresso, she continued. "This path, the one of motherhood and compassion, takes me back to Africa. Come to that, it's taking all four of us."

Everyone sat in silence, staring first at each other and then at the Orisha who gazed steadily back at them.

"You *can't* leave now."

Eleggua spread his expressive hands in a propitiatory gesture: "It is time, Madame Alix, we have done all that we can here."

"And more," replied Alix with asperity. She glared at each in turn, reserving her steeliest look for Oshun. "And what about your personal appearances?" she demanded. "We have you booked in every major city in the world!"

Oshun spoke placatingly, "Alix, you can't keep the product in stock as it is - you said yourself that it's flying off the shelves and you're back ordered for the next six months. You don't need me to sell *Oshun's Gold*."

"I know that," the cosmetics queen snapped. "This is about Glissando's image - not just sales. You – the goddess of beauty - are our figurehead and your personal appearance in the world's capitals will give us unparalleled cachet."

Oshun's conciliatory attitude vanished. Drawing herself to her full height she spoke in a voice edged with metal: "Yes, I *am* the goddess of beauty, and abundance, Alix Morton. It was *I* who gave you the success you prayed for all those years ago - it was *I who* granted your every wish and it was *I* who agreed to aid you in your latest venture: but I am tired of this life and so are the others. We are going home. But, before we do, it is time for you to make the payment I spoke of so long ago.

"The Honey Money Bush has great properties. You discovered some of them when you developed *Oshun's Gold*; now you must take the next step."

Alix looked at her blankly: "Next step?"

"With further refinement and more experimentation, the Honey Money gel can be used to regenerate damaged skin and bone - people who have been burned or injured- children with birth defects - war victims..."

"And you want…?"

"What would I want?"

Alix closed her eyes and took a deep breath. "You want me to donate the Honey Money gel to science."

"Exactly."

"All right, *Iyalode*. I'll call David Moss, he's the head of the Canadian Institute of Medical Science and offer them the gel. Then I'll have my PR department draft a statement of retirement and – "

Oshun cut in: "You aren't listening, Alix. I *said* that your retirement is a long way off. Nobody has such knowledge of the gel's properties as you and Christopher. With your help, research and development time will be cut by years. This is what I meant when I told you that you'll have your greatest fame in the last years of your career. It doesn't come from *Oshun's Gold* but from what you're going to do next."

"But I don't *want* to do it."

"What you want is of no concern. It is your path."

She turned to Angel: "I will be watching over you, sweet thing, and we will meet again, many times.

She enveloped Angel in a perfumed embrace, then gave her attention again to Alix, speaking soft words that seemed to uplift the older woman's spirits.

Eleggua leaned towards Keisha and looped a string of beads around her neck.

"It is a coleria," he said, in answer to her questioning look. "When you want me, turn it three times and I will come to you, wherever you are."

Keisha fingered the strand of red, back and white beads. They felt warm and protective against her skin. She smiled her thanks to the dreadlocked god who gazed at her with uncharacteristic soberness. "I will come to you." he repeated, gently touching her face. She bent her head, capturing his hand against her cheek and they stood, unheeding of the others.

"It is time." Oshun stretched out her arms, clasping hands with Angel and Alix who took Oya's right hand. Keisha linked herself to Oya and Eleggua, who grasped Brent's right hand. Brent took Chango's clasp on his left and Marc joined his hands to Chango and Angel, completing the circle.

Oshun looked at each of them in turn, eyes glowing through their thick black tangle of lashes. "We leave you with our constant love. Oluddumare will watch over you and may we be together again before too long."

"Be happy in your lives," said Chango.

"Stay strong in your dreams," Oya said.

"Keep your paths open to us and to each other." said Eleggua.

The air began to glow in soft rainbow colours that gradually brightened, swirling around the Orisha, wrapping them in radiant cocoons that strobed and pulsed, expanding and contracting. With each contraction, the lights became smaller, shrinking from life-size ovals to tiny spheres which danced around the table, touching each person on the forehead in benediction. The lights swept in a wide circle around the room and then vanished. The Orisha were gone.

Angel and Marc, Alix, Keisha, and Brent sat speechless, choked with sadness. Tears poured from their eyes, then their mouths opened and huge bursts of laughter thundered around the room. They laughed and cried until their throats ached and their sides hurt. Gradually, the tears dried and the laughter faded. As they looked at each other they saw that, like tiny movie screens, their eyes showed reflections of their lives –

what they had been, how they had changed since meeting the Orisha and lastly, what they would become.

They gazed into each other's eyes for hours, mesmerized by the images and when the pictures finally faded they sat in silence, humbled by the visions yet filled with hope. Into the silence, like a promise for the future, came a distant skirl from Eleggua's flute, the hum of Oya's whirlwind, a faint rataplan from Chango's drum and, lastly, the cool, clear tinkle of Oshun's golden bracelets.

THE END